5676 9408

P9-DBY-058

Praise for *Atlanta Burns*:

"[Atlanta Burns] is like Veronica Mars on Adderall. Chuck Wendig knocks this one out of the park as he so often does." —Stephen Blackmoore, author of *City of the Lost* and *Dead Things*

"Give Nancy Drew a shotgun and a kick-ass attitude and you get Atlanta Burns. Packed with action and fascinating characters, [*Atlanta Burns*] is a story that will captivate both teens and adults and have them clamoring for the next installment." —Joelle Charbonneau, author of *The Testing*

**Praise for *Under the Empyrean Sky*,
Book One in the Heartland Trilogy:**

"This strong first installment rises above the usual dystopian fare thanks to Wendig's knack for disturbing imagery and scorching prose." —*Publishers Weekly*

"Wendig brilliantly tackles the big stuff—class, economics, identity, love, and social change—in a fast-paced tale that never once loses its grip on pure storytelling excitement. Well-played, Wendig. Well-played." —Libba Bray, author of the Gemma Doyle Trilogy, *Going Bovine*, and *The Diviners*

"A tense dystopian tale made more strange and terrifying by its present-day implications." —*Booklist*

WITHDRAWN

BEAVERTON CITY LIBRARY
BEAVERTON, OR 97005
MEMBER OF WASHINGTON COUNTY
COOPERATIVE LIBRARY SERVICES

"*Under the Empyrean Sky* is like a super-charged, genetically modified hybrid of *The Grapes of Wrath* and *Star Wars*. Wendig delivers a thrilling, fast-paced adventure set in a future agri-dystopia. Fascinating world building, engaging and deep characters, smooth, electric prose." —John Hornor Jacobs, author of *The Twelve-Fingered Boy*

"A thoroughly imagined environmental nightmare with taut pacing and compelling characters that will leave readers eager for more." —*Kirkus Reviews*

"A lunatic, gene-spliced, biofueled thriller. Fear the corn." —Tom Pollock, author of *The City's Son*

"An imaginative, page-turning adventure that will delight science fiction fans and have them impatiently waiting for the next installment." —Joelle Charbonneau, author of *The Testing*

BEAVERTON CITY LIBRARY
BEAVERTON, OR 97005
MEMBER OF WASHINGTON COUNTY
COOPERATIVE LIBRARY SERVICES

ATLANTA BURNS

Other Skyscape titles by Chuck Wendig:

The Heartland Trilogy:
Book 1, *Under the Empyrean Sky*
Book 2, *Blightborn*
Book 3, *The Harvest* – Coming in July 2015

Short story based on the world of the Heartland:
The Wind Has Teeth Tonight: A Gwennie Story

The Atlanta Burns Series:
Book 1, *Atlanta Burns*
Book 2 – Coming in February 2016

ATLANTA BURNS

ATLANTA BURNS, BOOK ONE

SKYSCAPE

SKYSCAPE

This is a work of fiction. Names, characters, organizations, places, events, and incidents are either products of the author's imagination or are used fictitiously.

Text copyright © 2015 Chuck Wendig
All rights reserved.

No part of this book may be reproduced, or stored in a retrieval system, or transmitted in any form or by any means, electronic, mechanical, photocopying, recording, or otherwise, without express written permission of the publisher.

Part One of *Atlanta Burns* was first published in 2011 by Chuck Wendig as the novella *Shotgun Gravy*. Parts Two through Five of *Atlanta Burns* were first published in 2012 by Chuck Wendig as the novel *Bait Dog*. Published by Skyscape in 2015.

The quote on pages 70, 92, and 114 are from A.E. Housman's poem "To an Athlete Dying Young." In *Modern British Poetry*, edited by Louis Untermeyer. New York: Harcourt, Brace and Howe, 1920.

Published by Skyscape, New York

www.apub.com

Amazon, the Amazon logo, and Skyscape are trademarks of Amazon.com, Inc., or its affiliates.

ISBN-13: 9781477827109
ISBN-10: 1477827102

Cover design by Cyanotype Book Architects

Library of Congress Control Number: 2014912061

Printed in the United States of America

This book is for the bullied.

PART ONE: SHOTGUN GRAVY

Sometimes she wakes up at night, smelling that gunpowder smell. Ears ringing. A whimpering there in the darkness. Doesn't always hit her at night. Might be in the middle of the day. She should be smelling pizza, or garbage, or cat shit wafting from the house next door, but instead what she smells is that acrid tang of gun smoke. All up in her nose. Clinging there like a tick.

CHAPTER ONE

She hears the clanging, the echoing reverb of an open-palm slap on the side of a dumpster. Voices carry across the empty parking lot near Bogner's Produce: a mean cackle, a goofy *haw-haw*, the murmur of threats culminating in some pleading bleat. Atlanta Burns is on the way home from school, walking the five-mile stretch from town to country, for the burg of Maker's Bell lives on that line between rural and suburban, between farmland and white picket fences (with a crooked zigzag of trailer parks smack in the middle). She thinks, *Fuck it, fuck this, no,* no, *just keep walking, do not pass Go, do not collect two hundred dollars, do not go kicking over logs to see what worms squirm beneath.*

A few folks mill around. They ignore the sounds from the parking lot in favor of watching her. Ever since she got back, the eyes are always on her. As if she makes people uncomfortable now.

Whatever. They don't care about the noise. Neither does she.

But then she hears the laughs again. Crass and cruel. And the sound that follows: the sound of someone—a boy or a girl, she can't tell—scared shitless, maybe in pain.

Atlanta sighs. She pulls her tie-dyed bag—bought at a flea market some years ago when she was thirteen or fourteen and didn't know just how bad things could be—and crosses the street.

The sound's coming from behind the old garage. An abandoned husk of gray concrete.

Her mouth's dry. All the moisture gone to her hands: palms slick and sweaty.

Atlanta sees a rusted can of motor oil. Before she rounds the corner and heads behind the garage, she kicks that can—it clangs and skips across the blistery, cracked asphalt—just to let them know someone's coming.

Not that they'll probably give much of a shit. She heads out back, finds three boys from her school standing around the far end of a big green dumpster, its sides pocked with cankers of rust.

She knows them. Rather, she knows *of* them.

The tall one with the smashed-flat nose, that's Jonesy—a.k.a. Gordon Jones. The prick next to him is Virgil. Virgil's a juicer, the muscles of his upper torso looking like bulging balloon animals lashed together with ropy tendons. She's not real sure of his last name. Erlenmeyer. Erlenbacher. Something. The one hanging back behind the other two is Chomp-Chomp, his first and last name lost to her. He's average in every way. His hair is so sandy brown it blends in with the dirt lot behind the garage. One exception is his teeth: kid's got a wall of horse teeth shoved unceremoniously in his mouth. Big, flat biters in a too-small jaw.

They're not alone.

They've got a pudgy Latino kid held in the dumpster. Dressed well, this kid. Blue shirt buttoned tight to the neck. Hair slicked back like he's a gangster or a preacher's son. Jonesy's hemming him in with a flat-bladed shovel like the one Atlanta's mother uses to edge out her flower beds. Atlanta can see something sitting at the edge of the shovel.

A turd-curl of dog shit, by the looks of it.

The three boys—not boys, not really, given that they're all seventeen or eighteen years old, but boys because they're acting like mean little shits—stand and give her a real hard look.

"Hey," Jonesy says. He nods. Grins. Shrugs as if to say, *Yeah, what of it?*

The Latino kid—she thinks she's seen him at school, too. She figures him to be a sophomore, maybe a year below her. He gives her a look like he's not sure if she's friend or foe. He's got a cut across his brow, a line of blood running down the margins of his round, mocha-colored Charlie Brown head.

Virgil gives Jonesy a sharp elbow in the ribs. Jonesy waves him off and says, "Like the police say, nothing to see here. Move along."

"That kid okay?" she asks, lifting an eyebrow.

Jonesy nods a vigorous, almost comical nod. "He's great. We're just playing a game."

She looks to the kid in the dumpster. "Are you okay?" The gentlest shake of a head. No.

Again Virgil elbows Jonesy, but Jonesy retorts: "Fuckin' *quit it.*"

"Looks to me like you're trying to make that kid eat a shovel of crap," she says.

"It's chocolate," Jonesy says, stifling a laugh. "It's, ahhh, you know. Wetback chocolate. Made special. Just for him. Unless you want some?"

The third miscreant in the trio, the one she thinks of as Chomp-Chomp, is watching everything with a deliberate stare. Arms folded, hands tucked tight into his armpits. He's mule-kicked, she thinks. Or a sociopath. Or just scared of what he's gotten himself into.

She slides her hand into her tie-dyed bag. Leaves it there.

Virgil blurts in what he thinks is a whisper but what is instead just a really loud hiss: "Dude. Don't you know who that *is*?"

"What?" Jonesy asks. Then he takes a long look at her.

She knows what they see. On the surface, at least. Tangled red hair, a little too long, too frizzy, hasn't been cut. A patch of freckles across the bridge of her nose in the shape of a small Band-Aid. Old, ratty bomber jacket.

They don't all recognize her. Not yet. But Virgil does. He's got a wary look like he's watching a rattlesnake at a distance. And the kid in the dumpster looks like someone's been beating him up and trying to force-feed him a pile of dog shit. No telling if he's figured her out yet.

But then she sees the light come on behind Jonesy's eyes.

Now he gets it.

"Right," Jonesy finally says. "*Riiiiight.* Burns, yeah. Atlanta Burns. That's a name."

"Sure is," she says. "So, listen. Why don't you boys go home?"

"Is that like a Southern accent?" Jonesy asks Virgil. Virgil nods, but it's not like it's a secret. Up here, middle of Pennsylvania, her accent sticks out like a bent and broken toe. "Cool. My dad's got a rebel flag on his pickup."

"Then your daddy's a jackass." She says it before she means to say it, but that's how she is: it's like the bouncers who are supposed to be guarding the door to her mouth are on an eternal smoke break. Even still, she continues: "That flag's not just the emblem of being a racist asshole, a club to which your daddy probably belongs happily. But it's also the Confederate flag. The one carried by Southerners to say to the Yankees—that's your daddy, a Yankee—'Don't tread on me or I'll pop a musket ball up your ass.' Northerners driving around with the Dixie flag is like a Jew wearing a 'Go Hitler!' baseball cap."

Jonesy's smile has fallen off his face. He squirts a jet of spit from between his two front teeth, then hands the shovel to Chomp-Chomp, who takes it, shell-shocked. The ringleader then gives a look to Virgil and nods at Atlanta. It isn't subtle.

They both take a step toward her.

"You sure you wanna do this?" she asks.

Virgil doesn't retreat, but she sees him recoil. His body language is clear. He's *not* sure. He might be afraid of her. Now *that's* interesting. Jonesy, though, he doesn't give a shit. He licks his lips, comes another step closer.

There it is again: the smell of gun smoke. Damn near makes her sick. *It's not real*, she thinks. Not a smell, but the ghost of a smell.

"Last chance," she says. Her heartbeat is drumming in her neck. Every part of her brain is screaming for her to take those getaway-sticks she calls legs and run as far and fast as she can. But her body stays rooted. Her hand tightens in her bag. It's got other plans. "We can all just play nice. Go our separate ways. You can leave that nice Mexican boy alone—"

"Venezuelan," he peeps up from inside the dumpster.

"Sorry. You can leave that nice Venezuelan boy alone, and he won't tell anybody, and nobody will get hurt worse than he already has. Square?"

"I like her," Jonesy says to Virgil. "She's feisty. I bet the three of us could have a fun time together. Virgil at the front. Me at the back. Shaking hands in the middle."

Her stomach roils. She goes elbow-deep in her bag.

"I see you reaching in that hippie purse," Jonesy says, pulling Virgil along next to him. "What's in there? I don't think you can fit a *shotgun* in there."

Way he says *shotgun*, he knows. It doesn't scare him. And that scares her. *You're going to get hurt*, she thinks. *Maybe you do this to yourself.*

You go poking rattlesnakes, maybe you get bit.

But she bears down. Doesn't move.

"Nope, no shotgun," she says. "Hey, you ever been attacked by a bear?"

Jonesy pauses. "What?"

"A bear. Like, a grizzly. As I hear it, you get attacked by a bear, not much you can do. They run faster. They got teeth and claws like knives. You play dead, that might work, but not before the bear bats your body around like a cat with a dead mouse. You'd think a gun would do the trick, but that ain't necessarily true, either. A bear will take a round to the head and keep coming. And a scattergun mostly just pisses them off. What you need is a can of bear mace."

"Bear what?"

"Bear mace." She shows him. From her purse she pulls a tall, lean canister with a pull tab and a black nozzle. Atlanta points the pull tab at the three assholes and rips that tab off.

Bear mace isn't like other pepper spray. A can of dog deterrent sprays maybe five, ten feet. More a cloud than anything. But bear mace is a concerted blast—a geyser of pepper spray that shoots in a thirty-foot jet. Powerful enough that it doesn't blow back unless the wind's bad—and today, the air is still as a chair in an empty room.

The can empties in about five seconds.

For those five seconds, Atlanta can't see much. She knows that the Mexic—er, Venezuelan kid hit the deck inside the dumpster. Heard the thump of his body. The other three, well, she can see their shapes thrashing around—first standing up, then down on the ground—but that's all they are. Shapes. Screaming, howling shapes.

When the can is done, Atlanta wings it past the margins of the lot into the bushes.

The smoke clears, revealing the trio of assholes writhing on the ground. Faces red. Crying. Even from here she can see the blood vessels showing bright in the whites of their eyes. Jonesy's clawing at his face like he's got a rat chewing its way out of his sinuses. Virgil is blubbering, with dog crap on his face. He pounds the ground with a fist. The mute, toothy third, Chomp-Chomp, lies curled up like a baby. He whimpers like one, too.

She lets out a long breath.

A little voice inside her asks, *Is this who you are now?*

She doesn't want to find the answer.

So she turns and runs. Bag flopping at her hip.

———

She tries to cry, but it just isn't coming. She wants to. It's in there somewhere. But like a stubborn sneeze, she just can't make it happen, and that's somehow worse.

Up the long driveway, shoes crunching on gravel. Past the fallow fields on either side. Green starting to poke up, with spring trying to get sprung. In the distance is the Cat Lady's house. Atlanta doesn't know her name. Woman's old and frail, like a bundle of sticks bound up in a moth-bitten bedsheet. Her cats look that way, too: starving, rangy, half-mad.

Atlanta gets closer to the old farmhouse in which she and her mother live. Passes a dead brown Buick that sits off to the side, the car draped in the choking vines and soon-to-be-purple clusters of wisteria. It's not her mama's, that car. Was here when they bought the place.

Atlanta takes a moment. Her right hand is shaking. Her index finger in particular.

Then she goes in through the garage.

Mama's in there. Setting up the cot, pulling sheets over it, fluffing some pillow that looks about as soft and comfortable as a sack of grain. A long, lean cigarette is pinched between her lips.

Seeing Atlanta, she quickly puts it out. *I'm quitting*, she told her daughter a few days ago. Like that somehow mattered.

"You want dinner?" Mama asks finally.

"I don't," Atlanta says. "I got it covered." Which means some generic frozen entrée from the Amish store where they sell grocery goods that are either off-brand, out of date, or both. Froot Loops from two years ago, or Fruit Scoops only a month old.

Probably best her mother isn't cooking dinner. Mama can make a hell of a breakfast, but her dinners are at the end of the culinary spectrum reserved for roofing shingles.

Just to be a bitch, Atlanta walks over to where her mother is setting up the cot, opens the garage fridge, and pulls out a beer.

Coors Light. Tastes like watered-down cat piss, she thinks, but part of her just wants to see how far she gets to push.

Mama sees but pretends not to see, and that's all Atlanta needs to know.

Atlanta goes inside while her mother sets up a cot on the oil-stained concrete.

———

The age of the house shows in all the doorways—each tilted off-kilter like something out of a carnival fun house. Floors aren't level, either. Atlanta one time put a cat's-eye marble on the floor and it rolled away, down the hall and into an old iron floor grate. She never got that marble back.

Knock knock knock.

He about scares the spit out of her. Standing by the kitchen window like that. Atlanta goes and opens the back door and pokes her head out.

"What?" she barks.

The Venezuelan kid practically jumps out of his skin. Then he steeples his hands in front of him, looking nervous. "I just wanted to, uhh, ahh, say thank you."

"So say thank you."

"What? Oh. Thank you."

She nods. "Uh-huh." Then she slams the door.

But as she rips the cardboard zipper off the frozen dinner, she sees him still out there. He's no longer looking in the window, but he's on the back lawn by the rusted patio furniture. Pacing.

Fuck it. She ignores him. Perforates the plastic with a fork. Dinner in the microwave. She cracks the beer and takes a sip and makes a face, then dumps it in the sink. It's not skunked, but it might as well be.

The kid knocks at the back door. Moon face peering past floral curtains.

"Don't want any," she says. "Already have plenty. You're welcome. Scram."

When next she looks to the door and window, the kid is gone.

Five minutes later she's eating bad General Tso's chicken, each nugget so nasty it's like eating fried homeless people dipped in ketchup.

Door to the garage opens up. Mama comes in.

"Hon?" she asks. Atlanta's about to tell her mother, *No, thanks, I said I got dinner covered, so you go on back to your garage now*, but instead her mom beats her to the punch with: "I think a friend's here to see you."

Atlanta's about to protest, but it's too late. Mama's already letting the Latino kid with the oil-slick hair and the round acorn-storing cheeks in the door.

Mama waves like she did something nice, like this earns her credit or karma or something, and then she vanishes quicker than a lake monster.

Latino Charlie Brown doesn't say anything. They stare at each other in the cramped kitchen. Finally: "You want a TV dinner or something?"

He nods. "Okay."

She gets him something that looks (but probably doesn't taste) like lasagna.

CHAPTER TWO

They're watching one of those gavel-banging shows on cable. Blah blah blah. Dog bit my leg. Bitch dinged my car. Deadbeat won't pay for a paternity test.

The couch has as much give in the cushions as a body with rigor mortis, but what's even less comfortable is the space between her and the boy.

She hands him the remote. "You want to watch something else?"

"Nah." He pauses. "Well, I do like the Food Network."

"This is basic cable. We don't get the Food Network." She blinks. "You watch the Food Network?"

"Yes."

"Do you like to cook?"

"Yes."

"Then that lasagna you're eating probably tastes pretty bad. Like tomato paste pressed between layers of shoe leather or something."

He puckers his lips. "I wasn't going to say anything."

"Let's go back to the kitchen. You're going to cook me dinner for saving your tail today."

———

She can't lie. It's the best grilled-cheese sandwich she's ever had. Has a good crunch but isn't burned. Soft in the middle. A little sweet, too. She tells him so as they sit at the rickety card table that serves as a dinner table.

"The secret is to cook it low and slow in an iron skillet," he says as if he's been practicing this line for his own food show. He even waves his hands around, gesturing like he's on camera. "If you had Brie cheese, I'd make it with that. That's the best way."

"Brie. Sounds French."

"It is French."

"So, not cheap?"

"Not cheap."

"Your family can afford Brie?"

"Well. Uh. No."

Her eyes narrow. "You ever eaten Brie cheese?"

He hesitates. "Not exactly."

"Whatever. This is a good sandwich whether it has cheese made by French surrender monkeys or not."

"You know, that's a myth. That the French were all cowards. The French Resistance was instrumental in helping America win the war."

She just shrugs, keeps eating her sandwich.

"I put a thin layer of mustard in the middle," he says.

"Ish sho good." They sit and chew. She says finally, "I figured you'd make, y'know, Mexican food or something. A chalupa."

"A chalupa." Blink, blink.

"Yeah. Why? Is that racist or something?"

He thinks about it. "No, I suppose not." But the look on his face says he's not so sure. Atlanta figures that if that's the kind of racist she is, so be it. Last year, they found a dead Guatemalan kid under the bushes around the water tower at the edge of town. Beaten and kicked. Story goes that it was because he was dating a white girl. Atlanta doesn't truck with that kind of racism. She thinks people deserve whatever niceness they can squeeze out of this world no matter what their color or creed. But she also figured that, you know, you give a Latino kid a chance to cook, he's going to make a chalupa. Or an enchilada or burrito or whatever. Now that she's thinking about it, she figures that probably *does* make her a racist. Maybe it's all just part of a spectrum. Great. Now she feels like an asshole because of Mexican food. Or the assumption of Mexican food. *Dangit.*

"Thanks again for earlier," he says.

"Yeah. Well. They were looking to hurt you." She points to his head. "Guess they already did. How's the head?"

"Hurts, but okay."

"How'd you get cut?"

It's like he doesn't want to tell her, and she gets that, she really does. Finally he speaks. "The one, the muscle guy, he had a ring. A skull ring. He turned it to the inside of his hand and then he slapped me."

"Slapped you. Kind of a bitch-ass cheap shot, huh?"

"I guess." He watches her then. He seems on the edge of something, like he wants to say something, and finally she just turns her index finger in a barrel roll—a gesticulation meant to say, *Get on with it*. So he does. "Why's your mom in the garage?"

"She likes it there," she lies.

He blinks. "The story. About you. Is it true?"

"I do not have man-parts."

"Not that story."

"I did not bite the head off a bat on stage at a Black Sabbath show."

"What?"

She rolls her eyes. "Yeah. The story's true."

"Do you still—" But he stops. Then he leans in. Voice low. As if nobody should hear. "Do you still have the shotgun?"

"I do. Told the cops it was my mother's."

"And you didn't have to do time?"

She shrugs. "Felt like I did. Six months of therapy. Not here at home, either. But . . . away. Place called Emerald Lakes. At least I didn't have to go to school."

His mouth forms a reverent O.

"You should go home," she says abruptly around a huge mouthful of grilled cheese—it comes out *ooo shoul guh*, but then she swallows the big hunk of greasy goodness and says it again. "You need to go. We're good here."

"Okay." He looks confused, stung, but he gathers his bag. She plants a hand in the middle of his back and pushes him toward the door. He asks, then: "What do I do?"

"Huh?"

"If they come back. The three of them. They'll come back. I'm sure of it."

"What's your name?" she asks, changing gears. "I didn't get your name."

"Shane."

"Shane is not a Mexican name."

"That's because I'm Venezuelan. Like I said."

"Shane is not a Venezuelan name, either."

He shrugs. "My mom's Hawaiian. My dad's Venezuelan."

"What's your last name?"

"Lafluco."

"Okay. Fine. Listen, Shane Lafluco, here's what you do. Go to Cabela's. Online or take an hour drive south, they have a store there. Buy a big-ass can of bear mace. They come at you again, hose 'em down like a chargin' grizzly. That's what you do."

"Wait—" he says, but she's already pushing him out the door. She closes it, locks it. *Click.*

———

In the hallway upstairs, she sees the shotgun. Leaning against the door frame where she left it. It's a lean little bugger. A single-shot .410 bore scattergun. Winchester Model 20. Break the barrel open, pop in the shell—that's it. Pull back the hammer when you're ready to go. A chicken gun. Or a squirrel gun. That's what Guillermo—or Guy, Guy-as-in-guillotine—told her when she bought it.

It's been sitting there in the hallway since that night. She runs a finger along the mouth of the barrel. Pulls it away thick with greasy dust.

She lifts her finger to her nose. Smells like smoke and powder and oil. She feels like throwing up, so that's what she does. She goes to the bathroom and throws up, then takes a shower in her clothes because she doesn't think to take them off before she gets in. She finds no joy in the anarchy of the act. She removes her sopping-wet clothes and sits on her bed and stares at the wall for hours until she is reminded that you don't find sleep so much as sleep finds you.

———

Way she sleeps is like she's been shot in the head. A deep, fast sleep as if she's falling off an oceanic shelf and sinking into darkness. The dream that finds her there is squid-like, a kraken with many tentacles and mean suckers that drags her toward its biting beak. It's always hard to pull away—the dream feels so real, so alive, not at all recognizable as a dream.

Every time it's the same but different. Same feel. Same story. Different presentation. Like a morality tale with the same puppets but a different backdrop, or different voices, or different character names.

Here faces shift. Blood on the carpet. Her head shoved face-down in a pile of comforters that for some reason smell like the Cat Lady next door. A thumb wetted by a long, too-long, tongue and pressed against her cheek to wipe off a smudge. Again the shotgun goes off. Again the wicked stink of discharged powder. Again she awakens. Wet not from the shower but from her own sweat. Drenched, actually.

She needs to go see Guy on the other side of town after school tomorrow.

CHAPTER THREE

What's that they say about Pennsylvania? Philadelphia on one end, Pittsburgh on the other, and Kentucky in the middle? *Pennsyltucky.* Way Atlanta sees it, that's about right. She's from North Carolina and comes from a town where half the floor of the nearest gas station minimart is dirt, and even still, this part of Pennsylvania—the great gaping, pooch-bellied middle banded by the stretched asphalt elastic of I-80—fits the bill.

Her school, William Mason High, isn't straight-up Hicksville. It has its rich kids and its poor kids. Some kids are those of millionaires, some are kids who even at the age of fifteen know the ins and outs of the food-stamp program and need special assistance to afford a school lunch every day. The school has blacks and Latinos and a handful of Chinese, one Arab girl that she knows of, and more than a few Indians—not the casino kind, but the curry kind. But for every kid who drives a Lexus, you get three who can drive a tractor. For every kid who cares about poetry or science or the history of the world, you get five who know every driver's NASCAR number and not much else.

For every black kid, Latino kid, Chinese kid, Arab kid, you get a dozen white kids.

So it goes. None of them knows her, anyway. Not really. But all of them watch her as she walks down the halls past bands of lockers painted bright. She's only been back a week now, and it's like she's a ghost that everyone can see. Like she's a poisonous toad or toxic jellyfish—interesting to look at, but for God's sake, *do not touch.*

As she walks, she catches glimpses of old friends. Like Petra Bright or Susie Schwartz. Or her once-bestie, Becky Bartosiewicz (pronounced *Bart-o-savage*), a.k.a. "Bee."

Petra turns her bright blues toward Atlanta. Doesn't say anything. Not this time, at least. Sometimes she offers a polite *Don't forget we have biochem homework,* or maybe *Quiz tomorrow,* as if Atlanta's really gonna have to deal with homework for the rest of the year. Susie shields her face with a curtain of dyed-black hair, but through the scissor slit Atlanta can see her looking. Susie always looks so sad. Like the look you get from watching one of those Humane Society commercials with the crusty, one-eyed dogs and all that Sarah McLachlan music. Atlanta gives her a little nod. Susie doesn't return it.

Then there's Bee. Third in the trio, side by side, closest to Atlanta.

Bee, her old best friend, now not a friend at all.

Bee pretends Atlanta isn't even there. Eyes forward. Chin lifted. They used to be so close. Being a transplant, it wasn't like Atlanta was a big part of the ecosystem. Now she's on the shore of the pond. Dry when everyone else is wet. Standing while everyone swims.

Even the tadpoles and snails and water skeeters don't want shit to do with her.

———

After English class, Mrs. Lewis pulls her aside. Hands Atlanta a paper. Atlanta's own paper, by the looks of it. A one-pager on the subject of A.E. Housman's "To an Athlete Dying Young."

"What *is* this?" Mrs. Lewis asks. The woman's got some mean eyebrows. Like two fuzzy caterpillar lovers, straining to reach one another, trying to make out. Now those furry brows are scrunched up tight.

"Huh?"

"You heard me."

"It's my paper," Atlanta says with some authority. Because, duh, it is.

"It's one page."

"Thank you. Yes."

"I asked for a *seven*-page paper."

Atlanta blinks. "Yeah. I know. And mine's one page."

"Do you remember how you ended the paper?" Mrs. Lewis asks. "Do you remember how you reached the conclusion that resolves your thesis?"

Atlanta does remember. But she just shrugs instead, lets the teacher talk through it.

"This one sentence just . . . trails off and the ending is replaced by 'blah blah blah.'"

"I thought it was a nice commentary on the futility of collecting information and, uhh, synthesizing, ummm. Thought patterns." Atlanta nods, having settled that. "Yeah. Synthesizing thought patterns."

"You're messing with me." Mrs. Lewis's mouth goes from a tight line steadily melting downward into a mean scowl.

"Well. I don't mean to."

"I need you to rewrite this. Today's Tuesday. I want it by Friday. All seven pages."

Atlanta laughs. It's not funny, but she can't help it. "You're shitting me. Okay. Listen. Mrs. Lewis. I'm sorry. Maybe you didn't know or realize it, but I . . . went through some stuff recently? It was in the news, as I hear it. I was gone. For three months. And we've only got two months left of school. The other teachers—"

"The other teachers what?"

"They're giving me a straight B-plus. Across the board. Just to get me through."

It's the teacher's turn to laugh, but Atlanta can tell she doesn't think any of this is funny.

"Miss Burns, is that what you want? To just . . . 'get through'?"

She thinks about it, then nods. "Well. Yeah." She doesn't add that she thinks school is basically poop on a stick. That whatever they learn here isn't relevant to what's going on outside these walls. That all they're doing is teaching to the test and watching the stats. Case in point: the B-plus to shut her up and push her along with the rest of the mooing herd.

"That's not going to happen, Miss Burns. Let me tell you something. All we are is the measure of our work. You don't do the work, you're not worth the measure. You're a junior. You want to stay a junior, then keep treating my class like it's a blow-off. A paper like this won't fly with me. A paper like this gets an F. You fail this class, and I'll probably see you again next year. Are we clear?"

Atlanta feels rage in her heart, tries to bring it up like a bucket full of bile, and spits out, "I went through some bad shit, Mrs. Lewis, a lot worse than you've ever seen or had done to you, so why don't you wipe the sand out of your vagina and put on a nice smile and learn how to be a human being for once in your wretched life?"

For a moment, the teacher says nothing. Finally, she says:

"Tornadoes in the heartland. Child soldiers in Somalia. Homeless people on the streets worldwide. Everybody's got problems. Everybody knows tragedy. Life is short and hard. Do the work. Don't make me fail you. Have a good day, Miss Burns."

And then she waves her student off like Atlanta is the fucking janitor.

———

Atlanta sees only one of the three thugs from yesterday. Chomp-Chomp. Spots him in the cafeteria picking at a plate of taco meat with a plastic fork. He sees her, too, and he gets up and almost knocks his chair over and hurries out of the room so fast you'd think he was being chased by a cloud of yellow jackets.

———

She's still pissed when she walks to Guillermo's after school. Every stone or can in the road, she kicks into the corn or the soy or whatever grows in the fields she passes. It's coming up on late April, and she can't tell what little shoots are sticking up out of the mud, and she doesn't care.

Guy's got a little slice of farmland north of town, a parcel of land with dead fields and a gutted, burned husk of a farmhouse next to a red barn with a deep, drunken lean. Guy doesn't live in the farmhouse: place burned down a handful of years ago when a nest of squirrels got to chewing the old knob-and-tube wiring in the attic. Killed the older couple that lived there, and from what Atlanta heard, their two charred bodies were found still in bed like they didn't even know to get up. Then the fire spread to the fields. Took all night to put it out, the story goes.

His double-wide trailer is out back, behind the farmhouse. This time she finds him just past the trailer, taking potshots at cans and bottles on a fence rail with a little .22 pistol.

Pop, pop, pop, pop. A soup can jumps like it was bit in the ass. A bottle neck shatters. Two other shots miss, go off into the field or the trees beyond.

He drops the magazine out of the lean, black, snazzy-looking shooter, and then he turns and sees her.

Guy—Guillermo Lopez, or, as she sometimes jokingly calls him, "Guy-Lo,"—is a taut stretch of rope in a black wifebeater and urban camo pants. His head is shorn to the scalp, and even the day's barely there sun gives it a slight shine. The smile that spreads across his face is like two doors thrown open wide, and his arms move to match the gesture, spreading out in welcome.

"Oh holy *shit*, look who the fuck just came slinking up my six like an alley cat! What up, girl?" He moves in to give her a hug, and she extends a finger and presses it hard against his breastbone. All she has to do is give him a look and he gets it and backs off. "Dang, sorry, sorry. Stupid. The fuck was I thinking?"

She shrugs it off even though her body feels as if it just touched an electric fence. Irrational response, of course. She *knows* Guy. She does. Trusts him like she trusts few others.

More than her own mother, even. And yet. And still. Shit.

They stand there like that for a while. But Guy isn't comfortable in silence.

"I'm sorry to hear about what happened," he says. "Fucked up, man. Real fucked up. I, uh, y'know, I gotta ask and all—that shotgun, the little .410 chicken shooter, you didn't, it wasn't . . ."

"I did. It was."

His face goes ashen. She knows what he's thinking, so she gets ahead of it: "The cops don't care," she says. "They're not following the case. There's no case to follow. My part in it is . . . well, they saw it how it happened and they've got more important things to worry about. I spent a few months at Emerald Lakes. And the shotgun, they think it's my mom's, so."

"Cool, cool," he says. "Then I guess I'm glad you came by to buy that gun offa me."

"I need something else," she says. "I need drugs."

He waves her inside. "Let's talk."

———

His trailer is nicer than it should be. It looks like the home of a middle-aged housewife, with the kind of decor Atlanta's mother would've chosen. A pink wooden pig hangs by the front door to hold keys and mail. An Amish hex—a blue-and-red eight-pointed star—hangs above an old avocado-green stove. On the breakfast-nook table, the salt and pepper shakers are a ceramic sheep and goat, each framed by a cutesy wooden paddock made of popsicle sticks. Powder-blue curtains hang at the windows. Blue like a robin's egg blue.

"It came like this," he told her once upon a time. "But I kinda started to like it. Made me feel all cozy and shit. What, you think I was going to hang up the Puerto Rican flag all over the place? Soccer balls and rap posters and shit?"

What's funny to her is how clean he keeps it. He probably dusts. Her own mother doesn't dust. But her gun-and-drug dealer does.

He motions for her to sit at the table, then he plops down across from her and sets a beer in front of her. Yuengling Black & Tan.

"What you need, girl?"

"I need to not sleep."

"But sleep is awesome." He pauses. "Pretty much my favorite thing."

"Not mine."

He leans in. Smiling like he's solved all the world's problems. "You know what you need? You just need to sleep harder. Dang, that sounds like a movie and shit. *Sleep Hard 4: Sleep Harder.* Whatever. What I'm saying is, you get a little Ambien—that's like a baseball bat in pill form—you take that, and it's like *wham*, your head's a mailbox and it's hitting the ground."

"I don't know." She sips the beer.

"Plus—*plus!*—you do it right, Ambien can get you really fucking high, too. You push past the urge to sleep and next thing you know, you're, like, breast-feeding some other girl's baby while hang gliding over the Amazon River basin and whatever, man. You don't know what the hell happened."

"Teen pregnancy? Hang gliders? That does sound special. For now let's try something that *picks me up* rather than *puts me down.* A little more accelerator, a little less brake."

He nods. "Okay. Okay. Yeah. But don't be asking for meth. I don't sell that shit up in here. You want that, you head up Grainger Hill way."

"Grainger Hill—isn't that where the richies live?"

"Nah, that's *Gallows* Hill. Grainger's is where you find the drugs, the trailers, the dogfights. Ain't the underbelly so much as what's *under* the underbelly."

"I'm still figuring the area out a little." She sniffs, then says: "I didn't want meth anyway." She's seen what meth does to people. Bad skin. Worse teeth. Meth users end up looking like a pumpkin or gourd that sat too long past Halloween on someone's porch— mushy and rotten, the flesh puckered with pits and pockmarks.

"I got something for you." He disappears down the hall of the trailer. She hears one of the accordion doors slide open and slide back, and then he's back. The pill bottle rattles as he plunks it down in front of her.

She picks it up. It's unlabeled.

"Adderall," he says. "You know, for, like, hyperactive kids. I don't know why the fuck anybody would want to give an upper to a kid who's already acting like he just ate ten bowls of Sugar Smacks, but shit, once upon a time people thought the sun traveled around the earth."

"Some of them still do," she says.

"I know, right? Anyway. You take that. It'll focus you up real good. You know you gotta sleep at some point, though, right?"

"Of course," she lies. Her fingers work to peel the wet label off the beer bottle. Like peeling a sunburn, she thinks. "Yeah. Duh. I know that."

"Just in case." He reaches in his pocket, tosses her another pill bottle. "Ambien. If you decide to go the other way with it."

"Thanks."

"I normally get seven bucks a pill. You got ten Ambien there and twice that of the ADD meds, but let's call it an even hundred for the Adderall, and the Ambien can be my gift to you. For being such a badass chick and all that."

She pockets the drugs. Hesitates. "I'm not badass, you know."

"From where I'm sitting, you're one I wouldn't mess with."

"I don't have money right now. Soon."

"You can owe me. It's no thing."

"That's cool, Guy. Thanks."

Atlanta finishes her beer in one long pull, then gets up. She thinks to move in to give Guy a hug, but again the hairs on her neck and arms raise, and it's like she hears this keening frequency in her ears, and for a moment she thinks, *Oh, hell, I'm gonna pass out right here, right now—*

But then the sound goes away, and she's left feeling wobbly but stable.

She fake-punches him in the arm on her way out the door.

CHAPTER FOUR

It's gone dim by the time Atlanta gets home. Sky the color of a bruised cheek. Mama's in the garage, sitting on a cot, face lit by the little TV resting on top of a cooler. The cigarette between her two fingers has a long, crumbly ash hanging there like the head of a sleepy snake.

When she sees her daughter, her face lights up. "We got our check today." She fishes underneath her butt, pulls out an envelope, waggles it around. Then she notices: "Oh, shoot, this is the power bill. Gosh-dang PP&L, they didn't even read the meter last month. They just *estimated* a bunch of nonsense. Thieves, I'm telling you. And it's legal. But we did get our check."

"Super," Atlanta says, not meaning it. She moves to head inside.

"It's funny," Mama says a little too loudly. "I remember we'd go to the bank, you and I, and you used to love those little lollipops they had in a fishbowl by the counter. Like you were addicted to 'em. You wanted the blue ones, always the blue ones. I don't even *know* what they tasted like. Wasn't blueberry. I don't think anything in nature tastes like that, so I called 'em 'Windex Pops,' but Lords-a-mercy, if they didn't have any Windex Pops in the bowl you would go *unhinged*, so one time—"

"Great story, but I don't care," Atlanta says.

Her mother's face falls like a lightning-struck kite. "I'm just saying, I need to go to the bank to cash this. I thought you and me could hop in the Oldsmobile and go into town. Maybe check out the consignment store. Been wantin' a new mixer. I thought maybe I'd sell baked goods—"

"Here's an idea. Get a real job and then we don't need to rely on you getting money from the state. What a crazy idea."

Atlanta goes inside, ignoring her mother's stunned, stung face. She slams the door and pops two Adderall soon as she's in her room.

———

The Adderall is good. Real good. The high has no jagged edges. And it does the opposite of those anti-whatever pills they gave her at Emerald Lakes. Those little doodads, each the shape of a base-ball home plate, each the color of Pepto-Bismol, softened everything. Life through a pair of Vaseline-smeared glasses. It took the pain and smothered it under a downy mattress.

The Adderall takes the pain and straight up ignores it. It makes all the other shit going on so much more interesting. It kills the wasp by removing its stinger.

That night, she doesn't sleep because she doesn't have to. She cleans her room. She takes a walk down the driveway under the midnight moon, notices the windows of light still coming from the Cat Lady's house next door. She goes back inside and writes the seven-page paper demanded by that black-hearted hag, Mrs. Lewis. (Of course, it's a seven-page hate-fueled screed written in bold strokes with permanent marker. Which is to say, it's not much of a paper at all and ends up as a pile of crumpled-up boulders in her trashcan.)

Atlanta even cleans the shotgun. She doesn't have gun oil, so she uses WD-40 on the metal, olive oil on the wood. She doesn't have a barrel brush, but she does have a wire clothing hanger that she bends and breaks and corkscrews into a wad of paper towel.

She even pulls back the hammer and goes to clean it, but suddenly her heart feels like a jar of moths, and it's like she's standing on the edge of a building, teetering on the balls of her feet—the vertigo threatens to overwhelm her, to eat her the way a bullfrog eats a mayfly.

Atlanta hurriedly slides the shotgun back under her bed.

For the rest of the night she lies above it, staring at her ceiling with wide-open eyes, willing her heart to stop flipping and fluttering.

———

"Psst!"

Atlanta hears it but doesn't think it's about her. She's got her locker open and is going through the motions—pulling books down off the shelf and letting them tumble into her bag, even though at class time she'll just sit in the back and read her Stephen King novel du jour (today it's *The Stand*), collecting that sweet B-plus—and she's thinking, too, about how she didn't sleep one wink last night and doesn't feel tired. Sure, the Adderall's blissful ignorance failed her eventually, but really, that was her fault. C'mon. Getting out the shotgun? You handle snakes, you get bit by snakes.

Then: *"Psst! Tsst! Fsst!"* Again, ignorance is bliss.

She slams her locker shut, takes a long slurp from a Diet Coke.

Motion catches her attention at the corner of her eye.

"Atlanta! Hey!"

It's Shane Lafluco. Shane's dressed for—well, she doesn't know what, but it's sure not for high school: polo shirt, khakis, wing tips, not a hair out of place (so much so it calls to mind the plastic hair-helmets you snap onto LEGO figures). He's hiding behind the water fountain that nobody uses because the water tastes like weed killer. Shane tries to wave her over before ducking into the alcove behind him.

Yeah, no. She walks the other way.

But it isn't long before she hears the *clop-clop-clop* of his feet behind her, his stubby legs pinwheeling to catch up. "Wait. *Wait.*"

She spins. "Dude. C'mon. Just trying to go to class here."

"I need your help."

"Oh," she says. "Here." Then she musses up his hair. "High school makeover, complete. Now you don't look like some kind of golf-playing real-estate agent. We'll call that one a freebie. Bye-bye."

She turns, but he steps in front of her, desperately trying to smooth his hair back into its well-ordered place.

"No," he says, rolling his eyes. "I need you for something *else.*"

"Because me helping you the other day wasn't good enough?"

"You'll get paid," he says.

Through her teeth, she hisses: "What is it you think I'll do for money, exactly? Just because—"

"Oh! No. *No.*" A genuine look of panic hits his face like a bucket of ice water. Flustered, he holds up both hands. "I wouldn't—I don't—no, no, that's not what I mean—"

"Calm down," she says, voice low. Others are starting to look as Shane continues babbling. She says it louder: "I said, *calm down.* Just go. I'll follow. I said, go!"

———

She recognizes the boy waiting for her at the alcove's end, sitting there on the lip of a planter where a plastic tree "grows." Chris Coyne. One of the school's self-proclaimed Gay Mafia—La Cozy Nostra. Each of them gayer and more fabulous than the last. She knows a few of them—or, knew them once, since nobody seems all that interested in talking to her anymore—and they seem nice enough, if a little gossipy.

Coyne's all pretty eyelashes and pursed lips. He sits there with his legs crossed. Hands steepled in front of him. His chin is up as if to say, *I don't give a fuck.*

But when he sees her, that look vanishes in a powder flash. His face lights up when she enters the alcove, trailed by Shane. Atlanta's not used to this kind of attention.

She is, of course, immediately suspicious. "Oh, God," she says. "What?"

Coyne leaps up, beaming. He starts to move in for a hug, but she recoils as if he's coming at her with a pair of gory stumps instead of hands. He retreats, but the beaming doesn't quit.

"It's the Get-Shit-Done Girl," Coyne says. An eager, excited little clap follows.

"The who?" she asks, incredulous. "The hell does that mean?"

"I told him what you did for me," Shane says.

"And we all know what you did before that," Coyne says, laying it out there bold and bright as day, putting it on the table the way someone might drop a microphone and then walk off stage. As if she doesn't understand, he goes above and beyond to clarify: "The thing you did to your stepfather."

Ugh. Is that the story going around? Stepfather? Jesus.

"It wasn't my—" she begins, but then says, "You know what, hell with this. I gotta go."

But before she can escape, Shane exhorts her to stay, begging Coyne to lift his shirt and "show her, show her what you showed me."

Coyne takes a deep breath and turns around. He takes off his black sweater-vest and then begins to unbutton his shirt, which is an orange so bright she wonders if he's going hunting later in some kind of gay nature preserve.

When he lets the shirt fall, her breath catches.

From his lower back and trailing up his spine are a series of small circular wounds. Burns, she thinks. Each the size of a pencil eraser. They're still crusty and inflamed. One weeps clear fluid as the scab cracks. The burns go up to the base of his neck—around the point of his collar—but not beyond. Like the attacker didn't want to show off his handiwork. Like it was a message just for Chris Coyne.

"Cigarette burns," Coyne says over his shoulder. "They don't heal easy. Because of all the chemicals. Did you know in England they call cigarettes 'fags'? Here I am: a fag burned by a fag. Go figure, huh?" His words are glib, brave, but his tone doesn't match: his voice shakes a little. He's trying to cork that bottle, keep the fear from coming out.

It's a familiar feeling.

He puts his shirt back on. "They . . . did more. They took my pants off. Shoved a bunch of hot peppers up into my, ahh . . ." He clears his throat. "They spackled it over with peanut butter so it held the chilies up in there." He offers a weak, fakey smile. "Sounds funny, I know, and if it didn't happen to me, I might laugh, too."

Atlanta's not laughing. She says as much. In fact, she's pretty horrified.

"I bled down there for a week," Coyne says, matter-of-factly. Now she sees them: the tears at the edges of his eyes, glistening, filling up, but never falling down his cheeks. He blinks them back and massages underneath his eyes. "When they did it, they said . . . they said that this will teach me that it's an exit, not an entrance. Ironic given that they were sticking things in there, not taking them out, but I don't suspect that any of these fine upstanding citizens are in line for the Nobel this year."

"There was more than one?" she says.

He nods. "Four of them."

"And you know who they are?" Another nod. "And what is it you want me to do about this, exactly? Against four pissed-off gay-basher bullies?"

"You took down three bullies the other day."

Shane grins. "She did. You did. It was pretty sweet."

"You want me to scare them? Hurt them? Get revenge? That what this is about? Revenge?"

"Maybe," Chris says. "Yes. I don't know. What I really want is them to leave me alone. They told me they would do it again, or worse, if I didn't 'stop being gay.' As if that was an option I could select on the menu." He stares off at a distant point. "Even if they don't hurt me again, they'll hurt *somebody*."

She's chewing on her lip. This is a bad idea. No good can come of this.

Coyne's face is back to his untouchable, unfazed façade—any sign of tears is long gone. But his hands are still shaking.

Her hands shake, too, sometimes.

"I'll give you five hundred dollars," he says finally.

Whoa.

She owes Guy a hundred. The other four would be nice to have.

"Fine," she says. "Meet me at my house. Today. After school. Shane can bring you."

———

Final bell of the day. Atlanta's at her locker. Shoving in all the books she should be taking home, because she doesn't give two rats humpin' in a dirty gym sock what homework she has to do tonight. When she turns around, she sees them down the hall by one of the custodial closets.

Jonesy stands, hips cocked, lips in an amused sneer. Virgil's next to him. Big beef-cannon arms crossed so hard and tight the skin looks like an overcooked bratwurst, like it might split at any second.

She hasn't seen them in a week because they were put on suspension for something or other. Getting into trouble like cock-witted assholes sometimes do. But now she sees them.

They see that she's noticed them, and that's what they want. Jonesy does a little chin-lift, a little head-nod. He might as well drag a comical finger across his throat and point to her.

Then they turn the corner and go. She hears them laughing. Jonesy. That cackle.

Great. Just what she needs.

———

"So," she asks. "What's it like being gay?"

Atlanta walks along the edge of a barren cornfield, a field nobody plows year after year but whose clumpy rows still feature the
dead clusters of long-forgotten corn. Chris Coyne walks next to
her. He's twirling a rolled-up comic book in his hand while Shane
wades into the field, poking the ground with a stick, diligently
hunting for, well, something.

He shrugs. "I think I'm supposed to answer with 'fabulous.'
And then I should do a back flip and fire off pink bottle rockets or
something."

"Sounds like fun."

"What it's really like is moments of unbridled delight punctuated by long stretches of misery, uncertainty, and oppression."

She shrugs. "Same as any teenager, then."

"Say that if you want. And maybe it is. Maybe we all have our
own bullshit to deal with. But I can tell you that it sure ain't easy,
sister."

"Those YouTube videos would like you to know that It Gets
Better."

"Uh-huh." He laughs, but not in an amused way. Takes the
comic book out and unrolls it, then rerolls it: a nervous habit.
"Those videos. Good times. Nice enough, I guess. But that's like
whispering in someone's ear as they're getting raped: 'Oh, hey,
gosh, don't worry, it'll end eventually. Then it's all ponies and
bubble gum. For now, just lie back and think of England.'" He

stops walking. Eyes her up. Face sad. "Well. You know what I'm talking about."

She doesn't say anything and keeps walking, forcing him to play catch-up.

He continues: "I'm just saying, I could use a little less 'It gets better' and a little more 'Here's how to make it better now.' Or even, 'Here's how to stop bullying gay people just because they're gay, you fucking asshole thug prick-slit Nazi motherfucker.'"

"That sounds a little long for a catchphrase," she says.

"Maybe a bumper sticker?" He laughs.

"I found one!" Shane says from ten feet away. He holds up a small, black, flinty stone, his face a triumphant moon. He holds it close and squints, then sighs. "Never mind." He pitches the stone away, grumbling.

"How'd you two hook up?" she asks Coyne, gesturing toward Shane.

"We're not gay lovers, if that's what you're asking. I'm *done* with those. The last one did *not* end well, let me tell you."

"I . . ." She frowns, sticks out her lip. "I didn't mean that, now stop. I'm just saying, you two seem an odd pair of ducks. You're an agent of fabulosity—"

"While he sits in his basement building a 64-bit Ubuntu box?"

She crooks an eyebrow. "I don't know what the hell you just said, so I'm going to go ahead and assume that you're as big a nerd as he is, no matter how fashionable you look."

"Bingo. We met at the comic store in Bloomsburg." He shakes his comic book at her as if to demonstrate. She catches a glimpse of the cover: *Captain America.* Coyne must note her dubious face, because he adds: "What, did you think we all just sit around reading the homo version of *Cosmopolitan*? 'Nine Ways to Tickle Your Man's Taint'? 'The Cosmo Guide to Being a Power-Bottom'?"

She shrugs it off, but points to the book. "Seriously, though? *Captain America*? You find him sexy, don't you?"

"Please. I'll have you know, he's too muscular for me. I like thin little fey boys. Delicate as a wilting rose. No, I read *Captain America* because he punches Nazis and fights evil with a shield and because he used to be a little fey boy like me but now he's an ass-kicking pro-America patriotism machine."

"Didn't figure you for a patriot."

"Didn't figure you for al-Qaeda."

"Cute."

"Correction: the *cutest*." He beams, then kisses the air around her head. She swats at him like he's a fly.

"You're weird," she says.

"Uh-huh. So. You asked me, now I'll ask you: What's it like to be you?"

"It's fine," she says, plodding along. "Pretty boring."

He rolls his eyes. "Oh. Sure. I bet. The town of Dullsville, population: you."

"Now you're just being sarcastic. That's not cute at all. My daddy used to say, 'Darlin', sarcasm is the first refuge of bitter men.'"

"Well, I say that sarcasm is a minimansion in the middle of Awesome Town, and there's a pool and a room filled with puppies and a kitchen with granite countertops and a double oven. And a cabana boy named Steve." He walks in front of her and puts his hands on her shoulders, an act that earns him a malevolent stare. He doesn't pull away. "Atlanta Burns, you need to understand something. People are in awe of what you did. Jaw-dropping, pants-shitting awe."

"They don't know I saved Shane's ass."

"Not that. The other thing."

The *shotgun* thing.

She sighs. "I can tell, what with the way nobody talks to me anymore."

"I said *awe*, honey. In the truest sense of the word." Way he says "truest" is *tuh-ROO-est*. "Like how people have awe in God or government. Awe is respect, but it's fear, too. I think people are a little scared of you."

"Maybe they should be."

He shrugs and smiles. "Maybe so."

Shane totters back over and thrusts a sharp-angled rock in front of their faces. "Boom! Check it."

Atlanta squints. "It's a rock."

"A *fancy* rock," Chris adds.

Shane rolls his eyes. "Hello? Arrowhead? These fields are full of them. The local Indian tribe, the Shawnee, used to chip away at—"

Chris interrupts. "Nobody is *ever* going to pop your cherry, young Padawan." Then he snatches the arrowhead and tosses it back in the field.

"You're a dick and you're dead to me," Shane says.

Atlanta laughs, and they keep walking.

———

Back at her house, Atlanta has to root around her messy room for a while before she finds her yearbook. As she discards junk behind her—an Oak Ridge Boys CD ("Daddy used to sing 'Elvira' to me to get me to go to sleep"), a broken lacrosse stick ("I played one game one time, shut up"), a box of old Judy Blume books ("Somebody says they didn't read Judy Blume is a lying liar-faced liar who lies")—she finally finds it and plops it down in front of Chris.

"There. Yearbook. Point out your attackers."

He flips through the book. "Only two of them go to school with us."

"So show me those two, then."

Shane whips around a pair of nunchucks he found on Atlanta's floor, damn near knocking over a desk lamp.

The door to her room pops open.

Arlene Burns pokes her head in. Eyes flitting from Chris to Shane and back to Atlanta. "I didn't know you had friends here, 'Lanta."

"Mama, nobody invited you in here."

For a moment, a mopey look crosses Mama's face, but then it's gone again, dark clouds pushed aside. "You kids want anything? I can make you some snacks, maybe. I got cocktail weenies and croissant dough—"

"Mama!" Atlanta barks. "Jeez."

"Hi," she says to the boys. "I'm Atlanta's mother?"

Chris and Shane introduce themselves.

"It's nice to see my girl have some friends—"

Atlanta steps up, doesn't say anything else, just plants her hand on her mother's face like a spider squatting on a beach ball. She gives a gentle shove and then closes the door.

Then she sits back down in a huff.

"That was cuckoopants," Chris says.

"Yeah," Shane asks. "What's up with that? Your mom sleeps in the garage and you two are not . . . friendly. What's the deal?"

"There's no deal with my mom," she says. "She sleeps in the garage."

"That's weird."

"Not weird. Just her choice is all."

Shane frowns. "You get the run of the house?"

"I guess I do."

Chris—lying on his stomach on her bed, yearbook splayed out in front of him—doesn't look up when he says, "You should cut her some slack. Let her back in. Figuratively and literally. We look at our parents like they're supposed to somehow be impervious to stupidity, but the reality is, they make mistakes. They're people like anybody else, and, sister, people are dumb as a box of Frisbees."

"I *said*, it's her choice," Atlanta hisses through clenched teeth. "Now hunker down over that yearbook before I break it over your darn head."

"Okay, okay. Here," he says, stabbing his finger on a picture nestled amongst last year's junior class. Dude in the picture looks like a real skinhead type. Long, lean, hound-dog face with hard cheekbones. Hair shorn, showing the black ghost of a widow's peak. The collar of a gray jacket and a white T-shirt underneath.

John Elvis Baumgartner. Full name listed.

"I've heard of him," she says. "Skinhead, right? Always thought his name made him sound like a serial killer. Don't serial killers always have three names?"

"Yeah, but if you want to see the one that really *looks* like a serial killer . . ." He flips a few more pages, taps another picture. "There."

Mitchell Erickson. A real pretty-boy. Firm jaw like the swing on a swing set. Blond hair, well-coiffed. Big smile with white, shiny teeth. Atlanta knows him, too. Or of him. He's on student council.

And on the morning announcements. And a pitcher on the base-ball team.

He's one of *them*. One of the popular kids.

"No, no, no," she says. "You're just dicking around. You mean to tell me that John 'Fourth Reich' Elvis and Pretty-Boy Mitchell there attacked you *together*?"

Coyne's face is as somber as a lost puppy. "Them and two others. One of them a girl."

The skinhead and the student-council member. Buddies in hatred.

Ain't that just a peach.

CHAPTER FIVE

She's not sleeping when she hears her mother's scream. The Adderall makes sure of that. The drug is like a clean, warm finger thrust into the center of her mind. Once in a while, the finger wriggles, keeps her awake, keeps her focused. Until the scream.

When she hears the scream, it's like the finger's got a sharp, chipped fingernail dragging across her high. Atlanta's blood pressure goes up: she can feel the tightness in her neck, wrists, temples.

Heading down the steps, she almost falls—her feet are moving faster than her brain. But it's like she doesn't care, and before she knows it, she's through the kitchen. She slams her hip into the counter. Clips the fridge handle with her elbow. Then she's throwing open the door to the garage, where her mother's been sleeping.

Lights on. Mother in the middle of the room, crying. Not far from her feet: broken glass.

In the middle of the glass: a cement block with a dead cat wound around it with barbed wire.

Atlanta's first thought is that this is the handiwork of John Elvis Baumgartner and Mitchell Erickson, the Odd Couple of teenage homophobia, but that doesn't make a spit-bubble of sense. Unless the two of them have honed their homophobia to such an edge that it grants them psychic powers, she shouldn't even be on their radar.

No, suddenly she has a pretty good idea.

Jonesy and Virgil and maybe that other one with the big teeth.

Mama backs up to the cot, then sits down on it hard and heavy. She's struggling to light a cigarette, but her lighter isn't catching a spark.

"Someone threw a dead cat through our garage window," she says, blubbering.

"Yes," Atlanta says, her voice sharp with sarcasm. "Thanks for figuring that out, detective."

"Detective," her mother says, as if it pings something inside her thought process. "We should call the police. Is this about what happened? Oh, Atlanta, this might be about—"

"Shut up, Mama!" Atlanta barks.

Her mother gasps. At least it quiets her down.

Atlanta can't quiet her own heart, though. It's like an itchy jackrabbit thumping its back legs. She can hear her own blood. A rush in the deep of her ear.

"Poor kitty," she hears her mother say, just a peeping whimper, and she thinks, *Poor kitty, indeed*. Atlanta's not a cat person, not at all; not that she's much of a dog person, either. Even still, those two killing a cat like this—well, that means they're a lot more serious than she thought. She figured their antics the other day were amateur-hour karaoke: slap a kid around, make him eat dog shit? Ain't nice, but it also isn't the calculated bullying of, say, kidnapping a gay boy and burning him with cigarettes.

Killing a cat, though, takes it to a whole other—

Oh. *Oh.*

That's when Atlanta sees. It's a black cat, black as crow feather, black as a midnight specter, but she can see the smashed-flat tail and the tire tread on the rear half of the animal. The guts are poking out, too—or, rather, *squished* out.

It's then she knows that she's seen this cat: she saw it on the road a couple days before, hit by a car. Probably one of the Cat Lady neighbor's kitties—that woman is running a whole feral *colony* next door, accepting any and all felines regardless of demeanor or disease, and this one's probably just an escapee from that kitty-cat cracker factory.

Those idiots scooped up some roadkill and wrapped its mortified carcass around a brick.

Still ain't normal, but not exactly the plan of a cunning evildoer, either.

Either way, she's got to handle this. She can't have people throwing dead-cat deliveries through the windows of her house. And this on top of the thing with the Coyne bullies.

Atlanta glances at her mother. Mama's got out her clamshell cell phone and is trying to punch in numbers with trembling fingers. Atlanta takes two long strides over and snatches the phone.

"No cops," she says. "It's just a prank. Go to bed."

"It's gonna get cold out here with the broken window."

Atlanta clenches her jaw. Thinks, *So fucking what, you fucking scag hag jerk bitch I don't care if you catch hypothermia,* but she's not sure how much of that is her and how much of that is the angry Adderall squirrel that's doing laps around her brain.

Instead, she says through clenched teeth, "Fine, go inside, sleep on the couch or whatever."

Mama slinks inside like a guilty cat. One that didn't get run over and thrown through a window.

Though she deserves that, too.

Shut up, brain.

No, you shut up.

Atlanta goes back inside to do something, anything, but sleep.

———

Next day she finds that someone has put a Hello Kitty sticker on the outside of her locker. They've drawn comical, oversized dicks surrounding it. Some of the dicks are jizzing little jizz bullets. Underneath is the text:

DADDY WANTS DICK PUSY

PUSY presumably meaning PUSSY, but with these jackholes, who can say?

———

She about falls asleep in Mrs. Lewis's class. Which does not score her any more points with the teacher, but the Adderall is fading fast, and the woman is going on and on about someone named Wilfred Owen. Even the strongest upper is no match for the downer that is World War I British poetry.

After class Mrs. Lewis tries to flag her down, but Atlanta mumbles something about, "Oh, heck, I've got a . . . tooth . . . vasectomy . . . can't stay, sorry, bye now." And she ducks out.

And runs *smack* into Chomp-Chomp. She shoves him back and cocks a fist. "Wait!" he hisses, wincing, ready for the hit.

Instead she grabs him by his ratty Brooks & Dunn T-shirt and drags him through the nearest open door. Which is, of course, the girls' bathroom.

A girl with pink hair—Suzi or Soosie or something—yips like a spooked coyote and hurries out when she sees what's going on.

Chomp-Chomp yelps as Atlanta slams him against the sink. "I didn't do it!" he says.

"Do what, big mouth?"

"The cat. The brick. I didn't do it."

"So you knew about it."

"I was there! But I told them not to. Look, here . . ." His hand goes into his pocket and he pulls out a fistful of dollar bills. She sees a five sticking up out of there. "This is twenty-three dollars. I wanna help pay for the window."

She snatches the money. "Twenty-three bucks? Dang, do you know how much windows cost?"

"No."

She doesn't either, but she's not going to tell him that. "You're not very bright, are you?"

Again he answers: "No."

"Why do you hang out with those fuckwits, anyway?"

"I dunno. Because they let me."

Things start to click into place. Tumblers in a lock. She remembers hearing about this kid who will do all kinds of stuff for money. Nothing kinky, but he'll eat nasty garbage, he'll headbutt things, he'll say crass shit to teachers, all for a couple bucks. She looks down at the wad of ones in her hand.

"They make you do stupid shit for money. Don't they, Chomp-Chomp?"

"My name's Steven. And yeah." He protests, suddenly: "But I like doing it."

She shakes her head. "Then you're a dumb-ass, dumb-ass."

He shrugs. "Well."

It's hard not to laugh.

"Okay, Chomp—er, Steven. I'm going to bring hell down on their heads for this. I am not a happy girl, and I am eager to take out my unhappiness on those who pee in my Cheerios."

"They peed in your cereal?" She shoots him a look. "Never mind," he says with a flinch.

"Either of your buddies got a car?"

"Uhh." He hesitates but then sees her face. "Jonesy's got a Mustang. A '67 1/2, I think. Fastback or something? Green like a pine tree. Why?"

She doesn't say. She just winks and leaves.

———

Atlanta has a free period in the afternoon. She sneaks outside to the parking lot. Goes row by row until she finds that green Mustang. A restored classic muscle car.

She takes a piece of limestone gravel off the lot and keys a message into the driver's-side door:

BEAR MACE

She heads back inside.

———

She has a whole plan concocted. She's going to sneak into the administration office, and Shane's going to run interference because everybody there knows him and loves him, and then she's going to use someone's computer or get into a file cabinet and find home addresses for both John Elvis and Mitchell—but Shane tells her that plan is dumb.

"Haven't you ever used the Internet?" he asks.

"Sure," she tells him. "Cat videos and weather reports in case they're gonna cancel school for a day. But not Facebook. I stay the hell off that thing."

"No, I mean, have you ever used it to *learn* something?"

She shrugs.

He shows her that, if you know what digital door to knock on, you can find out pretty much anything. Finding out addresses is, according to him, "Easy like Sunday morning," which she's pretty sure is a Lionel Richie reference and strange coming out of Shane's big round head. She tells him so. But then he reminds her that she knew the reference, which makes her strange, too.

"My daddy used to like him," she says.

Regardless, they get the addresses. John Elvis lives in Grainger Hill. Mitchell's way on the other side. Up in the circle of minimansions on Gallows Hill. The Internet doesn't have any more information on John Elvis, but it has some more of the 4-1-1 on Mitchell: his father's Orly Erickson, and he, along with many of the other minimansion inhabitants, is a transplant. Erickson in particular is from Dayton, Ohio. Heads up some new "biologics plant" north of here, in Springtown. Some fifty-thousand-foot facility. TNC Biologics. She's not sure what biologics is, so Shane works more Google-fu.

"Looks like TNC does all kinds of stuff," he says. "Recombinant DNA. Stem cells. Vaccines."

She shrugs. Fine. The elder Erickson is a productive member of the business community. His son's still a gay-bashing bully piece of shit, and he has to be taught a lesson.

Still, though: she's a little nervous when it comes to creeping around the richie-rich types of Gallows Hill. Some of those are gated communities.

That means the first order of business is paying a visit to John Elvis Baumgartner.

To Grainger Hill. Trailersburg. Meth Town. The deep dark acre.

CHAPTER SIX

They head over on Saturday. Chris drives: he's got his mother's minivan, a 2004 Ford Freestar whose front end is mashed up like a boot-crushed Coke can.

Shane sits in the back, ensconced in a cocoon of kiddie toys. Chris isn't an only child. He's got two little brothers and one little sister, all under nine years old. Atlanta's not sure if both of his parents are really his or if there's a remarriage thing going on. Figures it's not worth it to ask.

She's up front. The shotgun in her lap. The barrel cracked in half, just waiting for a shell—and she has many of them rattling around the pocket of her camo pants.

Chris stares warily at it. "That thing's not gonna shoot me, is it?"

"It's not magic," she says. "Doesn't have a mind of its own, relax."

John Elvis Baumgartner lives even farther out than she does. Up Mill Road, past the "clean Amish." Left on Wagon Hollow, past the so-called dirty Amish. (Around here folks say that some Amish are lower-class than their peers, for reasons she doesn't quite get. Atlanta thinks it smacks of prejudice, but she has to admit that the dirty Amish *do* live on properties that look rotten and run-down: old barns, uncut lawns, ratty dogs wandering about.) Eventually they turn up the winding Indian Run Road, past the Blissful Acres Trailer Park, whose acres are blissful only in the heads of the drug addicts and meth cookers who frequent the place.

All the way at the end of the road sits the farm where John Elvis lives. Right at the base of Grainger Hill. The poor, podunk side. Like Guy says: Gallows for the rich. Grainger for the poor. Maker's Bell sitting smack in the middle.

They park on Indian Run Road, off to the side. The farmstead sits down a long, straight driveway, not all that different from Atlanta's own house. The barn is brown, not red, and has a roof that looks as if it might come tumbling down at any moment. The house is a smaller affair: water-stained buttercream siding, a sea-foam-green wraparound porch whose paint can be seen peeling even from here. The fields around are not fallow: they're freshly tilled for planting, in contrast to the rest of the property, which looks dried-up and forgotten. Someone else probably rents the fields from the Baumgartner family.

A dog lies chained to a tractor tire out front. A fat, scabby Labrador. He snoozes.

They hear music, though it's a bit of a stretch to call it that. It's a clamor of guitars, a speed pulse of bass drum and inconsistent cymbal-smashing. Some kind of thrash metal.

"We go up the side," she says, pointing along an irrigation gully. "You sure you're coming?"

"I *so* wanna see their faces," Chris says. His face is an eager, angry mask.

"I'm staying," Shane announces as if this were news. It's not. They told him he had to stay before they even got in the minivan. Then he says, "This doesn't seem like much of a plan. You're just marching up there with a shotgun? Isn't that illegal?"

Chris's face paints a wicked grin. "I think it's pretty badass."

"You know what's also illegal?" Atlanta asks. "Burning someone with cigarettes. I'd say it's even a little bit evil."

She thumbs a shell into the shotgun. Snaps the breach shut. That ends the conversation.

Together, she and Chris creep along the side, toward the barn. Toward the music.

———

John Elvis has a band. If the black spray paint on the kick drum is any indication, that band is named Warshed. She's not sure if that's "war shed," or "wars hed" or just a mispronunciation of "washed," though truth be told she doesn't give a rat's right foot.

The band—three members deep—plays loud, calamitous thrash music in the open back bay of the barn. The two doors are pulled back, and she and Chris walk up the earthen ramp—like where you'd drive a tractor into the belly of the building.

The trio doesn't notice them, so absorbed are they in making intensely shitty music. The guy behind the five-piece drum kit is another student from Mason High: a metalhead who Atlanta's pretty sure is named Travis, but she can't stop thinking of him as

"Manboob," given the fatty peaks rising behind his sweat-stained T-shirt. On the bass is a skinny chick in a torn, white, swastika-emblazoned T-shirt and a pair of acid-wash jeans slung so low you could tuck a fistful of pencils in her well-exposed ass crack. She faces away from them, thrashing her short bob of white-blonde hair, giving them a good look at the top of her moon cheeks.

John Elvis, he's on guitar. A cherry-red electric fresh out of a late-eighties hair-band video. Shaped like a cartoon bolt of lightning. It's pristine. He plays it with long, spidery fingers, but the grace of his movement doesn't match the sound that's coming out, which to Atlanta sounds as if someone is throwing their instruments into a wood chipper. *RAR RAR RAR JUGGA JUG JUG.*

He headbangs so hard she thinks his skull might come loose, go rolling down the hill. His one arm is inked from wrist to shoulder. Even from here she can see that it looks like a giant tattoo of a Hitler youth rally. *You stay classy, neo-Nazi douche-nozzle.* A cigarette hangs pinched between his lips. As he thrashes, embers whirl.

Her quickening heart matches the speed-tumble of the drums.

They don't stop playing. They don't even see the two interlopers standing there fifteen feet away.

Fuck it, she thinks and fires a shot toward the rafters of the barn. The gun barks. What's probably a handful of asbestos dust comes raining down.

But the gun's blast is lost to the music.

They keep playing.

JUG JUG JUGGA GRRAOW GRRAOW RAAAAR!

"Aw, what the heck?" she says, but her voice, too, is swallowed. In fact, her ears are starting to ring. Chris has his ears plugged with his fingers.

She pops the breach. The shell hops out like a spring toad, hits the ground. The smell in the air crawls up her nose: expended gunpowder. It's suddenly like she's falling sideways toward a memory she hopes dearly to avoid right now (*Smell is the most potent conjurer of memory*, she thinks, *and this is not a good time*), and so she pushes through it by popping another shell in the chamber, taking aim over the barrel, lining the bead just right—

And blasting one of the drummer's cymbals right off its stand. The birdshot sends the cymbal spinning into the wall. The stand wobbles but doesn't fall.

Manboob stops playing.

That gets their attention. They all look first at the cymbal as if it might've been possessed by a ghost or the devil or the spirit of Adolf Hitler himself.

Finally, they turn and see Atlanta and Chris standing there.

"Took you long enough," she says, and then she realizes she's yelling. Can't help it. Ears are still going *eeeeeeeee*.

The skank with the ass crack is like a rattler ready to strike: she's already got her bass guitar down on the ground and a baton in her hand—with a whip of her arm, it extends into a three-foot-long polycarbonate beat-down stick.

Manboob has fetched the cymbal—the golden metal is now pockmarked with birdshot. He holds it and looks sad, as if he just lost a friend.

John Elvis is nowhere near that fast. He's still throttling the neck of that Steve Vai special like it's a chicken, or his dick. His jaw is tightening and relaxing, teeth grinding: telltale signs of an addict. Meth, probably. *Shoulda figured he was into crystal.*

"What the fuck is this?" he asks.

"A friendly visit," she says. Atlanta cocks her head toward Chris. "Remember him?"

"Yeah," Chris says, voice shaking like he's going to lose it. "Remember me?"

Skinny Skank hisses at them, further completing the visual of the viper.

"I remember you," John Elvis says. "The Jew. And now, apparently, his Jew-loving bitch."

Atlanta scrunches up her face, looks at Chris. "You Jewish?"

He shakes his head and gives an uncertain shrug as if to say, *No?*

"Uh, yeah, he's not a Jew," she calls. "Not that it'd be a problem if he was, but we just figure, if you're going to hate on somebody, then hate them for the right reasons."

"Not a Jew?" John Elvis says, confused.

Skinny Skank fills in the blank: "That's the *faggot.*"

Atlanta's guessing now that Skinny Skank was one of the four who did a number on Chris. Certainly the way Chris is staring at her—as if he's burning her up with his own pack of psychic cigarettes—tells that tale.

"The faggot," John Elvis says, nodding, chewing on that information. "Yeah. Yeah. Uh-huh. Okay. What the fuck you doing, coming up into my barn with that shotgun—"

Manboob suddenly clutches the damaged cymbal to his chest. "I'm not with them!" he yelps, then barrels across the wooden floorboards—shaking the whole barn—and bolts out a side door.

"Goddamnit, Dave!" Skinny Skank shrieks after him. Voice like a fork scraping across teeth, that one. *Guess he's not named Travis.* "Pussy!"

"So whaddya want?" John Elvis asks. "Bitch wanna get burned like Homo Boy?"

Chris recoils a little, takes a hesitant step back, but Atlanta hooks his elbow and pulls him forward again.

"No, thanks," Atlanta says. "I'm trying to cut down. I'm just here to get a little payback for my friend. And also to deliver a warning that this bird won't fly. You leave him and everybody else around here alone or—"

"You gonna shoot us?" Skinny Skank asks with a laugh. "That's a one-shot shooter, you little dyke. Take your shot, one of us will be on you like white on rice. And if it's me, I'll take this baton and stick it so far up your coochie you'll gag on the end of it."

"I'm sorry," Chris calls out, "*who's* the dyke here?" It's like he can't contain his sass—but once it's out, he pulls back, turtles in once more.

Atlanta ignores that. Decides to clarify. "I'm pretty fast putting another shell in the breach, if that's what you're asking." She really is; she practiced in the mirror. "Maybe I get off a second shot fast, maybe I don't. That's on you to figure."

The two Nazi punks hesitate.

John Elvis has both hands off his guitar—it hangs by a black leather strap, the neck exposed. He gives a look to the Skank. Skank narrows her eyes, gives him a little nod.

Atlanta doesn't have time for this. What she does have time for: a demonstration.

She aims fast, pulls the trigger. The birdshot takes off the neck of the guitar right at the fingerboard. John Elvis looks like he's going to mess his pants. He howls and dances backward.

Skinny Skank doesn't flinch, though. Baton raised like a Valkyrie sword, she bolts forward.

Atlanta already has the barrel ejecting out its empty shell and is tucking another into the chamber—the barrel closes, her thumb pulls back the hammer, and she thrusts the gun up right in Skinny Skank's face. The girl skids to a halt.

"Wanna eat some birdshot?" Atlanta asks. "Because I'm talented with this shotgun. I'm the surgeon, and this here is my fuckin' scalpel." It's a lie, really. It's mostly because she's in pretty close quarters, and a shotgun is called a scattergun for a reason: you don't have to make one bullet count because you have a whole swarm of little lead bees to send at your enemies. That's what's great about it: no *need* to be surgical. "Unless you want your face erased, drop the baton, step back into the dang barn. Go on!"

Another hiss from the Skank, but she does as told. The baton drops. She slinks backward.

Atlanta tells Chris to pick up the baton. He does.

"We're gonna leave," Atlanta says. "Like I said, this friend of mine is under my protection. Whole dang school is under my protection. You come at us, I'll make shotgun gravy out of your tender vittles. Tell your friends, too. Mitchell Erickson and whoever else. This ends here." Skank and John Elvis don't say squat, but when she says Mitchell's name they share a panicked look.

Atlanta can't help getting in one more barb: "And by the way, your music's like someone set fire to my ears and then pissed on 'em to put it out. Talentless shitbirds."

Then she and Chris back away from the barn.

They leave the way they came, Atlanta keeping her gun up all the while. She sees John Elvis and the Skank standing there, watching them go.

They don't look happy. Well, boo-fucking-hoo.

———

On the van ride back, it's like someone uncorked a bottle of high tension and happy gas. Everybody's laughing. Giggling. The rush of courting danger. The uncertainty in the thick of it. The release of triumph, of slingshotting a stone into the eye of a giant, of still being alive to tell the tale. It's all *Did you see his face?* and *I know, right, what a skank, did you see that ass crack?* and Shane's leaning forward from the backseat over the center console, begging to find out what happened. "I heard gunshots! Did I hear gunshots? I *swear* I heard—"

Atlanta shushes him with a look, then nods. "You did. Chill out, man."

Shane whistles low, like a mournful *choo-choo.*

"Guess I owe you five hundred smackaroos," Chris says, cheeks pink, face giddy. "I like that word. *Smackaroos.* Sounds like a brand of underwear that comes packed with heroin. 'Hey, Mom, can I wear my Smackaroos today? Can I can I can I can I?'"

"Call it a hundred," Atlanta says, laughing. "I enjoyed that too dang much to take any more than that." And it occurs to her then that she *did* enjoy it. She feels higher than the Adderall flew her and like she accomplished something—like she really, truly accomplished something.

CHAPTER SEVEN

That night Mama says, "Atlanta, you want for me to go out and get some dinner? I'm fixin' to eat, darling, and we still haven't tried any of those . . . whatever they call those sausages."

She means kielbasa. Polish sausage. Lots of spice. This place is a big Polish area. Not just Polish, either. Lithuanian. Hungarian. Ukrainian. That means at all the diners you can get blinis and koshie and pierogies and pickled pigs' feet and all that good stuff. But the king is kielbasa. You go into town, you'll find three kielbasa shops within walking distance of one another. All run by old families, each with its own recipe, each with its own little old babushka-wearing ladies in the kitchen. It's not a competition. They encourage you to try each one. The area doesn't have much by way of tourism, but foodies come up now and again from Wilkes-Barre or Scranton or even Philly and New York just for the kielbasa.

Sausage tourism.

Being up north is weird, Atlanta thinks. Still, she's feeling—what's the word? Magnanimous. She tells Mama, sure. Go for it. Bring back some kielbasa. Which she does. They both eat the sausages—bright red from the paprika within—in silence, and when they're done, they go their separate ways. It's their first meal together in a long time.

————

It's nine at night when her head hits the pillow. No Adderall. She thinks, *Don't need it, feel pretty good, fuck it.* Sleep comes fast. Rushes up on her like a tractor trailer.

She goes down like a dog under a tire.

It's three in the morning when she wakes up to find Skinny Skank standing next to her bed.

Baton in hand.

Oh, shit.

She scrabbles to stand, but Skank has a hand over her mouth, and she shushes her. "Shhh, girl. Shhh. Don't cry out. Don't call for your mother. Don't wanna have to hurt her."

Skinny Skank teases along the hem of Atlanta's cutoff sweat pants, then runs the tip of the baton up the inside of her thigh and along the naked skin. Everywhere the baton touches feels like fire ants biting, and suddenly Atlanta is dizzy and sick and afraid in the way you get at the top of a too-tall roller-coaster peak, the fear of falling fast, the secret thrill of what's coming.

"I've been wanting to do this for a while," Skank says, smiling like she's doing Atlanta some kind of damn favor. "I think you've wanted it, too."

She thrusts the baton harder, and Atlanta gasps, her spine bowing so hard she feels it might snap—

And then there's a sound like a champagne cork blasting off the bottle, and before Atlanta knows what's happening, the Skank is staggering backward, her arm across the chest of her ratty T-shirt—she pulls the arm away and it's sticky with blood, and the shirt's torn open and so is the girl's chest.

The air stinks of gun smoke. It burns Atlanta's eyes.

"You shot my tits off," Skank says, her voice quiet and bemused. "Shot 'em right off. What man's ever going to want to suck on them again? Oh, God. How am I ever going to have babies? How am I ever going to feed them with these ruined tits?"

Skank makes a cry like a cat being kicked.

The blood flows hot, fresh, over the girl's hands. And then Atlanta wakes up.

———

She pissed the bed.

That's what she thinks at first, but then she realizes: *it's just sweat.* No way she could piss that much. It's up and down the length. Even the top sheet is soaked through.

First thing she does is feel around the floor for the Adderall and pop one.

No more sleep. Sleep can eat a bag of dicks is what it can do.

———

The next week goes by smoothly. She sees her old best friend Bee in the hall, and she sees that Bee is hanging out with a whole new crew. No more Petra, no more Susie. *Interesting*, Atlanta thinks. *I see your new friends, but do you see mine?* Does she even care? This new group of Bee's friends isn't the popular crowd, but it's one rung below—the B-Team to the popular crowd's A-Team. Soccer players, theater junkies, rich kids, smart kids. Bee gives her a look this time. Atlanta smiles at her because she's having a good week. Bee smiles back—a ghost of a smile—and then it's gone, and Atlanta figures, *That's all I'm ever going to get.*

But it doesn't ruin her mood. Things are good. She feels strong. In control.

The Adderall certainly helps. She even sits down to write that paper—for real, this time, even though it's way overdue. She re-reads Housman's poem "To an Athlete Dying Young." She doesn't need Shane's Google-fu to get to the point: sometimes it's better to go out at the top of your game, the poem's saying. The poetic version of *Live fast, die young, leave a pretty-looking corpse.* All with a lot of extra poetic horseshit thrown into the mix.

Chris sees she's doing the paper. He tells her that Housman was gay. She doesn't know what to make of that in terms of the poem—only that, hey, maybe he liked looking at boy athletes. No harm in that.

But then she wonders: maybe the poem is about someone. Some boy who died. And maybe Housman loved this boy. And used the poem to justify it, to find peace and meaning in death.

"You're probably just making shit up," Chris tells her.

She shrugs. "Ain't that how poetry works?"

Chris laughs. "I guess so, yes."

Later, they're hanging out at Chris's house. Just the two of them. Shane says he doesn't like to go by Chris's place. Got caught in the cross fire of some rant by Bill Coyne, Chris's father, about how at the factory where he works the "Mexicans" came in and took a bunch of the jobs, and worse, now they sent a bunch of jobs to Mexico. Standard racist angry white-guy stuff, but Shane wasn't really ready for it.

They go into the house through the garage—the house isn't much to look at, certainly doesn't match Chris Coyne's own fireworks dazzle and panache—and it's there that Atlanta meets Bill Coyne. She almost runs right into him as he enters the garage, overalls gunked up with motor-oil stains.

He sees her and smiles. His eyes flash. This isn't lust. She knows the lust look.

This is something else.

"Chris," he says, not taking his eyes off her. "Aren't you going to introduce your friend?"

And then she gets it. That look is *hope*. He thinks she might be a girlfriend. Or at least a heterosexual experiment. She's not really sure how much Bill Coyne knows—Chris doesn't like to talk about it—but it's not like the boy's homosexuality is particularly repressed. Two days ago he got detention for making out with Danny Corley outside the math wing.

Even still, hope springs eternal.

Chris introduces her. He says nothing more than "This is Atlanta Burns," but it's got that sullen-teen sublayer, that hidden text of *God, Dad, shut up, no, she's not my girlfriend, so don't even ask.* Might be something else there, too: a wariness.

Bill Coyne's mental antenna clearly doesn't receive teenage subtext. He just keeps smiling, shaking her hand too long. "Atlanta Burns. That's a . . . unique name."

She's surprised he doesn't recognize it from the news. "Thank you?" she says.

"Where'd you get it?"

"My parents gave it to me," she says.

"That's great," he says, nodding, still shaking her hand. "Just great. You two kids go on and play." Like they're going to whip out Monopoly upstairs. Or maybe he thinks they're going to get all sex-monkey—a far looser definition of "play," but there it is. And Bill all but confirms that: "Don't worry, I won't bother you two."

He then pats her on the shoulder with a creepy smile. And he heads over to a workbench. A tool-laden corkboard hanging above is bordered by a series of colorful license plates. Most of them for NASCAR or football teams. Two stand out, though. Each one black and white. No color. Stamped on one plate is the text 14WORDS. On another, just the number 88.

Doesn't mean much and she's not sure why it would. Chris pulls her inside.

In the kitchen, Chris pours her a glass of sun tea. Bitter. She hates the way they make tea up here. Tea should be sweet, gritty with sugar. Up here it's like the Yankees want their tea to taste like wash water.

"He knows you're gay," she says. "He's gotta."

"He knows."

"But the way he acted—"

"He thinks being gay is like a . . . decision. Like I chose to be that way now because I'm a rebellious teenager. But eventually the vagina will overwhelm me with its miasmic vapors."

"That sounds like the slogan for a really weird douche commercial."

He laughs.

"So where's your mom?" she asks.

He shrugs. "She left us when I was six."

"That sucks."

"Way of the world. Your daddy?"

A twinge of sadness in the real estate between her heart and her guts. "Died."

"Shit. I'm sorry." His face sinks like a stone.

Time to change the topic. "The fourth attacker. The ones who hurt you. We still don't know who he is?"

"I didn't really see him much. He stayed off to the side. Hard to even call him an attacker, honestly. Just stood there in the other room, sometimes hovering near the doorway. Watching. Overseeing."

"Couldn't get a good look? Got any details at all?"

"No. Not a big guy. Shorter than John Elvis, for sure. Arms crossed. Any time I tried to look, they pulled my head the other direction. Mashed it into the ground."

"Now it's my turn to be sorry."

He sighs. "This is bumming me out. Let's go find Shane and talk about boys in front of him to make him uncomfortable."

————

It's been nice hanging out with Chris and Shane. Even if she doesn't follow their conversations half the time. Blah blah blah, *Firefly* vs. *Star Wars* vs. *Star Trek*. Something-something *Glee*. Doctor Wholock. Superbatman. Faceyspaces. Something called "Linux."

Atlanta barely understands all of it. But their babble is comforting. It's like the warm wash of white noise. Womb sounds from fetal nerds. Helps her feel relaxed.

And like she already said, the Adderall certainly helps.

At least, it helps until it doesn't. By the end of the week, she's feeling torn up around the edges. Like she drank a football helmet full of black coffee, and now she's coming down but isn't quite at the bottom yet. Not tired, but not awake, either; floating in that uncomfortable space between.

———

Friday is when it goes sour.

Things were good. Suddenly, they're not.

It's like those two lines in the Housman poem:

> *And early though the laurel grows*
> *It withers quicker than the rose.*

———

Mitchell Erickson finds her as she comes out of the cafeteria.

"Do we know each other?" he says, face feigning obliviousness. Perfect teeth. Not a hair out of place. He's like a teenage Ken doll, which makes her think, *Does he have balls down there, or is he just smooth plastic?* But even thinking about that sort of thing has her feeling vertigo again, and she smells gunpowder and . . .

She shakes it off.

"I don't think we do," she says, and she starts walking away. But he steps in her path.

It occurs to her: *You've got nothing, you know that? Nothing with which to protect your fool ass. Did you ever order more bear mace? Did you bring that baton? Can't carry a shotgun into school. You were so goofed up on Adderall you didn't think about that, did you?*

Mitchell gets close. She tries to pull away, but he grabs her backpack straps—not violently, but with a grim authority that leaves her scared and angry at the same time—and holds her still.

"I *do* know you," he says, smiling, but his voice is soft and cold. "Took a little while for your message to get to me, but it found its way, like a lost puppy looking for home."

"That's a sweet story," she says, straining to sound badass, trying superhard not to let her voice go all shaky. "Does it end with the puppy biting off your face?"

"Nah. It ends with the puppy taking a big shit on the carpet when he wasn't supposed to. Sad how they had to put that puppy down. Hit him over the head with a shovel. Buried him in the backyard."

"I suspect we're not talking about puppies. I'm taking this English class about poetry, and we're learning all about metaphors. This is one of them, isn't it? A metaphor? You're like a poet."

"Shut the fuck up and listen." Smile still in place, but now he's speaking through those smiling white Chiclet teeth of his. "You kicked over a hornet's nest."

"Like that girl from that book."

"I said *shut up*. I don't care who you are. Or what you did. I just want you to know I got your message and give you a message of my own."

"White Power?" she asks, sticking out her chin. "Hail Hitler?"

"I'm going to make you hurt," he says.

He pats her cheek. She flinches—his touch disgusts her, dumps a cup of cockroaches into her stomach. Mitchell Erickson walks away then, joining the flow of kids in the hallway, merging with the stream, calling to some "bro" of his.

Atlanta goes into the girls' bathroom and throws up her lunch.

———

It's when she sees Shane at the end of the day that she knows how fucked it's going to get. His nose is swollen. Not broken, but bleeding. His whole upper lip encrusted with a blood mustache.

Shane's eyes are puffy, too. He won't say why, but Atlanta knows.

She starts to tell him she's sorry, Mitchell came up to her, threatened her, she had no idea—

"Mitchell? No," he says, but the way he says it with his nose all busted it comes out *Bitchell? Doh.* "Wasn't him. It was the other two. Jonesy and Virgil."

Shit shit shit shit shit.

———

"Shit shit shit shit shit," she says. She, Chris, and Shane are outside her house. Those two on the porch steps, she pacing in front of them like a nervous tiger. A tiger who's burned out on no sleep and lots of Adderall and who just got threatened by much bigger tigers.

"It'll be fine," Chris says, upbeat, but nobody really believes it.

Shane's nose looks like a bumpy turnip. Except scabbier. He says they surprised him around the side of the building, by the bus platform. Hit him across the bridge of the nose with a piece of smooth-sanded wood—like a chair leg or something from shop class. Then they ran off. A teacher found him, actually had the gall to yell at him. Like it was his fault he got bullied.

"That's how they are," Chris says when he hears that. "The adults don't care. It goes back to that rape thing. They think if we get bullied it's because we're asking for it. *Look at the way those nerds were dressed.* You're gay. You're Mexican—"

"*Venezuelan,*" Shane corrects.

"You carry comic books. It's like a bull's-eye. They don't ask, *How do we stop bullies?* Instead those assholes say, *How can we get these stupid kids to stop painting bull's-eyes on their foreheads?* They put the blame on the victims, not the victimizers."

"I'm sorry," Atlanta finally blurts out. "Y'all, this is my fault."

"Your fault?" Chris asks. "Oh, shit, excuse me." He takes a sip from the beer that Atlanta stole from her mother—Coors Light again, i.e., runoff from dirty rain gutters—and then spits it out in a comical spray. "*Your fault?* Sorry, wanted to do a spit-take on that one."

"I poked the bear. You don't poke the bear. I'm sitting here thinking, what? That I could just swoop in like some kind of gol-dang vigilante—"

"Like Batman," Shane says, holding a bag of frozen peas to his nose.

"—and all the assholes would be cowed? People are monsters for a reason. They don't stop being monsters just because you thumb 'em in the eye. Shit. Shit!"

Next to the porch sits a dead potted plant in a red clay container. She kicks it with her boot. It shatters. Shards and dirt clods everywhere.

Nobody says anything. Eyes wide, they watch her fume.

"Bad enough we got Jonesy and Musclehead. But now we've got a meaner set of fuckstains coming at us from a whole other side."

Chris holds up a finger. "Pardon. Can I get a clarification?"

"What?" She frowns.

"You'll say *fuck*. But not *damn*. Correct?"

She thinks about it. "So?"

"It's just weird, isn't it?"

"Well . . . *damn*'s a bad word!" she barks. "Especially when you put God up next to it. I don't know! That doesn't matter. What matters is, we got 'em coming at us from both sides, and it's because I couldn't leave well enough alone."

Shane speaks up. "You saved my ass that day. I'm still thankful you were there."

"And when I die," Chris says, "I will die satisfied by the look on John Elvis's face as you shot the . . . well, whatever that part of his guitar is called, off. The dick? The guitar dick? Let's go with that."

"If only we could get 'em all to bully each other," Shane says, "then they'd leave us alone."

Atlanta stops. She's tired. Bedraggled. All parts of her feel like a paper cut with lemon juice squeezed over it. Maybe she's crazy, but something there sounds pretty good.

"Bully each other," she says. Chewing on it. Noodling it.

The two of them watch her, obviously concerned. Finally, she says:

"I got an idea. C'mon."

CHAPTER EIGHT

She thinks they're going to have to coerce him—stick a shotgun under his chin or wave a hundred bucks in his face—but turns out, Chomp-Chomp is totally down with this. She meets him at the elementary-school playground Saturday morning, when the only eyes watching them are the crows lining up on the monkey bars.

"Those guys are kind of buttholes," he says, looking sad. She guesses it's because they're his only friends. "What are you going to do to them?"

Atlanta doesn't tell him everything. He might not like *every* little detail of the plan. All she says is, "We're going to teach them a lesson."

"Okay."

"So you'll tell them where we'll be?"

"Uh-huh."

"And when?"

"Yes. Yup." He gives her a thumbs-up.

She pats him gingerly on the back, way you might a child or an old person. "Thanks, Chhhh—" She's about to say Chomp-Chomp, but manages to pull out of the nosedive and end with, "—uuuuhsssssSteven."

———

"So," Chris says, "what's Mister Toothy going to tell those two thug-monkeys?"

"That we'll be out behind the old church playing D&D in the graveyard."

Chris laughs. "Dungeons & Dragons, wow." He does a theatrical bow. "Well played, milady. If ever there was a perfume that exuded the scent of weakness, it would be a fragrance that stank of multicolored polyhedral dice and fermented gamer sweat."

It looks like Shane wants to say something. They wait for him to finally spit it out.

He clears his throat.

"We could actually play D&D sometime," Shane says. Eyes hopeful. "What? Shut up! It's fun. Of course, we'd have to figure out which edition."

"Oh, Lord Jesus, don't get him started on the edition wars," Chris says. He forms his hand into a thumbs-down, then pulls on the thumb like a cow's udder and makes a fart sound. "We're not playing D&D. I don't want to lose my spot in the Cozy Nostra, 'kay?"

Atlanta ignores all that waffle. "Time for phase two." She looks to Chris. "You sure about this?"

"As sure as I am that Shane here will be a forty-year-old virgin."

Shane tackles him. They wrestle on the ground like idiots. Atlanta just shakes her head.

———

She and Shane watch at a distance, hunkered down behind a banged-up Jeep Cherokee.

The morning's cool. Fog slides between needled pines. The hardtop's up. Windows all closed.

Nobody here in the parking lot. Everybody's at the game. No cameras. No worries.

Mitchell Erickson drives a nice ride: a Lexus hardtop convertible, red as a matador's cape. He's got a baseball game that Saturday morning up at Werner's Field. Thing is, Erickson parks his car away from all the others. Paranoid, probably, about getting any scratches or dings on that cherry paint.

Chris whistles as he saunters up. He does these jaunty dance steps, whistling "Singin' in the Rain" as he twirls the tire iron.

He gets to the Lexus. Batter up.

He brings the tire iron against the driver's-side window. It pops and crumples inward. Even from their distance, Atlanta and Shane hear Chris squeal with what seems to be some combination of fear and delight as the window shatters and the alarm goes off. He looks over at them, giddy.

Chris holds up the origami boulder—a crumpled-up note he worked on all night by cutting out letters from an issue of *Cosmo* ("Okay, fine, I do read *Cosmo*, don't judge me, you monsters.").

He thrusts his arm into the window. Drops the note boulder onto the front seat.

Then hurries to meet his cohorts.

It's the second car Atlanta's messed with this week.

Phase two, complete.

————

Nestled in what Atlanta likes to think of as the armpit of the southern side, just before you go up into Grainger Hill and beyond to buy meth or hunt turkeys or whatever, is an old Episcopal church—the Church of St. Agnes. Way the church sits, it looks to her like a big stone middle finger, which is appropriate given her feelings on religion. Behind that church is a narrow graveyard. New graves at the back, and up front are all the old plots: broken headstones, many tilting or tumbled, the whole thing overgrown with weeds since it no longer appears to have any kind of caretaker.

Atlanta lies on the hill, looking down on the graveyard with a pair of binoculars she bought from the Army-Navy store a couple years back. Chris sidles up next to her, sitting there, and she fast grabs him by the shirt and pulls him down flat against the ground.

"Ow," he says.

"Stay flat. Don't want them to see us, do you?"

"By 'them,' do you mean the nobody that's down there?"

"It's not time yet. We're early." She looks around. "Where's Shane?"

"He's on his way. He wanted to bring snacks."

"Snacks."

"He gets hungry."

"Sonofabitch, if he gets here late, he's going to spook the—" But then she sees. Two figures moving past the side of the church and into the graveyard. It's them. Jonesy and Virgil. "Shhh. Look."

The two come into the graveyard, poke around. Virgil mostly just stands there on his phone, texting someone. Jonesy is fidgety. Wanders around. Kicks rocks. Kicks gravestones. Takes a piss on one. Checks his watch. Atlanta looks at her own watch and sees that time is fast escaping. They're not going to hang out forever. They think they're here to break up a D&D game and maybe give Atlanta "what she deserves," but they won't hang around forever.

Virgil pockets the phone. He and Jonesy have words. Atlanta can't hear them from up here on the hill—it just sounds like murmuring.

Jonesy shakes his head, moves back toward the front of the graveyard. Toward the exit. Virgil follows, still texting as he walks.

No, she thinks. *No, no, no.*

A new plan starts forming in her head—okay, she can't let them leave, so she'll sneak down there, call out their names, and then hide behind one of the big tombs, the ones with the stained glass in the doors, the ones with the thistles growing all around, and she's just about to dart down the hill—

When a car pulls into the church lot.

Oh, God. Not Shane. Please, not Shane.

It's a cherry-red Lexus. With a busted window.

Score.

———

The note that Chris dropped into that Lexus? It read:

FIRST WE FUCKED UP YOUR GUITAR NOW WE FUCKED UP YOUR CAR

MEET OUR BOYS AT THE ST AGNES CEMETERY 4:15 P.M. BECAUSE IT'S TIME FOR <u>YOU</u> TO GET FUCKED UP BOOM.

———

It's Jonesy who speaks first. She can't make out the words, but the volume of his voice goes up, like he's mouthing off. Virgil is the prudent one, pulling Jonesy back, shaking his head. He doesn't want trouble, that Virgil. Which is too bad, because Jonesy's got trouble in his eyes and self-destruction in his heart.

She thinks: *Where the hell is Shane?* He'd like to see this.

It happens fast. John Elvis jabs Jonesy in the bread basket with the tip of a Louisville Slugger. Mitchell steps up, too, flanked by the Skank. Just the three of them. No fourth, which means the last member of Chris's bully crew remains AWOL.

Virgil moves into the breach, says something just before shoving John Elvis.

Here it is, Atlanta thinks. *The title card. The sweet science. The big-ass beatdown.*

Way she imagines in her head, it's a cartoony cloud of fists and feet and headbutts, everybody taking a licking and ending up in an exhausted, bloody pile in the middle of the cemetery.

Way she imagines it is wrong.

It's not a contest. No competition here. That requires two sides, each with a fighting chance.

This is a massacre.

Virgil takes a bat to the chops. The hit spins his head around. She already sees his mouth, rimmed with red.

Jonesy cries out, tries to turn and run the other way, but Mitchell pretends he's on the pitcher's mound and scoops up a hunk of broken headstone and pitches it smack into the center of Jonesy's back.

Jonesy falls face forward.

John Elvis laughs wild and loud, a braying donkey, and he kneels down on Virgil's back and with the bat-as-rolling-pin presses Virgil's face into the dirt and weeds. Atlanta thinks, *Get up, get up, you big ugly ape*, because Virgil's built like an upside-down triangle, what with those steroids he's obviously gobbling, and yet here he is getting thrown around like a slab of beef.

Mitchell starts kicking Jonesy. In the side. *Boot. Boot. Boot.* Each time, Jonesy cries out, makes a sound like something inside of him is coming apart.

John Elvis stands, begins twirling the bat.

"They're going to kill them," Chris says, horrified, face white like a bloodless knuckle. "Atlanta, seriously. C'mon."

"They hurt Shane," she says, jaw set. "They deserve what's coming."

She thinks, this is how it goes. This is how it *has to be*. You want bullying to stop, you gotta take it all the way. Can't just make some threats. Can't just hose 'em down with bear mace. There's a line, and they're not afraid to cross it, so why should she be? If she hadn't had that bear mace that day, what would've happened? They probably would've come at her. Hit her. Maybe raped her. The look on Jonesy's face that day was plain as the pealing of a bell—he's a predator like all the rest.

John Elvis brings the bat down on the back of Virgil's legs. Mitchell kicks Jonesy in the face.

She hears Chris again, this time in her head: *They're going to kill them.*

The voice that answers is cold and unmerciful, a cutting and uncaring wind, and maybe it's the Adderall talking, or maybe it's really her true voice found after she's been stripped down to the quivering nerve endings:

So what?

And then finally the Skank steps in and her hand makes a motion and there's a glint of something and it's a knife—rather, a *switchblade,* bright and mean, and she's advancing toward Virgil with a look in her eyes that shows just how much she's looking forward to what comes next.

"Stop it!"

The scream comes across the cemetery, a hoarse shriek that surprises the hell out of her.

She stands up, waves her hands.

They all see her. Mitchell steps over Jonesy. John Elvis twirls the bat. Skank points the switchblade in her direction as if to curse her, as if to say, *Now I'm going to cut you.*

"Get up," Atlanta says to Chris. "*Get up.* We have to go."

The three foes are already clambering up over the side of the cemetery wall toward the hill, toward Atlanta and Chris, leaving Virgil and Jonesy bleeding and moaning amongst the dead.

"Run!" she says to Chris, and they both take off up the hill.

CHAPTER NINE

Atlanta bursts through the tree line at the top of the hill. Thorns grab at her clothes. She knows that on the other side of these trees is a road—Hilltop Road, which will take her back down into town toward Chris's minivan, which is hidden along the side of the road by the old half-collapsed covered bridge—and that's her plan. *Get to the road*, she thinks.

One minute she sees Chris running alongside her, darting through beams of sunlight coming down through the unfurling canopy of springtime trees above, whorls of dust and pollen in his wake.

The boy can run.

But so, it turns out, can John Elvis. He comes out of nowhere, his face a twisted rictus of meth-cranked rage. The neo-Nazi prick shoulders hard into Chris, slams him into a tree. Laughs.

Atlanta skids to a stop—but there, coming up fast behind her, is Skank. Doing the sociopathic adult version of running with scissors: sprinting with switchblade. Look on her face says she wants to cut Atlanta open and eat her heart.

It's fight or flight. But Atlanta doesn't have anything—no gun, no mace, no baton.

Her body makes the choice for her. She turns and bolts through the trees, the Skank hot on her tail.

One question remains unanswered:

Where's Mitchell?

She crashes through the tree line on the other side. Sees the road ahead. Jumps a soggy ditch, trips on a drainpipe, lands hard on her knee—the asphalt tears through her jeans like they're tissue paper, and pain blooms bright in her leg.

Atlanta leaps forward, can't care about her knee—she turns and starts to run down the hill, the pines and oaks rising up on each side of her.

It's then that she hears the gunning of an engine.

It's then that she finds out just where Mitchell Erickson's been.

The Lexus comes barreling up the hill, a bloodred flash of luxury steel, and it cuts hard on the brakes—the car drifts sideways, blocking the road and her path.

Atlanta turns to go the other way—up the hill instead of down—but here comes Skank. Grin cruel and sharp, like the knife in her hand.

Back into the woods, Atlanta thinks, and she goes to leap over the ditch once more, but she doesn't make it, and again she falls—hands forward into the ditch, into the muck, and then Skank has her feet and is pulling her out. Her fingers scrabble against asphalt as Skank drags her onto the road. Two of her fingernails break, one after the other.

Skank turns Atlanta over, presses the knife against her throat. Atlanta feels warmth and wetness creep down her neck and along her collarbone: blood.

"Wait!" Mitchell says, and for a moment Atlanta thinks, *He knows this is going too far and he's offering me a reprieve, maybe I should start believing in God after all because I sure do need to thank somebody for this*, but that's not what's happening, not at all.

Instead he throws Skank a black backpack. "Put that over her head."

Atlanta resists. Thrashes. Tries to throw a punch at Skank's head.

Skank turns to let her shoulder take the hit, then she returns with one of her own. A sharp pop against Atlanta's nose does her a world of hurt: she sees a bright firework flash of stars and feels her head snap hard against the road. Tears well up and drag the world behind a curtain of bleeding colors and blurring shapes.

Hands twisted behind her back. Wrists bound up with duct tape. Mouth, too.

The backpack goes over her head. The zipper closes to her neck, where it bites and pinches the skin.

She hears Chris nearby, crying.

The sound of a trunk popping.

And then she's pitched into darkness. Chris, too, as he's thrown against her.

Last things she hears are John Elvis panting, Skank cursing under her breath, and Mitchell Erickson saying, "Let's go. The others will be waiting."

———

It's tough to breathe inside that bag. All she has is her nose. Nostrils flaring to bring in air. Mouth stuck shut with duct tape. She imagines the tape is a hand. A hand that smells like gasoline and cigarettes. Atlanta almost cries at that, but then she thinks: *If I cry, my nose will fill with snot, and if my nose gets blocked, I'm dead.* And so she stops, she tries to relax, tries to breathe slowly and surely and not feel like the entire world is collapsing, swallowing her in a crushing fist.

When she breathes, she once again smells the ephemeral scent of gun smoke.

But for the first time, it brings her solace.

———

A tangle of smells has a gang bang in her nose. She's carried, blind and mute, and dropped onto a chair so hard her buttbone pulsates, but she can't help but notice the new smells: dust, must, stale cigarette smoke, a hint of cologne like old men wear, a tang of beer and sweat, and beneath it all, that greasy-yet-clean smell of gun oil. *The gun club*, she thinks.

She knows where the gun club is. Hard not to; it has its own road. Gun Club Road.

It sits south of town, just up in the piney hills—not far from where Atlanta got thrown into the trunk of a Lexus. She's been by the place once or twice. When she first moved here from North Carolina, she took to wandering to get the lay of the land. Eventually she became friends with Bee, and then Bee would drive her around instead of letting her walk, and they'd maybe sip beer or smoke a little weed as they drove around in Bee's certified POS, a Suzuki Samurai.

The gun club itself isn't much to look at. Blocky concrete building. Looks like a drain embankment you could live in for a while. American flag out front. A few boxwood shrubs. Bars on the windows.

And when they finally take the hood—the backpack *repurposed* as a hood—off her head, she sees what the inside looks like, too. It's nearly as austere as the outside. Wood paneling on the walls. Couple doors at the far wall. Tin tile on the ceiling. Folding chairs stacked against a wall, and a podium at the far end. In the corner sit boxes of blaze-orange clay pigeons and an old hand-thrower. On the wall: guns, framed pictures of members, war memorabilia, a handful of deer heads, a ram's head, a bear's paw upturned so it looks like it's giving the room a furry, black middle finger.

In the corner, a jackalope head.

Skank stands in front of her. Arms crossed. Smoking a cigarette.

Smiling as if she just took a real satisfying dump.

John Elvis paces. Itchy. Twitchy. Like either he's on fresh meth or he needs to be soon.

And Chris sits next to her. The capillaries have burst around his left eye, and when he turns toward Atlanta she sees the white of that eye is pink and veiny, too. John Elvis must've popped him one.

No sign of Mitchell.

"We're gonna fuck you up," Skank says.

"Mel—" John Elvis says, speaking what's apparently the Skank's name.

Skank ignores him. "That's a promise. Faggot and the fag hag. Sharing a single grave."

"Mel."

"Or maybe your bodies in a ditch somewhere."

"Melanie, shit!"

She wheels on him and screeches: "What? What, you fucking asshole, *what*? Can't you see I'm having a conversation here?"

It's then that everybody gets quiet, hearing raised voices coming from behind the one door. Male voices. Atlanta can't quite make out what they're saying, but the one voice sure as shit-fire sounds like Mitchell Erickson's. The other voice is a booming rumble of thunder. And the thunder god sounds pissed.

Then the voices stop, and Atlanta hears a sound like a dog yelping behind that door.

The door flings open.

The man who stands there is too big for the doorway. Got a chest like two beer kegs lashed together with fat and muscle. Square jaw. Beard not so much trimmed as it is sculpted onto his face.

Blue polo. Dark jeans. The signs of wealth: a ruby ring, a gold watch, a hand-cannon revolver hanging at his hip in an oiled brown-leather holster.

With thick fingers, the man turns the ruby ring from palm back to knuckle.

He scowls. "Melanie. Show the girl into my office, please. And cut her damn hands free."

"Sir—" Melanie the Skank protests.

"Just do it, Melanie. Miss Burns is smart enough not to cause any more trouble." Skank hisses something under her breath, then turns her mean cur's smile to a sweetness both saccharine and syrupy. First she rips the tape off Atlanta's mouth, then the Skank comes up behind her, flicks out that switchblade, and cuts through the duct-tape shackles.

Soon as Atlanta feels her hands free, she leaps up out of the chair and throws a wild, clumsy roundhouse punch—she doesn't know how to fight, doesn't know that this is one of the worst ways to hit someone, but frankly, it doesn't matter. Because Skanky Mel isn't expecting it. Skank's eyes are still cast floorward, and just as she's looking up, this long-traveled, around-the-world fist connects with her mouth.

Splits her lip. Rocks her head back. The knife clatters against the ground.

Atlanta goes for it, but she hears yelling behind her and the scuff of boots on the concrete floor, and before she knows it, John Elvis has wrapped his gangly arms around her and is pulling her back.

He's strong.

She snaps her head backward.

Feels it connect with his nose. Feels the nose *give way*, like squishing a coffee creamer.

His arms open. She steps out, reaches again for the knife on the floor—

The big man's hand grabs her around the scruff of her neck the way a mommy cat might carry its kitten. He heaves Atlanta hard toward the door, never letting go—it doesn't hurt, but he's strong and she can't do anything about the momentum, and her mind races: *What's he going to do to me once he gets me in that room, he's big and he's strong and he'll be able to take what he wants from me, scream, scream you stupid girl, scream.*

But then she's through the door and she sees she's not alone. Sitting in front of a desk is a chastened Mitchell Erickson, licking at a drying line of blood creeping from a small cut on his cheek. Leaning up against the corner in a folding chair is a smaller man, dark eyes sitting like hot coals beneath a unibrow that looks like the bristles on a shop broom.

"Get out," the big man says to Mitchell.

"Dad, listen, this girl—"

"You disrespect me by opening your mouth one more time, and you and I will have another talk, Mitch." Atlanta doesn't miss the not-so-subtle cue: the man, Mitchell's father, taps the ruby ring with the side of his thumb. Explains the cut on the boy's cheek. So that's how father and son "talk." Same way that Virgil talked to Shane behind that garage.

The communication skills of brutal men.

Mitchell turns his face away, then slinks out of the room like a whipped hound.

The other man, Mr. Unibrow, doesn't get up. He just sits there, staring. Eyes like shining nickels beneath that dark furrow.

Atlanta's seen him before. She's sure of it. Can't place him, though. The door closes.

She feels trapped. A cornered rat.

"Sit," the elder Erickson says, pointing to the chair just vacated by Mitchell. "Please."

The word is warmer, friendlier than she expects. She's sure it contains a secret vein of threat, a subtle promise to break open *her* cheek with that ruby ring, but it's so subtle she can't hear it.

Atlanta doesn't have much choice. She eases into the chair, legs shaking.

The big man sits behind his desk, framed by a massive elk head on the wall behind him. It's then she realizes: he looks the part of big-game hunter. She can picture him in a pith helmet and kha-kis, blasting blunderbuss rounds at escaping elephants, greedy for their ivory.

"I'm Orly Erickson. Mitchell's father."

Atlanta nods toward the man in the corner. "And him? Who's Unibrow?"

But Orly ignores the question.

"You made a lot of trouble, little girl," Orly says. His big voice calls to mind the distant rumble of a tractor trailer on the highway. Before she can protest, he adds: "My son and his friends have made trouble, too. They responded poorly. Nobody would disagree with that."

"Poorly?" she asks. "Oh, I think the police might have stronger words than *poorly.*"

"Not so sure the police need to be involved in this," Orly says. "Kids being kids and all that. You started something. They finished it. Nobody's a winner if the law gets involved. Isn't that right?" That last question posed not to her, but to Unibrow over there in the corner.

Atlanta turns, sees a small smile tease along the edges of the man's mouth.

It's then that she recognizes him.

He's a cop.

He was there. That night. The night of gun smoke. The night Mama's boyfriend . . .

Shit.

Her heart pumps faster: a cold rush of saline through her veins.

"I see," she says. And boy, does she ever. These snakes have at least one cop in the hole with them. Maybe more, who knows?

"Good. Very good." Orly sucks at his teeth. "The actions of children shouldn't be confused with the troubles of adults."

"And what troubles do you have, Mr. Erickson?" she asks, her gaze floating over the room. A black banner hangs on the catty-corner wall: on it is a white cross framed by a white circle, and above that the text: PRIDE WORLDWIDE. Next to the banner is a familiar-looking black license plate with the tag 14WORDS in white lettering. Next to that, a T-shirt with a white fist in the center of a horseshoe of laurel.

(*And early though the laurel grows. It withers quicker than the rose.*)

"Every man has troubles his children don't understand," the big man replies. "Not until they're older. That's how perspective works. For us adults, perspective is both a luxury and a curse."

Bite your tongue, she says to herself. And she does. She literally bites it hard enough where she thinks, *Just a little more pressure and I can bite clean through*. She tastes that coppery tang of blood.

The words, though, don't care for the taste of blood or the blockade of teeth.

Because they squeeze and squirm past like eager little ants in search of food.

"Troubles," she says. "Like Jews. Or blacks. Or let me guess— wetbacks, faggots, Chinks."

He cocks an eyebrow. "Those words don't sound very nice coming from a young girl's mouth. Don't confuse me with my son's friends. Like I said, children and adults have different concerns, different perspectives." He fidgets with the ring.

"That's a big ring," she says.

"It was my father's. It signified membership." Way he turns it and strokes it, letting light play across the ruby facets, she can tell it means a lot to him.

"All this wall decor signify membership, too?" she asks.

"Just symbols of one man's belief."

"And that one man's belief is that the white man is supreme. That about right?"

He straightens up, massive shoulders tensing, looking like logs rolling just beneath the surface of water. "A man can have pride in who he is. No harm in that."

"White power."

"White *pride*. Nobody begrudges black pride. Nobody says boo to feminists. And so why balk at pride in being white? One would assume that satisfaction with one's heritage and history is a good thing. As we say at work, it's a feature, not a bug."

"Being proud of being white is like being proud of being not-crippled."

"So those who aren't white are cripples?"

"What? No, I didn't—"

"Your words, not mine."

"But that's not what I meant." She feels frustrated. Cornered. "You know what? Fuck you."

"That how you talk to adults? Guess I don't blame you. After what happened to you." He relaxes again. The tension settles—he takes it off himself and gives it to her. A sharing of energy. Bad energy. He studies her face, must see it in her eyes. "So it's true, then. What you did. To your stepfather."

It's her turn to tense up. She shouldn't be surprised that this is where the conversation's heading, but even still, she's having trouble finding the words.

Again, the man in the corner—the cop—is smiling. Finally, she says in a voice smaller than she likes, "He wasn't my stepfather."

"Wasn't he?"

"Just a boyfriend. Of my mother's."

"She have lots of boyfriends?"

Atlanta says nothing.

"It's a shame what he did to you. I don't blame you. He's still alive, as I understand it?"

When the cop chimes in, it startles her, if only because he'd been sitting there quiet as a wart on a frog's ass. He says, "Alive as any man can be after having his nuts shot off by some teen cooze."

"He's in jail," Atlanta says through her teeth. "That's where kid-touchers go. There, and then hell." Not that she believes in hell, but for cases like this, she's willing to plead for an exception.

Orly holds up his hands. Massive palms, like he could crush a coconut with just a clap. "I don't blame you. I salute you. You took matters into your own hands. You and your gun. Somebody was giving you trouble and you handled it yourself. I admire that attitude and try to do the same. This man, this boyfriend of your mother's, was . . . broken. Deviant. Probably in how he was raised, but maybe even at the genetic level. So many deviants are. It's why I'm a bit surprised at the company you keep."

And there it is.

"Don't tie who *you* are to who *I* am," she seethes, lifting herself forward in the chair, hands planted so hard on the armrests she thinks she might break them off. "Don't tie my friends to him. I didn't shoot him because he was gay, because he was a different color or had different parts than me. I shot him because he was a bad person who did bad things, and sometimes bad people need a taste of their own awfulness."

Orly acts like he's chewing on that, like it's a piece of food that he freed from his teeth and now he's trying to figure out what it is. Finally he nods and shrugs.

"Well. All right, then. It was nice to meet you, Miss Burns. By now your mother should be here."

"My *mother*?"

"Indeed. I called all the parents to come collect their wayward children. I handle mine. They handle theirs. It's the way the world works. Or should, at least." He stands up. "That will conclude our business, then, Miss Burns."

———

When she goes back into the main room of the gun club, sure enough, there stands Mama, fretting over the cuts on Chris's face. Behind her, Chris's father paces, the flats of his hands shoved under his armpits. When Bill Coyne sees Atlanta come out of that room, ushered by Orly Erickson and his cop crony, he hurries over, scowling.

"Orly. Pete." That second name, he says to the cop. "What the hell's going on here? I thought this business was . . ." He scowls at Atlanta, and she feels a gentle push forward by one of Orly's big hands. Then the words of Chris's father are lost to her as her own mother steps in and sweeps her up in a big hug. She doesn't return it.

"Baby," Arlene says, "c'mon now, let's go, let's just leave this place behind."

Cold, glaring eyes watch from the sidelines: Mitchell, the Skank, John Elvis. All three of them watch the scene unfold with grim, gravestone faces.

Atlanta returns the look. She tries burying in there a not-so-secret psychic message: *This ain't over.* Seems her psychic message might've been received, because the Skank scowls and Mitchell shakes his head as if to disagree. John Elvis just seems lost, unfocused. Not surprising.

She pulls away from her mother, turns to Chris—Chris, who watches his father standing off to the side with those other two men, murmuring, arguing in whisper, maybe even conspiring.

"Chris, c'mon," Atlanta says. "We'll take you home."

He doesn't look at her. Instead, he calls to his father. "Dad?" The man doesn't look back.

"Chris—"

"*Dad.*"

His father turns, mouth a cocked line, and waves him on. "Just go on, get out of here. The girl's mother can take you home." Chris pleads with his eyes, but his father isn't having any of it. Instead he just points to the door. "I said go on, goddamnit!"

The look on Chris's face says it all. Like he just got slapped. Like someone reached in and gave his heart a hard squeeze with a rough hand. Like this, out of all the day's events, is the part that stings him the most. Tears roll down his bruised cheek.

Atlanta's mother pulls on her elbow. "Honey. Come on, now. Car's running."

"Chris," Atlanta says, not budging. "You coming?"

He does, finally, and the three of them escape the gun club.

———

Arlene's car is a boat. Not literally. An Oldsmobile Eighty-Eight from the mid-'90s. White, but dirty. Mama likes to joke that it has enough miles on it to get her to the moon and back.

Chris sits behind Atlanta. He's quiet. Mama grabs the steering wheel but makes a sound in the back of her throat like a wounded coyote—a low keening whine. Fingers tighten around the wheel, knuckles go bloodless.

"They hurt you in there," she says. Her hands are shaking worse than Atlanta's. "Didn't they."

It's a statement, not a question.

"It's fine, Mama," Atlanta says. "Let's just . . . get outta here."

"I said to myself, Arlene, you best never let anything happen to your baby bird again or she's gonna hate you forever. Because what kind of mother lets her baby bird get hurt? Huh?"

Atlanta doesn't need this. Not now. "I said, it's over. It's fine. Let's just go."

"I can't abide this no more. Can't sit idly by while people think they can do what they want. They can't. World's not supposed to work like that. I bought something. Something to make sense of everything. I brought it." Her mother plops her big fake-leather purse, pink as a baby pig, onto her lap and begins rooting through it frantically. "Something to make up for what happened, something that . . . that says this ain't gonna happen again."

She pulls out a small revolver. Blued steel. Rosewood handle. Fit for a lady—appropriate enough, given that it's a Smith & Wesson LadySmith. Guy had showed Atlanta one, but she didn't buy it—she went with the .410 scattergun instead.

All she can think is, *Holy shit, Mama has a gun.*

And Mama throws open her car door and starts marching back toward the gun club.

"Atlanta," Chris says from the backseat, "did your mother just pull out a—"

"Yes," Atlanta says, struggling to undo her lap belt. Damn belts in this car are stickier than a cocklebur. She finally gets it undone, hurries outside, and steps in front of her mother.

"Mama," she says, "you don't want to do this. Trust me."

"You did it," Mama says, eyes wet. She holds up the gun as if for demonstration. "You protected yourself when I couldn't. Or didn't. I made a mistake, baby bird. I let him hurt you. And you'll never be the same again." A look crosses her face, the look of a spurned dog ready to bite. "This time I'm not letting anybody get away with hurting you. Now move aside, girl."

The gun trembles like a living thing.

Atlanta gently places her hand over the side of the weapon. Eases it down.

"Please," her mother says. A sad plea.

But Atlanta just shakes her head, then takes the gun. "Let me handle this," she says.

"No," Arlene says, but the word has lost conviction. Fresh tears run.

"Mama, it's okay."

"Please don't get hurt."

Atlanta kisses her mother on the cheek. Smells the cigarettes and perfume. Finds comfort there.

Then she goes back inside the gun club.

CHAPTER TEN

Skank sees her, cackles, says, "Oh, the bitch is back," then starts to march over with her claws out. But that's before she sees the .38 in Atlanta's hand, and Atlanta makes sure the Skank sees it by sticking it up and pointing it at that mouth of hers—the one framed by the blackened, scabbing split in her lip.

"Back off, White Power Barbie," Atlanta says, drawing back the hammer on the gun.

John Elvis says, "Whoa."

"You don't know what you're doing," Mitchell says. "Poking a stick into a den of snakes."

"Poke-poke, motherfuckers." Atlanta pulls the trigger.

The Skank falls sideways. Not because she's shot, but because she's clutching her ear—after all, the gun went off only inches from her head.

What *is* shot is one of the pictures on the wall. Some hunter with a dead bear. Glass drops to the concrete, then the frame and photo follow with a clatter.

It had hung only a foot from Mitchell Erickson's head.

He drops to his knees. Fetal position. One hand out as if it could stop a bullet with the flat of his palm.

John Elvis skulks to the opposite corner and stays there, stiff and still as a broom. An epic task for a tweaker, she figures.

Atlanta knows what's coming next, so she levels the gun at the door to Orly Erickson's office. Orly's the first out the door, long-barrel revolver in his hand. His position is her advantage. Because when she yells at him to freeze, he does—and his prodigious bulk blocks the door. Behind him, she can see the cop and Chris's father, but neither of them can make a difference here, not as long as the big man stands in their way.

"You're back," Orly says. "And you brought a friend."

"My mama's friend, actually," she says. "Put the gun down."

"Don't think so."

Her arm straightens, as if to ready for recoil. "I said, *gun down.*"

Orly bites his lip, then eases the gun to the floor.

"You going to shoot me?" he asks. "Shoot all of us? Shoot the police officer standing behind me who, even now, has a service weapon in his hand? This is a gun club, little girl. Give us ten, fifteen seconds and we'll all have fingers around triggers."

Given the number of guns hanging on walls, he's probably right. Not that it matters.

"You're the only one I care about," she says. "I'm not afraid of anybody here. Because you're not going to let anybody get uppity with their trigger fingers. They do, you're a dead man. And all this will be exposed."

"I don't care about being exposed. Who I am and what I believe is not a hidden quantity."

"Even still, I suspect you don't want your *brains* exposed with a ventilating bullet. Am I right?"

He says nothing. Answer, confirmed.

"I want the ring," she says.

"The ring. My ring?"

She sneers. "What ring d'you think I'm talking about? The one around Saturn? The one the little hobbit carries? I'm saying I want the one with the ruby. The one what belonged to your daddy. That ring."

"It'll do you no good."

"Help pay for pain and suffering. Help make me feel better. Recompense and all that."

Just to make things clear, she cocks the hammer back once more.

"Fine," he says. He unscrews the ring from his finger with some difficulty—his knucklebones are big enough to be hooves on a kid goat—so he spits on it, and that grants it some give.

He tosses the ring. It bounces across the concrete floor and lands at her feet.

Atlanta stoops. Scoops it up. Never lets the gun barrel drift from its target.

"Then *that* concludes our business," she says.

"I don't think it does," he says.

She nods. "Not unless you feel like getting into a gunfight with a teenage girl. Hard to avoid the police attention that would cause, I figure. Maybe next time? I'll bring my shotgun. It's got a taste for the blood of monstrous men."

Then she backs out of the gun club and runs for the car.

———

It takes a while to convince her mother—and Chris, actually—that she didn't kill anybody in there, didn't even shoot anybody. Her mother drives erratically, weeping, babbling about how her daughter's going to have to go on the lam and that they'll head home now and pack their things and drive to Mexico because that's where they can escape the law, but eventually, *finally*, Atlanta makes it clear that the only casualty of war was a hunting picture of some fat asshole and a dead bear.

"Besides," Atlanta says, "what did you expect? You gave me a gun. Here! Pull over."

Her mother eases the car along the side of the road. Atlanta steps out. There, by the road, is a murky pond with algae already blooming green, thick with scummy clumps that look like foamy spinach. Past it is a pasture of cows. And crows dancing on fence posts.

Atlanta takes Orly Erickson's ruby ring and pitches it into the scum-topped pond.

He'll never find it in there. Were she to pawn it, he could get it back one day. But unless he feels like diving into dark waters and pulling it out from the belly of a hungry catfish, it's lost to him.

Small price to pay for what he did.

And she knows it was him who did this. Maybe not directly. But it was him.

A rotten apple doesn't fall far from its diseased tree. She gets back in the car.

———

They drop Chris off. She gets out with him. Together they stand by his mailbox.

He holds her hand. He gives it a squeeze. "Thanks," he says.

"It's like Mitchell said. I didn't do anything but poke a stick inside a snake's nest."

He shrugs. "Sometimes that's what needs to happen."

"I guess. So what now?"

"Maybe it's really like those YouTube videos say: *It gets better.*"

"Shoot, I hope so."

"Speaking of getting better—you need to make things right with your mom. She's hurting, Atlanta."

"I dunno. I just . . . I'll try." She chews on a lip. "What about you and your dad?"

"We'll figure it out." Way he says it, she's not sure that he really gets what's going on there. Or maybe he does but just won't shine too bright a light in that dark corner. Maybe that's a good thing.

Atlanta doesn't mind being the one to shine that light. Not at all.

They hug, and she gets back in the car.

———

Shane is sitting on the steps when they pull into the driveway. He leaps up and bolts for her, fast as a bowling ball tumbling toward the pins. He wraps his arms around her. "Uh, hey," she says.

"What happened?" he squawks, but then he sees Atlanta's mother getting out of the car. "Oh. Uhh. Hey, Missus Burns, I was . . . just asking your daughter about . . . what happened in class yesterday?"

Atlanta's mother smiles a sad smile and says she'll leave the two of them alone.

"Go home," Atlanta tells Shane. "Everything in class went . . . fine. I'll tell you about it tomorrow." She leans forward, whispers in his ear: "The whole thing went sideways, but somehow we got it righted again. Call Chris. He'll give you the scoop—but uh, give him a couple hours, okay?"

Shane nods, clearly confused.

She kisses him on the cheek. His eyes open up and his face goes red.

"Shoo," she tells him, and runs him off.

As her mother goes inside through the garage door, Atlanta hurries after.

"Hey," Atlanta calls. "Wait up."

Her mother looks at her expectantly and unsure.

"You want dinner?" she asks Mama.

"You want me to cook?" Arlene asks.

"Not so much, no." They both laugh. It's awkward and uncomfortable, but a laugh is a laugh. "How about we swing down to Dominick's, maybe get one of those Hawaiian pizzas?" Atlanta suggests. Up here in the Northeast, it's Italian joints every fifteen feet or so. You can't throw a shoe without hitting a cheesesteak.

"Sounds good, baby bird. Sounds real good." It's not until later that Atlanta realizes she kissed a boy on the cheek and didn't pass out.

CHAPTER ELEVEN

It's Monday afternoon—*quittin' time*—when Atlanta surprises Bill Coyne, Chris's father, by his pickup truck outside the factory where he works, a factory that makes little tools like tiny eyeglass screwdrivers and the itty-bitty screws that go with them. His truck is parked in the back lot, out by where the weeds come up through the blacktop.

When he sees her, his voice goes low, low enough to be a growl. "You."

"Me," she says.

Then he sees she's got the .410 with her. Leaning up against his driver's-side door.

"I don't think your son knows," she says.

He's cagey. "Knows what?"

"Don't be coy, *Bill*. You're a member of that gun club. I saw you in one of the pictures on the wall." She's lying about that. She didn't see that picture. But she knows it's true just the same, and the look on his face confirms it.

"I am," he finally admits. "So's a lot of people."

"I heard some things. Saw some things. See? I can be coy, too."

He keeps eyeing that shotgun. As if it might leap up off the ground and bite him. And it just might.

"Get to the point," he says.

"Back at your house. On the wall in your garage I saw this . . . license plate with the number eighty-eight on it."

Bill Coyne shifts from foot to foot. "Doesn't mean anything. It's Dale Jr.'s number. In NASCAR."

"Except that's not a NASCAR plate. Plus, you got that other one, too, like the one I saw in Orly Erickson's office. The one that says 14WORDS?"

"I *said*, get to the point."

"You're a neo-Nazi white-power asshole like the others. The number eighty-eight? I can Google. Learned how to from my smart little Venezuelan friend. Turns out, the eighth letter of the alphabet is H. Eighty-eight thereby corresponds with HH. And HH corresponds to 'Heil Hitler.' Same way that 14WORDS is some blah-blah Nazi bullshit about securing a future for white kids."

"You don't know what I'd do for my children."

"I think I do know. I think I know that you'd hire the children of some of your white-power dickhole fuckface buddies to try to scare your son into going straight. Not straight like, 'Don't end up in jail,' but straight as in, 'Stop liking the look of other men and start getting down with the lady-parts.'" He doesn't say anything, so she continues. "They burned him with cigarettes, Bill. They took hot peppers and . . ." The words die in her mouth.

"Unless you got proof of something, you best leave this alone."

"I got all the proof I need. It's right there in your face." She picks up the shotgun. Doesn't point it at him. Not yet.

"He's a good kid," Bill says. His voice has a ragged edge to it, like rusted saw teeth. His hands are shaking. He licks his lips. "Just needs guidance is all."

"You gave him guidance, all right. Now it's time for *you* to get some guidance, Bill."

She pulls a crumpled pack of cheap-ass Natural American Spirit cigarettes out of her pocket. The ones with the peace-pipe-smoking Indian on the front. She tosses the pack to him. "I bought those. Amazing how easy it is for a kid like me to buy cigarettes. I tucked a lighter in the pack for you."

"I don't smoke."

"You do today. Go on, light one up. Get it good and cherry." She lets the gun barrel drift toward him, though not at him, not yet. "Then put that cigarette out on your hand."

"What? Fuck you."

She cocks the hammer of the .410. Still doesn't point it at him. "Did you know, when you shoot the sack off a wannabe pedophile rapist, you gain a certain reputation? People know you ain't fooling around all of a sudden. Gets their attention. Do I have your attention, Bill?"

He says nothing. "Light up," she says.

With an unsteady hand he taps a cigarette out. Tries to screw it between his lips but drops it. He goes to grab it off the ground, but she tells him to just get another. He does. This time, he gets it between his lips, tries flicking the red plastic piece-of-shit dime-store lighter. It takes a few times to get a flame going, but then, just in time, it does.

He lights up, as commanded.

He inhales. Blows smoke.

"Looks like you smoke just fine," she says.

"I quit ten years back."

"Well, you can quit again in a couple minutes. A few more puffs. Go on."

Puff, puff, puff. The cherry glows atomic. The smoke stings her eyes.

"Now put it out on your hand."

"Which hand?"

"*I don't give a shit.* Just do it and stop jawing at me."

He takes the cigarette out of his mouth, holds it like he's ready to stub it out in an ashtray, or like a tiny spear with which you might nab a minnow. Bill Coyne winces, but she points the shotgun toward him, toward his crotch, and scowls.

Bill Coyne presses the cancer stick against his hand. His left. She can hear the hissing. Can smell the burn.

He cries out but chokes it back. Closes his eyes and stomps his foot. Whimpers.

When he opens his eyes again, she's already walking away.

PART TWO: BAIT DOG

CHAPTER TWELVE

On the north side of town, not far from the park and the water tower, away from all the homes of the wealthy, a pear tree sits on Gallows Hill overlooking much of Maker's Bell.

Given that it's springtime, the pear tree is in bloom.

It's there that a couple middle-school kids go to smoke a joint five weeks later, and there that they find Chris Coyne, in a sweater-vest and a pair of Yves Saint Laurent jeans, hanging by his neck, dead.

The rope isn't lashed around a branch. The branches of the pear tree aren't strong enough to hold that kind of weight. Rather, the hanging rope is wound around the trunk and cinched against the base of a branch—a rig-up for support. So that when hanged there, back against the trunk, Chris Coyne's legs would find only weaker, lighter branches that would not and could not bear his weight and save his life.

Many of those smaller branches are broken. From his kicking feet.

His tongue out, swollen. Eyes open, the whites full of blood.

A note tucked in his pocket, written in his own handwriting: *If you want a rainbow, you have to put up with the rain.* Then a second sentence: *It gets better.*

It's Shane who calls and tells Atlanta what happened.

He can barely tell the story. He mostly cries. Chris was his best friend.

And now Chris is dead.

CHAPTER THIRTEEN

They all stand around in the wet grass, everybody wearing sunglasses or squinting against the light. The thought running through Atlanta's head is *Funerals shouldn't happen on nice days.* Should be illegal. Doesn't seem right. Big bright sun and broad blue sky above. The night before saw weather far better suited to the day at hand: rain and thunder and clamor and clatter, and that's how Atlanta feels inside, like there's a tornado in a teapot screaming and howling so loud in her ears she can barely hear the graveside service. A service ringed in flowers.

Flowers on the ground. Flowers on tripods. Flowers on lapels. *And early though the laurel grows . . .*

Her friend is dead. Lowered into the earth. And she wants to be there with him.

With the worms and the roots. It's where she belongs.

———

The beer bottle breaks against the grave with a pop. Green glass lands in the grass. Atlanta has nothing against Nancy Tottlemeyer—the grave against which she's broken three Yuengling bottles so far—but it's the easiest target, and Atlanta doesn't give much of a shit right now. Because dear Nancy got a long life, damn near eighty years, and for that, fuck her right in her dead old-lady ear.

Atlanta rubs her eyes. Tightens her neck, her jaw, to ward off crying. Drinks more.

The bitter beer coats Atlanta's tongue like a soap-scum sheen. She fetches a bottle of cheap Polish vodka from her bag, spins the cap, takes a pull. Clean white fire. Liquid. Bright.

She sits like that for a while, next to Chris's gravestone, which is a modest stone that does not suit him. The stone shows a copse of pine trees and the silhouette of a mallard duck flying from the brush. Then his name and the dates that frame his life like a pair of parentheses.

A stone chosen by his father. One last spite by a man who did not understand his son. And didn't want to.

"I hate that stone," Shane says, walking up. His hands are flat and tucked into his pockets. He plops down next to her. His voice is raw, like it's been run across a cheese grater a few times. Like he's been smoking. He hasn't, she knows. He'd never touch a cigarette. Hell, he'd never touch a *candy* cigarette, much less a real one.

But he has been crying.

They both have.

"It's all wrong," she agrees.

He sighs. And he says with all seriousness, "It's not fabulous enough."

Like the vodka, Chris was liquid and bright. (Speaking of, she takes another pull that sets flame to the sorrow in her belly.) His life, cut short. And why?

Because of me, Atlanta thinks. A thought that deserves a third glug of bad potato juice.

"The flowers," Shane says. "They were all wrong, too."

She agrees. "All wrong."

"Roses, carnations. Roses, carnations. Chrysanthemums. Easel sprays, baskets, wreaths. Bo-ring."

She passes Shane the vodka. He sniffs at it. Raises an eyebrow.

"Just drink it," she says.

To her surprise, he does. Two seconds later he's on his hands and knees next to the grave, coughing, eyes bulging like they're trying to pop out of his fool head so they can roll away.

He spits in the grass but does not hurl. Drool hangs from his chin.

When he's done he hands the bottle back.

"Yummy," he groans, wiping his mouth.

"What kind of flowers would he have liked?" Atlanta asks. "You knew him better than I did." *And longer.*

"I don't know. He had an orchid plant, but he barely took care of it. I think for him it wasn't so much the flowers as it was the *arrangement.*"

"That sounds right."

"He would've wanted bigger."

She nods, fills her cheeks with vodka before gulping. After the gasp, she says, "More colorful, too."

"Like, he would've wanted it to be kitschy. Sparklers and tiki torches."

"And naked fire dancers," she adds.

"And a robot."

She snorts. "Okay, now you lost me."

Above their head, the sky darkens toward evening. A plane drifts, white contrail behind it.

Shane continues: "He liked robots. He had a bunch of old toy robots from the 1950s and stuff. Lot of them still worked. I mean, not as actual robots. He kept them out of sight, but they were down in the basement in boxes. He showed me. His eyes lit up when he did."

Atlanta stands, arms crossed. "He needed a better outfit, too. You see the suit they stuffed him in? Like a used-car salesman. Surprised they didn't go for the powder-blue tuxedo. A classic. You want kitsch, there it is."

Shane affects a haughty voice, holds his nose in the air along with an index finger thrust skyward. "I consider the lack of a sweater-vest to be a glaring oversight. A vicious error that will surely have Monsieur Coyne dancing the Batusi in his grave. Beware his fashionable zombie vengeance!"

They both get a laugh out of that, a laugh that's like a small light in a dark tunnel. But as the saying goes, sometimes the light at the end is really just a train, and that's true here: because opening the door to that moment of mirth—of feeling anything at all—also lets in a charging locomotive of grief.

"He looked plastic," she says, mouth dry. He did, too. Like a wax representation of him. Good enough for fake. But bad because it was real. "At least they didn't make his little brothers and sister see him like that."

She blinks away tears. It doesn't work. Shane sniffs, too. Blows his nose. Turns away as if embarrassed.

More vodka for her. And Shane takes another stab at the bottle, this time keeping it down.

A few quiet moments linger between them, stretching like taffy, collapsing like a Slinky left on its own.

"They murdered him," Shane says, suddenly. A bomb dropped on the conversation, a bunker buster punching a hole in the surface of the conversation, blowing it to hell.

Bad thoughts threaten to break down the doors inside Atlanta's head. All she thinks is: *Someone murdered Chris, but I'm the one who killed him.*

More vodka. Everything feels slow, sluggish, hot. The drunk is coming on now.

"Cops called it a suicide," she says, her mouth a grim line dragging. Those slurred words taste bitter like the beer. Sharp, but not sharp like the vodka. Sharp like a rusted nail poking up through a flip-flop.

"You don't believe that."

"I don't know." But she does know.

"You said it yourself. Orly Erickson's got a cop buddy in his pocket." The dark-eyed man from the gun club. Unibrow.

"What about the suicide note?" she asks.

"It was a message."

"But not from Chris."

"No. Not from Chris."

She wants to cry but suddenly finds that the tears aren't there. Her eyes hurt. Her brain wobbles inside her head. On one side of her the sun is melting into the horizon like a glob of orange sherbet oozing on a hot sidewalk. On the other, the ghost of the moon is already showing its face. Full, round, pregnant with all the nightmares that sleep will bring. Atlanta reminds herself to go to Guy

Buy more Adderall. With what money, she doesn't know, but he'll comp her. He always comps her. Guy's good like that.

"They killed him, Atlanta. They killed our friend."

There it is. The twist of the knife.

She gives the knife a twist of her own.

"I killed him," Atlanta says, finally.

"What?" Shane asks. Like for a second he's not sure if she's serious.

"I did it. I stirred up the shit. Mitchell Erickson warned me. Told me not to go poking snakes." She bites down on the inside of her cheek to stop herself from crying. The taste of blood brightens her tongue. "If somebody killed him, it's because of what I did."

"We all did it. It was all three of us."

"No!" she says, angry. Not at him, but anger is anger and he shrinks back. "I was the one with the shotgun. I was the one who marched into the barn, who set up Jonesy and Virgil . . ." She doesn't even mention that Jonesy ended up in the hospital with a broken nose and broken ribs, another vengeful spirit who will surely come looking for a pound of flesh. "It was me all the way—the hand on the stick, the finger on the trigger."

"Atlanta, we have to find out who killed Chris. Make them pay. Bring them to justice."

She laughs, but it isn't a happy sound. "Justice. Who are you? The sheriff? The lawman who wants to bring order to town? Wrangle up the outlaws and make things right? We tried that already, Shane. And let me tell you: *we were not up to the task.*"

"But Chris would want us to—"

"Chris is dead!" she yells. "Chris doesn't want *anything* now."

"Atlanta . . ."

But it doesn't matter. She doesn't want to hear him. She grabs her bag, throws Shane the vodka. Then she pushes past him and walks away, threading herself between the stones of the dead, walking the wobbly walk of the drunken and alive.

———

That night she goes to clean her shotgun. Back to the coat hanger with a paper-towel wad at the end and a little spray of WD-40. Crumbs of powder tumble out the end of the barrel, and she finds an empty .410 shell in the breach, green casing uncrimped and openmouthed from when the gun last coughed up a spray of pellets.

Halfway through, she has to put the gun away. Can't do it.

Can't do any of this. Can't solve Chris's murder. Can't bring him back. Can't help Shane. She's not equipped for any of this.

Her mother's been hovering over her like a cloud of gnats since Chris died, and tonight's no different, with Mama asking Atlanta if she wants anything at all, and Atlanta thinks, *I could really use a hug*, but for some reason she doesn't say that and instead just shakes her head. Then closes the door and feigns sleep. This night. The next. And so many others after.

CHAPTER FOURTEEN

It's the last day of school for the year. Atlanta passed. B-pluses across the board, except in Mrs. Lewis's English class, where she squeaked by with an untidy (but still passing) C-minus.

Atlanta goes by the English department, a dark little quad of classrooms. No lockers up here, and the day is almost done so it's mostly empty—a few kids laughing, passing around yearbooks, dumb shit like that.

She knocks on the door to Mrs. Lewis's classroom. The teacher looks up from a white carton of gummy lo mein, caught in a moment of embarrassment as she's got a squid's tangle of noodles dangling from her lips. She knits her dark brows and quickly slurps up the noodles.

"Sorry," Mrs. Lewis says, dabbing her lips with a napkin. "Kind of a tradition. Last day of the school year means a carton of Chinese from Happy Peking."

"They have good egg rolls," Atlanta says.

"They do. What can I help you with, Miss Burns?"

"Just thought I'd tell you to have a good summer."

The teacher smirks. "And here I thought you didn't like me much. From what I hear, I was the only teacher to buck the B-plus trend."

"Yeah. You were."

They hang there like that, in an awkward staring match, for ten seconds that seem to stretch into a geological epoch. Finally Mrs. Lewis says, "I'm sorry to hear about your friend."

"Mm. Yeah. Thanks." A sour feeling sucks at her guts. "Did you have him as a student?"

"I did not. He was in AP English. Mr. Shustack teaches that." Again the teacher dabs at her mouth with the napkin. "I'm surprised."

"At what?"

"That you didn't write anything for the yearbook. For your friend."

"Not much to say."

"Some wrote poems."

Atlanta shrugs. "I'm not the poetic type."

"Your analysis of 'To an Athlete Dying Young' was surprisingly incisive. Sloppy in execution, perhaps, but some powerful insight in there."

"Dying young's kind of a theme these days."

Mrs. Lewis doesn't say anything. Her pained, sad smile says it all.

"Housman was gay," Atlanta says matter-of-factly.

"He was. You should read all of 'A Shropshire Lad.'"

"Maybe." She pauses, then winces with the sting of truth. "I probably won't."

Mrs. Lewis laughs. "Well, at least you're honest." Then, in a fit of her own honesty, she says, "My son died. When he was five. Leukemia."

"I'm real sorry to hear that. I didn't know."

"Don't be. It was before you were born. But it's why I teach that poem. Among others. Life is equal parts strange and beautiful and horrible, and we're tossed into it without a map or an instruction guide. Poems and stories have a way of helping us make sense of things."

Atlanta's not so sure about that. She's not sure anything makes sense anymore. Even still, she offers a wan smile and a wave. "Maybe. I'll see you next year, Mrs. Lewis."

"Have a good summer, Atlanta."

But Atlanta knows the days of good summers may very well be over.

———

She hasn't spoken to Shane since the night of the funeral. Shane tried to reach out. Phone calls and e-mails and chasing her down in the halls. But she always got away, and eventually he stopped trying. She told herself it was best: he deserved better friends. Friends that wouldn't get him hurt. Or worse, killed.

———

People look at her now. Like, they actually *look* at her. Atlanta makes her way past lockers and the library and the administration office and out the front door toward the soccer field, and they watch her go by. Some even wave or say things to her. Eddie Peters tells her to have a good summer. Damita Martinez asks her to sign her yearbook. Kyle Clemons gives her a running high five without saying anything.

Takes her a little while to figure it out, but figure it out she does. Eddie is one of the La Cozy Nostra. Damita's . . . well, Atlanta wants to say Mexican because that's how all the white people around here see immigrants, but she's probably Guatemalan. Or Venezuelan like Shane. Kyle is a gawky, zit-sprung spaz in a Doctor Who T-shirt and checkered Converse All-Stars. A nice spaz, but definitely, you know, *spazzy*.

These are her people now. The downtrodden and disaffected. The beaten and bullied, the used and abused. The jocks don't talk to her. The pretty girls won't say boo. The party kids and student-council jerks and the rich pricks still won't give her a passing glance. But those beneath—the subterranean social dwellers, the mutants, the weirdos, the *exiles*—meet her eyes and, holy shit, actually *talk* to her.

But it isn't long before she's reminded how small this tribe of freaks really is.

She catches a whiff of weed, a skunky perfume plume that's gone when the wind turns.

Words rise from the other side of the bleachers:

"Dude," one of the voices, a boy's, says. "God *hates* fags."

Another voice: ". . . all should fuckin' off themselves."

"Obviously."

"Obviously."

Her bowels cinch like a too-tight belt. Sweat streaks the lines of her palms.

Keep walking, she thinks. *Go home.*

But even as she's picturing herself walking home down the back roads and through the cornfields, her boots are already taking her the other way. Toward the bleachers. Toward the voices.

Two shapes stand there underneath the stands, passing a joint back and forth in a gray-green haze illuminated by vertical lines of afternoon sun. She knows the one: thick little nub that he is, catcher for the baseball team. Charlie Russo. The other—lankier, ropier—plays on the team, too, though she doesn't know his name or position and doesn't much care. Both are friends with Mitchell Erickson.

The two boys continue talking. "I'd kill myself if I were gay," the lanky one says. "Especially *that* gay. Might as well be a fuckin' girl, man."

Russo laugh-coughs, a hacking blast as he exhales. "You got it all—" More coughing. "You got it all wrong. They're not tryin' to kill themselves, they just think the gun barrel is a dude's dick!"

Then he mimics a slobbery blowjob on a finger-gun where his brains come blasting out the back of his head. He passes the joint back.

They high-five: *slap.* Russo says, "Hey, you comin' to the fights later this—"

Atlanta comes up underneath the bleachers. Doesn't bother trying to hide her presence. The two guys do, however, try to hide the joint—but when they see who it is, Lanky brings it back out from behind his back.

"Yo, baby, you want a hit?" Lanky says, sticking the weed down by his crotch level and tweaking his two fingers so the joint waggles back and forth. Ash falls. He laughs. *Hurr hurr hurr.*

Normally Atlanta would be into some banter, maybe say something like, "My, what a tiny dong you have," but she's mad and her patience is worn down like a chewed fingernail.

Instead she just kicks him in the nuts. Hard.

Embers from the joint swirl. The air goes out of him. Lanky tumbles sideways. Russo's fast with his fists, but it doesn't matter, because Atlanta's ready. She has a new knife—a small lockback with a ruggedized orange handle and a fat little three-inch blade. A jerk of the wrist and the blade pops, clicks, glints in the sun.

A few swishes of the blade through the air, and Russo knows not to test her. By now they should all know not to test her.

A voice inside her mind screams and yells and tells her to go home, leave it alone—stop throwing rocks at beehives. But she stands her ground.

Lanky mumbles. Feels around the grass for the joint.

Russo blinks his bloodshot eyes. "You bitch."

"That's me."

"Should learn to mind your own business."

"Yeah, probably. But I'm going to need you to shut the fuck up when it comes to my friend." She feels tears threatening the corners of her eyes once more. *Not now, don't cry in front of these jokers, quit it.* "Chris was cool. The *coolest.* And it's people like you that make folks feel bad just for being who they are, just for living in the world the way they got to. Anybody should off themselves, it should be you dumb shits."

Russo takes a step toward her, but again she swipes the knife. It cuts the air with a hiss.

"Uh-uh," she says. "I'll pop you like a water balloon."

"You don't got the balls," he says.

"Don't much need 'em."

From the ground, Lanky moans. "She'll do it. Dude. *Dude.*" He tilts his head toward her. "We're sorry. Okay?"

But Russo doesn't agree.

"You'll get yours," he tells her.

"I figure you're right about that."

And then she backs away. Heart pounding. Throat tight. Eyes hot and raw.

She turns and runs home.

CHAPTER FIFTEEN

Atlanta walks down the long driveway toward her house, boots crunching on loose limestone gravel, dust kicking up since it hasn't rained in a couple weeks.

In the distance, in the woods far beyond the house, plump cloud-bulges rise into the sky. Steam from the PP&L power plant behind the woods. When winter comes and the leaves fall, you can see the cooling towers. Now it's all green and you have to squint to see the shapes.

Sometimes the clouds coming up out of there look like things. Hands or fists. Faces. A fox jumping. A person screaming. Right now they just look like lumpy piles of stuffing cut out of a pillow. Floating in zero gravity.

As Atlanta gets closer to home, she sees someone sitting on the steps outside the ratty screened-in porch.

A girl. Familiar but not too familiar. White-blonde hair. Peach T-shirt. Jeans, but not trashy jeans that hang low and show off the whale-tail of a thong. Pink lipstick. Good shoes. Rich girl, by the looks of her.

She's sporting an infinite stare, looking off at a fixed point in between worlds. Almost like there's nobody home in those eyes.

Atlanta lifts her chin in a bro-nod. "'Sup."

Blondie twitches, jarred from her reverie. "Oh."

"Yeah. Oh. You lost?"

"Are you Atlanta?" The girl stands.

"Maybe." Her encounter at school has her feeling standoffish, which isn't very fair. "Sorry. Yeah. Why?"

"I'm Jenny. Jenny Whitsett." The girl thrusts out her hand. It's like a mannequin's hand it looks so nice. Atlanta figures on not being rude, so she takes it. Blondie—er, Jenny—has a mannequin's handshake, too. Stiff but also lifeless. "I'd like to talk to you about something."

Atlanta rolls her eyes. "Listen, I believe in Jesus, I just don't know if he believes in me, and I try to be good but I'm not always so good at *being* good, so whatever it is you want to preach, it's gonna fall on deaf ears—"

"It's not about Jesus."

"Well, who else is there? You believe in some kind of space god, like Tom Cruise?"

"What? No." A flash of irritation. "I want your help."

Atlanta frowns, then gives in. She drops her book bag on the ground, goes and hooks a piece-of-shit white plastic patio chair with her toe, drags it closer, plops her butt down on it. Chin to her chest. Red tangle of hair over her shoulders.

"I need you to solve a murder," Jenny tells her.

Atlanta's whole body tightens, a flash of Chris's face in her mind's eye. "Murder."

"Yes. Murder. My dog. My dog was murdered."

She can't help it, but she laughs. It's not that she thinks dead murdered dogs are funny—but her brain concocts a really weird version of the board game Clue where a bunch of uppity rich white folks chase terriers and retrievers around a mansion with various found weapons. *It was Colonel Mustard who killed the Yorkie. In the kitchen. With a rubber doggy bone!* Jenny seems offended, though, so Atlanta just clears her throat and stands back up with enough force that the chair falls over.

"Jenny, was real fun meeting you. But I don't solve murders. Especially . . . dog . . . murders." She puts her hand back out, but Jenny just stares at it like it's a squirming tentacle instead of a human limb.

"But I'm Steven's cousin. He said you'd help me."

"I don't know a Steven."

"Steven Burkholder. Steve."

Atlanta narrows her gaze. "Mmm-nope."

Jenny shifts uncomfortably. "He has . . . big teeth."

"Chomp-Chomp!" Atlanta says, suddenly getting it. "I mean. *Steven*. Steve. Stevie. Sure."

"So you'll help me."

"Uh-uh. I like your cousin well enough, but I kinda sorta helped put a couple of his buddies in the hospital. We're not close or anything."

"But he said you help people."

"I don't help anybody."

"I can pay."

"Real nice meeting you," Atlanta says, already walking away. "Good luck with your . . . dog situation."

And she goes inside the porch and slams the screen door behind her. Jenny stays out there for a while. Atlanta thinks she sees the chick crying, and part of her thinks to go out there and console her, but in this life you need to learn to find your own consolation. Dog died? Harden up, Care Bear. Her friend died. A human friend.

People matter. Animals, not so much.

Atlanta's never had a dog.

———

That night she doesn't need Adderall. Sleep is evasive, ducking and feinting, slippery like a pig slathered in its own grease. The day was hot, but somehow the night seems hotter. The air thick and stuffy like she's a piece of French toast puffing up and sweating on the griddle. Summer's not even here yet, but the season has sent an early preview.

And all this thinking about food has her feeling hungry.

Restless legs kick off covers. Then she gets cold, drags the covers back. Hot, cold, hot, cold. Sometimes she almost falls asleep, but there it is: a sensation like she's falling down a flight of steps. Her arms jerk like those of a marionette operated by an epileptic puppeteer, and then her breath gets caught in her chest like a rat in a trap, and she gasps and sits up, again chasing sleep away with a swipe of panic. And guilt.

Guilt, guilt, guilt. Nibbling away at her. Every once in a while she can hear the voice of Chris Coyne in her ears, so clear it's like he's standing right there next to her. *Are you just going to let my bones rest? Sister, color me disappointed. Gray is the color of disappointment, in case you're looking for paint colors. Like gun-metal, that color. And here I thought you'd help me. My bad. Guess it really* doesn't *get any better, does it?* Somewhere outside a dog barks. Yappy little thing before it yelps and is gone. Chris clucks his tongue in her ear. *Tsk, tsk, tsk.*

She knows he's not really here. It's her own inner monologue made to sound like his. Not like a marionette but, rather, a ventriloquist's dummy: her throwing a voice to shadows and specters.

Puppets, puppets, she thinks drowsily, *we're all puppets, puppets and puppies*—an absurd thought right before she falls asleep in the final hour before the coming dawn.

———

Morning—well, late morning—*well*, let's just call it "noon"—arrives, and Atlanta awakens in a dreary, bleary-eyed sweat. Her spirits lift a little—not a full, bounding leap, but like a balloon whose helium hasn't gone all the way out—when she realizes that this is the first day of summer vacation. No more school. No more stupid kids. No more bullies. Just three months of sitting on her ass, watching bad daytime courtroom TV, eating cheap frozen pizzas and off-brand cereal from the Amish store, lining up cans on the post-and-rail fence out back and knocking them off with the squirrel gun. Freedom. Three months of do-nothing, think-nothing, mind-wiped, blissful teenage oblivion. *Hell. Yes.*

It's then she hears something downstairs.

A gentle sobbing, as if into a pillow. Or a couch cushion.

Her mother.

"Aw, shoot," Atlanta says. Then buries her head under her own pillow. Minutes pass. Once more she emerges—*peekaboo!*—and still hears the woman's weeping. "Dangit."

She's going to have to check on her mother, isn't she? The two of them have been getting along. Better. If not great. It's not like it used to be, where she looked up to her mother and wanted to be like her; that ship has long sailed. It sailed and hit an iceberg and broke apart when her mother invited that man into their house.

The sudden stink of gunpowder screw-spirals up her nose. Another ghost. Not present. Not real. She pushes it back, then makes her way downstairs, sees her mother from behind, sitting on the couch, her lap a clumsy cairn of crumpled-up tissues.

Next to her, a torn envelope and some kind of letter.

Her mother hears Atlanta come closer. "We're screwed," her mother says. Another honk as she blows her nose.

"Dang," Atlanta says, rubbing sleep boogers from the corners of her eyes. "What are you going on about?"

"I got the mail."

"So?"

"*Here.*" Arlene crawls up over the back of the couch and hangs there like a baby stuck on a crib rail, unable to escape her prison. She waves the letter in front of her daughter's face. "Acceleration clause, they say."

Atlanta grabs the letter, sent from the local bank. Montour County First National. *Adult problems*, she thinks.

Most of it is stuff she can't decipher. It's about the house. That much is clear. And something about the mortgage payments. She sees phrases like "risk-adjusted rates" and "forbearance" and "loan modification terms." Oh, and that one her mother just said:

Acceleration clause.

A lot of the details escape her. But she starts to get the gist. They want her to pay out the mortgage. Like, the whole thing. But if she pays ahead a little bit, they'll "reinstate" the loan.

Reinstatement comes with higher rates. Or something.

She keeps reading.

Failure to do any of that means foreclosure. Atlanta's not entirely sure what details orbit a foreclosure, but she sure knows the end result: sheriff comes and takes your house away, kicks your ass to the curb.

"Why?" It's a simple question, but one Atlanta feels she has to ask. Seems this is coming out of nowhere.

"I'm behind," is her mother's answer. Atlanta feels the hairs on the back of her neck stand up straight.

"What do you mean, 'behind'?"

"Behind on payments. By three months."

"Well, how the *hell* did that happen?" Atlanta can't help but raise her voice. A minimovie of them being locked out of their home and drop-kicked into a drainage ditch starts playing through her head on an endless loop. "I mean, you do know you're supposed to pay the bills, right? Not let 'em pile up like you're trying to win a competition."

Mama's face goes red. "I tried to pay the damn bills, girl. But we also need to eat! And keep the electricity running! And last month the well pump shit the bed and I had to pay to get *that* replaced." By now the woman's nose is plugged with snot and her morning makeup is running down her face like mud streaking down a dirty car door after it crashes through a puddle. "You do like water, dontcha? Showers? Drinking?"

"Yeah, but none of that matters if we don't have a house with a shower, does it? I mean, dang, I thought that would be the priority, Mama. What the hell?"

"The Internet said I wouldn't be punished until I let it go six months or more. It's only been three!" Her mother slides back to the sofa, crosses her arms. "*It's only been three.* You don't understand. We're screwed. That's all there is to it."

And then the woman descends into the kind of crying that's like a waterfall—once you go over, takes a long time to climb back up. It's all hitching sobs and shaking shoulders and murmured words of shame through blubbering, spit-slick lips.

Atlanta doesn't know what to say. Part of her wants to hug her mother; another part of her wants to cuff her upside the head.

Instead, she just goes and makes a call.

CHAPTER SIXTEEN

Atlanta sits across from the girl with the thousand-yard stare. Neither says much of anything. The girl's hand trembles over a manila folder. She starts to slide the folder to Atlanta, then stops abruptly and pulls it back.

"We should talk payment," Jenny says. "Before you . . . before you see this."

"Sure. Okay." Atlanta looks around, at Jenny's kitchen. Well, her family's. Atlanta walked the long trek over here, across town in the heat, up Gallows Hill, and into the nest of McMansions that form this neighborhood. Atlanta can see that this kitchen is as big as, if not bigger than, the entire downstairs of her own crooked farmhouse. It's all shiny granite and fingerprint-free stainless steel, lit by a light fixture that looks like a dangle of crystal teardrops. Above her hangs a pot-and-pan rack featuring cookware clean and spotless and surely never used. It's then that Atlanta comes to a number, and a crazy number, at that:

"A thousand bucks."

Jenny hesitates, but then nods. "I can make that happen."

Holy shit. Okay.

It won't buy out the mortgage, but it'll cover a couple payments. Time to print up some business cards that say *Pet Detective* on 'em.

"You think your dog was murdered," Atlanta says.

"Sailor."

"What?"

"Sailor. Her name was Sailor. Like Sailor Moon." Jenny clears her throat. "She was a Norwich terrier."

"Oh. Okay."

"Here."

She again slides the folder to Atlanta. This time all the way. But the hand lingers, still shaking. Staring out with those empty eyes. Sandblasted by trauma and sadness. Grief-struck as if grief were a hard-swung baseball bat.

Atlanta opens the folder, and it's then she understands.

———

Way the toilet flushes, it's like a vacuum on a rocket ship. A powerful *voosh* and Atlanta's puke is taken away, leaving behind a sparkling porcelain bowl once more. A bowl rimmed by a puffy taupe toilet seat.

Heated, if one likes. There's a button and everything.

She doesn't. Instead she leans back against the wall, hair matted to her forehead.

The folder. That dog.

In her mind's eye, flashes of white and red. White fur. And then blood. All that blood.

Looked like something an animal did. A fox. A wolf. A dang grizzly bear. But Jenny is saying a person did that. The vet called the injuries "inconsistent with an animal attack." The way one of the ears was cut. The way the neck was ringed with a rope-burn.

The way the teeth were all removed.

An act of torture, not rage. An act by human hands.

People are fucked, Atlanta thinks. She knows there are kids out there who do stuff like this—hell, back in junior high down South she knew a kid named Buck (who people called Bobo for reasons unknown) who would shoot frogs with a bow and arrow, then freeze them, then blow them up with firecrackers. What happened to Sailor was like a master class in that. Advanced Sociopathy for the Wannabe Human Monster.

Preying on the weak.

Eventually she crawls her way back to standing, makes sure there's no vomit curds hanging out along the edges of her mouth, then returns to Jenny, who sits in the kitchen, staring down at the closed folder. Again she snaps out of the reverie to ask Atlanta, "Are you—"

"I'm fine. I'll take it. The job. I'll find out who did this to your dog."

"To Sailor."

Atlanta nods, takes the folder. "I'll find out who did this to Sailor."

———

Outside in the driveway, between the pine-green Range Rover and the steel-gray Lexus, she sees a familiar mouth-too-small-for-his-teeth face. Chomp-Chomp. Steven. Standing there in a ratty black-and-red Slayer T-shirt and jeans spattered with . . . something. Motor oil, maybe.

He's got a Yamaha four-wheeler parked at the base of the driveway.

"Hey," he says, giving her a game little wave.

"Don't come near me," she says, putting the back of her hand against her mouth. "I probably got really bad barf breath."

"I know."

"What do you mean, you know?"

"Jen called. Told me you were kinda . . . I dunno. Sick."

"I'm fine now." She moves past him.

"Okay. Wait. I can give you a ride."

Atlanta turns. Cocks her hip and squints. "On that thing?" She points to the quad.

"I won't drive fast."

"You can drive fast, I don't care if you drive fast." A sudden spike of defensiveness and she's not sure why. "You don't . . . live around here, right?"

He shrugs. "Up the block."

"You're rich," she says. It's almost a condemnation, but she doesn't mean it that way.

"I dunno."

"No, you do know. You are. You're a richie-rich." She looks him up and down. "But you dress like you're poor."

"I do?"

"Kinda, yeah."

"Sorry."

She smacks her lips, tastes the pukey cottonmouth film on her tongue. "No skin off my knuckles. Hey, what do you know about the dog? The . . . dead one."

"I dunno. He was cute."

"She. Sailor was a she."

"Oh."

"Where'd they find the body?"

"They didn't find it."

She takes a step closer. "Huh?"

"They didn't find the dog. The dog came home."

"Came home? Looking like *that*?"

"Yeah. Scratching at the door wanting to be let in. I guess he— uhh, she—died about a half hour later on Jenny's bed."

"Holy crap," Atlanta says. "The dog came home."

"Yeah."

Maybe it's time to revise her assessment of dogs. Because that sounds pretty incredible.

Chomp-Chomp straddles the four-wheeler's saddle, waits expectantly. Atlanta goes to get on behind him, and he reaches back to pull her hands around his middle. "You need to hold on when—"

Alarm bells. Klaxons. Hands hot like they're touching a casserole dish without oven mitts. She staggers backward off the thing, bowlegged and nearly falling over. Every inch of her body feels like it's covered with spider legs doing a creepy little waltz across her skin.

That smell again: expended gunpowder. A ringing in her ears.

"You go ahead," she croaks. Voice dry.

"But you're not feeling—"

"I'm *fine*. I'm fine. Go on, now. Go. Don't want to lose my breakfast on the back of your neck." Not that she ate breakfast. And not that she's going to now. Chomp-Chomp hesitates, doesn't want to go, but she yells at him and that makes him drive off—slow like a sad donkey, head hung low, Eeyore in a death-metal T-shirt.

————

Atlanta has never been a big fan of dogs. You walk into the house of someone who owns a dog, you know it. You can smell it, and you can see it. Chewed corner of the coffee table. Musky, musty animal odor. Ratty toys on the floor. A half-eaten rawhide, gummy with saliva and stuck fur. And dogs are all drooly. Jumpy. *Needy*.

Atlanta doesn't like needy people, so she damn sure doesn't care for needy animals. Dogs are like that little kid in the grocery store who won't stop tugging on his mother's ovaries: *Mom Mom Mom Mom Mommy Mommy Mom*.

Not that she likes cats much better. Because, seriously, hell with cats, those dismissive emperors of the living room. You don't own a cat so much as you petition them for your time.

Plus, cat smell? Makes dog odor smell like fresh-baked blueberry muffins. Cat stink crawls deep. On a hot, windy day, the cross-breeze coming from the Cat Lady's house next door smells like a doom-wind, a rankling ammoniac smell heralding the end of days.

Animals. Ugh.

If Atlanta were allowed a pet, she'd choose a lizard. Maybe a snake, too. Or a tarantula.

Small. Not cute. Doesn't give a shit and doesn't need much.

And doesn't piss on your stuff.

But just the same, not liking dogs doesn't mean she feels good about what happened to Jenny's little lady. You just don't do that to an animal, whether you like animals or not.

———

Going back home doesn't sound appealing. Her mother will be making a nest out of ruined Kleenex, hatching little pity eggs like the saddest bird on the block. When the woman gets on a crying jag, it goes and it goes with all the energy of that stupid-ass battery bunny.

She wanders around town for a while. Not sure what to do next. Atlanta doesn't know what she expected: she'd turn the corner just past that little coffee café on the corner, and there, in front of Dosie Sawicki's kielbasa stand, she'd see some canine serial killer tying a noose around a Newfoundland's neck? Performing dentistry on a Chihuahua? Stuffing a Jack Russell into a cannon?

In the midst of her floundering, a kielbasa starts to sound pretty dang good. Throwing up does that to you, sometimes—leaves you hollow, ragged, but feeling like you need to be filled up again. Time, then, to eat.

She goes to the counter, orders up. The Sawickis have that coal-cracker accent going on, replete with all the dialect that makes Atlanta—with her muddy Southern twang—want to bite glass. *Y'wanna kilbo griller?* Kilbo for kielbasa. *Dincha want mustard wit dat? Come back tamarra!*

And they say Southerners sound dumb. If there's one thing Atlanta has learned, it's that hicks are hicks. Being red-in-the-neck is a global phenomenon, and everybody sounds stupid to everybody else.

It's Madge Sawicki behind the counter, big pink lips and cakey makeup and hair teased into a rat's nest, all in service to staving off the rigors of midlife. She's nice enough and wants to chat, but Atlanta's not in a chatty mood. She just orders—*yes, mustard with that, no, not spicy*—and goes and sits on the once-green, now paint-flaking bench around the corner.

By the time she's half-done eating the kielbasa—the skin with a sharp snap, the meat spicy and strange, the mustard doubly so—she takes a look at the folder sitting by her side, and suddenly the bottom drops out of her stomach and the food goes rancid in her gut. She gives it a couple minutes, but—still sour. Atlanta wads up the remains of her meal and pitches it in the metal trashcan next to the counter.

Madge waves. "Y'wanna wooder ice wit dat?" *You want a water ice with that?* That's another thing regional to the area. Water ice. That's what they called shaved ice. *Water ice?* What other kind of ice would there be?

She tells Madge no, then turns and sees someone across the street.

No, no, no.

Mitchell Erickson.

He sees Atlanta.

And then starts to cross the street toward her.

She's seen him around school a few times since Chris died but always stayed out of his orbit. Never mind the fact he might've been involved in Chris's murder.

Her blood boils. Her middle churns.

"Atlanta!" he calls over to her, waving and smiling like they're fucking yachting buddies.

She wants to run screaming, wants to dart around the corner or dive in a passing car or climb up into the food-counter window like a cat fleeing a house fire. But her boots stay rooted to the sidewalk.

"Been a while," she manages to say as he suddenly stands before her, smelling like soap and smugness.

"It has," he says, tongue probing the inside of his cheek. "Sorry to hear about your friend."

"I'm sure you sent flowers to the funeral and I just missed them."

"Totally."

"What do you want, Erickson?"

He leans in close, lowers his voice. The smile falls away like an ill-hung painting tumbling off a wall. "Just wanted to say, sorry to hear about your house."

"My house?" Her chest tightens. "What about my house?"

"Little mouse squeaked in my ear, told me that your mother's having a hard time paying the mortgage. Foreclosure, huh? Man. Symptom of the down economy, I guess." Sympathy so fake a breeze could knock the cardboard cutout down and blow it across the street, where it'd get hit by a bus.

She says through clamped teeth, "How do you know that?"

"Oh! Didn't I mention that my dad's got friends at First National? Golfing buddies. He keeps all his investments there, too—a sizable package."

"I'll rip off his sizable package and cram it down his throat." She feels dizzy. Like the world in front of her sits in supersharp focus but has gone blurry and greasy at the edges. Consequences again come crashing down upon her, the chain of action and reaction laid bare.

This tree she planted has twisted roots. Roots that want to choke her dead.

"Good luck with everything," Mitchell says. He reaches up and musses her hair; she swats his hand away.

"Wait," she says. He stops and smirks. "Let me tell you something, Mitchell Erickson. If I find out you had anything to do with Chris's death, *anything at all*, then you better run and you better hide, because your daddy or his banking buddies or his gun-club fascist freak-show friends won't be able to stop me from hurting you. I'll crash your car. I'll break your pitching arm. I'll find whatever it is you love—because even for a monster like you there's gotta be something—and I will tear it into screaming pieces."

Again his face falls. The smirk drops. "Coyne killed himself. It was suicide." But he says it as if he's not sure.

"That your story? That what helps you sleep at night?"

Mitchell grabs her, both hands around her shoulders, his face a sudden rictus of rage. "You listen to me, I didn't have a *fucking thing* to do with—"

"Hey!" Madge Sawicki yells from the counter. "Git off her! You wan' me to come out dere with my Louisville?"

She offers up a baseball bat, shakes it above her head like a monkey with a bone-club.

Mitchell relinquishes his grip. Steps backward off the curb, almost gets hit by a car. He says nothing else, just points at Atlanta and then crosses the street.

Atlanta lets out the breath she didn't realize she was holding. Goes back to the counter where Madge waits.

"Thanks, Madge."

"Nat a problum," she says. "Richie-riches are ruinin' this dang town. You go'n home now, 'Lanta. Go'n."

———

When she gets home, Mama's in the kitchen, which is never a good sign unless the waffle maker is out or there's an open carton of eggs, and this time she spies neither. What she sees instead is a fryer chicken. And a box of generic cornflakes. And a big, rust-cornered metal container of vegetable oil that's been in their pantry so long it's probably rancid.

"You're gonna start a fire," Atlanta says.

Arlene shrugs. Sniffles a little. Eyes so puffy the crow's feet are gone, like bird tracks swallowed by snow. "I want fried chicken, so I'm gonna make me some fried chicken."

"Do you know how to make fried chicken?"

"Well." Arlene blinks and looks around her at the fixings like an archaeologist staring at the icons of a lost civilization. "Sure. Coat the chicken in flour. Then cornflakes. Or maybe cornflakes, then flour. And I guess I need some way to make that stuff stick to the chicken. Ummm, and when that's done you dunk it in hot oil. For some . . . amount of time. Abracadabra, got us some fried chicken. See? Can't beat that with a stick."

Atlanta thinks that if she sees her mother go anywhere near a pot of hot oil she might *have* to beat the woman with a stick. Thing about Atlanta's mother is, when she gets in a mood, Arlene decides she wants comfort. And the way she gets comfort is with home cooking. Collard greens. Or red beans and rice. Or, heaven forbid, some ugly, sick-making facsimile of barbecue. That woman can't cook worth a shit. Unless it's breakfast.

Though maybe if she burns the house down, they'll get the insurance money and all this will be blood under the bridge. Provided they don't both die in the fire.

"Mama, we gotta talk."

"Can we do it over dinner?"

"I think we should do it now."

Arlene picks up the box of cornflakes, shakes it at her daughter dismissively. "Honey, I know you're thinking I'm going to burn the house down, but I promise I am not." She pleads: "Just let me have this."

"It's not about that. I mean, it is about the house. It's about the mortgage payments."

The woman begins to move about the kitchen, improvising this fried chicken recipe as she goes. Atlanta watches as she dumps an indiscriminate amount of flour and cornflakes into a plastic grocery bag—which has a little hole in it, so tiny streamers of flour drift from the bottom like dust from a broken vacuum bag. "I got that taken care of, sweet-cheeks, no problem. Mommy's on the case."

"You . . . are?"

"Uh-huh. I took what we had in the bank account and what I get from the state, and I put that toward a Wonderfully Delicious kit. Should be coming in a few weeks and then—"

"Wait, what's this kit and what's so wonderfully delicious about it?"

Arlene laughs as she uses a pair of metal tongs to deposit parts from the cut-up fryer chicken into the bag. "No, Atlanta, that's the brand. Wonderfully Delicious. I'm going to be a saleslady for them. You order the kit and then people come over and you demo their . . . culinary products . . ." Way she says *culinary* it's like she's feeling along a dark room as she walks through it. *Cu . . . lin . . . ary?* "It's going to be the bee's knees, sugar-pop."

Oh, crap-on-a-stick.

"It's like Amway," Atlanta says.

"It's not like Amway. Amway's a scam."

"It's *just* like Amway, Mama. For fuck's sake—"

"Now watch your tongue, girl."

"—don't you remember back home when that older boy next door got wrapped up in it? Ricky? Dicky? He had to spend more money than he got back. Amway's best customers are their own dang salesmen. That's how they make their money."

Arlene, indignant, shakes the chicken bag. Flour and corn-flakes do a herky-jerky polka inside.

"This is not that," Arlene insists. "I get to host a party and be a real saleswoman. Like with Avon. Or Tupperware. It's . . . esteemed."

"It's a pyramid scheme!" Atlanta's hands ball up into frustrated fists. "Shit, Mama, how much did you spend?"

Shake shake shake. "Not your business."

"I said, how much?"

"Like I said—"

"*Mama.*"

Arlene says in a much quieter voice, "Five hundred. Ah, five seventy-five. Shipping." She upends the bag onto a nearby plate, which rattles as a pile of gluey chicken tumbles onto it. Each chick-en piece has an uneven, clumpy coating of flour and maybe two cornflakes per piece. Three on the breast. The rest are still in the bag. "Oh, what the hell, I thought I did this right."

Atlanta sees her mother's eyes shimmering, like the first few raindrops before the storm hits. Sure enough, the woman starts to whimper, and her lips tighten like a closed-up coin purse, and the tears start to fall. Atlanta knows she's supposed to go and hug her, but she just can't stomach that right now. All she can do is scowl and stomp out of the kitchen.

———

Funny thing is, she was going to apologize to her mother. That was the talk she hoped to have. She wanted to say, "Mama, I'm sorry, but the reason the mortgage bill is due is because I pissed off a very powerful man who has ties to the bank and I'm going to try to help make this right and I got a job and it'll help pay a couple months and I'm sorry again."

But it didn't go like that.

It never goes like that.

Arlene stepped in it. Opened her mouth, stuck her pink-painted toenails all up in there. Wiggled 'em good, too. And now all Atlanta can think about is how mad she is at her mother and how this is actually Arlene's fault—it was Arlene who didn't pay the mortgage, which opened the door just wide enough for the rats to come creeping in. It was *Arlene* who had a bad boyfriend, a boyfriend who saw Atlanta as dessert under glass, a young girl who surely didn't mean those words she kept saying over and over again—*no, don't, stop*—and who cried so hard not because she was sad but because she was overwhelmed by the *strong emotion* of it all.

Again that gunpowder stink. The shotgun's in the closet, but Atlanta can feel it there, can almost see it through the wall like she's

got fucking X-ray vision or something. She hears a man screaming. Here, in this room, in her bedroom. But not now. *Then.*

The blast of a gun and blood on the sheets.

Atlanta rubs her eyes.

With an angry, darting hand she snatches the folder, opens
it again. Flashes of raw skin, wounds, blood. She slams the folder shut again. It's like a horrible drug, an ugly hit straight to her
soul—a car-battery jump, crass but effective. It focuses her, lets her
put Arlene and the house out of her mind.

It's then that Atlanta starts to put together a plan.

Or, at least, the first step of one.

CHAPTER SEVENTEEN

The vet's office smells like animal. All kinds of animal, given that this is a farm vet. Horse musk and dog shit and cat piss and rabbit fear. A big, poofy Persian cat that looks like Ron Swanson stalks the counter. Back and forth, back and forth, occasionally pausing to survey his leonine domain. Then back to pacing. His domain isn't much to look at. The waiting room has a floor of gray tiles, some cracked. The walls are white popcorn. Ceiling, too. Everything cast in a swimmy, fluorescent glow, lights occasionally buzzing and snapping like a bug zapper.

The woman behind the counter is a dainty thing with knucklebones where her cheekbones should be; they bulge out like sharp corners. She says, for the second time, "I'm sorry, but the doctor's with a patient."

Atlanta frowns. "By doctor, you mean the vet. And by patient, you mean, like, an iguana."

"Veterinarians are doctors."

"Okay." She really didn't know that. "When will Doctor—" Atlanta leans left to get a look at the name on the door. "Ch . . . Chenna . . . Pro . . . Pra?"

"Chennapragada."

"What kind of name is that?"

"She's Indian."

Atlanta drums her fingers. "So, the doc? Free soon?"

The woman flits her gaze toward a boxy old CRT computer monitor. "Not until two thirty."

"That's, like, two hours from now."

"That's her schedule. If you'd have called . . ."

"No, I'll . . . I'll wait."

Atlanta goes and sits back down, flips through some magazines. *Allure*—ugh, girls too skinny, skinny like those harsh, knobby cheekbones. *Field & Stream*—really? There's a magazine about fishing? Seems like there're magazines for everything. Jogging. Walking. Knitting. She spies a *Food Network Magazine*, thinks maybe to steal it and give it to her mother—either to teach the woman how to cook or instead to roll it up into a tube and swat the woman's nose any time she reaches for a kitchen implement.

Like the cat, Atlanta gets up and paces the waiting room. Across the far wall is a corkboard, and she goes over, starts perusing. John Deere tractor for sale. Free kittens, which Atlanta figures is about as redundant as it gets, because who in their right mind would *pay* for a kitten? (Probably the same weirdos who read fishing magazines.) Dog missing. Then another dog missing. A third. And fourth.

One's a cairn terrier ("Pepper"). Another a dachshund ("Oscar"). Third is a . . . vizsla puppy, whatever that is (no name given). Third a Lab puppy ("Lucky").

Three of the flyers have addresses.

And all three are up in Gallows Hill.

Atlanta's heart leaps the same time her gut sinks.

She goes to the counter, reaches over—ignoring the protestations of Little Miss Cheekbones—and snatches a pen, which she then uses to write the phone numbers on the inside of her arm.

"Here," Atlanta says, tossing the pen back to the counter lady. "I don't think I need to meet with the vet doctor anymore."

———

Pepper: The man is icy like a frosted-over windshield. Tells Atlanta over the phone that the terrier was a show dog, a regional winner and a state winner once, he'll have her know, and he'll pay whatever it takes to get Pepper back, and then he says his "partner" is the dog's trainer, and Atlanta thinks, oh, okay, he's gay—which adds up because he seems buttoned tight and has a clipped and lispy voice—but then she hears a woman's voice in the background calling for the man, and he ends the conversation with a sudden goodbye, cutting it short as if with a pair of scissors, *snip, snip, click.*

Oscar: The woman is destroyed, gibbering and blubbering, and it's clear suddenly that this dog, this dachshund, is not merely her dog but actually her "son," to the point where through the tears she even refers to him as "her little fur-baby," which sounds weird and somehow porny to Atlanta's ears, and for a moment that thought lets her escape the woman's grief—grief that is as deep and dark as quarry water, as hungry and wet as a chest wound, and when the woman has that glimmer of hope because she thinks Atlanta knows something, all Atlanta can do is panic and hang up on her.

The vizsla: Turns out a vizsla is, in fact, a dog, a red Hungarian retriever whom the man says he was breeding to be a hunting dog, but everyone around wanted pointers or spaniels and didn't know what the hell a vizsla was, and so nobody bit, and now the man doesn't know what to do, and Atlanta almost (*almost*) reminds him that it doesn't much matter now because the dog is gone, though he doesn't seem to care about the dog so much as he's pissed about the "lost investment," and when she gets off the phone she thinks, *Ugh, people.*

Lucky: It's a little girl who answers, maybe nine, ten years old, and she tells Atlanta that her mother is outside pulling weeds and her father's not home, and so Atlanta takes a chance, asks about Lucky, and then the girl tells a story that pries open Atlanta's breastbone and punches her right in the heart. The girl woke up briefly at night when one of her parents let Lucky out to go to the bathroom, and it was only five minutes later when the girl woke up again and heard Lucky yelping—in the girl's words, "screaming"—and then after that she heard people laughing and the screech of tires, and she even said that outside the house they found burned-rubber tire tracks on the street and curb, and does Atlanta have Lucky? Atlanta tells her no, and it punches her heart again to say it, and the girl doesn't cry but she says the saddest, quietest little "Oh" that Atlanta's ever heard.

Four phone calls over the course of an hour, and Atlanta feels tense, her guts pulled taut like a clothesline. And she feels sad, too—the sorrow heavy as wet clothes hanging from the line and pulling it down, down, down toward the ground.

But at least she learned something.

All four of the people on the phone told her when the dogs were taken.

They were taken at night.

And they were taken within a couple miles of one another up on Gallows Hill.

In the same neighborhood as Jenny and Sailor.

Atlanta starts looking through her closet for dark clothing.

———

Gallows Hill at night. Floodlights and sidewalks wet from spitting sprinklers, everything clean and walkable, a small playground every mile. The cars in driveways are a mixture of BMWs and Subarus, Mercedeses and Hondas, a Lexus here, a Porsche there. Atlanta wonders what it must be like: to buy gourmet food and to have migrant housekeepers and to know what it means to pump the really expensive gas. Then she wonders what it's like on the other end of the spectrum: to have no car to drive, no house to clean, no money for any food at all.

She's trying to figure out where she falls in this spectrum and whether or not she feels envious that she doesn't have all this or guilty because she's still a white girl in America, when she sees Shane riding up on his dingy, rust-gobbled ten-speed, panting.

"The hill," he says, gasping, leaning up against the light pole. That's the other thing—all the homes and developments in Gallows Hill are lit by bright white streetlights. Where she's at down in the valley—or, worse, on the other side on Grainger Hill with the trailer parks and dirty Amish—everything's dead and dark, so when you hear a sound in the woods you don't know if it's a skunk or a rabbit. Or someone come to hurt you. Sometimes she hears screaming in the woods, a sound like a woman getting killed, but everyone assures her it's just a fox's cry.

"You okay?" she asks Shane.

"Yeah." But it comes out as a breathy *gyeaaaauuhh.* He looks like he might throw up.

"You can throw up if you have to."

"I'm not—" Cough, cough. "Not going to throw up. So what's—" He gags a little, then spits. *Hawwwwwk, ptoo.* "What's up?"

She'd called him, left a message with his mother. Told him to meet her up on Gallows Hill around nine thirty. She's not sure if she's surprised he came. It's been a while. "I'm . . . doing something for someone."

"Could you be a little more vague?"

"I'm trying to solve a murder." Soon as the words are out of her mouth she knows she shouldn't have said it like that, because his eyes light up and he thinks she's talking about Chris. "Not Chris. A dog."

The fire in his eyes dims. "A dog murder. Is that a thing?"

"I dunno. I guess. Remember Chomp-Chomp?"

Now the fire's truly gone as Shane's brow darkens—his eyes smoldering black briquettes. Of course he remembers Chomp-Chomp.

"Him?"

"His cousin, Jenny, her dog was . . . tortured. Which I guess was bad enough to kill it." Behind her eyes flash images from the folder. Her breath catches in her chest like on a blustery winter day, even though the air is warm and sticky. "So she hired me to do this. And I thought maybe you might could help."

"Me."

"Yeah."

"But you're still not looking into Chris's murder."

"Well, no. I . . . I don't know. This pays. I need money, our house—"

"So it's all about money. Is that why you helped Chris the first time? Because he paid?"

She sucks air between her teeth. "Now, c'mon. Don't be that way. It's not like that. This girl . . . this dog . . ."

"They killed Chris and you don't want to do anything about it."

"Don't you dare say that. I did something already, and it was the wrong thing." Her nostrils flare. She feels her pulse in her wrist, her neck, the backs of her legs. "Now I'm doing something different. Maybe trying to help someone instead of hurt 'em."

"You don't even care that he's dead."

Pow. A hand—her hand, a hand she seems to barely control— slaps Shane hard across the cheek with a stinging *smack.* He recoils, touching the struck cheek with the gingerness one might use to touch a wounded bird. Eyes wide, he looks around like this is some kind of joke, like a camera crew might pop out and reveal this to be a YouTube prank. The panic on his face kills her. Because she made that panic happen. She gave it life.

"Shane—"

He fumbles with his bike, almost trips over it. She says his name again, reaching out and putting her hand on his tire to help him—but he pulls the bike away.

"I'll handle this on my own," he says. Way his voice shakes, she thinks he might cry.

"Please, Shane, I'm sorry as hell that I did that . . ."

But he's gone. His pudgy legs spinning, the bike bumping as it jumps off the sidewalk. She hears him for a little while even after she can't see him, spokes whispering, bike chains like bee wings.

She kicks the curb with her foot. Pain shoots up through her calf.

"Shit!" she hisses. "Shit."

———

Now: past midnight. Atlanta—alone and feeling it—hides behind a well-manicured boxwood shrub ringing a tennis-and-basketball court. Her legs are cramped and her back feels like it's on fire, but she makes no effort to move, in part because she's afraid that once she does she won't want to hunker back down again, and in part because she thinks she just plain deserves the pain.

The neighborhood is still. What's not still is Atlanta's mind. Guilt over Chris. Shame over Shane. Anger at her mother. A sudden spike of rage at the richie-riches who live here, who have too much. Flashes of white fur and red blood. Punctuated by the imagined sound of the Labrador puppy screaming in the night as someone steals it away.

That's when she realizes she's doing this wrong, waiting here in the middle of nowhere hoping . . . what? That some pesky dog thieves and canine tormentors will come winging by on a lark?

She needs to find a dog. A dog left outside, acting as an irresistible lure.

Dog thieves will go after dogs. Duh. Seems obvious now. So obvious, in fact, that a new, mean, bad thought comes slinking into her head like an alley cat: *You're stupid as all get-out, Atlanta Burns, dumb as a fence post but not nearly as useful.*

She emerges from her hiding spot, knees popping and back muscles burning brighter as they stretch.

Atlanta goes on the hunt, wandering the streets of Gallows Hill for the next hour. Aimless and restless. And worse, unable to find a single dog. Maybe the folks here know that someone's been taking dogs. Maybe they're keeping them in. And, of course, these are rich people. Their dogs are well fed and kept inside. These aren't barn dogs. These aren't dogs on chains made to sleep under the double-wide. These are . . . show dogs and Hungarian hunting dogs and the beloved well-fed puppies of little well-fed girls.

She's in her third development—from Fox Run to Palomino Farms and now to Clover Knoll—when she gives up. Decides, screw it, not finding anything, best to go home. And then she gives up all the way, at least mentally—she realizes that she's not cut out for this. She has no idea what she's doing. She's never going to find Sailor's torturers. She'll never be able to give Jenny Whitsett one ounce of solace.

Then: a distant barking. Not frightened. No panic there. Just a dog yelling at the night. Maybe barking to be let back in after a dump. Maybe bow-wow-wowing at a cat or a rat or some imagined interloper.

Atlanta takes a deep breath and figures, *I'll just check this out, and then I'll go home.*

CHAPTER EIGHTEEN

Takes her a while to zero in on the pooch, but zero in she does. Out in front of a real tacky Garage Mahal, with jagged rooflines and a salmon stone walkway, she sees a fat-bellied beagle with his butt planted on a lush, trim lawn. Barking at nothing. The moon, maybe.

She's across the street and about three houses down when headlights come from the other direction. The one headlight blinks, winking like a lecherous old man. An engine growls.

Atlanta ducks behind a blue mailbox and crouches there, darting a hand into her messenger bag.

It's impossible to tell make or model, but the coming vehicle is a white pickup pitted with rust and dented everywhere, giving it the texture of crinkled aluminum foil. The truck screeches to a halt in front of the beagle house, and the beagle goes from just barking to doing this . . . other thing. Something between howling and wailing, some mad banshee yowl that's probably meant to indicate alarm but sounds more like the dog fell in a well and can't get out.

Someone hops out of the back of the truck, runs toward the dog with a bag.

Atlanta feels the hoofbeat of horses in her heart—her skin prickles and everything seems suddenly hyperreal. Everything gone clear, clean, cold.

This is it.

She pulls the baton from her bag and bolts across the street, ducking low as she darts in front of the headlights, her long shadow stretched and bloated on the street for a hair's breadth of a moment.

Voices. Someone from inside the truck whoops. Male voice. "Get that dog, you fat clown!"

Another voice. Also from inside the truck: "Who the frick is that?"

Someone yells: "Hey! *Hey!*"

Atlanta ignores them. Chooses instead to focus on the dognapper.

The broad-shouldered trespasser ahead of her on the lawn is already doing a dance with the dog, coming at the animal with the sack—a feed sack by the looks of it—held out like a weapon, swooping low and trying to bag the beagle to no avail. The killer has on a black face mask, black shirt, black jeans, black boots, and, in contrast, a pair of yellow latex gloves. The kind you'd use to wash dishes.

The attacker goes for the dog again.

Atlanta bolts across the lawn, careful not to slip on the dewy grass. With a flick of her wrist and a button press, the telescoping baton snaps from its mooring, extends from eight inches to two feet. Last time she tangoed with the Skinny Bitch Nazi, the psycho came at her with a baton. So Atlanta bought her own. Ballistic nylon sheath, whatever that means. German steel. Fifteen bucks on eBay.

From the truck: "Watch out! Frickin' *watch out!*"

But Atlanta's target is focused on the dog.

Atlanta whips the baton against the stranger's back, right between the shoulder blades.

The kidnapper goes down, howling along with the dog. But something doesn't sound right.

The beagle, finally wising up and realizing that shit is going pear-shaped, takes off in the other direction toward the house. Behind Atlanta, tires squeal, peeling out as the truck belches a dragon's breath of exhaust, then barrels forward with a growl and grumble—and then it's all taillights and plumes of gray.

"Stealing dogs, huh?" Atlanta asks, and whips the attacker in the side again.

The bastard rolls over, face mask half pulled up from when he fell against the grass.

And Atlanta catches a glimpse of dark red lipstick. The whimpering dognapper can no longer see, paws at his face and pulls the mask up to his forehead and—

It's a she, not a he.

Atlanta recognizes the girl from school. Same year. Tattooed chick. Kinda gothy, but kinda rednecky, too. Husky, like a linebacker. Vanessa. Tessa. Something-essa.

"You," the girl squeaks.

"Me," Atlanta says, standing over her.

The girl kicks Atlanta in the crotch with a boot.

Anatomy lesson: girls don't have the low-hanging fruit of testicles, but getting kicked in the crotch is still no picnic. Pain shoots up into Atlanta's gut and she staggers left, doubling over.

Something-essa gets on her hands and knees, scrabbling on the wet lawn, and manages to move her dump-truck body up and forward—she runs the way a drunken moose runs, one leg almost caught by the other, boots stomping, braying as she goes.

Floodlights suddenly bathe the lawn in lights.

Inside the house, lights flick on.

Go go go go.

Atlanta pushes past the pain, raises her baton high like an angry monkey, and chases after.

She catches sight of Something-essa darting between a pair of boxy McMansions, heading east out of Clover Knoll, running like the out-of-control boulder as it chases Indiana Jones—way the girl moves isn't about grace or skill so much as it is about gathering momentum and then wildly tumbling forward until something gets in her way.

Atlanta intends to be that something.

Clover Knoll's streets are a bunch of horseshoes smashed together with a main avenue connecting them all together—and that's where Something-essa's going to have to come out. Atlanta bolts right, heads that direction. Knuckles white around the baton's nylon grip. Glimpses of white and red. The imagined sound of that baying beagle amplified times ten as someone cuts off its ears, pops out its teeth.

I'm going to mess you up, girl.

Atlanta, ribs stitched with pain, lungs burning, heads past countless prefab minimansions all smashed together on half-acre lots, then finally comes out on the main road—California Street.

She hits the sidewalk, is barely able to stop herself. Almost skids on some stone scree and slips, but catches her balance.

Just in time to see Something-essa stumble from someone's lawn about fifty feet away.

Between them, at a T-bone intersection, is the way out—the development entrance that leads to Gallows Hill Road. Atlanta grins. Something-essa will have to come this way to get out, because the only other option is to run to the hill and dart through the trees, and that's one steep-ass hill that really *will* turn her into the boulder.

Atlanta's about to yell something to her, some kind of cocky bullshit taunt. But then—sirens. Lights. Red and blue chase each other in a nightclub strobe. A cop cruiser—not just a sedan but a goddamn Dodge Charger—comes whipping up the drive into Clover Knoll, headed straight for the both of them.

Atlanta and Something-essa share a look.

Something-essa gives Atlanta the finger.

Then she heads toward the hill.

Atlanta thinks to go after her, but that'll force her to cross the path of the cops. No time for that. No time to think at all—her only mode is escape. Getting busted by the cops right now is not going to be good for her or for Sailor or for her mother. She already went away once; she doesn't want to do it again.

She turns and runs the opposite way. Back toward the McMansions.

———

Atlanta hides.

Again behind a blue mailbox.

Palms sweaty, mouth dry.

Making herself as small as she can. Appropriate, given how small she feels. Small and angry, like a pimple ready to pop.

The cops sweep back and forth time and again, spotlight sliding over houses and lawns and sidewalks. Part of her thinks, *Just go out there. Tell them what happened. Say,* I'm trying to find out who's taking these dogs and hurting them, *and then give them the details about the truck and Something-essa, and then be done with it.* But she does that, Jenny won't pay her.

Besides, she can't trust the cops. If one cop is sitting on Orly Erickson's shoulder like a dark-eyed hawk, then he may have others, too.

So, no. No trusting the cops.

Atlanta hides.

————

Every minute is an agony that gnaws at Atlanta like a rat chewing through drywall, because every minute when she's stuck behind a mailbox is a minute when the truck is getting away and that dognapping bitch is running farther and farther.

By the time the cops stop sweeping and go home, Atlanta's been there for another hour.

It's damn near two in the morning when she hoofs it out of Clover Knoll and back down the road toward the valley, toward Maker's Bell proper. The walk is only fifteen minutes, but it feels like forever—a long, dark journey past crickets chirping and the black shapes of oak trees and evergreens.

Eventually, through the trees, there's a fuzzy glow of the U.S. Gas at the bottom of the hill just before you turn onto Main Street.

It's the only place in town that has a pay phone. Atlanta thinks, *I have to get a cell phone.* Not that she has the money for that.

The U.S. Gas is four pumps under a cockeyed red, white, and blue roof. It's a dingy convenience store surrounded by a parking lot cracked and cratered as if peppered by tiny meteorites. Above, tinny speakers play some new country music—not old-school country music, but rather the kind that's basically just earworm pop crap sung by some rich kid who will never know true grief in her heart.

Atlanta slides into the phone booth, finds a phone book dangling by a red lacquered chain. What was Chomp-Chomp's last name again? Burkholder. Right. Only one set of Burkholders in the book, blessedly—unusual for a town where families breed like lusty rabbits (everywhere you go you meet a Troxell; those thick-witted bastards are like dandelions sprouting up and blowing their seed). She dials the number.

A man answers. Gurgles. Snorts. ". . . the hell is this?"

"Steven, please." She tries to be polite about it.

"It's two thirty in the morning." Another gurgle-snort.

More politeness made all the easier by her own Southern accent. "I understand and apologize, sir, but I'm a classmate of his, and I really need to talk to him."

The phone clunks and thumps as the person on the other end sets it down.

Atlanta tries not to listen to the awful Nashville pop, instead focusing on the crickets beyond and the buzz of the lights overhead, lights surrounded by little clouds of gnats and skeeters. Eventually someone picks up.

"Got it," comes Cho—er, Steven's voice.

Someone—the father—grunts and hangs up the phone.

"Hello?" Steven asks. Not groggy. Not gurgle-snorty. In the background: a TV with the volume turned down.

"Doesn't sound like I woke you," she says.

"I wasn't sleeping. I, uh, don't sleep much." Pause. "Atlanta?"

"Yeah. It's me."

"Hi. Wh . . . uhh. What's up?"

"Think I found the dog killers. Had one of 'em on the ropes and . . ." She neglects to mention the crotch kick because it seems unladylike, even for her. "She got the better of me. We went to school with her. Got a name like Vanessa or Tessa or something. She's dumpy, listens to that dopey clown-rapper duo—"

"ICP. I like ICP."

"Ick, whatever. She's covered in tattoos—like, I think her shoulder is covered in a . . . a . . . a fishing net or something."

"A spiderweb?"

"Oh." Blink. Blink. "Yeah, I guess that makes more sense. A spiderweb, then."

"That's Tressa Kucharski."

Oh, snap. She has to laugh. She didn't make the connection. "Tressa 'the Cooch' Kucharski?"

"Yeah, I guess they call her that sometimes."

They also say that having sex with her is like throwing a hot dog down a hallway. Or for the regional variation, waggling a kielbasa in a coffee can. "You know her?"

"She was doing Jonesy last year, but then they broke up and she threw a rock through his window and he took a dump on her front step and then they dated again and then more stuff got broken and I think she hit him? And I think he hit her back, and then she started hanging out less with us and more with the trash up on Grainger . . ."

A shape moves past the phone booth. Like a polar bear swimming past the glass in a zoo enclosure.

"Good story," Atlanta mumbles. "I'll call you back."

"Wait, where are you—"

She hangs up the phone and watches Tressa "the Cooch" Kucharski go into the U.S. Gas.

CHAPTER NINETEEN

First she thinks, *I'll go in after her.* Baton-whip the candy bar or whatever she's buying out of her hand, knock her teeth down her throat, make a real scene. But there might be cameras in there. She can't see any out here, so she decides to wait instead, standing next to the phone booth, anxiously extending and collapsing her baton.

Tressa's in there for five minutes, but it feels like five hours.

When she comes out, girl's got a pack of American Spirit cigarettes in one hand and a Monster energy drink in the other, with what looks like a big bundle of Slim Jims under one arm. The Cooch checks her cell phone, pops it into her back pocket, then begins tapping the cigarette pack before sliding one out and screwing it between her dark, sluggy lips. Thumb on lighter. *Flick. Flick. Flick.*

Atlanta steps up, pokes her in the back with the baton.

Tressa wheels, dropping her Bic in the process. The unlit cigarette hangs from her mouth, stuck to the inside of her lip the way a kid's tongue might get stuck to a frozen goalpost.

They stand that way for a while. In silence. Atlanta pointing the baton at her like it's a gun.

Tressa speaks first, and when she does, the cigarette falls and cartwheels into a puddle. "Oh. Hey, Atlanta."

"That's my name, don't wear it out."

"What's your deal?" Tressa swallows hard. Looks left, looks right. Finger tapping and scratching the top of the energy-drink can. "I don't mess with your shit."

"No, but I'm about to mess with yours. Lemme ask you—you like torturing animals? You one of those fucked-up people who likes to burn ants with match tips or stick firecrackers up a cat's ass? Make you feel all big and powerful when in reality you're just small and sad?"

"It's not like that."

"So tell me what it's like."

"I don't torture the dogs. It's not a . . . torture thing."

"Sure it ain't." She steps forward, lifts the baton under Tressa's chin.

"Before tonight, I . . . I . . . I didn't even touch the dogs. It's not my thing, I'm just there with . . ."

"With who?"

"Bodie and Bird."

"Who the hell are they?"

"The Haycock boys. Know 'em? Brothers. Irish twins."

"Like, from Ireland?"

Tressa shakes her head. She seems to be getting more nervous now. "No. Kids born so close together they might as well be twins. Born nine months apart. They call them Irish twins."

"Whatever. They go to school with us?"

"No, they're, uhh, they're 'homeschooled.'" When she says it she makes little air quotes, and in doing so, the Slim Jims drop from under her arm onto the asphalt.

"So they're the ones who like to hurt the animals."

"It's not like that, I told you—"

Atlanta scowls. "You banging one of them?"

Tressa tightens, doesn't say anything. Atlanta almost laughs.

The girl tries to change the subject. "So it's true, right, you shot the junk off your—"

But Atlanta has little interest in letting the girl finish her statement. "You're banging *both* of 'em?" Atlanta asks.

"I . . . I was with Bird, but then Bodie wanted to hook up and . . ." She suddenly looks confused, maybe even a little sad. "I still sometimes get time with Bird. But mostly it's Bodie."

Atlanta's about to ask another question when Tressa's gaze jumps like a leafhopper. Next comes the dingling bell tied to the top of the convenience-store door.

"Hey!" barks a man in a strong Indian accent. She turns, sees the little man brandishing a broom like a gladiator. "You stop messing around outside my store or I call the police! I call them!"

Atlanta scrunches her face, gives him an incredulous look. "You just sold this underage girl cigarettes. So go on, give 'em a ringy-dingy. I'll wait."

The man fake-laughs ("heh heh heh"), eases the broom by his side. "Oh! Oh, I think I, ah, hear a customer."

Then he ducks his head back inside. *Ding-a-ling.*

"That was cool," Tressa says while kneeling down and feeling for her lighter. Atlanta jabs her hard in the knee with the baton. Tressa bowls backward into a pothole. "Hey!"

"You don't get to tell me what's cool. I don't care to be admired in the eyes of a dog killer."

"I *told* you, we don't kill the—"

"You stole a white dog recently. Couple weeks back. Little. A . . . a terrier."

Tressa just sits in the pothole like someone who sat on the toilet while the seat was still up and ended up stuck. "Yeah. Well, I wasn't there. But we stole a couple little white ones recently."

"And where do they end up? Where do Bodie and Bird"—*those scum-sucking sumbitches*—"take the dogs?"

"The Farm." Tressa clears her throat, says it again louder. "They take them to the Farm."

"The heck happens at the Farm?"

"The fights."

"What fights?"

"The *dog*fights."

Didn't Guy say something about dogfights? Up on Grainger? "You don't put little white terriers in a gol-dang dogfight. That doesn't make a lick of sense. You use . . . I dunno, pit bulls and Rottweilers and—"

"Those dogs aren't for fighting. They're bait dogs."

"What the heck is a bait dog?"

Tressa tells her, and things start to add up.

Atlanta's shaking, the baton end quivering as it points accusingly toward Tressa.

"How much they pay you?" she asks.

"A hundred," Tressa says.

"Hundred bucks. That's it. That's how much the animal's misery is worth. How much your soul is worth."

"I told you, I'm not involved—"

"You better run," Atlanta seethes. Her voice barely sounds like her own. "You better run right now, because if you keep sitting there I'm going to knock *your* teeth out. Maybe break your fingers. Sell you to someone horrible for five twenty-dollar bills so they can do whatever they want to you. How's that sound? Huh? How's it fuckin' sound?"

Tressa backpedals like a panicked crab, manages to stand. "I'm sorry."

Atlanta whips the baton an inch in front of Tressa's face. Had it connected, it would've shattered her cheekbone, maybe cracked the porcelain bone protecting her temple. Tressa barks a sob, then turns and clomps away, clutching the can of Monster Energy like it's all she has left in the world.

————

This is what Tressa said about bait dogs:

They take the dogs and sell them to the humans who run the fights. The stolen dogs are worth more if they can't hurt anybody, so Bodie removes the teeth and claws with pliers. Then the little dogs—or sometimes cats if they can grab those, but they're worth less as bait—end up in an open cage or dangling from a rope or just thrown into a pen with the fighter dog. The spilled blood, the animal's cries—that's meant to rile up the fighter dog, get him thirsty and mean for the fight. The bait dogs train the fighter dogs to fight. And to kill.

Bait dogs go for a hundred bucks a pop.

A bait dog is *bait*. It's right there in the name.

And it makes Atlanta sick in a place far deeper than her stomach.

———

Atlanta runs through clouds of gun smoke. Through a field that's somehow also a swamp. A big moon overhead, bigger than you ever did see, pink like meat and fat like a pregnant woman's belly.

She chases a dog whose howls of pain echo over the grass.

The dog runs ahead of her. A white flash. Leaving wet blood on the grass.

Atlanta's foot steps into a hole as she runs. The ankle twists, snaps as she falls.

She cries out, and her cries are the dog's cries.

Someone reaches in, someone invisible, starts feeling for her teeth, starts pulling them out of her gums real easy, like they're weeds with shallow roots in loose mud. Someone starts removing her T-shirt, too, cutting it with a knife. Greasy hand feeling along her bra. Fingers working their way past the edges. Into her jeans and panties. The smell of cigarette breath and stale Rolling Rock. A voice in her ear, male, a voice too familiar:

"Your mother shouldn't know about this."

The dream ends, and she awakens cold and slick. She goes downstairs and eats cheap pretzel sticks with trembling hands until the sun comes up, a cairn of salt and crumbs piling before her.

CHAPTER TWENTY

It's like diving headfirst into a filthy pool. Dirtier and darker the deeper you go. Every link she clicks, every news story or website she reads, it just ruins her day that much more, until the moment comes where she feels like she's coming off a days-long stomach flu and she's not sure if she'll be able to eat anything ever again.

All the people around her here at the rinky-dink Maker's Bell Library, they don't know. They're going about their morning like it's nothing at all, taking out their bestseller books, bringing their kids to story time, searching for jobs or playing Solitaire or Candy Crush on the computers.

Earlier she'd thought, well, fine, Shane's not on her team this time, so it's time to act like him. WWSLD. *What Would Shane Lafluco Do?* He'd go Google something, that's what he'd do.

So, Atlanta went and Googled.

Search term: "Bait dog."

She started reading and sliding down that slippery slope, and now she sits, queasy.

Atlanta's learned more about the subject than she cares to admit in just a half an hour.

Bait dogs, like Tressa said, are meant to teach the other dogs—the fighters—to grow bloodthirsty, to go for the weaker animal, to go for the *kill*. Teaches the bigger dogs confidence. Teaches them how to be mean. If they don't go for the bait, they get hurt. Prodded. Poked. Shocked. Punished.

Little dogs make good bait dogs. Puppies, too. Plus cats or any other small animal.

Folks like Bodie and Bird steal the dogs from people's front lawns and backyards. Others answer ads in the paper—*free to a good home*. Puppy mills sometimes sell unsold dogs for just this purpose.

Seems, too, that some fighter dogs end up as bait dogs. A fighter loses a fight, gets mauled, sometimes the owner kills the dog. Other times he uses him as prey. Fighter dog won't go for a bait dog, he might end up as bait instead.

Sometimes they bet on bait-dog fights. How long will the bait dog survive? Will the fighter take the bait? Blood and money. Other times it's just training—no bets, no audience.

They use tools, gruesome tools. Cat poles. Bait cages. Flirt poles. Animals tied down, strung up. Bigger beasts having a go at smaller critters: possums, poodles, whatever. She sees a picture of a terrier pinned to the ground and torn apart like a chew toy—as if the mastiff who attacked it was trying to dig out the stuffing and the squeaker.

The images, like scissors, cut dark holes in her mind. Dark holes where she finds it hard to shine light.

Nobody feeds the bait dogs.

Nobody cares for 'em.

Most bait dogs die in the pen. Some don't. Those that don't, just get used again and again until they're spent up or dead. They're dumped after the fact—left in ditches, drowned in ponds, thrown in a hole somewhere.

Those rare few that get found still alive, either die from their wounds or are put to death by shelters who don't know what to do with them or don't have the money to devote to their care and rehabilitation.

Bait dogs are just about the lowliest form of creature on earth.

Used and abused and left to die.

Atlanta stifles a sob. Chokes it back. Toughens up.

———

Back home, she calls Jenny.

She says to Jenny, "I found out who stole your dog."

"Tell me."

"It's more than one."

"Tell me."

"I . . . don't know if they're the ones that hurt the dog."

"Please just tell me."

And so she tells her. She leaves out the details of the chase but gives her the broad strokes: Bodie and Bird Haycock, with their pig girlfriend Tressa Kucharski, stole Sailor and—she has a hard time telling Jenny this, and her voice cracks, but Jenny just says it again, *"Tell me"*—sold the dog to serve as bait for a dogfighting ring. She doesn't go into detail. Doesn't explain what that means for Sailor's last couple days on earth.

"Oh."

That's what Jenny says. *Oh*. It's not a dismissive "oh." It's a post-traumatic "oh." The "oh" of someone just told that they're broke, or their family is dead, or that the bombs will soon begin to fall.

One word because she must not have any others right now. One word because what else can you say?

"I'm sorry," Atlanta says.

"I want you to get even with them."

"What?"

"I want you to hurt them. And stop them from doing what they're doing. That's what you do, right? You get things done."

Atlanta feels hot and cold at the same time, like she's strapping into a roller coaster that, once it gets started, she won't be able to escape. "You don't know what you're asking. Let the police handle it."

"The police didn't care when I called them before. They won't care now."

She's right. They won't. That's another thing Atlanta learned when Googling all this horrible stuff. The cops don't much care about dogfighting. Sure, it's a felony in most states. But for the most part it goes underreported and poorly enforced. The laws are pretty clear: it's only punishable when caught in the act. That means infiltrating the ring, and podunk departments like the one in these parts won't bother trying.

"Jenny, I don't know—"

"I'll pay."

"I . . ."

"Another thousand. On top of the first. And I'll pay half up front."

Two grand. That money. The foreclosure. Their house. Atlanta feels the roller coaster starting. The click of the wheels on the tracks. The breeze turning to wind, her hair starting to blow.

"Okay," Atlanta says, the word coming unbidden. "I'll help you."

PART THREE: THE FARM

CHAPTER TWENTY-ONE

It's later that evening. Atlanta's sitting on the couch with the TV on and the remote in her hand, but she's not really watching TV—the news is on to her right, but it's just a flashy blitzkrieg of meaningless light, color, and noise. All serving as background to her troubled thoughts. Thoughts of bad people.

Thoughts of making those bad people pay.

Too many bad people. So little time.

In her ear, Chris's voice, soft and creepy-happy: *What about me?*

She shakes it off. Wonders suddenly where her mother is.

The woman's been gone all day. No idea where or why, but Atlanta finds out soon enough: she hears the Olds outside with its busted muffler, and it isn't long before Mama Arlene is coming through the side door and throwing her purse down on their little dining table, storming past with her hair a mess, her bosoms heaving. Atlanta catches a whiff of something—the smell of fryer grease. Suddenly she wants a hamburger real bad.

"They can't do that to me," Arlene says. She stands behind the couch with her arms crossed. She paces. Then stops. Then paces again. "They can't treat me like that."

"Mama, what *are* you going on about?"

Arlene thrusts a finger in her daughter's face. "They wanted me to clean bathrooms."

"Who? What?"

"Arby's! The Arby's. Down by the highway? Off the exit." She must mistake Atlanta's face for something else, because she continues to give directions: "You go down Broward, south out of town—it's the damn Arby's sitting there next to the Conoco gas, the one with the—"

"I know where it is. Why were you at an Arby's? And what happened with the . . . pyramid-scheme food thing?"

Arlene rolls her eyes. "I was looking for a job. I didn't think the Wonderfully Delicious thing was a good fit." Atlanta at first wonders if her mother actually took her advice, but then figures it's something far simpler: Mama thought it was too hard.

Truth is, Atlanta doesn't know if her mother is lazy or scared or what. She's not stupid. She can be very sweet. Maybe she's depressed, needs pills or something.

"You at least get any money back that you put in?"

"Well . . ."

Dangit!

"Mama, what the hell? You trying to bury us here?"

"Hey, now, I'm trying! I really am."

"Tell me Arby's at least gave you a job."

"They did." *Whew.* "But they wanted me to push a broom! They already got a young retarded girl—or maybe she's older, I dunno, they always seem kinda young even when they're not, on account of their lack of worldliness—and I told the manager, I said to him, I have more skills than a retarded person—"

Atlanta regrets it soon as she says it, but there it goes, falling out of her mouth: "Do you?"

"What?"

"I'm just saying, retarded people do jobs all the time. Hard jobs. Good jobs. But you mostly sit home and . . . don't. They probably have plenty of skills you don't have. I mean, not the really super-retarded ones, maybe, but—you know, I don't even think we're supposed to say that word anymore, *retarded*?"

"Who cares about the damn word? My own daughter is being cruel to me!"

"I'm not being cruel, Mama, I just . . . I'm just saying you can't go talking to the manager like that. And you oughta be nicer about people. Besides, why *can't* you push a dang broom?"

"Because I'm better than that!" Arlene yells. Face suddenly red and eyes suddenly glassy with tears that threaten to fall but don't. Her voice lowers. "Normally I'd have a man around the house, but ever since . . . well." Arlene looks away, and Atlanta feels a sudden stab of shame and anger all her own—one of her mother's many gifts, it seems, is taking her own shitty feelings and passing them along to other people the way you'd hand off a football or give someone else the flu. Arlene continues: "It's all right. I've got it figured out. I'm going to start my own business, be my own boss. You'll see. For now I need to . . ." It's like she's searching for the word. Then she finds it: "*Ruminate* upon it. Have a cigarette. Maybe a beer. And go sink into a nice hot bath."

And like that Arlene is gone, walking her way up the steps.

But she calls out behind her: "Hey! There's something on the front porch for you. A package."

Atlanta doesn't move at first. Soon she hears the pipes complain as Mama starts filling the tub. Atlanta heads outside.

Out there, she finds a wicker basket wrapped in red cellophane like a Christmas present that time-traveled to this warm and dry June evening. Inside are meats and cheeses and crackers and cookies. Summer sausages in their tubes, a brick of sharp cheddar, butter crackers and sugar cookies and more.

A little tag dangles from the arch of the basket's handle. Atlanta plucks it like a crab apple and flips it open:

I'm sorry. I'll help. –Shane.

Atlanta smiles.

It's a small smile, sure, but right now even the tiniest curl to her lips is a bright light in a very dark space.

——

Next day, at the little grungy café in the middle of town, Atlanta sits across from Shane and tells him everything, which feels good. There's comfort in purging all this horrible stuff she's been keeping stored up inside her, like it doesn't have to be all hers anymore.

Waitress brings her an iced tea, and as she talks, Atlanta upends a small dump-truck's worth of white sugar into it. Shane watches her over a coffee so black it might as well be ink poured out of a squid's ass. At the end of it, after he noisily sips the too-hot coffee, he blinks and says, "That sucks."

Two words, so simple, and so true. It does suck. All of it sucks.

She pops the straw in her mouth, slurps some tea. Still not sweet enough. *They do* not *know how to make iced tea up here*, she thinks. Glass of cold tea down South is like liquid crack. Iced diabetes and oh-so-tasty.

More sugar, then. It whispers as it hits the tea and sinks past the ice.

"So what do we do?"

"Well," she says, "that's why I need you. You're smarter than me, plain and simple. If I figure out anything it's because I'm lucky. If you figure it out, it's because you're smart."

"That's not true. You're plenty smart."

"I'm not saying I'm a dipshit or anything. You might be shorter than me physically, but you're taller than me if you figure your brain into the equation. Let's just leave it at that." She sips at the tea. Feels the sugar eating into her teeth—kind of a tingly sensation. Perfect. "That's why I need you. I'll pay you for your brain."

"You don't have to pay."

"No, I want to. Oh. Hey. Thanks for the basket of meat."

"It had cheese and other stuff in it, too."

"Yeah, meat is so good. I do not understand how someone can be a vegetarian." She blinks, and when she does she sees images from yesterday's Google search behind her eyes. The thought of meat suddenly flips her stomach. In her head she knows they're not the same thing, but her heart and gut don't care right now. Suddenly she gets vegetarianism. "Anyway, uh, I'm sure the cookies and crackers are good, too. So where do we start?"

"We gotta figure out where Bodie and Bird are, first."

"Sounds right."

"What are you going to do? When we find out who did this?"

Atlanta shrugs. "Jenny didn't say what to do. Right now I just want to find 'em. I didn't see them in the phone book at home. The Cooch said they were homeschooled, so it's not like they're in school records or anything. I don't know that I've ever seen 'em."

"So we're up the creek."

"Well, hold on, now, because here's our resident expert." Coming in through the front door is Chomp-Chomp, messy hair in his face, big teeth and tiny gums preceding him like he's some kind of mouthy horse. He sits down—flops down, really—and offers an awkward wave.

"Hey," he says.

Shane tightens. His head shrinks into his shoulders like a softball pressed into some mud.

She tells him, "It's all right. This is more Ch . . . Steven's area of expertise."

"You can call me Chomp-Chomp," he says. "Or Chompers. It's okay."

Atlanta kinda wants to, but it seems like being polite is the way to go. "Nah, we can call you Steven. Or Steve. Or Stevie?"

"Whatever you like."

That's not how a name works, she thinks, but Shane's still bristling, and they've got other things to worry about.

"Chris was our third," Shane says, his voice small and stiff.

She leans in, whispers to Shane as if Steven isn't sitting there, "He's not a replacement, dum-dum, he's just . . . he's just here to help, and I need help, so can we continue? Please?"

"Fine. You may continue."

"Good." Back to Chompers, then. "Steven. You know a pair of brothers named Haycock? Bodie and Bird. They were—or are—victims of the Cooch's cooch, so she says."

He nods. "Yeah. Bodie's the older one, but not even by a year. They live up on Grainger Hill past the trailer parks. But I called Adam Rains—he's the drummer for Hyperdoor—and asked, and he said they're not around this summer. Adam said they're staying with their . . . uncle or something up on his farm in Little Ash."

Little Ash is just one town over. On the other side of Grainger Hill. Atlanta's been through there—not much to look at. Not even a town, really, so much as a couple farms and hills, Amish and Mennonites here and there. "Uncle's farm," she says. "Wonder if that's *the* Farm. One Tressa was talking about."

"Could be," Shane says. "That where the dogfights are?"

"Maybe. I dunno."

"Then we need to figure out where the Farm is."

"Shit," Atlanta says. "If that's where they hold the fights, we won't have access. It's not like a town softball game or something."

Shane shrugs. "Why not ask your friend Guy?"

"Why? 'Cause he's Mexican?"

"*No,*" Shane says with a scowl. "Because he's into some . . ." For this, Shane lowers his voice, talks out of the side of his mouth. "*Shady. Business.*" Dang, just because she told him one time that she bought some prescription drugs from Guy, he thinks the guy is like fucking Scarface or something. Still. Maybe it's not a bad idea to ask. Guy *did* say something about dogfights way back when, so maybe he knows something.

"I'll ask. I need to see him anyway." Get some money up front from Jenny, get a hookup. She's about to tell them they need to settle up when someone else comes into the greasy spoon.

A cop.

The cop.

Orly's buddy from the gun club.

Not a big man, Unibrow. But he carries with him a sizable darkness. He's in uniform. Catches sight of Atlanta and the others sitting there, and his thin lips turn to a small smile. His single dark brow twists like a snake trying to find a comfortable way to lie, and he starts walking over.

Atlanta's blood and bowels go to ice water. The sugar tang in her mouth suddenly tastes bitter.

Shane sees him, too. He stares down at his coffee.

Steven doesn't get it. He mostly just looks up, confused.

"Everybody good here?" the cop asks.

Nobody answers. Steven finally says, "Yup." Nervous because it's a cop, maybe, but otherwise oblivious.

Atlanta stands. Moves fast.

She takes her iced-tea glass and smashes it over the cop's head. Sweet tea goes everywhere. The cop cries out. Jagged glass rends forehead flesh—blood and ice hit the cracked linoleum of the greasy spoon and—

The little minimovie inside her head stops playing, and the cop nods as he remains standing there, the iced-tea glass still sweating in front of her. The cop smiles again, watching her the way a black cat watches a spring robin at a bird feeder. "Hope so," he says, then heads to the counter.

Shane lets out a breath.

Atlanta can't take it. She has to get up and leave. Tosses her last dollar on the table and bolts.

———

Guillermo Lopez is nowhere to be found. Over the grass and the crooked post-and-rail fence surrounding his double-wide trailer, the thumping beat of Jay-Z rapping is causing the windows in the trailer to vibrate and hum—*bvvt bvvt bvvt bvvt*. She orbits the trailer a few times. Puffs her cheeks and lets out a breath.

Should've called first.

Maybe he's inside. She goes for the door—it's open, not locked—and pops her head inside. Same as it's always been: Amish hexes and cornflower-blue curtains and on the breakfast-nook table a little porcelain cow creamer.

"Guy?" she asks. "Guy-Lo?" Nothing. Just the muted bass of the music. *Doom. Doom. Doom.* The little cow creamer trembles with each deep beat.

She pulls her head back out—then hears something above her.

A shadow out of the sun—a hand appears, and in it the silhouette of a blocky pistol. Atlanta gasps, staggers backward, almost loses her shit and goes bristles-over-broom-handle.

It's Guy. He's up on the roof of the trailer, eyes hidden behind wraparound mirrored shades.

"Yo! Atlanta." He waves at her with the gun, like it's no big thing. "Ladder's on the far side. Come on up, girl."

She has to check herself, make sure she didn't accidentally pee. Shaking her head, she goes around the long side of the trailer and, by the little window that must overlook the kitchen sink, she sees a steel ladder leading up.

On the roof, Guy's got a boom box. He shuffle-dances over, turns it down. Atlanta spies a beach chair and smells coconut suntan lotion. Weirder still, she sees a small stack of paperbacks sitting next to the chair. Authors she's never heard of. Meg Gardiner. Patricia Cornwell. Margaret Atwood.

"What?" he asks, catching the look on her face. "I fuckin' like to read, you know?"

"Look like chick books."

"And you're a chick, so what's the problem?"

She laughs. "Well, you've got beans and franks, or so I assume."

"Hey," he says, suddenly all serious. "Reading books by female authors does not limit my macho vibe. Plus, bitches write the best characters, man. It's like they *get* people, you know?"

"I'm just saying, this goes against my image of you as a displaced, drug-peddling thug. Though that pistol you keep waving around is starting to move the needle back the other way." She cocks an eyebrow. "What is that, anyway? Looks like a .45. M1911?"

Guy sits on the edge of his beach chair. Kicks over an old plastic roof-tar bucket and flips it so she can have a seat. "This? Nah. It's a fucking Daisy. Pellet gun. I just keep it up here in case I want to try to shoot squirrels or groundhogs or some shit." His voice gets all faux-tough. "Or if some nosy bee-yotch comes poking her better-dead-than-red head in my damn trailer."

"Shut up."

"I'm just messin' with you. So whassup? Been a while, girly. Heard you got into some shit."

"Who'd you hear that from?"

"Word gets around when you tangle with the town Nazis."

"Yeah, I guess."

Guy's face suddenly falls. "Oh, shit, you know, I didn't say to you—I didn't say sorry. And, uhh, what's the word? Condolences. For your friend. The gay kid."

"Chris."

"Yeah. Him. That sucks."

"It's pretty much the definition of suck."

"He killed himself?"

"Yes." She pauses. "No. I don't know."

"So, ahh, what you need? You need pills, I don't have anything right now that's up your alley. I got a little weed if you want it, and between you and me I got some sugar cubes if you like acid—did you know that the penalty for selling LSD is, like, ten times worse than if you were selling heroin and shit? That's fucked up. Anyway, you don't seem like the trip-out kinda girl."

She shakes her head. "I don't want to feel my brain melt, no. I was hoping you had some Adderall."

"My hookup at Geisinger's gotten all paranoid. I think he's using what he takes, and it's making him a little loco, you know? I need to find a better connect there. Sorry, Burns."

"There's something else."

"'Sup."

"I need to know about dogfighting."

Guy leans back. Opens his mouth, waggles his tongue back and forth over his teeth. "Who told you that?"

"Who told me what?"

"That I could help you with that."

"Nobody. Well—you once mentioned dogfighting, and Shane had an idea—"

"Who's Shane?"

"What? He's my—you know, what the hell just happened here? One second we were talking, and now you've gone all squirrelly on me. I just asked—"

Guy stands. Puffs out his chest and tucks the gun under his armpit. "Who the fuck is Shane?"

She stands up to meet him chin to chin. "He's a friend who thought you might know people who know people."

"I don't do that anymore."

"Do what?"

"The fights."

"The dogfights?"

"Yeah. I don't do that anymore."

"You used to be involved in that shit?"

"Isn't that why you're asking?"

She gives him a hard shove. He staggers backward. Guy's ankle clips an exposed duct and suddenly his arms spin like a pinwheel in a hard wind, and next thing Atlanta knows he's tumbling over the edge of the trailer, yelling as he falls.

Then: *thump*. He cries out in pain.

Oh, shit.

———

She stands over him but doesn't help him up. Atlanta can see that his limbs aren't twisted or anything and that his biggest problem is trying to get air back into his flattened lungs. When he fell, he narrowly missed hitting a small, rusted picnic grill. Good for him.

He flails about with a hand, trying to get her to help him up.

"No," she says. And swats the hand away.

She's patient. She waits for him to finally gasp air back into his chest and sit up. Butt in the grass, he looks up at her with pathetic hangdog eyes. "You pushed me off my damn roof."

"That was an accident."

"You didn't mean to shove me?"

"I meant to shove you, just not off the roof."

He laughs, but it's not a happy sound. "You're lucky I'm not dead."

"I'd say that makes you the lucky one."

"Yeah. Good point. Listen, I don't do the dog thing anymore. That's something I did as a kid. And even then it wasn't that I wanted to do it. It was . . ." He rubs his eyes, groans. "Life is better now, is all I'm saying."

"But you know people."

"I didn't fight dogs around here."

She says it again. *"But you know people."*

"Of course I know people. Dogfights are like . . . they're like the oases you see on nature shows where all the animals come from hundreds of miles around to hang out at this one watering hole. At the fights, you find, like, drugs and gangs and guns. Hookers. All kinds of shit."

Atlanta's suddenly not sure she can trust him. Guy's part of that. He's not her people—he's one of the beasts at the watering hole. Before she thought of him as a friend; now she's a bit wifty on that point.

Still. What choice does she have?

"I'm looking for some people. Used a friend's terrier as a bait dog."

"Oof." He shakes his head. That means he gets it. He knows what that terrier went through.

"And I need to get some payback for her." *And for that poor dang dog.*

"I dunno, Atlanta. That's tough, but . . ."

She folds her arms in front of her chest. "You're gonna help me."

"And why is that?"

"Because next time I'll do worse than just push you off a roof." She grabs at her crotch, then says: "Remember the thing with my mother's boyfriend." She turns her hand into a gun, lets the thumb hammer fall. "Boom."

"Uh-huh," he says, his deep tan going suddenly pale. "Awright. Help me up. Let's go inside. I need some ice."

————

He doesn't have any ice, so he holds a tallboy of beer against the back of his neck. "I think I got, like, a slipped cervical disc."

"I didn't think you had a cervix."

"Not a cervix, a—you know what, never mind. You don't know what you're asking me to do with this dogfight thing," Guy says. He cranes his neck left, then right. Vertebrae snap, crackle, pop. "Ow."

"I'm just looking for two particular dickheads. Bodie and Bird Haycock."

"They're the ones that stole the dog?"

"Yup. They're staying somewhere called 'the Farm.'"

Guy winces. "Course they are. That's where they hold the fights. It's a fucking compound, yo. You're gonna need an in if you want to get within a mile of that place."

"You're my in."

"I'm not your in."

"But you said . . . it's like a watering hole for shitheads or whatever. And you used to . . ." She doesn't bother finishing the sentence.

"I'm nobody around here, and I like it that way. Got it? I sell my little pills and do my little thing, and ain't nobody thinks I'm more than just a stone in the tread of a sneaker. You want to head to the Farm, you'll need somebody to vouch for you, and I'm not that guy." He sets the beer down, cracks it with a *pssshhh*. Catches foam with his lip and slurps it up. "Especially if you're going up there to stir the shit. You don't wanna go up there, 'Lanta. That's nasty-ass business. You want just those two, fine, wait till those rats poke their heads outta their hole—they'll go buy smokes or beers or go try to get some trim somewhere, and when they do, you get 'em. Don't go up to the Farm."

"I need to," she says, and it's true, though she doesn't know why. It's like walking into a dark cave knowing there's something real mean sleeping down in the deep, but you keep walking anyway, because you have to *see* it with your own eyes. "I'm going to the Farm one way or another, so it might as well be with your help."

"Please." Way he says it, it sounds like he's begging, really begging. "Don't drag me into this."

"Consider yourself drugged. Dragged. Whatever."

"Shit."

"Don't you want to do something good?"

He just shakes his head. "Nothing good's gonna come out of this, Atlanta Burns. Nothing." He tells her he'll put together some names, figure out a way in, he'll call her. Then he slams back the rest of the beer and doesn't bother offering her one.

———

She doesn't have any Adderall so she goes into her mother's medicine cabinet, but she doesn't find much in there, either. Mama's not exactly a fan of most prescription drugs these days, claiming she used to be addicted to . . . it was either Xanax or Valium, she can't seem to remember which (and that leads Atlanta to believe it was probably both at one time or another). Most of what's in the cabinet is allergy meds and Motrin.

Fine. She goes downstairs and nukes a cup of instant coffee. It tastes like dirt from the bottom of a workman's boot, but it's hot and it's caffeine. Just to be sure, she drinks three more cups before the sun comes up.

When it does, she's not sure what to do with herself. She washes some of the dishes in the sink. Makes herself breakfast, which is really just ramen noodles—the ambiguously named "Oriental" flavor, which she suspects tastes less like anything Oriental and more like soy sauce. Ramen noodles have been a breakfast staple of hers for years, on all those many days when her mother did not come down to make anything. Cheap. Easy. Oddly comforting to an anxious stomach before another day at high-school hell.

As she's slurping noodles, she hears footsteps upstairs. Then a toilet flush. Then footsteps back to bed. Atlanta almost misses having the run of the house. Since the woman moved back in upstairs, Atlanta's reminded how much noise Mama makes.

Atlanta sits and finishes her noodles. Putters around. Feels useless. Like a pair of fake nuts hanging from the back of a pickup truck—ornamental, stupid, a worthless decoration.

It's an hour later when the phone rings.

"It's on," Guy says. "They got a fight next week. We're in."

Atlanta's heart plummets through the floor like an elevator.

CHAPTER TWENTY-TWO

They call it a farmers' market, but it's no such thing. It's a dirt mall—a big, concrete rectangle with stall after stall smashed together in a big U-shape. They have farm stuff, sure. Amish sell jams, jellies, jars of chowchow, red-beet eggs, pickled everything. A few stalls compete for produce—curiously, little of it is actually local. But then you have the homely, elderly twins who sell old electronics and appliances—tape decks, decrepit vacuums and vacuum parts, old RC cars. Or the pet-food store that has a live alligator in the back that they like to show off (his name's Arthur). Or the butcher counter whose meats smell a little too sweet, a little too sour, like they're on the edge of going south if they haven't already. And the food stalls: everything from fried chicken to Cuban sandwiches to Kenyan food to sugar-crusted elephant ears big enough to use as a trash can lid. Food smells mingle together with body odors to make a confusing olfactory experience.

Shane travels behind Atlanta, ogling and oohing.

"You really never been here before?" she asks.

"Huh?" Shaken from his reverie.

"I said, you've never been here before?"

"Nuh-uh. No. I just thought it was . . . I dunno, a farmers' market."

"Name's kinda misleading."

"Whoa!" Shane runs over to a table outside a dimly lit stall, finds a real oddity—some taxidermist threw together a true chimera: a frog's head on a bunny's body with what looks to be a tabby cat's tail. It sits beneath a cracked jewel lamp that is also for sale. "Look!"

Atlanta makes a face. "I'd put that down. You'll get fleas or something." She snorts. "Maybe that's why they call these things flea markets."

"It does smell."

"I bet."

Suddenly his eyes shift, catch light, see something else that fills his fool head with excitement. "Comic shop!" And he's off like an Iditarod husky. She rolls her eyes and follows after, finds him rifling double-time through a long box of dusty old comics. She sees titles she doesn't recognize—*Outsiders, Starman, New Mutants*— alongside a few she does—*Batman, Flash, The Avengers*.

Shane looks like a miner who just found a rich vein of gold, and Atlanta has to hook him under the arm and drag him back out. "That's not why we're here, geek-boy. I need stuff." Yesterday she nabbed an advance of cash from Jenny. Soon as Jenny started writing a check, Atlanta said she needed the real deal instead— cold, hard greenbacks, thanks. She paid a bit to Guy for his troubles, and now she's here, prepping for next week's trip to the Farm.

They muscle past a pair of superfat middle-aged housewives in too-tight sweat pants (on the one is emblazoned the word "Juicy" in pink glitter, which Atlanta assumes is supposed to make you think of sex but instead makes her think of ham) and there she finds what she's looking for: Keystone Mobile, a grungy, overstuffed stall full of mobile accessories and headsets from the early 2000s, plus a ton of old phones crammed together in a glass case.

Dude behind the counter is a lanky sort with crow-slick hair and a patchy beard poking up out of his face like a bed of bad weeds. She tells him she needs a burner—no plan, just a pay-as-you-go.

"Something that's all phone, though. I don't want to play fruity little games on it."

Shane chimes in: "Angry Birds is pretty cool."

"They don't sound cool. They sound angry."

"What provider is this?" Shane asks. "AT&T? Sprint? Boost?"

Atlanta doesn't know, so she just shrugs. Shane asks the scraggly-beard, who says, "We're an . . . independent provider." He starts boxing up a basic, gray, candy-bar phone: a little brick of forgotten technology. He goes into a spiel, sounding rehearsed and mechanical: "Keystone Mobile. You'll hear about us in a few years when our patented 5G signal goes—"

"That's not a real service," Shane whispers in her ear, but she shushes him and pays for the phone.

Then she drags him on toward their next stop.

This stall: weapons.

And here, again, Shane's eyes go big and bulgey.

Atlanta taps the counter. "I need a box of shells."

Shane's not paying attention. Instead he recites a litany of what he sees: "Tonfa. Sais. Manrikigusari. Wakizashi. Katanas! Oh, dude, whoa, katanas." He scurries over to a wall clad in a velvet drape with various implements of ninja destruction hanging there. Then he spies a wall of medieval weaponry—swords and maces and pieces of armor—and dashes over to that. The guys behind the counter, who look like carnies, watch him and snicker.

"Eyes up here," Atlanta says. "I said, I need shells. Gimme the .410s."

One of the carnies, a scruffy ginger, reaches in past a display of Zippo lighters and butterfly knives and plunks a box out on the glass. "Shooting squirrels?"

"Rats," she says.

"Cool."

————

The parking lot looks like a scene from the end of the world: beater cars and certified POSes left and right, molester van sitting cock-eyed next to a pimped-up Cadillac. Lots of rust and second- or thirdhand rides. Atlanta and Shane weave between crap-bucket cars. He finally gets the advantage and scoots in front of her.

"You have to let me go with you," he says. "I wanna go."

She slides past him, almost knocks the long, velvet-wrapped package out from under his arm. "I can't believe you bought that thing."

"It was only a hundred bucks." He tucks the fabric-clad katana tighter. "It's awesome."

"It's a flea-market katana. It's pretty douchey."

"Is it?"

"Kinda. Like, if you smelled of Drakkar Noir and wore gold chains and pretended to meditate and were in your midforties and stuff, I would totally expect to find a katana on your wall."

He hurries after her again. "Maybe it's for home protection. You ever think of that?"

"A shotgun is for home protection. A katana is for dudes who want to pretend to be a ninja. And by the way, a cheap-shit katana won't cut through a bubble bath, much less a burglar or serial killer."

"It seemed pretty sharp to—" Shane growls in frustration. "You're changing the subject."

"Correction: I already changed the subject."

"Well, I'm changing it back! You should take me to the fight."

They reach the edge of the parking lot. Shane's bike— somewhat miraculously—remains locked up around a bent maple tree. Atlanta hoofed it from home. Another two-hour walk awaits her. "What? So you can protect me with your garage-sale katana?"

"C'mon. Atlanta. Please. I can be helpful. I can . . . carry ammo for you. I can watch your back."

"So you're like a mule?" She looks left, looks right, then crosses over the road after a pickup passes. "It's a bad idea."

"I want to help, and I can only help if I'm there. You want my big brain? Then the big brain goes with you. C'mon. *Pleeeeease.*"

"Fine," she says. It's still a bad idea, and she stands there on the other side of the road pinching the bridge of her nose and fighting a headache. "But you need to wait in the car."

"Again?"

"Again."

"Okay."

———

They're bringing Donny out on a stretcher and he's not screaming anymore because they must've given him something. His one hand dangles off the stretcher and it's coated with blood. His. From where he cupped the wound. Atlanta's not sure how bad it is or what kind of damage she did, only that he bled like a throat-slit goat and screamed for a long, long time.

Mama's on the porch, crying.

Everything is red and blue lights, painting the house, the windows, the field. It goes slow, then fast, then slow again.

Crackle of radios. Wind across the grass and the corn. Atlanta shivers. Wants to cry but can't, and is worried that not crying is a real bad sign. Like now she's broken or something, irrevocably, irretrievably, never the same girl again.

Detective Holger puts a blanket across her shoulders like they do on television and hunkers down. She's a bulldog of a woman, hair cut short and mouth in a permanent frown, but her words don't match the frown, and she says, "Honey, I know this is hard, but you're going to need to come with me, now."

"I know," Atlanta says, shaking like a leaf in a hard wind. "I'm sorry for what I did."

Holger leans in. "Between you and me, I'm not. I'm not saying what you did was right, but I'm not saying it was wrong, either. And I'm damn sure not saying I would've done differently. You hear me?"

Gamely, Atlanta nods.

Then she's up and ushered to the car, and Holger opens the back of the car—not a cruiser but a dinged-up gray Ford Taurus many years out of date—and sitting there in the back is Chris

Coyne holding the little terrier, and he smiles that winning smile and says, "I hope you're ready for all this."

And she says, "I'm not." And then, "This is a dream, isn't it?"

He winks. The dog barks.

She wakes up, soaked to the bone in sweat. Teeth chattering like they did on that day.

———

Week later, Guy's outside in his boxy Scion, honking the horn. Atlanta reaches into her closet, plucks the .410 shotgun from inside. Her hands tremble as she picks it up. Finger alongside the outer edge of the trigger guard. Part of her thinks, *Just put it away. No good can come of this. Park it. Forget it.* And that's what she decides to do.

But her body goes the other way. Even as her mind is telling her the Winchester belongs here at the house, she's walking downstairs with the shotgun resting on the soft of her forearm, her pocket stuffed full of green birdshot shells.

CHAPTER TWENTY-THREE

"Music's too dang loud," Atlanta says, spinning the volume knob the other way. Guy shoots her a look as the Scion zips through the asphalt ribbons of nowhere road. Trees and cows and silos. The smell of chicken shit. Sunlight through pollen.

"You know not to mess with a dude's stereo, right?"

"It's making me queasy. I can feel the bass inside my belly. Like a . . . baby kicking or something." It's not the bass making her queasy, but it sure isn't helping. Again the feeling of being strapped into a roller coaster hits her. Guy's driving—fast, one-handed, taking curves wide with the tires scraping gravel.

A hand darts out from the cramped backseat. Shane holds out a bag of red licorice splayed out like octopus tentacles. "Twizzlers. Want any?"

Atlanta takes one, sucks air through it without chewing. She's not sure if it's helping or hurting her nausea.

"I can't believe we had to bring him," Guy says.

"I have a name," Shane says from the backseat.

Guy inhales through his teeth. "And I've already forgotten it, little dude."

"Shut up," Atlanta barks.

"Yeah," Shane says, waggling accusatory licorice. "Shut up."

"I mean it for the *both* of you." Her hands curl tighter around the stock and barrel of the squirrel gun. She's got the barrel up by her ear. Atlanta leans her head against it. It feels cool.

Guy gives her a sideways look. "And I can't believe you brought that. Keeping it up by your ear like that—girl, you gonna blow the roof of your head off."

"It's not loaded." *Yet.*

"Still shouldn't have brought it."

"I need it."

"It's trouble."

"You said all kinds of bad people are going to be there. I bet they'll all be packing."

"Some will," he says, taking a few hairpin turns that bring them back down Grainger Hill on the other side. Through the trees she sees the tops of trailers laid out in a trailer park like white dominoes. "And that's exactly why you don't want to be carrying around a goddamn gun like you're—who was the female cowboy?"

"I dunno. Calamity Jane? Annie Oakley?"

"Whatever. You ain't them, 'Lanta. The way some of these guys treat the dogs, that should tell you just what they think about the sanctity of life and shit. My mamá always used to say, 'Don't throw rocks at the moon because one day you might knock it down.'"

"I'll throw rocks at the moon if I wanna." She pouts a little.

As they round the last switchback, Guy punches the brakes. Everybody lurches forward—Atlanta has to brace herself so she doesn't smack her head on the dash. Guy whips the car into the middle of a three-point turn.

"Hell with this," he says. "This is a bad idea. I'm not doin' it."

"Wait!" she yells. "*Wait.*" The car stops in the middle of the road, pointed perpendicular. "I'll leave the gun in the car. I'll hide it in the backseat. Happy?"

Guy is silent for a moment. Then: "Yeah. Yeah. Okay." He reverses again, points the car once more in the direction. "Turnoff is up ahead."

———

The drive to the Farm takes them down a bouncy track of limestone gravel, the Scion ill-made to handle the dips and bumps. Atlanta's teeth rattle as they pass a tall-grass meadow to the left and, on the right, a boggy tract of trees—sunlight caught in the surface of murky pools.

Soon they start to see the No Trespassing signs. All handpainted on boards that are nailed to the trees. "TRESSPASSERS WILL BE SHOT. BEWARE OF DOG. TURN BACK. FUCK OFF."

They pass a guy in a backward John Deere hat pissing against a weeping willow.

That's when they get to the fence. Chain-link. Topped with coils of razor wire. The gate's locked by a loop of heavy-gauge chain with a padlock that's so big you could beat a horse to death with it.

The car sits there, idling. "What do we do now?" Atlanta asks.

They don't need to wait long for an answer. The willow-pisser comes back from his bathroom break. He heads around the front of the car, comes up on Guy's side, and raps on the window with the back of his knuckles.

Guy buzzes the window down. "'Sup?"

The guy peers in the window. Midforties, maybe. Pitted cheeks like he once had real bad acne. His left eye is tight behind puckered, puffy skin—scar tissue not suffered by the other eye. He takes off his tractor cap, runs his fingers through a length of greasy brown hair. "Fuck ya want?"

"Here for the Show," Guy says.

"Uh-huh." But Winky doesn't budge, just keeps staring in the car, both eyes lingering on Atlanta.

Guy reaches gingerly into the console compartment, pulls out a big freezer baggie, which is in turn filled with a bunch of smaller Ziplocs, each one packed with a variety of pills. Little blue ones, little pink ones, capsules the color of chocolate milk. He shakes it. "I'm here to make a deal. Guillermo Lopez."

"You're cool," Winky says. But then he snorts and starts chewing on something. Phlegm, maybe. "But these two? They're not on the list."

"That little shithead in the back is my brother—"

"Hey!" Shane protests.

"And her, she's an associate looking to buy a dog."

"This ain't fuckin' PetSmart, pal."

Guy nods to her. "Show him."

She reaches in her pocket, pulls out a baggie all her own—as planned, it's full of twenties. A portion of her advance from Jenny. All part of the ruse. She won't be spending it, but they don't know that.

Winky rubs his scalp again, then screws the cap back on his head. He once more moves around the front of the car and comes up on Atlanta's side. He waits as she hits the button to lower the window.

"The boys can go in," Winky says. "You can stay out here with me for a little while."

"Like he, uh, said, I'm his associate, so. I better go with him."

"They'll be okay without you for five, ten minutes."

He leans in his head. His tobacco breath is dark, earthy, acrid. He takes a sniff of her.

"Hey," Shane protests again.

Winky ignores it. "I like your shampoo."

"It's called soap," she says, voice shaky. Suddenly she wishes the shotgun wasn't in the back of the car. Stuffing the barrel up under his chin would go a long way toward getting him out of her personal space. Everything feels suddenly tense, uncertain. A spinning dime moving toward the edge of the table. She has the collapsible baton on her. How long to reach in the bag and get it? Snap the button, pop the baton? No room to move in here. Open the door? Push him back? She's starting to feel claustrophobic. *Do something.*

But it's Guy who does something. He grabs the bag of money, flips the zipper, and takes out a handful of twenties. He thrusts them up under Winky's chin. Then says, "I forgot there was a toll. Can we go, yo?"

Winky smiles a mouth full of ochre teeth, then nods. "Sure thing, *ese.*" Then he goes up to the gate, pops the lock with a key, and swings it wide over the gravel.

They drive forward, and Atlanta feels as if they're heading into the mouth of hell through the front gates, pulling right up to the devil's own palace for valet parking.

———

It's not far past the front gate that the Farm comes into view. A quick glance shows that its simple and earnest name is true: it's a farm, all right. A red barn dominates, standing tall like a demon's church. On the other side is a Morton building—a big metal structure with a corrugated roof—that has an old, grungy farm tractor sitting outside and a pull-behind brush mower next to it. Grasses and weeds and wildflowers growing all around. Atlanta can see another structure, too, off in the distance—a white stone farmhouse tucked away in the trees.

But the centerpiece is the pit.

It's smack-dab in the middle of everything, and that's where all the people are. The pit looks to be plywood walls affixed to metal stakes forming a big dug-out octagon, dozens of people standing at the perimeter and watching whatever's going on inside, and another dozen more milling about like ants that wandered from the colony.

Guy parks the Scion at the edge of the lot. Atlanta stays, draws a deep breath. The encounter with the man in the John Deere hat has left her shaken—like someone stuck an ice pick through the links of her imaginary armor and got her right in the lungs. She pulls it together. Another breath. Another. *Toughen up, you dumb girl.*

"Stay in the car," she says to Shane.

"But—"

But nothing. She's already out and closing the door behind her. Her bag remains in the seat where she left it, but she takes the collapsible baton and tucks it into one of her oversized pockets.

The sun is bright. Hot. The day is starting to cook the earth, dry it, and split it like chapped lips. Guy stands in front of her and pops on a pair of Wayfarer sunglasses. "You good?"

"I'm good."

"You got a plan?"

"Nope." And with that, she starts walking. Heading right for the big stage, the main event, the really big show. That's what they call it, Guy said. Those in the know don't call it the "fight" or "fights." It's the Show. Capital S.

Stones crunch under her boots. Guillermo walks next to her, hands tucked into pockets, trying to look tough, or like he just doesn't care, or maybe those are the same thing for him.

The crowd, like the assemblage of cars in the lot, is a wild mix. And fairly segregated. A cluster of black dudes on this side—some of them looking like gangbangers, a couple others hanging out in uniforms that suggest they work up at the local rendering plant. Hispanics on the other side, and some of them look like bangers, too. A few look like maybe they just came from a kitchen somewhere, with dirty aprons still on. The whites ring the other side, and they're a mix all their own—a clot of hillbillies, a handful of sweaty suit-clad business types, and then on the other side, the fucking skinheads. Some of them are punky: tatted, Mohawked, wild-eyed. Others are clean, conservative, real Hitler Youth types.

Not many women, that's for sure. Those that *are* here appear to be pros. Short skirts, too-tight jeans, lipstick so red they look like vampires fresh from a feeding.

Then she sees something that really bakes her lasagna: three students from her school. One of them is Charlie Russo, the weed smoker under the bleachers. Next to him: Carlos, another from the baseball team. And wandering away from those two: Maisey Bott. Atlanta knows Maisey. Shit, they're in biochem class together. Or were before the school year ended. She's a nice girl. Dumb as a bag of coconuts, but nice.

Maisey might be someone she needs to talk to.

"Still good?" Guy asks her.

"Yeah," she lies.

Atlanta's feet carry her forward with an irresistible gravity. As if she's not moving forward but rather everything is moving toward *her*.

They find a space in the crowd right between the whites and Hispanics—as if the two of them form connective tissue between the two groups.

Her hands hold the plywood wall, a wall that stands about waist high. A splinter bites into the meat of her index finger and she pulls it away, a bead of blood already swelling up like a little red balloon.

Nobody's in the ring right now. It's between matches. The parched earth of the arena is scratched and furrowed from earlier fights. A few tumbleweeds of dog hair blow around in the faint breeze. The ground is stained dark in a few places. Or maybe Atlanta's just imagining things.

Suddenly, commotion. Someone moves through the crowd at the far end, close to the skinheads: it's a thick-necked white guy wearing a black wifebeater and showing off biceps that bulge with a pair of swollen swastika tats. The creature he hauls into the ring calls to mind the old adage of how dogs and their owners start to look like one another. His tawny pit bull's bristling with fat and muscle, a beast wreathed in mean gristle. Around the dog's neck is a rusted chain wrapped again and again, the ends trailing in the dirt. The dog's got empty eyes and a muzzle marred with a mesh of pink scar lines.

Thick-Neck brings the beast to the far end of the arena, celebrated by the hoots and hollers of the skinheads.

The second dog comes into the arena. A brindled pit bull who enters and sits right away, its body making the shape of a pyramid—thick base, thin shoulders, tiny brick head. The dog seems happy. Mouth open. Pink tongue out. Panting in the heat, blissfully ignorant. Its handler—owner? trainer? torturer?—is a big black dude in a loose-hanging Chicago Bulls jersey and has one of those helmet-strap beards that looks like someone drew a line along his jaw with a permanent marker. He gets down, nuzzles the dog, gives it a few slaps on the haunches. The dog leans into the attention. The joy of a well-loved animal, ignorant to the boos of the skinheads nearby.

"That dog's dead," Guy says.

"What?"

"Man, look at him. He's docile. A pet, not a fighter."

Her middle tightens. "That's messed up."

"That's dogfighting." He sniffs. "Besides, over there, the skinhead? That's Karl Rider. His dog, Orion, hasn't lost a match. Trains him with those chains. Makes him drag around tractor tires. Makes him tough as balls. He's probably outside his weight class or close to it. But money makes that a moving target. Bribes make the world go 'round. This world, anyway."

"Orion." Her teeth clench. "Figure he'd name it something more Hitlery. Adolf. Himmler. Something."

"Nah, check it. Orion. O-R-I-O-N. Our Race Is Our Nation."

"Oh."

"Yeah. Here. Look—the ref. Match is about to start."

The ref isn't very ref-like. No black-and-white stripes, no whistle. He's just a potbellied yokel with a fat nose over a big black beard who comes out and gesticulates with his hand almost like he's whipping around an invisible lasso: "Orion versus Omar. To your corners!"

Each handler brings his dog toward its respective corner.

The ref goes and, using a screwdriver, carves a semicircle line in the dirt before each dog, saying, "Behind the line, face away." And both the skinhead and the black dude turn their dogs away from each other, toward the wall, toward the crowd. The ref asks each man to bare his arms, then his calves, and then he pats each dog down.

"The heck's he doing?" she asks.

Guy says, "Checkin' for cheats. Some guys hide shivs or razors. Or stuff to throw in a dog's eye like sand or whatever. I've even seen it where they try to put razors on the dog's paws or in their mouths. That's amateur-hour bullshit, though. Doesn't happen too often, but Cajun Rules says you gotta check."

"Face your dogs," the ref calls. Another lasso motion.

Each handler forcibly turns his dog to face the center of the arena. The animals stand just behind their handlers, head and shoulders poking through the men's legs.

The ref shouts: "Let go."

The men step aside—and the fight's on.

Atlanta's heart's racing and she expects the tempo of the fight to match it, figuring these two beasts will barrel forward and slam into one another like two cannonballs, but that's not how it happens. The battle unfolds slowly and clumsily, the animals hesitant—if it's a car crash, it's one set to a slo-mo crawl.

Gristly Orion trots out into the middle like this is old hat. The other dog—Omar, apparently—circles right, still panting, still wearing that giddy, dumb dog's face, oblivious to the thrashing that Atlanta is now certain he's going to get. Omar's handler gets off to the side, starts yelling at the dog and waving his hands like he's trying to telekinetically move the animal. Handler gets too close, and the ref taps him: "Back up. No touching, no touching."

Karl stands back, arms crossed, showing a broken-toothed smile.

Omar turns back toward his handler and the ref yells out: "Turn!"

"Shit!" the black dude says.

Karl just laughs as the ref whoops out: "Handle your dogs!"

Both handlers grab the dogs and head back to their corners.

"That's a turn," Guy explains. "Dog faces away from the fight, that's a cur move. Curs are losers. Winners are champs. Dog makes a turn—meaning he turns away from the fight—three times, match is over. Dog loses. Bonafide cur, yo."

Atlanta's stomach flutters. That's what needs to happen here. Omar isn't up for this. He's not a fighter. *Keep turning,* she thinks. *Keep. Turning.*

The ref whips his hand around again, calls out the same as before: "Face your dogs." Dog head and shoulders show again through handler legs. "All right. Let go."

Once more the dogs are free.

Again Orion boldly steps into the middle. He knows the drill, and Karl doesn't have to do anything to egg the animal on. But the black dude—Atlanta hears someone in the audience tell him to

"Whip that bitch, Deshawn!"—stands behind his dog, clapping his hands and snapping his fingers.

It works. Atlanta grips the plywood as Omar moves to the middle. But not like a fighter. The brindled pit's got a lean, slack posture—a happy doggy face like he's going to greet an old friend and maybe tussle in the dirt over a chew toy. Orion just stands there, head low, shoulder hair starting to stiffen. A hellhound ready to pounce.

The crowd is whooping it up. The skinheads cheering. Everybody else gasping or booing. It's like watching a lamb bobble off toward a waiting lion.

Orion moves. Fast. Scary fast.

His jaw wraps around Omar's muzzle and he pushes the smaller pit bull down into the dirt. A plume of brown dust rises. Omar squeals, cries out—a sharp, keening whimper. The crowd is loud now—Atlanta's own strangled cry is lost amongst all the catcalls and monkey hoots.

Omar's wriggling, trying to move, trying to roll over. But Orion isn't letting it happen. As Omar whines and thrashes, Deshawn hops up and down, wide-eyed and screaming, the corners of his mouth wet with spit froth: "No! *No!* C'mon! C'mon, son! Get up!" Deshawn hunkers low, suddenly waves his hands like he's a man drowning at sea. "Fanged! Fanged! Omar's fanged, yo! Ref, ref— you listening to me?"

The ref hurries over, hunkers down, then yells out: "Fang. On Omar. Handle your dogs, back to corner."

Karl finally shows some life—and he's pissed. He gets up in the ref's face disputing the call, banging his two fists together. The ref acts like Karl isn't even there.

"I said, *handle your dogs.*" It's then Atlanta sees that the ref has a sparking stun gun in his hand. Karl backs off.

As the two handlers go for their dogs, Atlanta asks, "What's 'fanged' mean?" But the answer becomes clear. As the handlers break the magnetic blood-bond between the two dogs, Atlanta gasps as she sees Omar's face. The muzzle is ragged and looks like ground meat. She thinks: *Go now. Get away. Stop watching.* Or better still: *Get the gun. Put these rabid animals down.* And by rabid animals, she doesn't mean the dogs.

But she stays. Transfixed. Held fast in the quicksand of her own horror.

She barely hears Guy telling her that being fanged means that the other animal's tooth gets stuck in the other dog's skin. *Like that splinter in your hand.*

She's trembling now.

The dogs move back behind the scratch lines.

"Water test," ref says.

Deshawn pulls a bottled water from the corner, uncaps it, pours a little into his own mouth. The ref gives him the thumbs up, then looks to Karl, who waves off the opportunity. With shaking hands, Deshawn pours the water over the dog's face and then into the animal's mouth. Omar leans in against his handler, whining in the back of his throat. Water and blood, water and blood. The earth below the brindle damp with both.

Guy leans in to her, "Handlers test the water first. Make sure it's not juiced."

"That dog. He's really hurt."

Guy nods, grim as the grave. "It's only going to get worse."

It all unfolds again. Face the dogs. Let them go. Back to center. Atlanta wants to run in there, turn the smaller dog away before he gets his throat ripped out.

The two dogs move toward one another. Orion is slow and methodical. And once more Omar waddles out there like he's going to make best friends, like that whole muzzle-biting thing was just a casual misunderstanding between two old friends.

Orion aims to end it now. The big beast lunges again.

And his jaws snap closed on open air.

Omar snarls, moves fast. The smaller dog gets up under Orion, clamps down on the animal's throat. The crowd gasps. The skinheads go nuts—banging and kicking the plywood, screaming every racial epithet they can muster; Atlanta's from the South and even she hasn't heard some of them before today.

It's over fast.

Orion rolls onto his back, and Omar bites down, head shaking like he's trying to clear his head of an infection. And then it's done. Game over.

The worst part is, a little voice inside Atlanta had chosen a side. She wanted to see Omar win. Which means she wanted to see Orion lose—Orion the bully, Orion the beast, Orion who gets what's coming to him. But he's just a dog, a dog who didn't want this, a dog who was *made* into this . . .

It's then that everything goes nuts. Karl comes at Deshawn with fists out, the tendons in the skinhead's neck popping out like bridge cables. Deshawn backpedals, laughing like a donkey, egging the Nazi on. The ref gets between them before the two human beasts clash, pushes them apart. Atlanta can't watch anymore. She turns and flees the ring, trying hard to find her breath and failing.

―――

"Rough and tumble stuff, isn't it?"

She runs into a wall, and the wall speaks.

The man is huge. Six-six. Wide shoulders, long gray hair, and a big snarly beard are just the top of the mountain, a mountain formed of the remarkable bedrock of his barrel chest and the round granite of his massive gut. His beard is the kind that birds might use for a nest, and the tangled salt-and-pepper carpet parts as he smiles.

"I . . ."

"First dogfight, then."

Behind her, she hears the ref call a winner—"Orion is the cur. Omar is the champ!"—and the crowd surges forth on a tide of victory and hate, of adrenaline and dopamine. The human mountain laughs again.

"That fight was a quick one," he says. "They can go for hours. Depends on the dogs and their handlers. I run some dogs now and again. Beautiful animals, these beasts."

"Yeah." She's in his shadow and even that feels like it has weight. She thinks, this guy could give Orly Erickson—who is himself a big sonofabitch—a run for his money. For a moment she's lost in the minimovie of those two fighting in the plywood ring, beating the piss out of each other like a couple of Kodiak bears.

"You from the high school?" he asks her.

She doesn't know why she's honest, but she is. "Yeah."

"Uh-huh. You place any bets yet?"

"No, I . . . no."

He winks. "Shame. Seems if you had money on Omar you'd be rolling around in cash right about now."

Money. Cash. Foreclosure. One bet on the right animal—

Is she really thinking about betting on these fights? Putting money on this horror show? Watching the fight had her invested. Got her blood churning, rooting for Omar. And now she's thinking of buying in all the way? *No.* A black hole of shame blooms in her middle and draws all the rest of her toward it.

"This here is my farm, so I'm glad you found our humble operation," the man says, clapping her on the shoulder with a hand so big he could probably crush a cantaloupe with it. His touch is gentle, however.

Then the mountain moves past her, into the crowd.

She suddenly finds Guy at her side.

"Yo, you met the big man," he says as they both start to walk away from the ring. He sounds in awe.

"He was . . . big, all right."

"Yeah, and he's also the guy who runs this whole place. Ellis Wayman. The Mountain Man."

"The man who is a mountain."

"Word. All right. Listen. I gotta go sell some shit. Might as well make some bucks. You good?"

"I'm good." But she's not, not at all, not even a little.

CHAPTER TWENTY-FOUR

She wanders, feeling lost and angry, the rage burning hot—an iron skillet of hot coals searing heart-meat. She knows she has to find Bodie and Bird. Has to finish what she started here. But where to begin? What to do? Who to ask?

The sun has reached its noontime apex and started its slide back down the other side of the sky.

Current fight's over, so the crowd's starting to mill about. Over by the parking lot, a couple kids are buying a baggie of something from a dealer who's younger than they are. She passes a pair of rich white guys in polos—one of them has his phone out, showing off some video on the screen. She hears porny noises. They laugh. She keeps walking.

Atlanta finds herself nearing the Morton building. As she gets closer to it she passes a little shed—a pump house, by the looks of it—and through the cracked door she sees a girl and an older fellow putting on clothes. She catches a glimpse of the girl's face: Maisey Bott. *Dang.* She wonders if Maisey's been coerced into something, but then she hears Maisey's goofy-ass laugh and the click-snap of a bra closing shut, and so Atlanta just hurries past.

She sees Karl carrying Orion toward the big metal building, his face a twisted rictus of grief and anger. Forearms wet with the dog's blood.

Two familiar faces come out of the Morton, heading toward Karl.

John Elvis Baumgartner and his Skanky Bitch psycho-girlfriend, Melanie.

Horror seizes every muscle in Atlanta's body. And rage. Always more rage.

John Elvis flicks his gaze in her direction.

No no no shit shit shit.

Atlanta ducks behind a donut stack of tractor tires, hunkering down in the weeds. A tick crawls on her leg. She flings it away and bites her lip.

Don't see me don't come over here don't see me shit shit shit.

She waits. And waits.

Hears footsteps approaching.

Her hand moves toward her pants, toward the baton stashed there.

Maisey Bott pokes her head around. "Atlanta?"

Wince.

"Hey, Maisey."

Maisey shows herself fully, stands there, bright-eyed and beaming. "Hey! What are you doing here?"

"Same thing you are," Atlanta says, instantly regretting that. The words just came out—she didn't think before she said 'em, and now there they are.

Maisey laughs—guffaws, really, she's got a goofy kind of gulp-snort donkey laugh—and starts to unwrap the foil around a stick of spearmint gum. "Cool, man. There's good money to be made here. This is fun, isn't it?"

All Atlanta says is, "Yeah. Yep. Great money."

"You want a piece?" Maisey asks around the wad of gum. *Oo wanna piesh?* She waggles the Doublemint pack.

"I'm good." Atlanta clenches her eyes shut. "Hey, is anybody coming over here?"

"Huh?"

"Behind me. From the Morton building. Anybody heading this direction?"

Maisey peeks her head out. "Don't think so. Ooh. Someone you're hiding from?"

"Old boyfriend," she lies. "Don't want him to see me here. You know."

Another donkey laugh. "Yeah, I hear that. Boys get so jealous. I think you're good. I didn't know you had a boyfriend. Lemme ask you something." And Atlanta knows the question is coming, because anytime she gets into close contact with someone from school and they have just enough rope with which to hang the conversation, they always ask. "Did you really . . . you know?"

"Shoot my mother's boyfriend."

"In the—" And suddenly Maisey lowers her voice and squats down next to Atlanta. *"In the beans and franks?"*

"Yeah."

"Was he . . . touching you?"

"He wasn't a good person."

She neglects to say: *He came to my room three times. He told me to do things for him or he'd tell my mother that I was hitting on him. Or he'd leave her. Or he'd hit her. He made me do things for him, all kinds of things that left bruises and made my jaw hurt real bad and then the next time he came to me I didn't want to do it anymore or ever again and so I was ready and waiting and I shot him and the birdshot tore his scrotum clean off. Or maybe not so clean.*

She adds: "So I did what I had to do."

"Cool."

Atlanta has to clench her whole body not to give Maisey Bott a hard flick to the eye. Instead she just nods. "Yeah. Real cool."

"Hey, why you heading toward the murder building?"

"It's a Morton building. It's like a type of farm building."

"No, I mean, that's where they Vick the—"

Just then, a gun goes off inside the building. *Bang.*

"The dogs," Maisey finishes, wincing. "I hate that part."

"Vicking a dog."

Maisey nods. "You know. Killin' it? Like the, uhh, football player."

Killing it. Atlanta has to get out of here before she finds a way to set fire to the whole place.

But she has something to do first.

She says, "Maisey, you know a Bird or a Bodie?"

"Haycocks. I know those two. Couple-a dopes. They're over at the barn."

"The barn."

"That's where they keep the dogs before the fight."

Her hand dips into her pocket. Feels the baton there again—a small source of comfort, that baton, like a match flame on a cold day. But it's better than nothing.

She doesn't know what she's going to do. She has no plan. But her anger doesn't need a plan—and it probably wouldn't care if it had one.

———

She leaves Maisey in the dust and heads toward the barn, a massive peaked building with windows like eyes and a big broad door like a hungry sideways mouth. Barn's got a fresh coat of paint that marks it with the color of a slaughterhouse floor, but Atlanta tries not to think about it that way.

Inside, the floor is hay-strewn. Big spears of sunlight beam in through windows and skylights, motes of swirling dust and pollen suspended there. She's surprised at how calm it is, given the dozen or so dogs stuck in wire cages—cages that are piled one on top of the other. Whatever fighting instinct these dogs have is neatly contained, bottled up and somehow saved for the fights. What she sees are mostly pit bulls of various sizes and colors—black and brindle and fawn, big and small. At the far corner is a boxer, gooey drool hanging from its flappy jowls.

Handlers mill about, some of them tending to their dogs, others talking. Still others stare each other down from across the barn. It's quiet, yes; but behind the apparent serenity lurks a thread pulled taut.

Atlanta wants to kill all these people.

Not just hurt. But *kill*. She tells herself that's just the anger talking. That she doesn't really want to kill anybody. Kids say that all the time, right? *I'll kill you if you touch my beer! I'm going to kill her for stealing my man. Teacher gave me a bad grade, and now I want to kill her ass.* They don't mean it, right?

But she really, honestly wants to kill someone.

It's not the first time she's felt that way, and that's worrying her most of all.

Someone shoulders into her—a dirtball kid with ash-blond hair that segues into a mullet that *then* segues into an even longer rat tail braided and hanging down to the middle of his back. He smiles with pebble teeth and blinks his tiny eyes at her. "Oh, shit, I'm so frickin' sorry."

He clutches a choke chain leash to his chest.

"It's awright," she says. He seems to be the least threatening person in here—he looks nervous, awkward, maybe even bewildered. Good place to start. "Hey, I'm lookin' for someone."

"Sure. Whozat?"

"Bird and Bodie Haycock."

The kid's eyes bug out, and his jaw drops like he's seeing a pair of braless breasts for the first time in his life. "That's me! Well, I'm one of those two, I'm not both of them. Man, how frickin' crazy would *that* be? To be two people?" He offers his hand. "I'm Bird."

"Bird." She says his name, doesn't take his hand, feels a hot gush of bile geyser up from her belly and into her throat. Images of Sailor the little white terrier flip through her mind. But at the same time she's having a hella hard time reconciling the person who could do such a thing to a helpless dog with the gawky, marble-eyed, thimble-dicked hick in front of her. "*You're* Bird."

"Yup!" So proud of it, too.

"And your brother is Bodie."

"Yup!"

"Where's he at?"

"Oh, he's out back. Trainin' one of the dogs at the cat pole."

Hit him now. Break his stupid dumb face.

But she doesn't. "Can you . . . take me to him?"

"Sure, c'mon!"

Bird heads to the back of the barn, waving her on, rat tail bouncing between his shoulders. Atlanta's hands ball into fists, her chewed-up fingernails digging into the flesh of her palm.

———

As they walk behind the barn, they pick up a small trail that leads into the woods. Rough pavers mark the way.

Bird won't shut up. He's a squawky one.

He's all, *So where you from?* and *You go to the high school?* and *Yeah me and my bro we're totally frickin' homeschooled, it's awesome.* He's like a broken spigot—much as you want him to turn off, he won't. *I like the woods. It's frickin' peaceful and whatever. I got allergies though and they frickin' suck and my uncle is what got us the job here and man it's sweet and I like to work outdoors even though I got allergies oh I already said that and you seem really nice I like nice girls man some girls are frickin' not frickin' nice and y'know, you got, like, the coolest red hair and—*

She's about to whip out the baton and give him a good whack in the kidneys just to shut him up. But then a sound cuts through the woods—a half-growl, half-scream, all-panic animal cry. In the tree cover above, a pair of startled turtledoves takes flight.

"Yo, those frickin' things are *loud,*" Bird says, waving her on.

"Those things."

"Yeah, like, one time my frickin' aunt decided to take one in as a pet and stuff? I was five or something, and I was just, y'know, doin' my thing and playing with my Tonka truck and stuff, and then here comes the coon, and he's all frickin' fired up about *something* and scratches the *hell* out of my arms and legs. Stupid coon."

They come into a clearing that's paved with concrete.

She knows it from her research. It's a training ground for fighting dogs.

Tractor tires. Heavy chains. Two big cages dangling from a pair of chestnut trees, both cages empty. Atlanta spies a rusty washtub. A small shelf with soaps and sponges. A car battery and cables.

The concrete is spattered brown in places. Maybe blood. Maybe animal waste. Probably both and definitely like that spot in the Shakespeare play: never to wash out.

Out, out, dang dogsblood.

Bodie's the only one standing here, and he looks like an older, better-put-together version of Bird. He's taller than his brother by a good six inches. Handsomer, too, though given how Bird looks a little like the son of two close cousins, that's not saying much. Bodie's hair is cropped short, though just as blond.

A metal pole sticks up out of the concrete, and from an eyebolt hangs a long, lean chain. A skinny raccoon is attached to the chain via a collar. All around the pole in a circle are little footprints, wet and red.

A dog sits off to the side. Not a pit bull, by the looks of it. All white. Flat black nose—comical, like a Snoopy nose, like it was put there by a blob of paint. The ears are cropped, and they don't just stick up—the tips of the ears each turn inward, like the points of Batman's mask.

"Fuckin' dog," Bodie says. He turns toward them. Atlanta sees he's got a lockback knife in his hand. Like her own. The blade greasy with blood. Coon's blood, she figures.

"Bodie," Bird says. "This chick was totally lookin' for you, bro."

Bodie's disgruntled face brightens. A mean smile spreads across it like a puddle of gasoline just before someone lights it on fire. His blue eyes—little sapphires—seem to flash and catch the light. "What's up?"

She thinks to haul off and hit him right now. Baton out, crack him across that asshole smile. Teeth broken.

Instead, she says, "What're y'all doin'?"

Bodie laughs, "Ohh, haha, shit, listen to that accent. That's cool. I like that Southern thing. Sexy. What am I doing here? Just trying to train this dumb piece-of-shit dog of our uncle's to take the fuckin' bait."

"But he won't," she says.

"Nah. Stupid bee-yotch just sits there staring. I stuck the fuckin' coon, ran him around the pole. Nothing. Not a goddamn thing." He turns and screams at the dog: "Kill the coon! Kill it!"

The dog just watches, looking a little confused, if Atlanta's reading that right.

"That dog won't frickin' hunt," Bird whines, shaking his head. "Uncle's gonna be pee-oh'ed, Bodie. He paid a lot for that one, tell you what."

"Uncle shouldn't have bought a dumb cur."

Atlanta's hands are twitching. She shoves them in her pockets to hide them. "Doesn't look like a pit bull."

"That's 'cause he's not. He's a rare breed or some shit. Supposed to be good at fighting, but to me he ain't good at doing anything but being a—" and here again Bodie gets mad, screaming at the top of his lungs: "—a *fuckin' retard!*" The dog cocks his head. "Yeah. You heard me. I think you're a fuckin' retard, retard." Bodie turns his full attention to the dog. "Maybe you need a little encouragement. Huh? *Huh?*"

Flash of the blade. Bodie moves toward the dog.

Bird says, "Bodie, bro, wait . . ."

But Bodie raises the knife.

She can't let this happen.

Baton in her hand, thumb on the button, snap of the wrist. Atlanta moves fast. Bird starts to say something else, but all he really gets out is a llama-bleat, "Whuh?" Bodie goes at the dog with the knife, but before the blade lands, Atlanta brings the baton hard against the side of his head, right against his ear, *bam.*

Bodie staggers sideways. The knife drops, clatters against the spattered concrete. He cups his ears and wheels back, a look of betrayal and horror on his face. A line of blood snakes down his jawline.

Bird backs up, waving his hands. "Whoa! She's frickin' crazy, bro!"

Bodie growls, comes at her. She swipes the baton in open air—and he backs away.

"You're dead," he says.

"You like hurting animals, don't you?" she says.

"I'm gonna like hurting you."

Again he comes at her. *Swish, swish.* The baton connects with the back of his hand and he recoils, hissing breath.

"Gah! *Fuck.* You dumb crazy bitch. You have no idea what you've done. Bird, get her."

But Bird's eyes flick back and forth. He shifts nervously from foot to foot. His heart's not in this. "Bro, she's got a . . . whatever that is. She's gonna frickin' hit me!"

The dog sits back, watches it all.

"I'm here for Sailor," she says.

"Who the hell is that?" Bodie asks.

"Little white dog. Terrier. No teeth. No claws. Chewed half to death. Died on his owner's floor."

"Who cares about a stupid little creampuff piece of shit?"

"I do," she says, and whips the baton at him again—he barely dodges it.

From the woods comes a sound—a snapping of branches. Louder. Faster. Someone or something is coming.

Atlanta darts her gaze in that direction.

Oh no.

It's the Cooch, Tressa Kucharski, barreling forward like a stompy moose except this time it's a stompy moose with a *gun* in her hand—where'd she get a gun? Where'd she even *come* from?

Atlanta turns, steps back, almost trips over a loose restraint pole that she didn't see.

Tressa has the gun up. She's making a sound that's half-growl, half-scream.

Everything's gone suddenly pear-shaped, reality off its leash.

Twenty feet and closing.

Atlanta staggers, stands, runs.

Fifteen feet.

Bodie laughs. Bird just shrinks.

Ten feet.

The gun fires.

It barely makes a sound.

Just a little *snap*.

Something hits Atlanta in the meat of her lower back—no more pressure than a flicking finger. She bolts forward, feeling with her hands where the bullet hit her—she expects a hole, some blood, something, but all she finds is a little nub that wasn't there before. She runs into the woods like a panicked animal, the nub coming off in her fingers, and as she crashes against a tree her head starts feeling woozy, everything sliding sideways like the earth is tilting, like it's all loose furniture on a sinking ship.

She sees that what she's got in her hands is a small tranquilizer dart.

The forest collapses inward.

Tressa crashes into her.

CHAPTER TWENTY-FIVE

The world goes woozy, like Atlanta is drunk and tired and lost inside of herself. Her body doesn't respond to the commands her brain gives it. Limbs sit dead, disconnected from the rest of the human machine. She tries to speak. It only comes out slurred gibberish.

Atlanta can hear *them*, though their voices sound like they're talking through a long metal pipe—echoing and hollow, close but distant. Tressa outs her as the one who stopped them from stealing the beagle. Bird panics, says they should get their uncle. Bodie says no, they can handle it, and besides, he has an idea. His hands find her face, grips her chin and cheeks hard—it should hurt, but it doesn't. Like she's at the dentist, all numbed up.

Bodie whispers in Tressa's ear. Atlanta sees the two of them smash together like blobs inside a lava lamp. Hears the sloppy sounds of them making out. Bird just mumbles and moans, the sad cry of a kicked puppy.

Tressa and Bodie grab her under her arms. Together they drag her across the concrete.

The forest is a blotchy mess. She sees someone in the woods watching. It's Chris. He waves at her—a chipper five-finger waggle, as if to say, *Toodle-oo.*

More animal noises. Bird again? No, the raccoon. Bodie has the animal—the collar's off, the chain against the ground. He sticks the knife in its neck and throws it into the woods where Atlanta sees the brown shape run about ten feet and then drop. It's just a lump, but she sees its haunches twitching. Hears it whimpering.

Then: Fingers around her neck. The jingle of a collar. The rattle of a chain.

They're hooking me up to the pole.

I'm the coon.

I'm the bait.

She finds the slack in her mental rope and pulls it tight—she's able to get her hand up and swat at Bodie and Tressa, but it's a dumb, numb paw, and the fingers still don't work. Tressa slaps her once, twice, a third time. It doesn't sting, but it rocks her head back against the metal pole and *that* hurts, and she thinks the pain is good because it means maybe, just maybe, the tranq is starting to leave her system.

"Get her hands," Bodie says. Tressa moves behind her, winds another chain around her hands. The metal is cold, and Atlanta tries to pull away, but her body still isn't listening.

Bodie gets between her legs. Eyes glide over her. That mean smile. A grim chuckle. He lets his hand fall to her thigh, and it feels like a heavy weight *and* like it's not there at all, and inside she's a barn full of horses catching on fire, but outside she can't do much more than shift her weight and moan against her teeth.

Tressa punches him. "Hey."

"Whatever," he says. His hand leaves Atlanta's thigh.

There, in the woods, Atlanta sees a shape in the trees. A shadow hanging. A body. She sees Chris's face—purple-bruised, tongue thrust out from between dead lips. He winks.

Then—a white blur, a snowy shape, a hot humid blast. Bodie brings the big white dog over to her, shoves its face into hers. He tells the dog: "Maybe you just need better bait. Since this bitch lost us our last bait dog, seems like she wants to volunteer. Ain't that right?"

The dog sniffs her. Stares. Lip curls up showing one pink canine fang. *Fanged*, she thinks, *fang stuck in skin,* and she envisions that happening to her.

This massive beast is gonna tear her apart.

Omar and Orion all over again, except she can't run, can't move her hands, can't protect her face. Dog's got a set of jaws that could peel back a crumpled car roof. And he's staring at her like she's a plate of steak left on the patio.

She knows she's crying. But she can't feel her tears.

What she *does* feel is the knife.

Bodie's there with the blade, and he sticks it in the meat just below her collarbone. She doesn't know how deep, but it feels deep—at first it doesn't hurt at all, like her flesh is just an old car seat and he's sticking his finger through a rip in the leather. But then the pain shows up—late to the party but there just the same, a bright flash of hot agony with long tentacles that wakes her up full tilt. The pain is a hard wind that blows away some of the clouds of the tranquilizer, but she knows it doesn't matter now.

She's able to wriggle her hands free from the chains, but then they just lie there like dead fish—free from the net but useless.

The dog growls. But still doesn't move.

"There you go," Bodie says. "Get that blood stink up in your nose." She sees him present the knife under the dog's flaring nostrils. "No? Not yet. Fuckin' retard. Let's stick her again and see."

Flash of the knife, wrist back, blade pointed forward.

He moves to stick her again.

White flash. Avalanche. The dog growls and moves fast, and suddenly Bodie's screaming, a blood-curdling banshee wail as the dog's mouth clamps down hard on his hand and wrist. The knife drops. The dog's head shakes like he's got a whistle pig in his mouth whose neck he wants to break. With every shake, Bodie screams louder, beating at the dog with one open hand at the same time he's trying to crab-walk away.

Then Tressa starts to scream, and Bird makes a scared noise and runs off into the woods.

The Cooch grabs the knife, goes for the big white ghost-hound ripping up Bodie's hand, ready to stab the dog in the neck.

Atlanta focuses everything she has on moving. She pulls her hands completely out of the chains just in time to give a clumsy shove, pushing Tressa Kucharski to the ground. Again the knife falls. And this time, Atlanta grabs it.

She hooks the knife blade under the collar around her neck. She feels a nip of pain, but then she saws back and forth and the collar pops off. When she stands, the dog lets go of Bodie's hand— and all she sees is a red mess at the end of his arm. He's still got fingers and a thumb, but everything south of them looks like crow-picked roadkill.

Tressa's getting to her feet.

Atlanta doesn't know what to do.

So she runs. She runs hard and she runs fast, passing Bird in the woods—he's just sitting there against a tree, crying into his hands like his mother just died.

———

The dog is chasing her.

She thinks, *He's coming for me, now,* and any second he'll bite into the heel of her foot, and when she goes down it'll be face-first. The dog will rip her to ribbons.

Atlanta stops, wheels on the dog. Better to face the hellhound than give the beast her back.

But when she pivots, the dog skids to a stop. And sits down.

Panting. He even gives his head a little dip—to say what, she doesn't know.

It's surreal. He's got a head like a cement block, and his jaw is stained pink and red. Teeth, too. But he looks docile as a sleepy lamb.

"Go away," she mumbles, mush-mouthed, lips barely able to form those words.

The dog continues sitting.

"Stop following me."

Pant, pant, pant, pant.

"Seriously, quit it."

The beast licks his lips. Blinks. Then burps a little.

"Whatever," she says, exasperated. No time for this. She still feels groggy, like her parts are disconnected from the whole. But her job here is done. Revenge has been achieved. Bodie's hand looked like a grenade went off in the palm. That's good enough for her.

She turns again and runs. Time to find Guy and get the hell out of here.

———

Into the crowd. Another fight must be on—everybody is fixated once more on the ring, and she hears snarls and whimpers from within the octagon. She searches the throng, body by body, face by face, looking for Guy but not seeing him. Someone bumps into her leg—

And it's not a someone but a some*thing*. The dog. The white hellhound with the cement block for a head. The dog looks up at her. The face of innocence, except for that bloody muzzle. She doesn't even bother saying anything; he'll figure out sooner or later that she doesn't want him around.

Movement from over by the barn: Bodie—his face twisted by pain, his hand under the crook of his opposing arm. Next to him, Tressa, the tranquilizer pistol in her hand. Both of their eyes searching the crowd.

Shit! Where's Guy?

She moves away from the barn, around the far side of the ring, the dog still plodding after her—his snow-white coat sure to give her up. "Shoo," she says. "*Shoo.*"

Everything feels like a nightmare. She's still moving slow from the drugs. Can't find Guy. Her enemies are here and looking for her. Pursued—dogged, literally dogged—by a red-mouthed hell-creature.

It's then the nightmare really opens its mouth and shows its teeth.

Ahead, toward the parking lot, she sees John Elvis Baumgartner talking to somebody.

It's the cop. It's the goddamn dark-eyed, unibrowed cop. Plain-clothes, no uniform. He's easy to spot—he's like a crow on a power line, a shark's shadow under the sea's skin, a melanoma *right there* on the back of your hand.

Why is he here?

A voice answers: *Maybe he's here for you.*

Gotta get out of here.

Now.

But she doesn't know where to go. Danger in each direction. She feels caught, like she's still collared to that pole. The dog nuzzles her wrist, and she almost thinks to swat the animal away, but she's too afraid to touch him. Then a voice reaches her ears, and that voice is like a song sung by all the angels in one big chorus:

"Atlanta?" Guy asks.

He's shoving a baggie—now half-empty of its pharmaceutical booty—into a back pocket. "Hey, what's up with the dog—"

But she doesn't have time. "We gotta go," she hisses.

"Aw shit, you're bleeding. What did you do?"

"I'm fine. Talk later."

She starts dragging him toward the parking lot. He protests— "I've only sold half of what's here"—but she shushes him and gestures toward the cop.

"That's a *cop*," she says, quiet as she can manage over the whoops and boos of the crowd.

"What? You kidding me?" He suddenly gets it. "Gotta go, yo."

"This way," she says, taking the long route through the parking lot, ducking behind as many cars as she can. Gravel crunches under feet.

As they duck behind a powder-blue Chevy pickup, Guy says, "That dog's following us."

"I know, shut up."

"Where'd he come from?"

"I said shut up, dang."

Ahead sits the boxy Scion.

And Shane's not in it.

Atlanta stands, slaps her hands against the back window, and peers in, thinking that maybe he's lying down or hiding in the backseat somewhere like a scared mouse. But he's nowhere to be found.

"Bitch!" comes a voice across the parking lot.

Tressa Kucharski. Bodie next to her, his forearm dripping. The two of them start winding their way through the lot. Atlanta looks the other way and, sure enough, there's John Elvis Baumgartner, squinting in her direction, the flat of his hand forming a visor to block out the sun.

"Let's go!" Guy barks, skidding around the front of the car while hitting the keychain button to unlock the doors.

Atlanta yells, "We can't leave without Shane!"

"Maybe *you* can't," he says, then hops in the car.

Now John Elvis is really leaning in. "Hey!" he yells, like he's still not sure it's her. Of course, he's dumber than a stack of firewood. But the cop sees her.

He stares right at her, eyes like two cigarettes, burning holes in her.

From the other direction, Tressa and Bodie are hurrying around cars—fifty yards and closing.

Tressa raises the pistol again.

Where the hell is Shane? Atlanta calls out: "Shane! *Shaaaaane!*"

And then, as if she possesses some kind of person-summoning magic, boom. There he is, walking up from behind the car, hands in his pockets like it's no big thing. "What? I had to take a leak."

She grabs him, pulls him close.

Just as a little tranquilizer dart *thwips* into the fat of Shane's bicep.

"Ow!" he says, and swats at it like it's a bee.

Atlanta shoves him in the car. Before she can close the door, the big white hell-beast hops in after him—which causes Shane to scream like a Tasered Girl Scout. Atlanta slides in through the passenger's-side door just as the tires bite into limestone scree and spin stones.

The car jolts forward.

———

Shane's screams last for about thirty seconds. Then they wind down like a child's toy with dying batteries—he slumps against the seat, the tranq taking hold. The dog sits next to him, panting, oblivious. Occasionally rebalancing his big white body as Guy takes the turns and skids across gravel toward the exit.

Ahead is the gate. Closed.

Winky in the John Deere hat is already up, barking into a walkie-talkie. He flings down the radio and goes dipping a hand into a rusted red toolbox under his metal folding chair.

Next thing they know, he's standing straight again.

With a pistol pointed at them.

This one doesn't look like a pellet gun. Or a tranquilizer gun. It's the real deal.

Guy doesn't say anything—he just makes a sound that's halfway between a scream of anger and a yelp of fear, then he steps on the accelerator. Winky doesn't have time do anything but jump out of the way as the car crashes into the gate, flinging it open.

The Scion's tires skate across gravel, the ass end of the car going left while the rest of the vehicle tries to go straight. They fishtail, ending up perpendicular to the road, leaving Atlanta facing the ruined gate.

The car drifts to a stop.

Winky's back on his feet, gun up and out.

Guy hits the pedal—tires spin uselessly on stone.

Atlanta ducks, fumbles for the shotgun in the backseat.

Hands on cold metal.

She brings the gun up.

Realizes the window isn't down.

Winky fixes that. One shot through the glass—passes through, hits the driver's-side window, breaking both. Glass everywhere. Guy cries out. The dog howls. Atlanta uses the butt of the squirrel gun to punch out the rest of the passenger's-side window and then leans out, thumb pulling back the hammer on the single-barrel .410.

The pistol's up again and about to fire. But Winky's either smart, a coward, or both—because he throws his body into the ditch next to the gravel drive. Atlanta doesn't even have to pull the trigger. She just keeps the barrel aimed out the window, staring down the sight.

Guy reverses the Scion—again the tires spin. But then, suddenly, miraculously, they catch. The car whips backward into a laser-fast K-turn.

Two minutes later, they hit the road. Literally—the Scion slams up onto the asphalt with a bang and a rattle.

CHAPTER TWENTY-SIX

Nobody says boo. Only sounds are the car's engine, the wheels on the road, the dog's breathy panting. Occasionally Atlanta shakes herself loose from the shock and glances into the backseat to make sure the dog hasn't chosen Shane as a meal.

Shane lies slumped, flycatcher mouth lolling. The dog sits, staring ahead. When Atlanta grabs her own seat to turn around and see, the beast takes his dry-blood muzzle and licks her hand.

She turns back around.

Eventually, Guy speaks.

When he does, it's under his breath. "Shit." Then louder. "*Shit.*" And finally: "Shit!"

He bashes the steering wheel with the heel of his hand.

"Yeah," Atlanta says, because she's not sure what else to say.

"*Yeah?* Yeah doesn't cover it. So I'm sitting here thinking, right? I'm thinking, that's a dog back there. From a dogfight. Except, that ain't no normal dog. That's no pit bull. That's a rare breed. You know that?"

"Kinda."

"Kinda? It's an Argentine Mastiff. A *Dogo Argentino*." On these last two words he throws a little spicy accent powder, rolling that r like a ball bearing rolling across a snare drum. He says it again: "Dogo. Argentino."

"Sure. Okay. So what?"

"I heard something there today. I was sellin' some vikes to some hillbilly cracker with a bum leg, and you know what he said? He said that someone had bought and was training just such a dog. You know who that someone is? Do you?"

"Just get to the dang spoilers."

But she already knows the answer, doesn't she?

They went and are staying with their uncle or something up on his farm in Little Ash . . .

This here is my farm, so I'm glad you found our humble operation . . .

Just trying to train this dumb piece-of-shit dog of our uncle's to take the fuckin' bait . . .

"It's Ellis Wayman's dog," he says. He says it again: "Ellis fucking Wayman."

"Oh, that's not good." Panic claws its way through her.

He hits the steering wheel again.

"Pull over," she says. "Hurry."

Guy steps on the brakes. Shane's drug-slumbering form slumps forward, his head thunking against the window. Atlanta hurries outside, opens the back door.

The dog—the very special dog breed, the Dogo Argentino—stares at her.

"Go!" she says. "You're free. Look. Out there it's . . . trees and farmhouses and a bunch of walking hamburgers." The dog just stares. "Liberty! Freedom! This here is your Emancipation Proclamation. Go!"

The dog's massive body fails to move.

She reaches in with ginger hands, grabs the dog in a tricky stealth hug, uses the fake affection to try to drag his white ass off the seat. But he's heavy, a statue moored to a concrete slab. There's that age-old question, could God create an object that He Himself could not move? The answer: yes. This dog.

The dog licks her ear. The tongue is wet and dry at the same time, like drooly sandpaper.

"C'mon," Guy says, snapping his fingers. "They could be on us soon. We gotta roll, Atlanta."

"Dangit," she says, getting back in the car.

———

They manage to get Shane out of the car, carrying him over to one of the white plastic patio chairs in front of her house and dumping his butt into it.

The dog hops out of the car and plods after.

Guy doesn't say much. She's not sure if he's mad or scared or something else, but he's stewing and simmering, and she knows to leave well enough alone. He doesn't even say good-bye—she thinks he's just going over to turn off the car engine, but instead he gets in and peels out. The Scion rockets down her driveway toward the road.

The dog sits in front of her, panting and licking his chops. In effect licking the blood that stains his muzzle. Bodie's blood. From Bodie's ruined hand.

"I have got to clean you off," she tells the dog.

She heads inside, hoping that while she's in there he'll decide to wander off into the corn or the weeds. Instead, he follows her inside, her own white shadow. At the sink she runs the faucet over a wad of paper towels. When she's got them good and wet, she squats next to him, hesitant.

"You're not gonna bite my hand off, are you?"

He thumps his nose into her forehead.

"I hope that isn't secret dog language for 'yes.'" She sighs. "Let's get you cleaned off."

She wipes his muzzle, the paper towels turning pink her hands. A shudder grapples up her arms, to her spine, and then to the rest of her body. *Don't think about that.* Soon she has the creature's face clean.

Back outside, the dog at her every step.

Shane is awake, wide-eyed and staring down the driveway, hands clutching the sides of the patio chair in a mortified grip. He hears her coming, starts talking: "I remember a dog. Like, this monster from Hell. Cerberus, the three-headed hound that guards—"

Then he tilts his head and finally sees that the dog is hot on her heels, and he squeal-yelps and pulls his arms and legs up tight like he's floating on a buoy in shark-infested waters.

"Yeah, the dog's real," she says. "Sorry about that."

"Whuh . . . what happened?"

And she tells him. About the fight, about seeing John Elvis and the Skank and the cop, about Bodie and Bird and how the Cooch tranquilized her and then him. About the dog crunching the bones in Bodie's hand, rending the flesh. Turning it to a glove filled with ground meat.

"That dog's evil," Shane says.

The dog pants and whines in response.

"He seems all right," she says. "I think he saved my life, actually."

She clumsily pets him. Meaning, she taps him on the head with her open palm. Clumsy or no, the dog seems to like it and leans into her, eyes closed, a sincere moment of canine bliss.

"So he belongs to who now?"

"Ellis Wayman," she says. "Big sumbitch. They call him the Mountain Man, though whether that's because he's from the mountains or big like one, I dunno. Maybe both."

"You have to give the dog back."

"I can't do that."

"What?"

"This dog saved my life, Shane. What, I'm supposed to repay him by sending him back to that place? I saw just one fight and it was the most miserable thing ever. All the blood in the dirt. Both animals in pain. I can't do it. *Won't* do it. He's not my dog, but he's not gonna be theirs, either."

"He's gonna want that dog back."

"I know." Worry fills her up—gallons of spoiled milk in all her empty spaces. "I don't know what to do."

"Do you think he'll come for you?"

She shrugs and takes a seat. "Maybe him. Maybe Bodie." A sudden realization strikes her: "Aw, dang, and those other Nazi assholes saw me, too. That's not good, Shane."

They sit quiet for a while. The afternoon sun sinks, sliding like a plump egg yolk toward the edge of a tilted pan.

The dog leans his head on her knee. She scratches his ear. He whines a happy whine.

"You're not my dog," she tells him, "so don't get used to this."

He pokes her with his nose.

Soon Shane says, "Those Nazis. They were the same ones who messed with Chris."

"Yeah."

"Do you think they did it?"

She knows what he means. Chris. The hanging.

Atlanta offers a small nod.

Shane sits up straight. "That means this whole thing with the dogs is starting to meet up with Chris's murder."

"Yeah, I guess it is."

"That's not good."

"No. It ain't."

Takes a while, but Shane finally asks: "Are you going to make them pay, too? Way you made those guys, Birdie and Bodie, pay?"

She exhales, hoping the breath will make this feeling go away, but it doesn't.

"I don't know," she says. "I'm not real good at that part. I mostly just make things worse." Feels like she's sinking in a bed of lake mud, and with every struggle she sinks that much deeper.

"Atlanta, I did some research. Newspaper archives and whatever. Local county business? Chris isn't the only gay kid who killed himself. There's three more in the area—and one who was beaten to death underneath the water tower just outside Danville." He pauses. "That one had cigarette burns on him."

Cigarette burns.

"And there's been a rash of Hispanic kids killed, too. All of them beaten to death."

"We don't know that it's connected."

He shrugs. "No. But it makes sense."

It did. It does. Her insides curdle.

———

Shane goes home. Atlanta heads inside—the dog again trotting after—and eventually she calls Jenny. She offers only the vaguest of details, explaining that the boys who hurt Jenny's dog have been hurt in return.

"I don't know how to get you proof of it, though," Atlanta says.

Jenny breathes loudly into the phone. "I need proof. I gave you a lot of money."

"Oh. Okay." She pauses. "I don't know how to do that."

"What happened to them? You said the one's hand was . . . hurt."

"A dog chewed it up, actually. Yeah."

"'And if your right hand causes you to sin, cut it off and throw it away.'" Jenny pauses. "That's from the Bible. From the book of Matthew. One of the gospels."

"I've heard it before."

"This place you went to. It was a . . ."

"A farm. They had dogfights there."

"That means they're going to keep hurting dogs."

"Well, these two knuckleheads won't."

"I can't . . ." Here Jenny's voice breaks down a little. Just a hiccup, a croaky stutter where the voice goes high-pitched like a ricocheting bullet. "I can't think of other dogs getting hurt."

"I don't know what to tell you, Jenny."

"Fix it."

"I don't know what that means."

"Shut it down. I'll pay you the rest of your money and then some."

"I can't. I can't go back there. It's dangerous."

"Imagine what it's like for the dogs."

Atlanta tries not to yell, but she does anyway: "I *saw* what it was like for the dogs, okay? I saw. I saw the fight. I saw the barn where they, they . . . *Vick* the dogs. I saw blood and heard dogs in pain and there was this raccoon . . ." Her voice trails off, softens again. "I can't go back. I don't have good reason to."

"Then you won't get the rest of your money."

Shit. "Fine. It'll just have to be that way."

Atlanta hangs up the phone.

————

She paces the house for a while, the dog trotting in her wake. Afternoon fades and evening steps in, and at a certain point Atlanta is surprised to discover she wants her mother. Wants to see her, wants to talk to her, wants her to make pancakes, because hell if a stack of Mama's pancakes isn't the most comforting thing in the world. Like a golden pillow slathered in warm, buttery syrup. Atlanta goes to the fridge to see if they have the fixings for just such a golden pillow. It's there on the fridge that she finds the note.

It's in her mother's handwriting and it's held fast to the fridge by a Dunkin' Donuts magnet. The note reads:

Atlanta

Gone for few days. Cousin Harley is down in Richmond and hes a lawyer now so I'm visit with him to help with forclosure prob.

Luv

Mama

Atlanta plucks the message. Reads it a few more times just to make sure she gets it.

She should be happy about this. House to herself, for one thing. But more importantly, if the Mountain Man comes looking for his dog or the Nazi shitbirds come home to roost, Mama won't be standing underneath the sky when it comes falling down.

But that's not how Atlanta really feels. What she feels is anger at her mother running away. And sadness over being alone. And above all else, fear. She's scared of what's coming, scared of having to face it all by herself. Just once she'd like to be a little girl again, crawling up into her mother's lap and watching television and eating M&Ms and popcorn out of a big bowl. That can't happen. Not now, maybe never again. It's hard realizing your parent is just another crazy, screwed-up human being.

Just like everyone else ever.

CHAPTER TWENTY-SEVEN

The next day, Mama calls, and Atlanta thinks to yell at her, to open up with not one barrel but two, but somehow she just doesn't have it in her. Day after the mess at the Farm and Atlanta's feeling sore all over. Groggy, too. Like she was a little bit drunk. Or maybe like she was chained up to a metal pole and hit in the back with a canine tranquilizer.

Instead she just tells her mother everything's fine, it's quiet, no problem.

It's not fine. Atlanta's twitchy now. A shoot-out will do that to you. She keeps thinking she sees movement by the windows—just a shape, just a blur—but nobody's ever there. Sometimes when the house is quiet she suddenly hears breaking glass or the bang of a gun, but it's all in her head. Shakes her up just the same.

Two days later, and Mama's still not home. Called again on the evening of the third day just to say that Harley's got a job he's doing, but when he's done he'll sit down and go over the house situation. In the meantime she's "hanging out" there.

Atlanta doesn't say anything about the money from Jenny.

For now, she sits in the screened-in porch. Nobody's come for her or the dog. The first fireflies of the night flicker to life. Cicadas complain in a curtain of sound. The dog rests his head on her lap and makes a low, satisfied whine in the back of his throat.

She says that out loud: "The dog."

Last few days she's been feeding him whatever she could find around the house. Out-of-date Ritz crackers. Generic-brand Cheerios ("Ringy-Os"). Ramen noodles. Microwave pizza. He ate it all. No complaints. Of course, that means *she's* damn near out of food. Atlanta makes a mental note that tomorrow will be a food-shopping trip. Last year Mama was able to get food stamps, but they changed the rules, and now if you're under sixty and you have too many assets—like, say, a falling-down old farmhouse— then no food stamps or assistance for you.

But she'll be okay. She's still got some of Jenny's money left— though the rest sure would be nice. She thinks that tomorrow could be a kick-ass shopping trip. Won't have to go to the Amish store for off-brand or expired food. She can hit the Giant instead, pick up some fancy cheese and lunchmeat, some soft white bread. She'll still have enough for a month or two of the mortgage, help stave off the foreclosure a little while longer.

"I guess I ought to buy you some proper dog food," she tells the dog.

The dog looks up at her from his resting place on her lap. His eyes move, but not his head. His jowls are pooled underneath him like bedsheets.

"Don't get excited. It's not gonna be, like, some kinda fancy organic food or anything. We're talking Alpo, here. And don't forget: you're still not my dog."

The dog closes his eyes.

"Though I suppose it wouldn't hurt to name you. Just so I'm not running around saying, 'Hey, dog, come here,' or, 'Hey, dog, quit lookin' at me like that.'" She thinks on it. "I could just call you Asshole or Shithead. Because you're kinda both, you ask me." One eye opens and the dog whines. "Okay, okay, just kidding. For a man-eater you're awful sensitive. You got a head like a cement block, so we could go with Blockhead. A little nicer, at least, won't get me too many looks out in public." She pauses. "But I figure since you're Velcroed to me every doggone step I take, let's just go with White Shadow. Whitey for short."

The dog's eyes close and Whitey starts to snore.

"Yeah, naw, it's not like I was talking or anything." She rolls her eyes. "Have a nice nap, Whitey."

Whitey. What a blockhead.

———

Ends up that she has a nice nap, too. Falls asleep in the chair on the porch. Eventually Whitey slides off her and lies on the floor splayed right at her feet, occasionally letting loose these noxious puffs of fly-killing dog-fart that wake her from her slumber long enough for her to make a sour face and curse him and the rest of his litter. Then, back to sleep.

At around nine at night she wakes up again.

This time to the crackle of gravel under approaching tires. Headlights slice the darkness as a car eases slowly down the driveway toward the house.

No, not a car. An SUV. A big one, too. Chevy Tahoe. White.

Atlanta's not sure what to do. She thinks to go hide. Lots of places to do that—into the corn, out back of the house, in the cellar with the doors all locked.

The dog—White Shadow—starts to growl in the back of his throat. He stands, stiffens. She sees the hairs on the back of his neck go sharp like the bristles of a boot brush.

Hell with it. Dog's ready to meet this head-on. So's she.

Atlanta feels around the side of the wicker chair she's sitting in, finds the squirrel gun leaning there. On the other side, a box of shells. She dips her hand in the way you'd reach into a bowl to grab some cheese doodles, pockets a bunch, and saves one.

That one goes into the broken barrel. She snaps the gun closed, the vibration running along her hand.

By the time she nudges open the screen door with her shoe, the Tahoe's here, sliding to a stop. Feels like her heart's a microwave clock after a power outage—frozen in time and forever flashing. What happens now? Men come tumbling out of the car? Guns at the ready? Winky and Bodie and Ellis Wayman? A hail of gunfire? The other day leaving the Farm was her first real shoot-out—something no teen girl should ever think, much less say—and she's not eager to repeat the experience.

And yet, here she stands. Gun up, hammer cocked.

Car door opens and a big man gets out of the front.

But it's a different big man than she expects.

Orly Erickson.

He's still got that sculpted beard, that big logjam chest beneath a too-tight powder-blue polo. He's not big like Wayman is big—Wayman is a feature of the landscape given flesh and bone and life, like he woke up in the forest one day under a big carpet of moss and left his Sasquatch brothers to come live amongst men. Orly's like a big-game hunter on safari. Wayman's fatter, sure, but he looks to have earned his body. The elder Erickson forged his—like something you build, not something you are.

Orly holds up both hands, smiles teeth that are like his son's: broad, too white, too even.

"Atlanta Burns," he says. "You ought to put that thing away before someone gets hurt."

"Seems this is the second time we're in this situation," she says, trying to keep her voice from trembling. "You want me to steal another piece of jewelry from you? Maybe take your shoes, your watch?"

Orly's smile disappears for a moment, surely thinking about that ring. But then it comes back, like a flash of lightning in an otherwise dark sky. "Heard you were up at the fights the other day."

"Must've been someone else."

Whitey sidles up next to her, coiled like a spring. Orly's about twenty feet away, and she wonders suddenly if the dog's going to make a move. She puts a hand on his haunches, and he relaxes. A little.

"You keeping tabs on us?" he asks.

"Now why would I do that?" She knows she's entering the rattlesnake's den on this one, but she can't help herself: "Not like you killed one of my friends or anything."

"Hey, now, watch your mouth with accusations like that. We're just having a polite conversation. Besides, that boy killed himself. Police reports say so. Suicide is a hard thing."

"Suicide must be a disease that's going around. Heard tell of other gay kids catching it. Maybe a few Mexicans, too. Thank the Lord no straight white dudes are getting hurt. That happens, folks'll be gathering in town-hall meetings and calling up drone strikes."

To this, Orly says nothing. Instead his eyes wander to the dog at her side.

"That's a nice dog, there."

"Who, Whitey? He's all right. Stinks up a room pretty bad, though. His butt smells like a bunch of squirrels climbed in an old jockstrap and died. Maybe it's the frozen pizzas I've been feeding him."

Orly laughs. "Whitey. That's a good name."

Suddenly she gets it. "Oh, see, no. I'm not being racist, you old bastard. It's not a white pride thing, it's a 'he's a dog and he happens to be all white' thing. Dang you people got one mind about stuff, don't you?" Her lip hooks into a sneer. "What are you doin' here, anyway? You're sure not here to talk to me about dogs."

"Actually, I am. *That* dog in particular."

"Go on."

"I want him."

"Because he's white?"

"Because he's a rare breed. You don't see too many Argentine Mastiffs around." He steps in front of his own headlights, his massive shadow darkening the house. "May I come up and talk?"

"You may—" He starts to take a step forward. "Long as you don't mind picking birdshot out of your shiny teeth."

He steps back. "I'll stay down here, then."

"Your call." She shrugs. "Not much to talk about, anyway. This dog ain't yours."

"He's not yours, either."

"If you say so." Time to figure out how much he knows. "So whose dog is he, then?"

Orly chuckles. "I think we both know who that dog belongs to. I'm surprised Wayman hasn't come for him yet."

Again the dog growls, ears bristling. Atlanta says, "If you know who owns this dog, what's your angle? You want to return him to his rightful owner?"

"Nope. I want him for myself."

"Figured you were friendly with Wayman."

Again that smile drops. "Sure. Real friendly."

"Way you just said that didn't *sound* real friendly."

"We compete, sometimes."

"Ohhh. That why your toadies were up there the other day?"

"Just carrying the flag for the cause."

It's then she gets it. It clicks like the satisfying hammer of the gun in her hand. "I wonder if you don't like Wayman's operation because he invites the undesirables. Meaning, folks who don't look like you or me or Whitey here."

"I'm not here to go over that again with you." She can tell by now Orly's getting tired of this conversation. The smile hasn't come back. His voice has a cheese-grater edge to it. "I'm here to make an offer on that dog, plain and simple."

"Not interested."

"Don't you even want to hear the offer?"

"Like I said, not interest—"

"I'll talk to the bank. Fix the little problem I *hear* your mother's having with the mortgage." He shifts in the light of the Tahoe, shadow puppets on the wall dancing behind her. Every time he moves, the lights hit her eyes, make her squint. "Hell, maybe I'll even get them to lower her rate a little bit—might be a little wiggle room there."

"For the dog."

"For the dog."

Temptation dangles above her head, tantalizing as a bunch of ripe red grapes. All she has to do is shake the devil's hand and send Whitey on his way. Probably to train. And to fight. And maybe to die. She's not sure if Orly just wants to exert some grudge against the Mountain Man or if he really wants to see this dog in the ring. She's not sure if that even matters. The fight is the fight no matter why it takes place.

She looks down at Whitey. He doesn't take his eyes off Orly.

So easy. So easy to just give in, let the dog go. Watch her problems—or at least one problem—melt away. She's got no loyalty to dogs. Doesn't even like them much.

But this dog . . .

This dog saved her life.

Putting him back there? Giving him to the man who may be behind Chris's murder?

Aw, crap.

"It's up to him," she says. "Whitey, you wanna go with the man in the fancy white car? Go and be a big bad dogfighter? You can go if you want."

But Whitey doesn't budge. Of course he doesn't.

She shrugs. "Guess he's not interested."

"You're making a mistake. I'm handing you the keys to your cage."

"You come back here again, I'll be handin' you your balls in a cereal bowl."

Orly nods, resigned to it. He heads back to the Tahoe, throws open the door. Before he steps up into the full-size, he calls out over the top of the door, "You better watch out, Atlanta. If you burn everything down around you, don't forget that people you love will get burned, too."

"Is that a threat, Mr. Erickson?"

"Well, Miss Burns, you take it to mean however you—"

She shoots one of the Tahoe's headlights. Orly cries out, hurries into the car, and throws it in reverse. The SUV wibble-wobbles backward, bounding in and out of the shallow ditch along the driveway, then back up the driveway until it's gone.

Atlanta lets out a breath she didn't even realize she was holding in.

She hunkers down and hugs Whitey.

"I think I just screwed up," she tells the dog.

The smelly beast licks her ear. Sandpaper and slobber.

———

"That dog's still freaking me out," Shane says, staying about fifteen feet away from Whitey at all times. He rubs his hands all nervous-like. "Are you sure you're keeping him?"

Whitey sits, panting. Atlanta waves Shane off. "I'm not keepin' him. I'm just . . . holding onto him until this storm blows over. That's all. I don't want a dog."

"Did you call a shelter or anything?"

"No, not yet. And I can't take him to a shelter, anyway. He's some kinda . . . rare breed."

"You could sell him on the Internet."

"To some stranger? I don't think so."

"You bought dog food for him."

"And a dog bed," she adds.

"I'd say he's your dog."

Again she waves him off. Whitey drops to the ground on his back, squirming around. Maybe itching his back or pretending he's rolling in gopher poop or something. She's not a dog psychologist and doesn't care to find out what's going on in that bowling ball he calls a brain.

Shane says he'll make lunch. Though Atlanta hit the grocery store this morning, it's not like she knows what to do with most of the ingredients—so she was figuring again on a packet of ramen noodles, or maybe a microwave pizza (though admittedly a higher-grade microwave pizza than she's normally used to). But then she called Shane and told him what happened and here he is. Offering to stay over for a couple-few nights until Mama comes home. She asked him what good he would be if Orly came back, and he said he'd "bring his katana."

Sure enough, he brought his katana.

He cooks up another of his famous grilled-cheese sandwiches. Way Shane cooks is very focused, hovering over the skillet like an artist or an archaeologist, brow knitted and mouth pursed into a tight pucker.

Eventually he plops a sandwich on a plate for her, garnished with a little green sprig of parsley.

One bite and her eyes close and she can't help but make a *mmmmguuuhhh* sound around the bulging cheekful of bread and cheese and—a little bit of mustard? "Besht shandwich effer."

Whitey stands there and starts to drool. Big, glistening ribbons of saliva hanging from his jowls. Shane scowls at the dog and scoots his chair around the other side of the table.

"So you going to talk about it?"

"Whut?" she asks, still chewing.

"Orly coming over here."

"It's fine," she says, swallowing a delicious clump of sandwichy goodness. "I ran him off."

"He threatened you. You shot at his car."

Atlanta sighs. "I know."

"And you didn't give him what he wanted."

"*I know.*" She pokes at the half-eaten sandwich, her hunger vanishing. "He's a bully. They're all bullies. What would you have done? Would you have given him the dog?"

"Yes." He blinks. "No! I dunno." Suddenly he sees what she's doing and he yelps—"Hey!"—but it's too late. She tosses the last half of her sandwich to the dog, who catches it in his mouth and basically just dry-swallows it without chewing. *Gulp.* "That's a good sandwich!"

"It is and was. He sure seemed to enjoy it."

Shane pinches the bridge of his nose like a frustrated librarian. "You think Orly killed Chris?"

"He said it was a suicide, same as Mitchell said, same as the cops said. But then he went and threatened me. Told me that . . . basically that I was burning the house down with all my loved ones in it." She mimics Shane and pinches her nose-bridge. It's oddly satisfying. "I dunno. Maybe he's right. I just keep making trouble for myself and everyone I love. Why can't I just be a normal girl who doesn't know what spent gunpowder smells like? Why can't I just . . . dick around on Facebook and chase after boys and . . . I dunno, just quit stirring up the shit?"

Shane shrugs. "Why can't I be six foot tall and built like Captain America? We are who we are."

"Well, I don't wanna be me, then."

Whitey, seeing that he's not getting another bite from Atlanta, shifts his butt sideways and scoots over closer to Shane. Shane recoils. The dog gets closer. And again starts to emit ropy, gooey drool.

"He likes you," Atlanta says.

"He's a monster."

"He's a cute monster."

"He ate somebody's hand."

"Kind of. A little bit of it."

Shane picks up a corner crust of the sandwich the same way someone might pick up a dead mouse or a dirty tampon and flings it in the general direction of the Dogo. Whitey's head ratchets back and the jaws snap closed on the sandwich piece, making it disappear. "Can you imagine those jaws closing around your throat?" Shane asks.

"No," Atlanta says. "But I can imagine them closing on Orly Erickson's."

CHAPTER TWENTY-EIGHT

Later that day she calls Guy. Figures by now he's done being mad at her. But his cell just rings and rings. He's still mad. *Whatever.* She decides to get ahead of that problem. She gathers up Shane and Whitey and takes a walk to visit with her friendly neighborhood drug dealer.

The day is hot and the walk is long. It's not technically summer yet, but summer's here just the same, biting deep and breathing hot, dry breath.

Atlanta brought a bottle of water and occasionally tilts it back and lets Whitey slurp and lick at it.

Shane brought his katana, attacking anything and everything. Deadheading wildflowers. Hacking at a log. Chasing a white cabbage moth like it killed his mother and he's out for vengeance.

Along the way, after beheading some thistle, Shane says, "Hey, I looked up that dog of yours."

"What, he got a criminal record or something? Maybe win a spelling bee?"

Whitey pants as he walks.

"No," Shane says, rolling his eyes. "I mean the *breed* of dog. The Dogo Argentino."

"What about it?"

"It's just funny that everyone wants to use him as a fighting dog is all."

"Okay, you're making me pull teeth here—just spit it out."

"They're not very good at it. See, they mixed a whole bunch of breeds in there—Great Dane, boxer, bull terrier—but also an extinct breed thought to be the world's best fighting dog, the Cordoba Fighting Dog. The Cordoba was *so* aggressive toward other dogs, if given a choice the males would choose fighting instead of mating every time."

"Fightin' instead of fornicatin'. Okay. I don't see the disconnect here, dude."

"With the Dogo, though, they bred the Cordoba traits *out*. The Dogo's a pack hunter, not a dogfighter—so dogs that exhibited *any* aggression toward other dogs didn't get to breed. Couldn't have the dogs, like, tearing each other apart on a boar hunt. They needed them to work together and be loyal toward their people."

Whitey looks up, drooling. As if he knows they're talking about him.

Shane continues: "But still the dogfighters think that the ghost of this legendary Cordoba breed is still in there. So they try to tease it out—or do worse. But it's a futile effort."

"So, he's just not a good fighter."

"Not unless something is threatening his pack. I guess you're his pack."

She pats him on the rump. "That's fine by me." Whitey's tail wags.

———

Eventually they get to the little plot of land Guy owns, tucked behind a couple trees and a tangled wall of blackberry bush and rose briar. Soon as she turns the corner, she sees, feels her breath catch.

The windows are broken in the trailer. And in the Scion. The front door of the double-wide is open, hanging off one hinge like a drunk hanging onto a chair rail. The grill's overturned. The wooden front steps have been smashed. Most of the trailer's decor is scattered across the lawn—an Amish hex, a wicker basket, a blue checkered tablecloth, all the country bullshit that Guy so unexpectedly adores.

Guy. *Guy.*

Atlanta breaks into a run, shouting his name. Whitey bounds after.

She knows what she's going to see before she even sees it.

He's going to be inside the house. Beaten. Burned with cigarettes. Hanging there from the light fixture.

But what she finds instead is him sitting on a chair next to an overturned table, holding a bag of frozen sweet corn to his head. His lip is split. Blood on his chin. Blood down on his neck.

"Atlanta," he croaks. "'Sup."

Whitey wriggles his way into the trailer. Ears up. Shoulders forward. Looking around.

"Guy," she says. Her eyes feel hot and they start to sting and she quickly wipes tears away before they form and fall. "What . . . what happened?"

"I was gonna call you, but they bashed my phone to shit."

"They? They who?"

"Who you think? Wayman. And his little inbred white-boy nephews."

She moves toward him to hug him, but her skin crawls and cymbals crash in her head and she pulls away suddenly—the panic comes fast and without invite as it always does, leaving her feeling cold and clammy and freaky-aware. Feels like she's having a stroke and a heart attack all at once. In her mind she hears a shotgun blast. She sees blood on a bed.

Shuddering, she backs away from Guy, mumbles a mousey, "I'm sorry."

"Yeah. Sorry." He sighs. Pulls the frozen corn away to reveal a busted-up eye. The white's gone red, the whole eye ringed in a knotted bruise. "Doesn't matter."

"It's my fault."

"Yo, I drove you up there. My choice, not yours." Way he says it doesn't sound like he means it, though. He won't look at her, either, gaze drifting near her but never at her.

Shane finally stomps in through the door, panting. He takes one good look around: "Holy crap."

"'Sup, *vato*," Guy says.

"Uh. Hey. Um. You look bad."

Guy flips him off.

"Did Wayman say anything about me?" Atlanta asks.

"'Cause it's all about you, right?" Guy's nostrils flare. "Sorry. Yeah, we talked about you. He wanted to know where you lived and shit. Wanted to maybe pay you a visit. I didn't tell him. I don't give nobody up. I'm no snitch, not to cops, not to crooks."

"Thanks," she says. But then adds, "That doesn't make sense, though. Kucharski knew who I was."

"She doesn't know where you live, and I guess they figured best way to get that information was to beat it out of me." Guy again molds the bag of corn to his eye. "Or maybe they just wanted to send a message. Big man wants his dog back."

"He can't have him." *Nobody can but me.* She's surprised at her own stubbornness on this point as her mental heels dig in. She scratches Whitey behind the ear. His head tilts and his eyes close.

"Yeah. Well. Guess you gotta wonder how far you're gonna take this, then."

"I guess I do gotta wonder." She chews on the inside of her cheek. It's a question she doesn't want to ask, much less answer. "Did he give you a way to contact him?"

Guy winces as he stands, feels around the countertop by the microwave, comes back with a slip of paper. A phone number sits scrawled across it in hasty black marker. "There."

She takes it, nods. "I'm gonna go make a call."

As she passes Shane on the way out, he looks up. "Wait, hold up. What are you planning?"

"I don't know yet." It's not a lie.

———

She stands by the busted Scion, pacing like a zoo animal. A pair of mockingbirds chase one another in the nearby briar. A red-winged blackbird hops along the fence.

Atlanta chews her lip. Runs her fingers through her hair.

Takes the phone. Looks at it. Waits. Puts it away.

Finally she takes it out again and makes the call.

Ellis Wayman picks up on the first ring.

"Was wondering when you'd call," he says, voice gruff, growly—but also hidden there is a vein of amusement. "Quicker than I figured."

"Do you even know who this is?"

"The girl with the great name. Atlanta Burns."

"How'd you know?"

"Says so on my phone."

"Oh." She really should figure out how to turn that off. "I got your message. You hurt my friend pretty good."

"He broke my gate. You stole my dog."

She starts pacing again. "I didn't know it was your dog. Your nephews attacked me."

"Not before you attacked them."

"They hurt dogs. They were going to hurt your dog."

This seems to give him pause. "Then I'm going to have to have a chat with them. I'm old guard, sweetie. I like to keep my dogs healthy. I'm not in it for the blood. I'm in it for the sport."

"Don't see how you can separate the two." The mockingbirds flit above her head.

"In the ring you can't, but outside it is a different story. The niggers and Nazis like to kill their curs if they don't perform. Shoot 'em or use 'em as bait for other, meaner champs. Like that big-time fancy football player who electrocuted his dogs. Not me. Then again, I don't buy bad dogs. I buy champs. I buy into strong legacy breeding lines, bloodlines with a history of wins. Like that dog you have in your possession as we speak."

"He's not much of a fighter."

"My nephew's hand says different. Got nerve damage, you know that? Doc said his fingers won't work so great after this.

And the last two fingers—the pinky and whatever the other one is called—may never get the feeling back in 'em."

"Pardon me while I cry into my pillow over your dog-torturing bully of a nephew."

"Not asking for sympathy, just stating facts. Way I figure it, he had that coming to him."

"On that we agree."

A hot wind, dry as the air from an open oven, spills across the meadow. "I paid ten grand for that dog," Wayman says finally. "That's a lot of money. You gonna pay me that?"

"I'm not. I can't."

"Then I need that dog back."

"I'll bring him back," she says, getting an idea. "When's the next fight?"

"Two weeks. And I'm not interested in waiting that long."

"You may not be interested in it, but you'll do it anyway. I'm gonna train the dog for you."

He laughs, a big grumbly sound like if you threw some ice into a garbage disposal. "That's sweet, but no thanks."

"It's not an option. It's an offer and the only one on the table. I'm going to train him to be a fighter, and then he's gonna win his fights and you're going to owe me instead of me owing you."

"You're no dog trainer."

"Your nephews were doing *such* a fine job of it."

"Sarcasm doesn't suit a pretty girl like you," he growls. "Still. You got a point. So. You bring me a champ, then what do I owe you?"

"I want revenge on someone," she says. "Someone you don't much like."

"Who's that?"

"Orly Erickson."

A bigger, meaner laugh from Ellis this time around. And with that, she knows the hook is set. She just hopes she can reel in such a big dang fish.

She stands there for a while after he hangs up. A rare breeze blowing. She then dials another phone number and tells Jenny's mother she'd like to talk to her daughter, please.

Jenny is stiff on the phone. "It's you."

"You said you wanted it all shut down."

"I do."

"That you don't want dogs hurt anymore."

"I don't."

"Is the money still on the table?"

"Anything I can offer."

"Good. Because I'm gonna do it. Couple weeks from now, I'd keep a close eye on the news if I were you. Then you'll see. Everybody will."

———

Back inside the trailer, she tells them what happened. What she did and what she said. They look at her the same way some folks look at really nasty YouTube videos, like a guy taking a skateboard to the nuts or a couple girls doing the cinnamon challenge—wide-eyed disbelief, disgust. They ask her what's wrong with her? Why did she do that? And she tells them it'll be fine. She has a plan. It came to her like—she snaps her fingers—like *that*. As she tells them the plan, a plan so simple and so elegant it cannot fail, she feels the hairs on her arms and neck rise, feels the sense of driving in a fast car down a dark road with no headlights on. Exhilaration and fear holding hands and running toward the edge of a cliff. Guy and Shane nod. They still look worried. But the plan is the plan, and there's no turning back now.

PART FOUR:
KISSING FIRE

CHAPTER TWENTY-NINE

Two weeks later. Night before the dogfight.

Her mother still hasn't come home. Atlanta's spoken to her a few times. Hasn't told the woman about the money, because when Arlene hears that, she'll be throwing open the front door fifteen seconds later. Atlanta doesn't want her to come home. Not now. Not in the middle of all this. Meantime, Arlene told her a story about how Harley and his wife Tuyen (she's Vietnamese) have twins and were having a helluva time watching those rambunctious little rug rats, so while Harley went over Mama's "case," she figured she could stay there and help out, and that'd pay for the legal consultation. Atlanta told her it was fine even though it was most certainly not fine, told her to have a good trip even though she felt pissed to high hell about it. She may not want her mother to come home, but she still wants her mother to *want* to come home. Atlanta hung up on her.

So tonight, she's having a party.

That's what kids do. They have parties when the parents are gone. They trash the house. They smoke and drink. They have sex in the parents' bedroom. Atlanta's never done any of that, and she figures it's high time to start.

She envisions one of those parties where it's wall-to-wall people, where the bass is booming and some wasted cheerleader is doing body shots out on the back porch, where somehow the couch ends up on the lawn and by midnight the dang thing is on fire—burning bright, bringing the cops, *woop-woop.*

Thing is, Atlanta is Atlanta. So the "party" ends up being six people and her, sitting around a small campfire, drinking peach schnapps and vodka and Yuengling beer. Oh, and one dog—Whitey snoozes at her feet. Sometimes on his back, showing his balls to the moon.

(Not exactly in fighting shape, this one.)

She invited Jenny, but no go. Jenny said she "doesn't really like people anymore." Which is a shame. Though just the same, Atlanta gets it.

Well, whatever. Party's on.

Guillermo holds up a baggie. By the orange firelight it almost looks like a bag of little candies, and at first she thinks that's what it is because he announces, "Yo, I brought trail mix if anybody wants any." He shakes it at them. "Not sure what's in here. Got Vikes. Oxy. Perks. Ehhh . . ." He shakes the bag, peers into it. "Maybe some Vitamin R?"

Eddie Peters—of the school's Gay Mafia—makes a "hmm" sound, and he hops off the folding chair. He sets his beer down, then goes and lets Guy pour a couple pills into his palm. With a finger he starts poking through. He holds up a little blue pill that looks like home plate at a baseball game. "Is this Viagra?"

Guy squints at it. "Think so."

"I *so* don't need a three-hour erection." Eddie puts that one back, then fishes out what looks like a little lemon-flavored Pez block and pops it in his mouth. He dry-swallows and laughs. "The definition of irony: perks do not make you feel perky."

Then he sits back, plucks his beer as if he's plucking a flower from the earth, then takes a swig.

Shane leans over, whispers in Atlanta's ear. "Should I try drugs?"

"What?" she asks, loud, maybe too loud. She lowers her voice. "Uh, no."

"Are you sure?"

"I'm sure." The image of Shane ramped up on Ritalin or gone goofy on Percocet is something she could go her whole life without seeing. He's already on a drug called Vitamin Shane. She snaps her fingers at Chomp-Chomp, who passes her the schnapps bottle, which she in turn passes to Shane. "Here, just drink this instead."

He takes a drink, and when his mouth pulls away, the bottle makes a hollow *ploomp* sound. "Oh, that's good."

Suddenly, bright-eyed geek-boy Kyle Clemons hops over. He pushes his head out like a turtle and inserts it into their conversation. "Hey. You guys watching *Sherlock*?"

Shane's whole face lights up like an arcade machine struck by lightning. "*Oh my god*. Dude! The end of season two where you think Sherlock is—"

Atlanta clamps her hand over Shane's mouth. "Kyle. Can I have a word with Shane for one hot minute?"

"Yeah. Sure. Okay."

She forcibly turns Shane's head back so he meets her nose-to-nose. "You don't need to be doing drugs and you don't need to be talking to Kyle right now."

"But I like Kyle."

"Do you think Kyle's pretty?" she asks.

Shane makes a face like he just ate a spider. "What? No."

"And do you think Damita over there is pretty?" she asks, pointing to Damita Martinez, who sits talking to Eddie. She's got a pretty face, if maybe a little too much makeup, and she's got hips that go on for miles in those jeans of hers. "Well?"

"I . . . do."

"Then you should go over and talk to her."

Shane suddenly narrows his eyes. "Is this because we're both Venezuelan?"

"No, it's because she's the only other girl here besides me, and you need to get laid." His eyes go wide. "Dang, fine, if not laid, then third base. Or second. Or at least batting practice outside the dugout."

Before Shane can say anything else, Atlanta calls over, "Hey, Damita. C'mere."

Eddie shoots her a look and says, "Rude," but then he starts laughing and she figures it's okay. Damita hops up and shakes those hips on over.

"Hey, girl," Damita says.

"Damita, you ever meet my friend Shane?"

Damita extends a hand with nails painted pink like bubble gum, each rimmed with a ridge of crusty silver glitter. Shane takes it delicately and, like a gentleman, kisses her hand. Atlanta notices his own hand is trembling.

Atlanta says, "I met Shane a few months ago—"

But then Shane interrupts, blurting out one rapid-fire question, "Hey-do-you-ever-watch-that-show-*Sherlock*-it's-on-PBS-but-it-comes-from-the-Beeb-uh-the-BBC-and-it's-pretty-awesome-so?"

And there pops the balloon. Except it's not even a dramatic pop—more like the knot comes undone and the balloon flutters and flubbers around the room, gassy hiss as the air leaves and the balloon dies.

Damita says, "I freakin' *love* that show! Holy crap, Moriarty! Right?"

Which is not what Atlanta expects to hear. Suddenly the balloon is buoyant and bobbing once more.

"Well, okay, then," Atlanta says, offering a smile. She hops up, pats the chair. "Damita, you can take my seat." The girl sits. And suddenly Damita and Shane are talking about Sherlock Holmes.

People are weird, Atlanta thinks. Everybody's someone different than you suspect. Guy likes country decor. Damita likes Sherlock Holmes. Chris liked comic books (*though now he doesn't like much of anything, does he?*).

Chris.

Chris.

He should be here.

I miss you.

The gravity of sadness pulls at her insides.

Deep breath. For a moment the voices around her fall to background noise—a bubbling murmur, a hiss of static on a broken radio, and all she hears is the snap-crackle-pop of the logs on the fire, and then next thing she knows she's standing next to Guy.

"Gimme something from inside the bag," she says. Time to break this piñata.

"You sure? You got a big day tomorrow."

"Yeah. I'm sure."

He hesitates. "Atlanta, maybe it's not such a good idea—"

"I said gimme something. Something to keep me going. I don't want to sleep tonight. Got any Adderall?"

"Nah, but the Ritalin will do you right."

She holds out her hand. He fishes out a classic capsule—tan on one half, white on the other—and gives it to her. Into the mouth and then she rescues the vodka from Chomp-Chomp's feet and—

Down the hatch. She feels it crawl down her esophagus, sliding on the breathy vodka burn.

"I'm gonna go inside, get some chips," she says. The dog starts to get up and she says, "You sleep. Big day tomorrow, Whitey."

Whitey's cement-block head thumps against the earth and he commences snoozing.

———

The kitchen is dark. She doesn't bother turning on the light. She doesn't even try to find a bag of chips. Instead Atlanta plants her hands on the counter and stares at the window, which is a square of darkness brighter than all the darkness around her. Speckled stars sit in the sky above. The Cat Lady's house is a distant square with pinpricks of golden light—it's midnight and the old woman is awake. She's always awake, that one.

Atlanta drums her fingers on the counter. The Vitamin R hasn't taken hold yet. She wants it to because she's tired, and tired

means sleep and sleep means erasing eight hours from her life—
and when tomorrow comes . . .

Tomorrow's going to be a bad day. No way to change that. The
fights are horrible. She'll be wading into murky waters thick with
moccasins and copperheads, all lookin' for a taste.

Still. If everything goes to plan—and the plan is so simple it's
foolproof—then the bad day will at least end on a good note. It
won't fix everything. But it'll go a long way toward doing what
needs doing.

She's lost in the thought of it when she hears the scuff of a shoe
behind her.

Atlanta doesn't move fast enough.

She turns—

A shadow standing there. Reaching for her.

She starts to cry out—

A mouth finds hers. Lips. Teeth against her teeth. Schnapps
breath.

Her skin crawls. Her brain screams. She shoves the person
back hard. Cries out. Kicks. Connects with his gut.

Chomp-Chomp *oofs* and doubles over.

When she sees it's him, she cries out in frustration and rage
and shoves him again.

"Ow," he says, holding up his hands. "I'm sorry, I'm sorry, I'm
sorry."

"Shit!" she says, breathless, skin still feeling like every inch is
swarming with ticks. "You stupid asshole."

"I swear I'm sorry."

She rubs her face. "The hell were you thinking? Don't you know
who I am? You think cornering me in a dark kitchen would be a
good idea? I hate to be touched, Steven. *Hate it*. Because it makes

me think of . . ." She can't finish the statement. Won't. Doesn't want to. Whatever. Suddenly she feels a blanket of shame settle over her, hot and smothering. She *hates* this. Makes her feel weak and woozy. Like she's a victim—or worse, like she *wants* to be a victim, like this is the costume she wears. It's real. It's not fake. It's no costume. But that doesn't change how she feels. Steven keeps apologizing, but she can't even hear him.

Her body resists. Every part of her wants to run the other way. Feels like she's stepping toward the ledge of a building and is about to step off. As she reaches for Steven, vertigo overwhelms her, but she pushes past it.

She pulls him close and kisses him back.

Again their teeth clash. Lips mash. Her tongue finds his, and it's as if he can't believe this is really happening—but then his body settles into it and he leans closer. It's awful and wonderful at the same time. A thousand synapses fire in her head like a missile battery—*voosh voosh voosh voosh*—and she has no idea how she can feel unwound and knotted up all in the same moment. Maybe it's the Ritalin. Maybe it's all the memories. Maybe it's what's coming tomorrow.

It goes like this for a while. One minute, then two, then five. Then ten.

Eventually she pulls away, face red, lips chafed.

"Guh," Steven says.

"Yeah," she answers. She feels like a sparking wire jumping on the ground.

"I thought . . ."

"Don't talk," she says. "Let *me* talk. I don't like you—wait! No, I mean, I don't like you like that. You're just—you and me—we can't. And I don't want anybody right now. But this was good. This was nice. I needed this. I still feel like—I mean, I think I want to throw up? In a good way. In a real good way."

Steven blinks. Like he doesn't know what to do with what she just said.

Instead she just kisses him on the cheek and says, "Thanks."

Then she hurries back outside.

———

The night accelerates toward morning like a hard-driving truck with wonky headlights.

Atlanta drinks.

The Ritalin sets her up; the alcohol knocks her down.

She's a set of bowling pins rolling loose.

Whitey chases her as she chases fireflies into and out of the corn.

She talks with Kyle about how she doesn't understand comic books, and Kyle tells her she's just not reading the right ones, the ones about girls and women doing kick-ass girl-and-woman things. Batgirl, he says, or Ms. Marvel.

She goes to the house to bring back chips for real this time, and then Steven's gone but Shane and Damita are making out—Damita's in his lap and she's way taller than he is, so Atlanta has to cut short a laughing jag as the two of them mix spit and slap tongues.

At one a.m. she teaches Eddie to shoot.

At two a.m. Eddie teaches her to pirouette—he's a dancer, you see, trained in ballet and apparently quite good (though him being drunk and high makes for an interesting show). They spin together and laugh, and at one point he whispers to her how he misses Chris, how they never dated but they would've been good together.

By three a.m. Steven still hasn't come back, and so she and Guy do some shooting as Eddie dances behind them and Damita and Shane go off into the house. Guy's got a little .22 target pistol—a Ruger—and they set up cans and bottles and some of Mama's magazines and they shoot in the dark and sometimes hear the rewarding *krish* of a bottle breaking or the metallic *clung* of a can jumping off a fence rail and hitting the ground.

At three thirty a.m., Atlanta thinks she sees Chris standing there in the corn. Watching her and waving. But it's just a shadow, a trick the moonlight plays on her, and then he's gone because he was never really there.

At four a.m., Atlanta passes out in one of the patio chairs.

CHAPTER THIRTY

"It's time."

Guy wakes her.

She blinks. Her mouth tastes like fireplace ash. Wisps of smoke drift from the logs in the fire. Her skin crawls.

Atlanta lurches over the side of the patio chair and pukes. The chair is shit for balance, though, and as she throws up, the chair tilts left and she damn near falls in her own sick, just barely managing to roll out of the way.

Her head pounds. And spins. A hackey-sack kicked in the air again and again.

Atlanta steadies herself. Nudges an empty schnapps bottle out of the way.

Guy helps her up. Whitey sits back and watches.

"You look like a hairball that dog coughed up, yo," he says as she gets her balance under her feet.

"I figure you're bein' generous," she gurgles.

"Let's go with *dog shit*, then."

"That's more like it." Her lips smack together. The corners of her mouth feel dry and crusty. "It's time?"

"It's time."

"I probably shouldn't have had all that vodka. Or the schnapps. Or the Ritalin."

Guy laughs. "I been there, 'Lanta, I been there."

"I gotta go pee," she says.

"Thanks for sharing."

――――

Her bladder is like a water balloon about to pop. She tries to make a beeline for the bathroom, but suddenly there's Shane jumping up like a gopher at his hole. Big grin on his face. Mouth smeared with lipstick. Damita's. His eyes might as well be goggly and on springs.

"Damita's great," he says, his voice dreamy and lost.

"Uh-huh," she says, skirting past him. He trails after her.

"I got to touch her boobs," he says.

"She let you?"

"She let me."

"I'm real excited for you."

"It's all thanks to you."

"You and her boobs are very welcome. I gotta pee. And maybe throw up again."

His face scrunches up. "Yeah, you don't look so hot."

"Please move."

"Sorry."

Inside the bathroom, she pees like she's trying to put out a house fire.

At least she doesn't puke again.

———

She pukes again on the way. Guy yells at her not to get any on the car, and so she hangs out the open window—a window that no longer exists thanks to Winky with his John Deere hat and pistol— and somehow manages to miss the side of the banged-up Scion.

For a few minutes, she feels better again. Barfing is funny that way, she thinks. You never want to do it, and you try so hard not to, doing whatever you can to keep it from happening, all the while feeling like a stack of dishes ready to topple. But then you do it, and it's horrible for those thirty seconds, but afterward you feel cleaned out, freshened up, like all you need to conquer the day is a splash of water and a capful of mouthwash.

Whitey sits in the back, panting. After she hauls her head back inside, he licks her ear. She reaches back with a clumsy hand and scratches behind his ear.

"You've really taken to that dog," Guy says.

"He saved my life. Or something close to it. I figure I owe him some ear-scratchin' now and again."

"It's more than that. You two are bonded."

"He's all right and I'm all right and we're even more all right together. But he's just a dog."

"You say that, but you don't *act* like that."

She just shrugs.

"You sure about today?" he asks.

"I'm good," she says. "My guts no longer feel home to a pissed-off family of raccoons."

"That's not what I mean."

"I know. I'll be fine. The plan is about as easy and as dumb as they come."

"You'll be in there alone. No gun. Nobody with you."

Again she scratches Whitey. "I got him."

———

Guy drops her off at the base of the driveway like she asks. Atlanta doesn't need him getting any more wrapped up in this than he already is, way they wrecked his trailer and his car—oh, and his face. She hoofs it with Whitey in tow.

The day, like all the days lately, is hot and dry, and it isn't long before she starts to feel like a piece of meat left too long on the grill. The trees and the grass all feel a little less green, like the sun has decided to stop feeding the plants and start feeding *from* them instead. It's doing the same to her—sapping her strength, robbing her of her confidence and stripping her bare like pulling all the insulation off a wire. Fear sparks hot and electric.

The hangover isn't helping, either. Her whole body pulses.

Sick, slick, sweaty, and weak. Say that a hundred times fast.

Her boots crunch on gravel. Not far off she sees the fence and the gate.

Sure enough, Winky stands there, his green and yellow John Deere hat easy to spot.

This is it. Beginning of the end, she thinks. This is where she finds out if they're going to let her back in or just shoot her at the gate and steal the dog. As she gets closer, Winky sits forward in his chair and eventually stands, radioing in with the walkie-talkie.

He grins. Tips his hat. "Morning, Miss Burns."

"Hey."

His right hand hangs at his thigh, occasionally drifts toward his ass—she figures he's got that pistol tucked in the back of his jeans.

"You want to go in?" he asks, teasing her.

"I do." Whitey senses it. Steps forward. Head low. A low grumble coming from his throat.

"That dog better not come at me."

"Then *you* better not come at *me*."

"I'll shoot him."

"And I suspect that Ellis will shoot you as a reward."

He smiles. Nervous-like. Offers an awkward laugh: "Heh heh heh." Then says, "Lemme just get that gate for you, if you'll hold one second."

Winky backs toward it. He lets Atlanta and the dog pass. Whitey growls at him the whole way.

———

She feels like she might throw up again, but whether from the hangover or the nerves, she's not sure.

As she walks up to the Farm, a massive shape crosses the parking lot to meet her halfway. If he were a little higher in the sky, the Mountain Man would block out the sun and cast darkness all across the earth.

Through his tangled beard she can make out a big, yellow-toothed grin.

"Atlanta Burns, as I live and breathe."

"Mr. Wayman."

He puts out a hand. She remembers watching this video with Shane about a big-ass spider: a Guatemalan bird-eating tarantula. His hairy knuckles and knobby fingers make her think of that spider. They shake hands, and she's afraid he'll rip her arm out of the socket. But while his hand is rough with calluses, the grip itself is soft. The shake, gentle.

"There's my prize," he says, the mountain shrinking and stooping to Whitey. He holds out the back of his hand. Whitey sniffs it. Doesn't growl, but hesitates. "He's suspicious. That's good. How'd training go?"

"Just fine," she lies. Only things she's trained this dog to do are chase houseflies and catch Doritos in his mouth.

"Walk with me," Wayman says.

She nods. Reticent as she follows along.

Ahead and to the right, the crowd has gathered. They're milling about—the fights haven't started yet. The crowd's shuffling feet kick up puffs of dust as the onlookers murmur and whoop and posture.

Wayman heads off toward the barn. Thankfully not the Morton building. Atlanta wants to see that building burn to the ground with all the human monsters in it. *Contain yourself*, she thinks, trying to swallow her angry heart in a tide of . . . well, if not compassion, then patience.

In the barn, he flags over a man—it's the potbellied referee. Got a pair of eyeglasses sitting low on his bumpy nose. Reading glasses. Wayman calls to him: "Charlie, got one here." Charlie holds up a finger as he stares over his nose at a clipboard.

"Where're your boys?" Atlanta asks. "Your nephews."

"They're not cut out for this," he says with a sniff. "Bird's too frail. More sparrow than sparrow hawk. And Bodie, well. Bodie's maybe a little *too* cut out for this. I figured he needed some time to himself."

The ref—Charlie, apparently—comes over with a choke chain, moving toward Whitey.

Whitey no likey. He lowers his head, shows his teeth. Charlie pauses.

Wayman just laughs. "Thatta boy. That's the fighter spirit for which I paid most handsomely."

"What's going on?" Atlanta asks.

"Need to put the dog in a cage," Charlie says, real matter-of-fact.

"What? I didn't agree to that."

Wayman claps a hand on her shoulder—less gentle than the shake. Feels like she might collapse under his hand like a jacket knocked off its hanger. "Miss Burns, this is how it's done. The fighting dogs can't be wandering around. They wait in the cages till the Show starts. Safest place for the animal is in one of those cages."

She seethes. "Until the fight, you mean."

"Now, you're not having second thoughts about this, are you?"

"And what if I am?" Her body, starting to tremble at his touch, quivers with the fear that she made a big mistake.

"Then I'd say it's too late for all that because here you are and here I am, and we had a deal that I'd hate to see fall apart at the last minute. My disappointment would be *keenly* felt."

"No second thoughts," she says.

"Good. Charlie, give her the choker, let her take the dog over."

Charlie squints at her from behind those reading glasses, sizes her up, then hands her the bundled chain. She waves it off, instead going over to an open cage and calling Whitey over with a quick whistle. The dog complies, keeping an eye on the others as he walks over.

She scratches him behind the ear. "Into the cage," she says. "I won't let anybody hurt you. I promise."

Whitey licks her face.

Then he steps into the cage.

Seeing him in there about chops her heart in half. A log split under a heavy axe.

Wayman walks over. "Your fight's in about an hour, provided the one before doesn't go long. First up is Jasmine versus Tuco, and that'll be an interesting one. Jasmine's a boxer, though some folks call her 'the poodle' because she's got bows around her ears. Tuco's a straight-up bull terrier run by the spics." He snorts. "You, well. You're going up against the Nazis—they're running a new dog this time around. Amstaff mix. Name of some German World War Two horseshit. Charlie, what in the hell's the Nazi dog's name?"

"Panzer," Charlie says. "Though I heard one of the Nazi boys call the dog 'Jew-Biter.'"

Wayman shrugs. "There you go, then. Boss versus Jew-Biter."

"Boss?" It takes her a second to realize that's what Wayman calls Whitey. "I call him Whitey."

"He's not your dog to name, Miss Burns."

"In training, I called him Whitey, so he's Whitey."

Wayman laughs again. The sound calls to mind an avalanche just starting up—ground shifting, trees breaking. "Whitey it is, then. Have a good fight. I'll be watching you two in the ring, sure as shit."

Then he's gone. No longer eclipsing the sun or taking up all the oxygen in the room.

Atlanta takes one last look at Whitey, whose pointy ears flatten back. He makes a sad face.

"I'll be back," she says.

It rips a hole in her heart as she exits the barn.

CHAPTER THIRTY-ONE

Whitey will never get to fight. This'll be over before that happens, if Atlanta has her way.

She mills around outside. Licks her lips. Feels the electric buzz of adrenaline pushing back the grabby fingers of her hangover, loosening its grip. Time to make sure all the pieces are in place, then.

Yesterday, she made a call. To Orly Erickson. Told him before he could get a word in edgewise that if he wanted the Dogo he could have the Dogo and she'd meet him here. Then she hung up on him.

Atlanta hurries over to the parking lot. Peers at row after row, feeling her gut sink further and further as she's not seeing what she's looking for—

Ah.

Hell yes.

There it is: a big white Tahoe. The front headlight shot out, the chrome around it peppered with dings from the .410 scattershot. A surge of joy and triumph jolts through her.

Gotcha, you sonofabitch.

She goes to make a call.

Flips through her contact list.

Under *H*—ahh, there we go.

Detective Holger.

Same cop who helped her through the thing with Donny. Same cop who made sure she got time at a mental-health facility instead of in juvie (or worse).

Atlanta makes the call.

Only problem. The phone's not dialing. It's not doing a damn thing.

It makes an angry *beep beep beep*. On the screen: NO SIGNAL.

She waves the phone around. Still no bars. "No, no, c'mon," she mutters. "Don't do this to me, you piece of crap, don't you dare."

She moves to the far end of the lot. Nothing. Back the other way. Nothing again.

Everything here is flat. No way to get to higher ground, unless she's interested in climbing up on top of the barn. Or worse, up onto Ellis Wayman's shoulders—man's probably got a whole cloud layer around his ears. But seeing as how that's not an option, she keeps roving. Back to the front of the barn just as one fight is starting to get going—Charlie in the ring, two fighters: Jasmine the boxer versus Tuco the bull. Still no signal.

She heads to the back of the barn, where Bird took her on her last trip here.

There. One little half bar. A stub of a signal, but should be enough.

She redials the detective, quick before the signal can fade.

Just as she hears a click behind her ear. Then the pressure of something round and cold.

In her ear she hears the phone ring.

A voice behind her, scarily familiar. "You dumb twat."

Skinny Skank. Melanie.

"Hang up that fuckin' phone," Skank says, "or I'll pull the trigger. Unless you're not a fan of that ear. *And* you don't mind being deaf for the rest of your probably short life."

On the phone, Atlanta hears the detective's voice answer: "Holger here."

Skank reaches over with her free hand and snatches the phone, killing the call with a thumb.

"Turn around," Skank says.

Atlanta hesitates, but turns—slowly.

And there stands Skank, holding a Luger pistol. Leather pants vented with knife slashes. Torn black half shirt with a white swastika emblazoned upon it, what little cleavage she has thrust up and out, pale as couple of cave crickets. Her hair a briar tangle of platinum branches.

"You overplayed your hand this time," Skank says. Lips the color of spilled wine peel back to show her feral smile. "I've been *waiting* to do this."

Atlanta sticks out her chin, defiant. "Do what?"

Skank clubs her on the side of the head with the gun. Atlanta goes down. Dizzy. Feels the Nazi girl's fingers wind around her hair and yank her forward.

"Let's go, fag hag," Skank cackles. "We've got business."

———

Skank drags her by the hair around the back of the Morton building—the *murder* building—and throws her up against the metal wall with a bang. To her left she sees a bale of barbed wire and a metal washtub. To her other side, a heap of moldering plywood, rusty nails sticking up like beckoning fingers.

Atlanta feels a trickle of blood run along her jawline. Fingers fumble along her temple, finding the skin torn where the gun barrel—or the sights of the gun barrel—bit her. Skank just cackles again.

"For someone who thinks she's so smart, you're dumber than dog shit," Skank says, licking her lips. "You really thought you could pull one over on us? Set some kind of . . . what? Trap?"

"I'm just here for the fight," Atlanta croaks.

"Mm-hmm. Sure, sure. Just a *coincidence* that we're here. Guess you didn't call Mr. Erickson last night, try to lure him here? Oh, hey, here comes an old friend."

Around the back of the building walks John Elvis Baumgartner, scalp freshly shorn, arms inked with the scenes and symbols of a Hitler rally. He's not just smoking a cigarette, he's practically chewing it. Agitation and anxiety bleed off him—he's on something other than nicotine, Atlanta thinks. Coke, meth, pills, a combo pack.

He storms up, stopping short of stepping on her. She kicks at his knee, but he dances out of the way.

"Worse than a dog," he says. "A dumb bitch dog."

Skank leers. "Somebody needs to put you down like they put down your faggot friend."

"That your official statement?" Atlanta hisses. "Somebody put him down? You? Him? *Who?*"

John gives Melanie a look, backhands her shoulder. Skank punches him in the gut, and for a half a second Atlanta thinks she has a shot at getting away because he gives his girlfriend a look like he wants to go toe-to-toe with her—he even half lunges with a fist cocked, then stops.

He gives Atlanta a twitchy look. "Your friend killed himself."

"Go to hell," she says. "That what I'm gonna do? Kill myself?"

"You just might," Skank says.

"Your boss sign off on this? Where is the big man, anyway? Where's Orly? I saw his Tahoe. I know that sonofabitch is here. Or maybe Mitchell's planning on showing his face."

John Elvis rubs his eyes, laughs, claps his hands hard like a crazy toddler. Atlanta feels like she's watching a monkey rage at the zoo—railing against the bars, attacking the tire swing. Then he seems to pull it back together.

"You *really* think he'd show up? At an illegal dogfight? After your clumsy-ass attempt to trap him? He knows you ain't gonna give him that dog. Not on Wayman's property. Stupid slut. *Stupid fucking slut.*" He pitches his cigarette into the woods. "I'm gonna go get Petry. He'll know what to do."

"Let's just handle it ourselves," Skank says. "Drag her in the woods. Shoot her in the head, leave her for dead."

"I *said* I'm gonna go get Petry!" John Elvis says—more petulant than pissed. Like he's tired of being emasculated. "Don't make a move without us." Then his voice gets cold and quiet and he points an accusing finger: *"Don't."*

He storms off, leaving the two girls alone.

Skank paces, never taking her eyes off Atlanta, like a predatory cat watching a little kid from behind the zoo glass. Crows caw. Cicadas buzz. On the other side of the Morton building the crowd roars.

A dog yelps, and the crowd gets louder—booing, cheering, jeering, hooting. The fight's on. Is it Jasmine or Tuco? Champ or cur?

Time is ticking down. Atlanta feels the candlewick burning and the flame guttering—and with it, any hope of coming out on top. Orly's not here. Atlanta doesn't have her phone—and, even if she did, it has the cell signal of a broken toaster. The plan, so simple, so elegant, so rock solid, is now just sand in her hand sliding between the gaps in her fingers. All she needed was to place the call to Holger. Get her to show up with some cops and shut this place down. And lock up all the monsters big and small.

Now? That won't happen. *Can't* happen.

Worst of all, these people are going to hurt her.

She has to get away. The only weapon she has is the baton, waiting in her baggy pocket. If Skank looks away . . .

"You and me, we're not so different," Skank says. Burning stare. Faint smile.

"If you say so," Atlanta says.

"You really did it, huh." A statement, not a question. "Blew your stepdaddy's yam bag off?"

A weak nod. Atlanta clarifies in a throaty mumble: "Wasn't my stepdaddy, though. Everybody thinks that, but he wasn't."

"Just a boyfriend, then. Whatever. Bet he got to you a bunch of times before it pushed you that far, right? Yeah. Me too." She lights a cigarette. "I had an uncle. Married in, not blood. Uncle Lincoln." She laughs and snarls at the same time. "Lincoln, Lincoln, I been thinkin', what the hell have you been drinking? Whiskey, that's what. Cheap-ass hot-piss whiskey. He raped me three times and like they say, three times is the charm because the next time he came at me I stabbed him in the thigh—three times, actually, go fuckin' figure—with a steak knife. Hit an artery. He bled out, *almost* died. The stains never really washed off the porch—that's where he liked to do it, outside on the porch before my parents got home from work. In front of God and everybody." She shrugs. "I should've taken a lesson from you and cut his nuts. Like an apple from a tree. Monkey steals the plums."

"Sorry to hear all that."

"No, you're not. You're thinking just what everybody else does—*this crazy bitch probably deserved it.* I didn't, because no-body deserves that, but whatever. I don't blame you for hating me. You should hate me. I hate you. I got enough hate to go around. And see, that's where our paths go two different ways. I see you making friends with the faggots and the wetbacks and picking up every other downtrodden piece of garbage that goes floating by, cradling it to your breast like a teddy bear. You still feel bad about what happened to you—you see yourself as a loser, and so you hang out with losers. Bunch of turds bobbing in the same toilet bowl." But here Skank stops, eyes shimmering. She gestures with the gun, punctuating each word with a thrust of the barrel. "But I found *power* in what happened to me. Found out that I was *strong* and I don't have to swim with garbage. I see trash, I call it what it is and then I throw it away. *Homos* and *niggers* and *spics.*"

Atlanta narrows her eyes. "Let me guess. Your not-blood uncle wasn't white."

Skank clucks her tongue. "Cute. Fine. Yeah. Lincoln Sternberg. He was a fuckin' Jew. Rich-ass, big-nosed kike. Just like all of them."

"Man who touched me was white. That mean all white people are that way?"

Skank's jaw drops. "Whoa. Wait. You know, I . . . damn, I didn't even think about that. I didn't even imagine that white people could do bad things and that maybe I've been prejudging people based on . . ." But she can't contain it anymore and starts cracking up. "Whatever, like I've never heard that one before. White people can be shit, too. But they learn how to be an animal from the animals, you dummy."

She looks away for a half second, shaking her head and laughing.

That's when Atlanta moves.

Baton out with a button press—*snick*. She leaps up, baton raised.

Skank's elbow catches her across the bridge of her nose. Everything is white flashes and dark shadows swirling together, an army of ghosts pulling at her. Skank grabs the baton, cracks it hard against the Morton building wall, breaking it into three pieces. Atlanta tries to run, but her eyes are watering and her vision is smeared, and by the time she starts to move, Skank's got her by the hair again.

Wham. Back against the wall. Atlanta crumbles. Wipes her eyes and holds her nose—her palms come away red.

"You won't surprise me this time," Skank hisses. "I own you."

"Girls," comes an admonishing voice. Atlanta looks. Even through her bleary, smeary vision she knows who it is.

The devil has arrived.

The cop. The dark little man with the furrowed black brow. Again in his civvies: red polo, jeans. She doesn't see a gun, but she figures he has one on him somewhere. Ankle, maybe.

"Mr. Petry," Skank says with some measure of respect, then steps back.

Petry. That's his name. Officer Petry.

He sniffs, looks Atlanta over. "You."

"Me," she says. Then spits a little blood into the grass.

"You don't know when to leave well enough alone."

"What can I say? I like to pick scabs."

He nods. "Which means you like to bleed."

She shrugs.

He says to Skank, "Panzer's going to fight soon. Karl and Hiram are heading there now. You go over. I'll handle this problem."

"I want in on this," Skank says. "You can't take this from me."

They start arguing, but Atlanta's head reels. Panzer. Jew-Biter.

Whitey. That means her dog will fight. Wayman will want that fight whether she's there or not. Won't he? Whitey isn't ready. Isn't *trained* for this.

Gotta get up, gotta move, gotta do something.

". . . can just shoot her in the woods, nobody would know . . ."

". . . don't need you for this, Melanie . . ."

". . . they'll think I'm just shooting a dog . . ."

Melanie gesticulates with the pistol. Petry tries to calm her.

Atlanta reels. Her face pounds. Her nose bleeds.

There.

That's it.

What she learned back in the hospital? Back at Emerald Lakes? Where they locked her up, tried to make her not crazy? Blood is power, just not in the way Skank thinks it is.

They took her weapon and gave her a weapon.

She holds her face to her hand. Bleeds into her mouth. Tastes the greasy, salty red. Over her tongue. Under. Holds it there. Then she stands up.

Skank sees, says, "Oh, hell no, bitch, sit your ass down—" And comes at her with the pistol.

Atlanta spits a mouthful of blood into Skank's face. Into the eyes. Into the mouth. It's enough.

I'm not gonna be surprised by you again.

Oh, yes, you are.

Skank staggers, wiping at her face, shrieking like she just caught AIDS—and it's all Atlanta needs. She grabs the hand with the gun and twists the wrist and—

She has the Luger. She hits Skank across the nose with it and the psycho goes down, rolling around on her side, moaning and sobbing and clawing at her face.

Petry is already dropping to one knee and ripping the Velcro flap off his ankle holster—but before he can grab the stubby revolver tucked there, Atlanta has the gun leveled at his head.

"Don't," she says, voice shaking, but her hand steady.

"You don't want to do this."

"I am doing this. Take the gun out. Throw it into the woods."

He stares with dark, pinprick eyes, like holes cut in a blanket. "I'm not going to do that."

"Then I'll give you the worst haircut of your life."

"You shoot, they'll hear."

"They'll think I'm offing a dog."

"I'm a cop."

"You're not a cop. You're a killer in a cop suit. A monster in man-skin. Now throw that gun away or I swear—"

He gently pulls the gun out by the holster. Lets it dangle. She gestures to the forest with her head and he tosses it into the brush. She hears it crash and thump.

Atlanta stoops.

Grabs her phone off Skank's belt loop.

"Come after me," she says, "and I'll kill both of you."

She runs.

CHAPTER THIRTY-TWO

The first impulse is a fist reaching into her heart and pulling its strings—*Go get Whitey, stop the fight, do whatever you have to do*—and it takes everything she has to do differently. She tucks the gun in her waistband and skirts the woods with the burner phone in her hand—no bars, no signal, no bars, no signal, *c'mon c'mon c'mon.*

She's ready to take the phone and pitch it into the woods, throw it to the ground, bite into it like a candy bar—but then she thinks, *The barn, the barn, go back behind the barn.* That's where she had her limp-noodle signal, and that's where she heads, tearing ass and watching over her shoulder to make sure nobody's following her.

Atlanta holds the phone up. Her arm an antenna.

Still nothing.

She tries dialing Holger's office.

NO SIGNAL.

"Shit!" she says, trying not to cry—*keep it together, keep it together*—and she starts waving the phone around like she's trying to catch butterflies in a net.

She hears a twig snap—she spins, gun out and up, ready to shoot.

A chipmunk darts into the tree line.

She almost laughs.

When she next looks at the phone: one meager bar.

She has no interest in squandering whatever chipmunk magic that woodland varmint conjured up, and she quick fumbles with the phone, redialing Holger's number.

Ring, ring, ring.

Ring, ring, ring.

Please answer please answer please—

"Holger here."

Atlanta laughs. Weeps. Utters a vanquished, strangled cry.

And then she tells Holger all the details: dogfight, the Farm, Ellis Wayman, guns, Nazis, drugs, the whole nine yards, every bad thing under the sun.

Come, she tells her. *Come now. Hurry up.*

Bring everyone.

———

Her first urge is to crack up, to collapse and sob, or maybe to spin around like that girl in the meadow in *The Sound of Music*. But then comes a sound that cuts to the quick: a dog's yelp, a cry of pain—a cry she *knows*.

Whitey.

She's too late.

The fight's on.

Oh, God.

Already it feels like she's a scarecrow with the straw torn out, tired and floppy and without anything left inside, but that cry spurs her forward—and once again she runs, this time toward the fight, not away from it.

Ahead, the crowd masses around the octagon. She can't see in; she sees only the throng. Bodies and the backs of heads. She hits the crowd like a crashing wave, pushing through and throwing elbows—someone shoves her, and she shoves back and keeps pushing. A hand yanks at her hair, and she kicks out with her boot and catches someone in the knee—right person, wrong person, she doesn't know, but the hand relinquishes its grip.

She slams against the plywood side.

She sees—

Red blood on a white coat.

Whitey's blood. On Whitey's fur.

His shoulder's bitten. And bleeding. Ellis stands behind him, spurring him forward with red cheeks and bulging eyes—gone is any semblance of cool, now it's all rage and spit and the vigor of the fight. An erupting volcano instead of a calm and tireless mountain.

From the other corner rushes an animal that might as well be the love child of a dump truck and a pit bull—cigarette-burn eyes and trailing drool and hell blazing in its heart. The beast's handler is a middle-aged, clean-cut Nazi with a tight, pockmarked face and fists jabbing at the air.

The dog known as Panzer charges Whitey—but Whitey, unfazed, just lowers his head and tosses the Nazi dog aside. No bite, no blood, just derailing the freight train. Panzer rolls into the dirt, kicking up powder, but lands back on his feet. The bull bolts forward with renewed fury.

This has to stop.

Atlanta climbs up over the plywood. Worst idea ever. And the only one she has.

Ellis sees, splits his attention between her and the two dogs.

Holds his hands up—starts yelling for the ref, "Charlie! Charlie, goddamnit!"

Again the two dogs clash. This time Whitey fails to turn the beast aside.

They rise together, standing on their haunches—Panzer tries to bite, but Whitey holds the Nazi hellhound at bay with his paws: pushing, dancing, shoving. A gnashing canine waltz.

Atlanta runs toward the dogs.

Ellis moves to stand in her way—tectonic plates shifting, an earthen wall in the shape of a man pointing at her.

"He's not your dog!" he growls, as much a beast as the two dogs in the ring.

Panzer's jaws go wide, about to clamp down on Whitey's muzzle. Whitey's not cut out for this, not a fighter, that part of his bloodline is dammed up and pinched off.

She can't abide it.

Atlanta points the Luger in the air and fires.

One two three, *bang bang bang.*

Panzer's gun-shy. Whitey isn't. The pit bull yelps, pulls away, and hightails it to the corner and between the legs of his trainer.

Everyone shuts up. No cheers. No boos. They don't run, they don't scream.

They just stare. At her.

She has a half a second at best before folks start reaching for their guns, decide to start shooting—and the shape of the fight pit means it'll be a blood bath, a race war, and that's not what she wants. But she knows what to do.

She points the gun at Ellis.

With her other hand, she pats her thigh.

Whitey trots over, favoring his one front leg over the other.

Ellis's hands tighten to fists—two fleshy wrecking balls sitting at his side, waiting to knock down buildings. He screams at Charlie: "Don't you let her leave this ring!"

Behind her, Charlie stands in front of the ring gate.

"You don't wanna do this," Wayman snarls.

"I already did," she says. All eyes on her. She feels like an ant under a magnifying glass.

"You're bringing hell down on your head."

She nods. "I know." *I'm good at that.* "Now let me out of here."

"I can't do that."

"He can," she says, pointing the gun at Charlie, the potbellied ref.

Charlie hesitates. Ellis takes a step toward her—she jerks the gun in his direction, then back to Charlie, then to the Nazi trainer behind her, then back again. The gun shakes. Threats on all sides of her, like water rushing in through doors and windows— she feels flooded, drowned, like she can't swim. Worse, then she sees John Elvis pressed against the plywood wall, lip in a fishhook sneer. No Melanie. No Petry. Not yet.

A whole lotta eyes watch.

High tension. Everything perched on a wire like a sharp-beaked bird.

A terrible thought crosses her mind: *I'm going to have to shoot someone.*

Please, not again.

But then finally Charlie mumbles, "Sorry, boss," and steps away from the gate. Ellis bellows at him, but it's too late: the path is open, the way is clear.

Atlanta pats her leg and Whitey stands at attention. She moves briskly toward the gate, keeping the gun sights roving from target to target.

As she gets closer to the gate, Ellis yells: "Do *not* let her leave this ring!"

Ahead of her, the crowd fails to part. They instead tighten around the exit. The octagon ring wall is open, but the human wall remains closed.

I have the key, she thinks.

She raises the pistol at the crowd and fires off two shots.

At least, it looks like she's firing at the crowd. She's really firing just over their heads, but in all the sound and clamor and panic, nobody's figured that out yet. And like Moses parting the Red Sea, Atlanta parts the ocean of bodies as they start to scream and yell and run the other way.

Chaos. She needs chaos.

Atlanta runs into the crowd, firing off another two shots, a cowboy moving his herd. She darts into the throng, moves through it, away from it, lost within it. And soon as she can't see the octagon anymore, she bolts for the woods with Whitey swiftly in tow.

———

The wound looks worse than it is, she thinks—a few teeth marks, still bleeding but the punctures are shallow, so she and Whitey hunker down in the woods not far from Wayman's farmhouse. She sits behind a stack of firewood and holds the dog close.

He sniffs her ear and licks it.

She cries. First just a little. Then great big gulping sobs. She yells at herself inside her own mind to stop, but that only opens the floodgates wider.

It takes time to wind down, for the sobs to hitch and stumble and hiccup before eventually quitting. All the while, she holds the bleeding dog close. The day is hot but she's got the chills. Trauma. Shock.

Soon she's still. And the forest goes still with her. Noises of the Farm are present but distant, as if in another world. Once in a while she looks over the stack of wood corded between prongs of rusty rebar and she can see the Farm. Folks mill about. Crowd looks a little thinner but not by much. She doesn't see anybody looking for her, but then, why would they? She can't go anywhere. Whole property is fenced in. One way out, and it's the same way she came in.

They're going to wait till the day is over. Then they'll come find her.

But she knows the cavalry will arrive long before that.

Holger will bring her people, and it'll all be over.

Except . . .

Time seems to tumble forward like falling rocks, and still nobody's coming. No Holger. No cruisers. It's then the panic hits her guts like she just quaffed a shot of battery acid—they're not coming. *They're not coming.* The cops are crooked. Aren't they? All of them. Petry was able to get ahead of it somehow. Here he was, walking around without a care in the world. He knows he won't get caught. Holger's crooked. They're all crooked.

She suddenly feels very alone and very scared. With a trembling hand she pops the Luger's magazine, thumbs the bullets into her palm, and counts—

Three bullets left. Little golden 9-millimeters catching dappled sunlight from above.

Whitey stiffens. His head perks up and he starts to growl.

Behind her, a radio squelches at the same time as a branch snaps.

She wheels around—one of the three bullets rolls off her palm into the leaves. Panic makes her clumsy; she tries to press the remaining two 9-millimeters into the magazine, but she fumbles the first one and it catches the spring mechanism and launches itself out of her grip like a jumping bean. She curses under her breath and presses her teeth together so hard she's afraid they'll snap. The final bullet slides into the magazine, and she jacks it into the gun—

Just as Ellis Wayman steps into view.

His face is ashen and rage-struck, like he made a mean face and now it's stuck that way. He steps forward. Whitey lowers his head but doesn't growl—this is his old master.

Atlanta points the gun.

Ellis takes another step forward.

"Stop where you are," she says.

"You called the cops," he says, voice a haggard rasp.

"What?"

He holds up the radio. "Randy just called from the front gate. Said the cops are there." As if on cue, she hears the distant sirens warbling, gravel grinding under tires. "And now they're here."

Another step forward.

Whitey starts to growl.

"You need to stop," she says. "I'll shoot. I swear I will."

"I figure you will."

Another step forward.

She pulls the trigger.

Click.

"You didn't pull the toggle," he says. She tries to rack it like a pistol, fumbling for the slide but suddenly finds there is no slide—her hands move over the old German pistol and she doesn't know what to do. He tells her. "You lift up on the bolt toggle, toward the back of the . . ." He sighs. Waves her off. "Don't bother. They're here. It's over. I don't hurt little girls even if they want to kill me. Even if they steal my prize dog."

Whitey whines.

"I . . ." She searches for words. All she comes up with is, "I'm sorry."

He shrugs. "I'm going inside the house. Get a glass of whiskey before they come. You want one?"

"I don't."

He starts to walk away, but then he stops and turns back around. "I liked you. Still do. I thought maybe we had an under-standing. But you screwed me pretty good here."

"This is a bad place."

"Maybe. I'm not a bad man, though." He offers a ghastly, mis-erable smile. "I'll see you on the other side, Atlanta Burns."

And he plods back toward his house, head hung low, big feet tromping over branches and briar. A bear heading back to his den to wait for the hunters.

CHAPTER THIRTY-THREE

Eventually, when it seems safe, she steps out. She leaves the gun hidden under a pile of leaves—last thing she needs to do is approach a shitload of police with an old German pistol in her hand. And hell if there aren't a lot of police—three cruisers, two paddy-wagon vans, two animal-control vans, couple unmarkeds.

Atlanta's first true reward: as cops lead folks into the vans, she spies Melanie's blood-crusted face disappearing into one.

And there's Holger. The detective's dressed like it's early March, even though it's as hot and dry as the devil's own breath out here—Holger's got on jeans and a long-sleeve shirt and a Phillies cap pulled over her too-short haircut.

From there everything's a blur—Atlanta feels relieved but numb. Holger sits her on the bumper of one of the unmarked cars, an old-school Crown Vic that looks like it's seen a thousand better days and none worse than today, and it's there she plants herself for a good hour and a half as the cops, like termites, start to chew apart and break down the wood of this criminal operation. Dogs in cages head to the animal-control van. Cops seize drugs and guns. Two state paddy wagons leave, and a third—this one from two towns over—pulls up. She sees familiar faces—Karl the Nazi, the pockmarked fucker, Charlie the ref, John Elvis—all loaded into cruisers or vans. When they see her they all look at her the same way, each offering up a cold stiletto stare that says, *You did this to me.*

Some cops try to take Whitey away, but before Atlanta says anything, Holger calls over that it's okay. *That's Atlanta's dog,* she tells him. "That dog's safe."

Safe. That's a good word.

Atlanta smiles.

"I guess you *are* my dog," she says to Whitey.

He pants in approval of this fact.

———

It's not long before they bring out the big fish. Ellis Wayman. Trudging forward, hands behind his back, big head and bigger beard bobbing with each step. He sees Atlanta and gives her a boozy, woozy smile.

"You missed out," Wayman calls over to her. He whoops: "I broke out the good whiskey!" He offers a booming laugh.

They load him into a cruiser—which looks so difficult as to be comical, like they're trying to shove a grizzly into a phone booth—but eventually they get him inside, and he gives Atlanta one last look through the glass. She can't tell if the look is sad or mean or just drunk. She wonders how much whiskey it must take to light up a man like that. One bottle? Two? A claw-foot bathtub filled to its brim?

As the cruiser pulls away, she realizes she still hasn't seen Petry. That squirmy, slimy sonofabitch. He must've known what was happening and found a way out. She should've known he'd slip the noose.

Holger meets back up with Atlanta, tells her, "You did all right."

"I guess."

"This was a big operation. Not pro league, but one rung down. Might let us trade up and catch some even bigger fish."

"Dang, this thing has leagues?"

Holger nods. "Amateur. Semipro. Pro. Big money at the top."

"That's scary. And a little bit sick."

For a moment, Holger just looks old and tired. Like this is all she sees and it's the cross she bears, a cross that weighs her down and pushes her closer to the earth day after day, year after year. She finally says, "It is, and sometimes it feels like you're just kicking sand at the tide. But we did good today, thanks to you."

"Will it make a difference?"

"It will." But the way she says it, Atlanta's not so sure. "Anyway, now that we're wrapping up I should get you out of here. Thanks for waiting. You made us kinda busy." She smiles.

"I'm ready to go home."

"You mind coming by the station first? Make your report? I want to tie up all the loose ends on this thing." Way she looks at Atlanta, there's a flash of something: suspicion? Irritation? Straight-up confusion as to why a girl like her is here at fights like these? "I'll be quick about it. Better to pull the Band-Aid off fast than rip it slow."

Atlanta hesitates—she really *is* ready to go home. But she nods. "Yeah. I can do that."

"I appreciate that. I'll get someone to take you, and I'll be along soon enough." Holger starts looking around, then her eyes fall on someone over Atlanta's shoulder. "Petry! Petry, hey, c'mere."

Petry.

Atlanta's blood goes ice cold.

And here he comes. Petry. In full uniform. He comes over, takes no obvious notice of Atlanta. He's all business. "Detective. What's up?"

"Can you take Miss Burns here back to the station? I want to get through the paperwork. We get that started, we can start making the case."

Atlanta feels like she's got a string of firecrackers under her feet. *No. Not him.* She runs through the possibilities, plays a series of minimovies in her head, like the one where Petry drives her somewhere you can't find on any map and puts a bullet in her head, *bang.*

Whitey's feeling it, too. Staring up at Petry. Licking his chops.

Before Petry can say anything, Atlanta blurts: "I can get a ride." They both look at her. "I'll call somebody. They'll come. They can drive me." Her words are short, clipped, a little breathless. All doing a poor job of masking just how her skin crawls, how her heart feels like a moth trapped under glass.

Holger shakes her head. "Nah, this is fastest. Safest, too."

"How about the dog?" Petry asks.

You leave my dog alone.

"Take the dog, too," Holger says. "You can put Atlanta in my office and the dog . . ." She seems to think on it. "Break room downstairs, maybe. Give him a cookie or something."

Petry waves her on like he didn't just have a showdown with her behind the Morton building. "Miss Burns, follow me, please." So polite for a sociopath.

Atlanta looks to Detective Holger. Thinks to say something. Anything. Maybe just run. What if she tells them Petry was here? That he was a willing participant in all of this? That he threatened her? That she stole his gun and tossed it into the woods?

Would they believe her?

They'd take his word over hers.

And saying any of that right now opens up a real bag of snakes. More snakes than she can kill.

A thought strikes her: *He can't do anything to you. Not now. Not like this. Everybody will see him put you in that car. This is on the record. On the books. Holger knows.*

Holger looks at Atlanta expectantly. "You can go, Miss Burns. Unless there's something else?"

Atlanta wants to tell her everything else. All of it. But she doesn't. Instead she pats her thigh to get Whitey's attention and follows ten feet behind Officer Petry.

The killer in a cop suit, the monster in man-skin.

He opens the door to a cruiser—his cruiser—and says nothing as he points toward it.

It's a little miniprison, she knows. She's seen movies and TV. Those doors close, they only open for him. It's a portable cage, a jail on wheels.

Whitey hops in the back.

Atlanta holds her breath—not by choice but because she can't seem to let it out—and gets in, too.

———

For a while the car just drives, humming along the back roads, occasionally rocking as one or two tires hop in and out of a bad pothole. Like before, it's all trees and barns and horses behind fences. The trees seem to sag and wilt. The paint on barns peels in long leprosy strips. All the horses look like the animals at the zoo on a hot day—tired, wasted, like they just want to lie down, roll over, and die. Sunlight comes through the trees, a bleach-white light—not warm and comforting but empty and hot. The eye of hell watching.

Petry doesn't say a word.

Neither does she.

Even Whitey doesn't pant. He just stares forward, his eyes like lasers burning holes in the back of Petry's seat.

The dog knows. Has a sense of the man's malevolence.

Atlanta feels trapped. Like she's one of the dogs before the fight. Locked away in her crate until it's time for the scuffle. Until it's time to die.

Comes a point when to head back to town, toward the station, Petry should stay straight on this road—Boxelder Road—but turns off instead onto Old Orchard Road. Not toward the town of Maker's Bell in the valley, but rather onto a road that loops back up toward Grainger Hill. Toward the trailer parks and dead barns and shitty little ranch houses where grungy motorheads sell bad weed or crystal meth.

That's not good.

She pulls out her phone. No bars.

Whitey growls, real low.

Finally, she says in a croaking voice: "Where are we going?"

But Petry, he doesn't answer. He just drives forward, eyes front.

Ahead, a dirt lot. He pulls into it, the tires conjuring up a plume of dust. Doesn't turn the car off, but leaves it running instead. Through the windshield Atlanta can see a burned-out house—a charred briquette that was once someone's home and is now just a skeleton of black bones.

Petry turns around. Faces her through the wire.

"If you touch me," she seethes with false bravado. But she can't finish the words. She's too scared.

He says nothing in response. Instead he pulls out a phone—no, not a phone, but some kind of MP3 player. He's already got it cued up to play what he needs. He thumbs a button.

Sound fills the car. A conversation.

First voice: "Something's wrong with my son."

Second: "We've noticed that. Wondered if you'd come to us."

Two men. Atlanta recognizes both of them.

"I worry that who he is . . . is who he is," says the first man. Bill Coyne. Chris's father. "That it's something he can't change, you know?"

"He can change." This one, Orly Erickson. "It's a choice he's made. Whether out of teenage rebellion or something else, I don't know. I'm no psychologist. But I know that God did not make us this way. And I know that the devil gives us choices and tempts us so that we choose poorly."

Bill: "I want something done."

Orly: "Are you asking me to do something about this?"

Bill: "I . . . I don't know."

Orly: "You are. Aren't you." A statement, not a question.

Bill: "Yeah. Yeah. I guess I am."

Orly clears his throat, says, "I think we can get the boys on it. They got that program for troubled kids, kids who are lawbreakers. 'Scared Straight,' they call it. This is like that except far more *literal*. They'll scare him straight, all right. Beat those improper feelings right out of him. Throw the devil out the window and leave room for the goodness of God. We can do that, right?"

A few moments of silence. Orly's asking someone other than Bill Coyne. Petry. It has to be Petry. He doesn't speak on the recording—trademark silence. Probably just nodding.

Orly again: "It'll cost you a little something. Not much. Since it's for the cause and all."

Bill: "I can do that. I can pay. I'm happy to pay."

"Then thy will be done." Orly laughs. Then the sound of a drawer opening. Glass against glass. Maybe a bottle pouring—*glug glug glug*—sharing a drink. "Hail victory."

Bill: "Hail victory."

Another clink of glass. A toast.

Then the recording stops.

Petry again says nothing. He just removes the MP3 player from the cage.

"I know all that already," she says. She can barely keep from yelling. "You're not telling me anything new."

"Oh, but I am," Petry says. "I played that for him. For Chris. So he could hear. I took him from his home. I drove him up to Gallows Hill, to the pear tree as it bloomed, and I gave him rope— already tied like it needed to be tied—and I played that recording so that Chris knew what his father had done."

The air, robbed from her lungs. A gut punch. A horse kick. She plays through it in her head. What that must've been like for Chris. To learn your own father had orchestrated the worst and most humiliating moment of your life. Thinking you were broken. Thinking you could be *fixed* through pain and humiliation.

"You made him do it," she says. Voice quiet. Again Whitey growls.

"Not really. I just marched him to the door and gave him a reason to walk through it."

"You *forced* him," she seethes. Tears wet her cheeks. "You pointed a gun at him. Made him listen. Made him climb up there and hang himself."

"The gun was just to get him in the car and to the tree. Then the recording became my weapon and so I holstered my piece. I was right. It was enough. I didn't make him do it. I just gave him a reason."

"That's the same thing. I'll get you for this."

"You're missing the big picture, Atlanta. You're not thinking straight. Why am I telling you this? Why play that recording?"

"To torture me like you tortured him."

He shakes his head. "Wrong. To *show* you. Like I *showed him*. I'm showing you that I can get to anybody. I can hurt the people you love. You're a troubled girl, and troubled girls make trouble for everybody else. I can't have that. *We* can't have that. This is a warning. It may not be my last, but you're nearly at the end of your rope just as Chris was at the end of his. Cross us and get in our way, and I will hurt everyone around you. You want to blame somebody for Chris Coyne's death, blame yourself. You had to go shaking the trees, and now you're wondering why the branches came crashing down on your head."

She growls, cries out in grief and rage, bangs the heels of both hands against the wire.

Then Atlanta buries her face in her hands.

Petry says nothing and backs the car out of the dirt lot and back onto the road, leaving the burned-out building behind and heading back toward Boxelder Road.

——

Atlanta sits at Holger's desk, waiting. Trying not to shake. Trying not to scream. Her hands hold onto the detective's desk, fingers gone bloodless like she's holding the safety bar of a rollercoaster.

When they arrived at the station, Petry left her alone. Just walked off like it was no big thing. Another officer, a young buck with a wispy mustache, took the dog away toward the basement steps. Whitey didn't want to go, but she knelt and kissed his brow and promised him they'd get someone to look at his shoulder soon. Here under the lights the wound didn't look too bad—she hopes a few antibiotics will be good enough.

Whitey rested his head on her shoulder and made a small sound in the back of his throat—a growl of sorts, but not aggressive, not really. She took it to be a promise, or something like one: he's got her back.

"Go on," she told him, and the officer—Landis was his name— took the dog away.

Down the hall, Petry stood by a coffee machine and gave her a look and a small, sinister nod. A reminder. *I can get you wherever you are.*

Now here she is. In Holger's office. Waiting for the woman to arrive and trying her damnedest not to grab a stapler off the desk, march over to Petry, and staple his mouth and nose closed.

In her mind's eye she keeps replaying Chris's suicide. The march to the tree. The slow, creeping realization afforded by that recording. The rope. The decision. Choking and kicking and emptying your bowels and then—

Holger enters.

"You okay?" she asks Atlanta.

"Fine," Atlanta says. She knows that one word doesn't sound fine, and that the very word may be the only one in the English language that everybody says but never means—if you meant it, you'd say *good*, but when you don't mean it, you say *fine* like it's a joke that everybody's in on. "Just fine."

"I want to talk to you about how all this . . . went down."

"Okay."

"There's gonna be some questions, and you might have to talk to a district attorney. Someone may want to coach you about things to say."

"You telling me to get a lawyer?"

Holger shakes her head. "Not at all. It's just that this is a big deal. Big operation like this gets busted, there's gonna be accountability. And a man like Ellis Wayman may seem like some redneck rube, but he's going to lawyer up in a big way. And those lawyers are going to look at you . . ." Here her voice trails off.

"I'm a troubled witness. Given the things that have happened."

"Could be."

"I get that. Well. Whatever y'all need."

"Thanks, Atlanta."

Holger asks. Atlanta answers. As honestly as she can tell it. She leaves Guy and Shane out of it. Says she was looking into some missing dogs for a friend. That put her into Bird and Bodie's orbit. Here she leaves out what they did to her and how she stole Whitey. She mostly just plays it like she was there sniffing for information and when she saw what she saw, she couldn't abide it—and so she called Holger. It's a simplified version of the truth, but it works. No real gaps to speak of, long as nobody else tells Holger differently.

When they're done, Holger nods and says, "You're a tough little girl."

"I'm not little."

"No, I suppose you're not. Girls grow up faster than ever."

"I guess we have to."

"Let's go get your dog and get you home."

———

The way it all happens seems like a nightmare. It's impossible and unthinkable and yet it happens just the same.

She and Holger walk down past the cubicles and desks of this middling police department and they head to the stairwell—metal door opens, clangs, cement steps down toward the basement.

Holger's making small talk, something about how there's an ice-cream place just down the road that has pink bubble-gum ice cream and how she used to love that flavor when she was a girl. Then she starts talking about Teaberry Gum.

Atlanta doesn't know why they're talking about it or how they even got onto the subject of ice cream and bubble gum because all of that escapes her head when she hears the gunshot.

The shot, loud. A quick, echoing *pop*. Just one. From downstairs in the basement.

Atlanta's whole body feels like it's falling through itself.

Upstairs, she didn't see Petry.

Where had he gone?

This is a warning. It may not be my last . . .

She breaks into a run, Holger after her.

The downstairs is all cement blocks and concrete floors. Functional. A hall with many doors, one of them open.

Atlanta calls to her dog, starts yelling out for Whitey to come to her.

No dog answers.

She hauls ass to the break-room door.

It's there she finds him.

On his side. Pool of blood under his head. A red hole in the ridge above his eye.

Petry leans against the back corner of the break room. Gun set on the counter. His hand is bleeding, and he's swaddling it in napkins. "Don't know what happened. Dog came at me. Bit my hand—"

But then Atlanta is screaming. The sound that comes out of her is like a banshee, a wail like a storm wind through a broken shutter—it drowns out his voice.

She clambers up over the break-room table like a rabid animal. Claws for him. Shoves him against the counter. Thinks to grab the gun. Grab it, stick it under his chin, pull the trigger—

Hands find her. Holger. Pulling her back. Her hip bangs into a chair. She screams. Weeps. Yells again and again how he killed her dog, he killed her dog, he killed her dog . . .

Other cops come into the room. Alert. All hands on deck. Full-tilt boogie. But Atlanta doesn't care. She can't get to Petry, but she can get to her dog. She drops next to Whitey and feels him and holds him and kneels in his blood. She cradles his limp head to her own. The dog made a promise to her—he had her back, and she thought she had his, but soon as she turned her eyes away . . .

Atlanta lies upon the dog, wetting his side with her tears.

Whitey is dead.

PART FIVE: BAIT GIRL

CHAPTER THIRTY-FOUR

Atlanta was there when her father died. He had an aneurysm out in his workshop. Blood balloon swelled at the base of his brain, and just as he was about to hammer another nail—he was out there in the dust and the cobwebs, fixing one of their dining-room chairs—the balloon went pop and Daddy dropped.

Atlanta was the one who found him. Lying on the stone floor. Bits of sawdust in his hair like the snow they never saw much of down South. And the thing she remembers most about that moment is how she knew he was dead. Was like something had left him—and now what remained was just a department-store mannequin of meat and bones but no soul, pale and tight and missing that essential human spark that makes us who we are.

All that was made worse at the funeral when she got a look at the man in the box. Her father had turned into a museum display, preserved and plasticky, waxy like a McIntosh apple. Dead eyes and too much blush and his mouth forcibly arranged in a slight smile that wasn't his smile at all. A portrait the artist got wrong.

As she lies there across Whitey, she feels it here, too—the sense of lifelessness, that something vital has vacated the animal. A spirit, a ghost, a soul: gone.

Hands try to pull her away, but she won't—*can't*—leave him behind. She wants to curl up and lie in the blood and hold the dog tight until she starves and leaves behind her own Atlanta-shaped mannequin. Voices—Holger, maybe—call her name, but she doesn't listen and doesn't care about what they have to say, because all that's good in this world has failed her. The police are corrupt. They can't protect her. They can't protect an innocent dog. She doesn't know why Whitey bit Petry—did Petry egg the dog on? Slap him? Kick him? Or did Whitey just know to sink his teeth into the flesh of an evil man?

It doesn't matter because it happened, and now Whitey is dead.

She bends down and presses her face against his face and kisses his muzzle.

She hears it—her own heartbeat, *thump, thump, thump*—but then she thinks, that's not her heartbeat, not at all, it's not even a heartbeat. It's a tail. Thudding dully against the floor.

Whitey's tail.

Wagging. Weak. Barely there. But wagging.

She says, "He's alive," certain that her own words are a lie, that this is just a false flag and one last moment of life before Whitey wanders off to the eternal fields of his happy hunting grounds—but the tail thumps again. And his tongue snakes out over his jowls and lies there like a tired slug.

This time she doesn't just say it but screams it, letting the world know that her dog is alive.

———

The siren wails. The single blue light atop the old Crown Vic spins. Holger floors it.

Atlanta sits in the back, Whitey's head cradled in her lap. His eyes are glassy and unfocused. His breathing, fast and shallow, like he can't get enough air. One paw twitching. The cratered hole in his skull isn't bleeding anymore—just a few black rivulets of drying blood stark against his white fur. She feels his neck, his ribs; his pulse is there, but only barely. The tail no longer wags.

It's then the dog's body seizes, stiffening in her hands. Whitey's eyes roll back into his head and he takes one big gulp of air— holding it, holding it, no more breath, frame tight and legs sticking out like broomsticks—

And then the eyes roll back and the dog's breathing returns— fast, shallow, *pant-pant-pant-pant.*

"Drive!" Atlanta cries from the back. "Please please *please.*"

She can barely see through the tears. She kicks the backseat. As if it matters, as if it means anything at all.

———

Time dilates, then expands, then falls back in on itself until it's meaningless mush. Atlanta sits in the waiting room of the veterinarian's office, waiting to hear something—anything—from Dr. Chennapragada. Holger came and went. Told Atlanta that she's sure Petry had good reason, but she'd look into it, and if she needed her to call Atlanta's mother she would—but Atlanta didn't say anything, just sat there quaking and hoping that if she sat real still, time might be kind enough to fast-forward itself on her behalf.

Eventually the vet comes out. The fabric of her white coat red along the sleeves. Chennapragada is a small woman, but round, hippy—her face the shape of many lush fruits in a netted sack.

She sits next to Atlanta and holds her hand. Tight. Atlanta feels her jaw tighten and the tears start to well up, but she growls— literally growls, a sound she does not expect to make but makes it anyway—and bites back the tears.

"I'm going to say something to you now that you may not want to hear," Chennapragada says.

"No," Atlanta says, firm. "Don't you tell me he didn't make it."

"Your dog is stable." The words, a lift—her expectations countered. "The bullet lodged above his eye. He will have to lose that eye. There will be some . . . other reconstruction necessary." The doctor pauses. "He has a very hard head, this dog."

Atlanta almost laughs. "Me too. I have a hard head, too." She doesn't understand why the vet said she doesn't want to hear any of this—it's good news. It's not the best news, the best news would be, *Your dog didn't get shot in the head*, but considering the circumstances—

"I think you should have the dog put down," the vet says.

A wall slams between them. "What? You said he's stable."

"But he's going to lose an eye. And some of his skull. The brain is intact but . . ." She pauses, finally gets to the heart of the matter. "This is going to be very expensive."

"I don't care."

"It will be thousands of dollars."

"I said I *don't care*. I got a couple grand." *The mortgage money. You need that to live.* "I . . . can pay for some of it now and, and, and you can bill for the rest."

"Please. There are no guarantees. The world has many dogs. It is painful, but if you were to put the animal down . . ."

Atlanta narrows her eyes. "You put that dog down, I'll put *you* down. You fix him. You hear me? *You fix him.*"

Chennapragada nods, clearly taken aback by Atlanta's fervor. "As you wish."

———

Four hours later, Atlanta's lying across the chairs in the waiting room, head extended over the back of a chair, hair touching the floor like the fronds of a dry mop. Anxiety gnaws at her like a dog chewing a pig's ear.

This is, once again, all her fault.

She just keeps pushing. And pushing. And *pushing*—and in her head it's because she tells herself *This is the right thing to do* when really it's because *You're angry and you want everyone to pay for what was done to you.* She's making all the bad people pay for the crimes of one. One voice inside her justifies it—after all, that's probably what drives most cops or soldiers or abuse counselors, right? Some specter haunting them from their past, a single hinge on which the whole door swings. But then she's reminded of the cost: Chris dead, Whitey almost dead, their house soon gone. Is the result worth it?

Thing is, no matter how much she recognizes her part in all of this, she keeps thinking of Petry. And she thinks about how *he* needs to pay. Not a little bit. But a lot. He needs to bear all the costs. All the *burden.* He needs to hurt like he makes others hurt. Because now he knows he can get what he wants from her. He can keep coming back and hurting all those around her—Shane, Guy, her mother. She's got Whitey, but Orly Erickson has Petry—Petry is a rabid dog on a long leash, and the only thing to do with a dog like that is put him down.

That way lies madness. A road lined with the trees of bad ideas. And yet she keeps walking it.

This is a warning. It may not be my last . . .

A shadow falls over her. Atlanta, jolted from her reverie, sits up straight.

It's Miss Cheekbones. The girl from behind the vet counter. She has a bottle of water and a plate of cookies—store-bought, not homemade, but Atlanta's stomach suddenly tightens and gurgles. Hunger hits her like a wave, as if until now she forgot that she ever needed food. The hangover from earlier and the insanity of the day have scraped her clean from the inside out, and now she's staring at those cookies like a wolf staring at a baby deer fumbling through the forest.

"Hungry?" Cheekbones asks, but by the time she adds the question mark to that one word, Atlanta's already got a cookie shoved in her mouth. "Oh. Okay." Cheekbones sits while Atlanta eats. She's three cookies deep by the time they form a wad of masticated dough in her throat, so she quickly uncaps the water and chugs it.

"Thank you," Atlanta gasps, wiping her mouth. "I don't know your name."

"Betsy."

"Hi, Betsy. Sorry for . . . camping out here. I just don't want to go home."

"It's no big thing. It's a slow day." Earlier a woman with a twitchy dust-mop—a *shit zoo* is the only way that Atlanta can spell the breed's name in her head—came in, but Betsy turned her away, said the vet would be in surgery all day. Beyond that, the place was dead. "Your dog is pretty amazing."

Another gulp of water and mouthful of cookie. Atlanta nods. "Yeah. He is." She sighs. "Dogs aren't supposed to survive a shot to the head, right?"

"No, not really. It happens more than you'd think, I guess, but it's still unusual." Betsy shakes her head. "We had a cat with an arrow through its head come in last year. Some kids were shooting animals at the park—ducks, geese, squirrels. They saw the cat and, well."

"The cat live?"

"Yeah, but not well. The cat was kinda . . . weird after that."

"Oh." Her skin goes clammy. "Will Whitey be . . . weird?"

"I don't know. I'm sorry."

Atlanta stares off at a point that doesn't exist here in this room. "No, it's cool."

It's a thousand miles from cool.

"Your dog's breed is rare," Betsy says. "I was doing some reading. You know those dogs used to hunt mountain lions?"

"I didn't."

"Yeah. They chase their prey and just keep throwing themselves against the animal again and again until the prey falls down—and then the rest of the Dogo's pack joins in, both dog and owner. Hunting mountain lions like that? Lord. That tells me your guy back there is one tough cookie." She looks at the now-empty plate. "Um, no pun intended. I'm just saying, if any dog's gonna make it through this, it's yours."

"I hope so." Atlanta forces a game smile. "Thanks."

Betsy pats Atlanta's shoulder. "If you need another water, just say the word."

———

It's another three hours when Chennapragada appears and says five words.

You can see him now.

Atlanta does not hesitate.

Going into the back is a slow-motion walk. She wants to hurry, but Chennapragada moves slow with a trundling hip-sway— Atlanta wants to shove her out of the way but wouldn't know where to go once she did.

The vet takes her to the final door. It swings open, no doorknob. The smell back here is strongly antiseptic, a medicinal sublayer and beneath all that, the smell of musk and fear and animal piss.

There, in the center of the room, on a shiny metal table, is Whitey.

He looks dead.

"He's not dead," Chennapragada says, obviously aware of how it looks. "He's under anesthetic."

The bullet hole is now hidden behind a square bandage. Below it, the eye is a tight pucker, the fur around it shaved down, stitches suturing the eyelid edges closed.

His face seems to sag on that side. Like he's got a palsy.

But his chest rises and falls. Slowly. Steadily.

"Here," Chennapragada says. "Souvenir. If you want it."

She rattles a metal tray—a 9-millimeter bullet rolls around in there. It smells strongly of rubbing alcohol. The lead has mushroomed, like a muffin that blew up and out of its tin.

"He's going to be okay?" Atlanta asks.

"He should be, yes. I'll give you antibiotics and some pain pills."

"I can take him home today?"

"No. He should stay here for a couple nights. So I can monitor him. But you're free to visit with him." The doctor eyes her up and offers a small, wry smile. "You can go over to him. He won't bite."

Atlanta didn't even realize it, but she'd been hanging back. Afraid to touch him like he was a pile of dust and if she got too close he'd blow away on the wind of her breath. She hurries over, wraps her arms around him gently. He's warm. The rise and fall of his breathing gives comfort.

Then: a stink fills the air.

Atlanta's nose crinkles. "Something's wrong. That smell . . ."

"Gas," the vet says with a chuckle. "He farted."

"Oh."

Chennapragada shrugs. "Welcome, Miss Burns, to the joys of dog ownership."

Whitey remains asleep, but his tail thumps against the metal table: *clong clong clong*. Happy in gassy oblivion.

———

Home again, home again.

By the time she makes it home—on foot—evening's creeping in. Not yet dark but will be soon, the paint of twilight already spilling slowly across the sky. A few early fireflies light up their butts across the driveway and above the corn. Should be peaceful. She should feel settled. She doesn't. She feels on edge. Like she's stepping on the ragged tail of an Adderall high, but she hasn't had Adderall in weeks. Itchy. Twitchy. Angry.

Inside, an answering-machine message from her mother. Things didn't work out with Cousin Harley. Coming home soon. Couple more days, then she'll be back. Hope everything is good there, whatever, blah blah blah.

Yeah, Mama, things are peachy-keen here. One big dollop of ice cream on a giant shit sandwich.

Mama coming home soon. Whitey, too.

Atlanta's alone.

She should feel scared, but she doesn't.

She calls Shane, and then she calls Guy.

It's time to do something.

―――

After she tells them the whole story, they both sit and look shell-shocked. She expects that from Shane—that's one of his default looks. You tell him there's pudding pops in the freezer or that it's the day that the new comic books come out, and he tends to get that deer-in-the-headlights-of-an-oncoming-tractor-trailer look. Guy, though, he's sharp, snappy, ready for all the crazy shit life throws at folks—and he's got the same look, as if he just saw something you're never supposed to see, like a lion eating a baby. Or worse and weirder, a baby eating a lion.

"Oh my god," is all Shane can say.

"I can't believe that dog's still alive," Guy says. "Yo, that's messed up. And you put away the Mountain Man? Damn. *Damn.* That's some shit right there."

"The cop killed Chris," Shane says, staring at the floor. It's like he wanted to know, but now that he does . . .

"I want payback," Atlanta says. "And I want it now."

"Girl," Guy says, "you gotta leave this one alone. Let that bird fly free."

Shane shakes his head and finally looks up. "No, she's right. He needs to pay. We let him keep going, and he'll mess with all of us. What do you think's gonna happen when he finds out Whitey is alive? He'll find a way to finish the job. Maybe he'll just kill him. Or maybe he'll have the dog put to sleep. That's the law, right? Dog bite means euthanization."

"The dude's a *cop*," Guy says, incredulous. "You saw what happened—he was able to shoot that dog inside the damn police station. He's untouchable. And did I mention he's a *cop*?"

"I'm the bait dog," Atlanta says suddenly.

They both look at her like, *whuh*?

"I'm the cat on the cat pole. The coon in the cage. Petry knows he's already got a piece of me. He's got blood in his nose. I dangle in front of him a little more, he'll come for me. He'll come to make me hurt. Maybe he'll hit me. Or try to do to me what my mama's boyfriend did. Or maybe he'll just kill me. But I can make him come here. And when he does, I'm gonna kill him."

"Whoa. That's crazy," Guy says.

Shane nods. "Yeah, actually, that is crazy."

Her jaw sets, her mouth a hard line. "It's the only way."

Shane frowns. "There might be another way. Guy, can you drive us somewhere?"

CHAPTER THIRTY-FIVE

Night comes. They drive.

"You okay?" Guy asks, looking over at Atlanta in the passenger seat. "Maybe you need time to cool down."

"Don't have time," she says, gnawing a fingernail to the quick. She gets it to a hangnail and uses her teeth to wrench it free from its mooring. Blood wells and the wound stings. "This has to happen fast. He can't know it's coming."

"Yeah, but are you *okay*?"

"I'm fine." Chew, chew. The taste of licking an iron skillet.

"Is your nose broken?"

She touches it. She'd forgotten about it, actually—the pain receding like low tide, but now that she's thinking about it again her nose feels like a radio powered on, full volume, dialing up a loud frequency of pain. "No. Don't think so."

"You can't go like this forever. At some point you gotta be a normal girl."

"If you say so."

Guy looks over at her, obviously worried. "I'm serious."

"This part has to happen first. This man shot my dog and killed my friend—and I don't buy that line of bull that Chris killed himself—that's not what this was, not for one dang second. I let that slide, and soon he'll come for you. Or Shane. Or my mother. I'm tired of people taking power that's not theirs to take. Evil keeps on keepin' on. At some point you gotta stand in the headlights and take your shot."

And that's the end of that conversation. Guy nods. Says nothing else. Just drives.

She eventually points ahead: "Turn here."

The night sky is a kind of green-dark, like the algae waters of the pond that is now the murky, mud-bogged home to Orly Erickson's heirloom ring. A pond they just passed.

As they get close, Atlanta tells him to cut the lights. He does, and he slows the Scion so it's quiet. And so they don't go driving into a tree.

Up ahead—moonlight on windows, like ribbons of light caught in pools of oil.

The gun club. Where Orly Erickson and his cronies meet and talk about powder loads and the NRA and, oh, right, *white power heil Hitler let's hurt anybody who doesn't look or act like we do.*

From behind Atlanta, a blue glow rises, fills the car. She looks back, sees Shane sitting there, nose practically pressed against the screen of a very small laptop—what he calls a Chromebook.

"You can do this?" she asks.

"I dunno. It depends."

"Depends are what old people wear to hold in their pee," she says. "I thought you said you could do this."

"I can. *If* there's even anything here."

Way Shane put it was this: Petry played her a recording, but it wasn't played on a handheld digital recorder. It was an MP3 player. Which means that conversation between Orly and Bill Coyne was contained within a digital file—like, duh, an MP3.

Good bet that Orly does his business—er, more to the point, his really nasty business—out of the gun club, since doing it at his house or his company would put him at risk. That, then, must be where the recordings come from.

Where the recordings live. Recorded there. And stored there.

Easy-peasy, George-and-Weezy.

"So you're gonna hack a computer in there," she says.

"Huh?" Shane looks up. "Oh. No. Just the network." His computer *boops*. "There. Wireless network. And . . ." He taps on the touchscreen. "Like I figured, not very well protected. No WPA or WEP, just a straight username and password. I looked at the gun club's website, and it's pretty much a big old piece of crap—like, GeoCities-era terrible," he says, continuing with words that Atlanta only barely comprehends. "I figured they didn't exactly have a robust network, and I was right. Still. We need to figure out the password. Maybe they use the default . . ." More typing. "Admin, no. Administrator, no. Password, no, 1234, no, Comcast, no. Damnit."

"What's the problem?"

He gives her a *durrr* look. "I don't know the password."

They start going through possible passwords. Mitchell, since it's his son. TNC Biologics, since it's his company. Gun club. Gunclub. Wife's name takes a bit of Googling: Mary. No, not that, either. Shane frowns. "I wish he had a Facebook profile. Could find out his birthday, maybe."

"I don't think Orly's the type to be on Facebook." She almost laughs. "Is there a racist white asshole version of Facebook? Hitler-book or Bigotface or something?"

That's when it hits her.

She says, "Wait. These racist pricks are pretty much shoved up Hitler's ass every hour of every day. They're Nazi fetishists, it's got to be tied to that." And so they start firing off Nazi-themed stuff—everything from Hitler to Himmler, Adolf to Eva, Panzer to Jew-Biter. Wehrmacht. Warshed. Blitzkrieg. The names of concentration camps. The names of high-ranking officers. Shane's pretty good with this stuff, because he studies and knows his history—but then Atlanta snaps her fingers.

"It's not old Nazi stuff. It's new Nazi stuff. I saw a license plate at Bill Coyne's *and* in the gun club on the wall behind Orly's desk: 14WORDS, it said. It's a neo-Nazi thing, counting the words in one of their mottos—something about securing the world and future for white children. Try that. All one word."

The little computer *bings*.

Shane's eyes light up brighter than his netbook monitor. "Bingo was his name-o."

Atlanta starts biting another nail—this time, her thumb. Guy looks impatient. "So what now? You, like, take over their computers and shit? Hack the files?"

"I'm not really a hacker," Shane mumbles, staring at the screen like a sorcerer peering into his cauldron. "And I'm not gonna be able to hack the computer—if I were better than this I could maybe put out a packet sniffer and see what comes and goes, but we don't have time for that anyway. I just need access to the printer. And . . ."

Tap, tap, click, click. "I do. Via the IP address. Adding it now."

"You said you needed a message from me. You got it ready?"

He nods. "All ready. Is it go time?"

"It's go time."

He stabs a key.

"Your message is printing, milady."

———

The wait is the worst part.

Will someone come? Tonight? Tomorrow? No way to know. Nobody was at the gun club, and so the message on the printer should go undiscovered until morning.

Just the same, they've no way to know when the axe will fall.

Or if it will. She starts to worry—maybe he won't take the bait. Maybe he's too smart a monster to go for the low-hanging fruit.

So they wait. Or, she and Shane do, at least. Guy leaves her with some Adderall and heads back home. He wants to stay, he says, he really does, but he's already had enough trouble, and these are cops and . . .

Atlanta tells him it's okay. She needs his car gone from the driveway anyhow.

When he's gone, she takes the Adderall.

Doesn't kick in right away, but when it does everything seems crystal and bright—she finds a sense of hyper-alertness, easy and electric. All the world under a magnifying glass. Her mind wiped free of fatigue. She tells Shane to sleep, and he lies down on the couch. One leg draped over. The house is humid. He's got a sheen of sweat on his brow.

"Do you think he'll come?"

She nods. "I figure. We all set up?"

"Yeah. Won't take much to get it all going. You sure this'll work?"

"No."

"Oh."

"Just remember, whatever happens—stay out of the way. Hide in the coat closet and *don't* come out. I don't need you in the cross fire in all of this. Just say in there and stick to the plan."

He pauses. Draws a deep breath. "What do you think he'll do?"

"I've been nesting on that. At first I figured he'd come after one of you. But then I got to thinking, he knows I'm vulnerable. Mama's gone. Dog is at the vet—far as he knows, maybe dead. Day after I shut down a major dogfighting ring I might have some folks who want to come at me, make me pay, so he could pretty easily make it look like something it's not. Plus, we dangled the bait. So, he'll come. He'll come. He'll try to kill me."

"I'm kinda freaked out by all this." He flops his head back on the couch. "I'm scared."

She lies and tells him, "Me too." But she's not scared. Not right now, at least. The Adderall smooths over all the sharp edges. It wears the mountain of fear down to a smooth, comfortable hill.

"I don't want to die," he says.

"We're not gonna die." Another lie. She doesn't know.

"I got to touch a girl's boob."

"At least you got to do that before you died."

"At least."

He stares up at the ceiling for a while and eventually falls asleep.

For Atlanta, sleep is just a dream.

CHAPTER THIRTY-SIX

Four o'clock in the morning, Atlanta hears it. She's not asleep. She's been in the dark, sitting across from Shane the whole time, staring not so much *at* him as *through* him. Her mind wandered onto the subject of Steven and of their kiss and if she could ever really see him as more than a friend, more than just a sad boy with big teeth, and here her thoughts hovered like a mosquito over a barrel of brackish water.

But she's ripped free from those thoughts as she hears the creak of a board upstairs.

He's here.

He's in her room.

———

The message they wrote and then printed on the gun club printer was this:

ALL YOUR AUDIO FILES ARE BELONG TO US.
YOU'VE GOT ONE WEEK.
MEET ME AT THE WATER TOWER, SATURDAY, MID-NIGHT.
BRING TEN GRAND OR I SEND THE FILES TO EVERY-BODY.
--AB

Shane assured her that there was a joke in there somewhere and that it was a good one. She didn't get it and didn't much care to.

That was the message. An upgraded version of when they lured the Nazis to the graveyard by throwing a note through the broken car window. That worked. Sort of.

This message, like that one, is a lie. They don't have the audio files. And they never intended to meet him at the water tower. They knew he'd come before then. To get the files back on his own. To handle the problem.

And now here he is.

Upstairs.

She's surprised that he's here so soon, though. They only set the letter to print six hours before. Somebody must've gone to the gun club and seen it. Orly, probably. Late-night meeting.

Doesn't matter now.

Atlanta hurries to Shane, shakes him awake, and at the same time clamps a hand over his mouth so he doesn't cry out. She hiss-whispers: "He's here. Closet. *Go.*"

He whimpers, then rolls off the couch—and bangs his knee on the coffee table.

Upstairs, the creaking stops suddenly.

Atlanta shoots Shane a real lightning bolt of a look and jerks her head toward the closet. Shane darts toward it like a soldier in a war zone—head down so it doesn't get shot off.

Her bare toe feels under the couch. Finds the cold metal of the shotgun barrel. Then she reaches for the iPod Touch on the rickety old side table. The iPod isn't Atlanta's. It's Shane's. She flicks it on, does what needs doing, and then waits.

Again the creaking. Toward the steps.

And down. One by one. The house is old, and every floorboard is a complainer.

From here she can see the staircase through the wooden railing.

Can see the first shadow—deeper black than the rest of the dark—step onto that top step.

She thinks suddenly: *Screw this.*

Drop the iPod.

Pick up the gun.

Just kill him and be done with it.

But Shane has a plan. And despite her very worst and hungriest instinct, she holds still, standing there by the couch in the dark of her own home.

Petry continues to walk down those steps.

She sees his feet. Then legs. Torso.

And then his arm and hand and in that hand—

His gun.

The same gun that shot Whitey in the head and came an angel's whisper away from killing her dog.

The same gun that probably forced Chris out of his home and to a pear tree on a hill.

The gun that aims to kill me, too.

Soon as he reaches the bottom of the stairs, she speaks. She means for her words to sound confident and badass, but instead they come out a shaking, quaking croak. "I knew you'd come—"

Muzzle flash, gunshot, the lamp on that rickety side table pops and jumps to the floor with a crash.

Atlanta falls backward, her buttbone nailing the wooden floor. She cries out and presses her back flat against the wood, sandwiched between the base of the couch and the legs of the coffee table.

This wasn't supposed to happen. They were supposed to have a . . . a chat, a *conversation*—like they do in the movies where the good guy and the bad guy square off one last time and—

Petry fires again. A pillow ejects feathery guts into the air. Motes of white snow against the dark room. All Atlanta hears is the ringing in her ears. All she smells is that gun stink, oil and powder and murderous intent.

"Wait!" she screams. "Stop! *Stop!*" Silence. No more shots. She cries, her words fast like machine gun chatter: "You-kill-me-you-don't-get-the-files-please-stop."

"You don't have any files." His voice is slow and cold. No emotion. No anger.

"Do too!" It's a childish response but all she can think to say. What's next: *You're a nanny-doody-head?*

"Those files don't live at the gun club. Orly's got 'em elsewhere."

She almost sobs, but a hard surge of hot anger burns away the tears before they fall. "Wrong. I have proof you hurt Chris. Proof you and Orly been killing off Mexicans and gay kids and anybody else who gets in your way." She's stringing one lie after the other now. "All your neo-Nazi bully white-power bullshit. The money. The guns. Everything."

Petry doesn't say anything at first. She hears a faint scrape of a shoe—*is he moving? Oh, Lord, where is he?*

Then he says, "I don't speak on most of those files. They can't prove anything. Besides, I didn't have anything to do with any of the other gay kids. That wasn't me."

"Chris was you."

"You already know that."

Keep talking keep talking keep talking.

"And the Mexican kids?"

"I do as I'm told. Mr. Erickson has a very clear vision for the future of this town, and any outsiders are not a part of that. That includes you, by the way."

And suddenly there he is. Standing at her feet between the couch and the coffee table, gun up—

But she's got a gun up, too. Shotgun up and out from under the couch. Shell loaded. Hammer back.

Boom.

The shotgun goes off, and a framed photo—her seventh-grade photo, gawky Atlanta with big braces and tangle of red hair even meaner and wilder than it is now—drops off the wall as Petry darts left.

And then silence again. He's somewhere on the other side of the couch. Single-barrel shotgun means she's just used her one shot. Atlanta rests the iPod on her chest and breaks the barrel, fishing in her pocket for a shell—

All the shells leap free of their pocket prison and roll across the floor. Just out of reach. Her hand flails to find some, one, any.

"Just admit you don't have the audio files," Petry says from the far side of the room somewhere. The floor groans. He's on the move again. Her hands feel for shells—but they've rolled past the coffee table and she can't get any without moving and making herself vulnerable. "You can't prove I killed any of them."

"But you did."

"Some of them. Others I just watched."

"Fine. You're right," she says, voice so haggard and worn to the nub she barely recognizes it as her own. "I don't have audio files, plural. I have one audio file. I thought this would go a little different, but it doesn't change the fact—I've been recording this, you sonofabitch." It feels good to say that. She imagines the look on his face—cracking that stony veneer, a kidney stone burned to dust by a surgical laser.

He says nothing in response.

She needs ammo.

She needs it *now*.

She stretches—muscles burning—fingers touching one of the green crimped shells—

Another gunshot. The floor shudders near her hand and she feels a cough of stinging splinters—she jerks her hand back like it got bit by a snake. Feels blood from the splinters. And still she has no shell.

Petry's up. No longer making a secret of his movements. Footsteps—*thump thump thump*. She shouldn't have given away the plan, shouldn't have gotten cocky—

Atlanta cries out, scrambles to stand, the iPod clattering to the floor—

There he is. In the dark. Flash of teeth. Gun up.

She swings the shotgun like a bat. Barrel in her hand, stock slamming against his shoulder. The Winchester stock breaks in half with a bony *snap*—suddenly Petry is lunging for her, no gun in his hand—did he drop it? No time to worry about that now—his hands close around her throat and drop her back to the floor between the couch and table, thumbs pressing tight against her windpipe, fingers crushing the blood flow to her brain.

She's been here before. A man on top of her. These hands are tighter, much tighter, but the feeling is still the same—heavier than the compressed density of a black hole, his knee between her knees, his breath hot in her nose and mouth. This is an act of anger, not of lust, but to her it matters little. The shotgun is out of reach. Everything is out of reach. She's alone. No dog. No mother. Chris is dead.

A deeper darkness bleeds in from the edges, a puddle of tar threatening to smother . . .

Atlanta starts to shut down. Stops struggling. *Just let it go.* It's all her fault. She opened the door, and the demon came in. Invited. What did she think would happen? Is this what she wanted all along? Does she deserve this?

Maybe she does.

But then Petry's eyes flash, a shimmer of sudden hunger. Not at her. At something else.

He lets go of her neck. Reaches to her side, pulls up the iPod.

She has no idea if it's still recording. Atlanta sees fireworks behind her eyes.

Oxygen rushes to her brain. Her skull a pulsing blood bag.

It brings renewed vigor. It carries fresh anger.

She gets her arm, loops it around the leg of the coffee table, and pulls it hard right toward her. The side of the table jams into his temple, and she thinks, *Here's my chance—*

But it's not enough. He takes the iPod in his hand and smashes it against the top of her head. Again she sees stars spinning dizzily in the dark of her eye as plastic sticks in her skin and pain kicks her like a horse. Everything collapses inward—moments shuddering, shuttered.

The iPod's broken . . .

Her thoughts, broken.

No longer recording . . .

His weight is off her.

Tries to stand.

Can't.

Hand out, steadies her against the couch.

It's too late, should've killed him when I had the chance.

Her plans all broken . . .

Here he comes . . .

Footsteps . . .

There . . .

Dark shadow dark eyes mean man in monster-skin.

He's got the gun.

Fine kill me end it get it over with.

She kneels.

I'm all alone.

Gun up, black eye staring her down, open mouth.

Pointed at her.

Shape, movement, shadow.

Petry doesn't see.

Shane.

Shane.

Shane is there—mouth in a silent O, cheap-shit flea-market katana raised up over his head like an executioner's axe—and he brings the weapon down on Petry's wrist.

The blade breaks in half like a dry spaghetti noodle.

Petry howls—

The gun goes off.

Another photo—this one of Atlanta as a little girl standing knee-deep in a muddy hole with a doofy smile on her face—leaps from the wall.

The gun hangs limp in Petry's hand. Atlanta rushes. Drives a knee into his balls. Gets her arm under his arm and twists—the gun drops to the floor, and she hurries to pick it up.

The sound that comes out of her is like a rabid animal, crazed and wild.

She staggers backward. Petry advances—

She points the gun at him.

She sees in the dark his pale face. Shane's, too—he backs away, hands out like he's trying to fend off a lion. Both have a similar look—hair askew, plastered to forehead and thrust up like the feathers of a car-struck crow.

Moments pass. Big moments, full of expectation. Could shoot him now. Could just end it. He broke in here. Nobody would be the wiser. A justified act.

And yet.

"Outside," Atlanta says, panting.

Petry sneers but doesn't move.

She shoots at his feet.

"I said, *outside.*"

She gestures with the gun.

Petry marches. Atlanta sniffs, blows a shock of red hair out of her eye. Tells Shane, "Get my shotgun. And a couple shells. Then follow me."

CHAPTER THIRTY-SEVEN

Moon's up. Big and bright over the corn. Petry creeps forward slowly. She tells him to keep his hands up, and when he does she sees his wrist is wet with blood. A real sword might've done a lot worse, but blood is blood and right now that blood makes her happy.

He gets to the edge of the corn and she sees movement off to the right—one of the Cat Lady's cats out hunting for mice or chipmunks. The cat *mrows* and darts between the stalks.

"Your turn to kneel," she says. "But you gotta face me, first."

Shane catches up, her gun with the busted stock in one hand, a pair of green .410 shells in the palm of his other.

Petry turns and kneels. He stares up at her with eyes that might as well be carpenter nails. Cold and dark and sharp.

Atlanta points the gun at his head.

"Whoa," Shane says, the word as much a gasp as it is anything. "Atlanta, what are you doing?"

"Finishing what he started."

"You don't have to do this."

She swallows a hard knot. "I reckon I do."

"Atlanta—"

"The recording is gone. He broke the iPod. We don't have a dang thing."

"The cloud," Shane says. And she's not sure what he means so she darts her gaze up—no clouds tonight, the sky is dappled with stars. But then he says it again: "The cloud! It's saved on the cloud. I set that app to back up all recordings—off the device."

Petry's eyes narrow.

"So we have it?" she asks, a flutter of something eager and insane inside her gut.

Shane nods. "I checked. Yeah."

"Oh. *Oh.*" She eyes Petry. Small dark man in dark clothes. A human stain. A hunk of coal ruining a puddle of ink. "You. Lie down. Chin against the dirt."

The wind kicks up. The corn hisses and murmurs. As if it's alive.

"Atlanta," Shane says, not understanding. That's okay. He will.

She tells Shane, "The shotgun. Load it."

"It's broken."

"Just the stock. The important part still works."

He fumbles with the action—eventually breaking the barrel and clumsily thumbing a shell into the chamber.

"Close it," she says.

"Atlanta—"

"I said, *close it*." She hears her own voice and it's too dark, too ragged. She adds: "Please."

The *click* of the gun snapping shut.

"Let's trade." She hands Shane the cop's pistol, and gingerly he hands her the Winchester.

The wind dies down. The humid air comes back—hot, damp, choking. The gun is lighter in her hands—the stock now broken off a couple inches past the trigger guard at its narrowest point. Now just the jagged teeth of splintered wood. She thumbs the hammer back. It makes a satisfying *click*.

"This is how it's going to work," she tells Petry. "We've got you on record saying some very bad things. Things that would get you into some deep and awful shit. Maybe the way we did it wasn't legal, but you and I both know that doesn't matter one whit. It'll still put eyes on you. Eyes you don't want. And when those eyes look at you they'll start to look at Orly Erickson, and then the ghost of Hitler himself couldn't save you from what's coming." She draws a deep breath, blows it out through flared nostrils. "So you're going to leave. You're going to pack up your stuff and disappear from this town, this world, this life. I don't care where you go. I don't care what you do. Long as you're nowhere near here. Because that recording? It's gonna get out. And you don't want to be here when it does."

Petry lies there, face-down against the dirt.

"I'm gonna need you to acknowledge what I just told you," she says.

"Fine," he mutters.

"Come again?"

"I said fuckin' *fine*. Whatever you want."

"I want something else."

"Don't push your luck."

"Don't push *yours*. You ever read the Bible, Officer Petry?"

"I go to church."

"Ain't the same thing. Most folks go to service but never crack the Good Book. Devil can quote scripture and all that. Well, think of me as being the devil on your shoulder, and let me quote a bit of scripture to you, something someone said to me recently. *If your right hand causes you to sin, cut it off and throw it away.* It's from one of the gospels, though I'll be honest, my memory is lapsing as to which one. Guess I'm not a very good devil. Or angel. But I am a spectacular human being, and we human beings love our punishments."

Shane steps back. Watches, rapt, scared, arms folded over like he's suddenly cold.

"Get on with it," Petry says, voice muffled by the earth.

"Put out your hand," she says. "Your right one. Same hand that held the gun that ushered Chris up onto that hill. Same hand that gave him the rope. Same hand that shot my dog in the head. A dog that *lives*, by the way. Hey, let me ask you something while you're here. They found a note in Chris's pocket. Where'd that come from?"

"His journal. Open on his desk the night I took him from his house. I ripped it out. Seemed a good enough suicide note."

"Fine. Now put out that hand."

Petry hesitates.

She jabs him between the shoulder blades with the barrel. "Either your hand or the back of your head. Your call."

"Please," he says.

"Pleading, now? That doesn't seem like you."

"I have a wife and kids."

"How sad for them."

"Fuck you."

"Hand. Or head. I'll count down from five." She starts. "Five . . . four . . ."

His arm moves. The right hand—already with a bleeding wrist from where the cheap katana lacerated the skin—creeps out like a pale spider, fingers walking it along.

"Extend your arm all the way," she says.

He tenses, then does just that.

"Chris was my friend. He was Shane's friend. He was a *lot* of people's friends. He lit up a room like a birthday cake stuck with Fourth-of-July sparklers. And you took that away from all of us." She blinks back tears. "This doesn't end for me. But it does for you."

She pulls the trigger.

Gun's loaded with half-ounce birdshot. Six BBs in each crimped shell. The .410 is a squirrel gun. Doesn't blow a squirrel apart, and it doesn't blow apart Petry's hand, either. That's not to say it's pretty, though the range is close and the birdshot stays in a tight pattern. The back of his hand blooms red; the skin flays, opens up like a torn bag of chips. His hands curl inward. Blood spatters the earth, gleaming in the light from the moon and stars.

Petry screams. Rolls onto his side. Fetal position. The hand may not be ruined. But it'll never again work the way a hand is supposed to.

Like Bodie's hand, she thinks.

Hammer back.

"Now you run," she says. "You run or the next shot opens your neck."

Petry tries to stand—foolishly plants his hand, his *shot* hand, on the ground in a panic and wails again as he falls over. But somehow he manages to get his legs up under him and spring forward.

Sure enough, he runs. Down the driveway. Toward the road. There's no car here—must be parked somewhere else, somewhere on the road. Or maybe he walked. It doesn't matter.

Atlanta breathes in the warm air. Fireflies orbit one another.

She collapses, crying. Shane wraps his arms around her, and he cries, too.

EPILOGUE: THE MESSAGE

"Is this how I do this?" she asks. "I just point the—"

Shane comes over, tilts the little laptop up. With his finger he taps a tiny pinhole over the screen. "Look here when you talk."

"That's a camera?"

"That's a camera."

"Ain't technology grand?"

He smiles. "Yep."

Sun comes in through the window, illuminating a plate of cookies on the bed. Cookies Mama made—meaning, cookies you don't want to eat 'less you plan on chipping a tooth. Mama's been baking a lot recently. Nervous habit. It's late summer and they're going to lose the house, or so she thinks. A house that now has a few bullet holes hanging, plus two broken picture frames. That was a tough one to explain. Atlanta admitted they were bullet holes, but lied about how they got there. Said they were from when a coon got into the house. Arlene was either too dumb to figure differently or too smart to look any deeper than that.

She said it didn't matter anyway, what with the foreclosure coming. The little money she has left from Jenny that didn't go to the vet bill won't be but a Band-Aid on a bullet wound.

But Atlanta has a recording from a couple months back that suggests the foreclosure might not come after all. Soon as Orly Erickson has a listen.

Orly. Must be wondering where his beloved enforcer got to. Atlanta wonders, too. Thinks maybe she shouldn't have let that bad man go. Hopes against hope he doesn't pop his head back up out of whatever hole he crawled into.

But that's a problem for another day.

Today is a different barrel of monkeys.

Shane taps a key. The screen comes on. Atlanta's on it. The camera's already showing her own face—everything she does, her digital doppelganger does at the same time. She pulls her red hair back and through a blue rubber band. "I feel like I should be wearing lipstick."

"This isn't a dating video."

She *hrms*. "Yeah, you're right." There's a part of her that wishes Steven had come. As a friend, at least. She called him—multiple times, actually—but he never called her back. She hopes that bridge didn't burn beneath her feet. She still remembers the kiss.

"You sure you don't need a script?"

"I don't need a script."

"Okay. Just hit the space bar when you're ready."

Her tongue snakes out over her teeth, then her lips, to moisten them. She shifts nervously. The space bar looms—she almost hits it, then doesn't, then finally stabs it with a finger.

A red circle blinks on the screen. Next to it in white text: RECORDING.

She takes a breath. Looks up. Then at the pinhole.

She starts talking.

"They say it gets better, but that's a load of horseshit. Like one day you wake up and things are just easy. That bullies come and bullies go and eventually everything sorts itself out. It doesn't. That's not how the world works, and it won't ever work that way. Somebody's always going to be there to try to hold you down against the ground and kick you while you're there. They'll find a reason for it. An excuse. You're black. You're gay. You're a girl who said no, or a boy who wants to be a girl. You're different from them, and they make *themselves* feel better by making *you* feel like dirt."

She stares hard into the camera.

"It *doesn't* get better."

Another deep breath.

"I know what you're thinking. Sounds like I'm saying there's no hope. This girl's a bummer, you're saying, maybe I should put a gun in my mouth or a rope around my neck or take whatever pills I find in my mama's medicine chest. That's one road you can take. But that's the coward's way. That wrecks the world for those you leave behind. Those who you think don't care, but who really they do. Suicide is selfish. Doesn't do squat but leave behind a lot of mess. Worst of all, it makes sure that the bullies win. Because now they live in a world with one less person they hate—in a world that looks suddenly a little more like them."

Now she leans closer, narrows her eyes.

"I'm saying it doesn't get better on its own. But I am saying you can *make* it better. You can fight back. You can kick and scream and shove and make sure nobody gets the better of you. You can vote. You can punch. You can stand your ground and stick out your chin and take pride in who you are.

"That's how you really get 'em. By being proud of yourself. By owning it and being awesome and giving them a big old middle finger that tells them no matter what they do, it won't change you one teensy tiny little bit. Let them be uncomfortable. Let them squirm. They don't like who you are, then fuck 'em.

"You defeat them by being undefeatable. By being you."

Now she smiles. A mean, fox-faced grin.

"But I know it's not easy. Standing tall. Fighting back. So I'm here to help. Sometimes you need a hand just being who you are and keepin' the bad folks at bay. You do, you call me. You go to my school, you already know me. You live in this town, *you already know me*. You already know what I did. What I'm capable of. It won't get better on its own, but together . . . well, maybe we can *make* it better."

The smile drops off her face like a framed photo dropping off a wall.

"To you bullies out there? To the haters, the monsters, the Nazis and criminals, the tyrants and tormentors? I've got a message for you, too—"

Suddenly, from off to the side, a series of fast footsteps.

Whitey jumps up in her lap. Almost knocks her off the chair. On the laptop screen she sees his big doofusy, droopy face. One eye missing and one ear cocked away from the other in a permanent forty-five-degree angle. Little starburst scar above his gone eye. But he's got a sloppy grin on his face and a goopy string of drool hanging from his jowls, and he starts panting like the happiest dog on Planet Earth. He licks her cheek. She kisses his nose.

"You bad guys and bullies got it real good right now. You have all the power. But that's over. *Done.* For you, it doesn't get better. In fact, from here on out?"

She offers the camera a middle finger.

"It gets a whole lot worse."

She nods at the camera, then hits the space bar again.

The red light goes away. Recording, over.

"We good?" she asks Shane.

He comes, checks the laptop, gives her a thumbs-up. "We got it. You nailed it. I'll get that on YouTube by the end of the week. Just in time for the new school year."

"Cool. Want a celebration cookie?" she asks, pointing to the plate on the bed.

Shane makes a face like he just ate a lemon rubbed in dog dirt.

They both laugh, and Whitey lays his head on Atlanta's shoulder.

Everything feels a little bit all right.

For now.

ACKNOWLEDGMENTS

I'd like to thank everyone who supported this Kickstarter way back when. Because without you, this book just plain doesn't exist. Maybe the world needs Atlanta Burns, maybe it doesn't. But she sure needed you, so thank you.

To learn more about hate crimes:
Partners Against Hate: http://www.partnersagainsthate.org

To learn more about dogfighting:
Humane Society: http://www.humanesociety.org/issues/dogfighting /end_dogfighting.html

ABOUT THE AUTHOR

Michelle Wendig

Chuck Wendig is the author of The Heartland Trilogy and the Atlanta Burns series, as well as numerous novels for adults. He is also a game designer and screenwriter. He cowrote the short film *Pandemic*, the feature film *HiM*, and the Emmy-nominated digital narrative *Collapsus*. Chuck lives in "Pennsyltucky" with his family. He blogs at www.terribleminds.com.